THE THRONES OF ENGLAND AND OF FRANCE DURING THE LATE 13TH, 14TH & 15TH CENTURIES

VALOIS

CHARLES
Count of Valois

Isabella = EDWARD II King of England 1307-27

PHILIP VI
King of France
1328-1350

EDWARD III
1327-1377

JOHN 'The Good'
1350-1364

CHARLES V
1364-1380

Louis
Duke of Anjou
d.1384

John
Duke of Berry
d.1416

PHILIP
The Bold
of Burgundy

CHARLES VI 'The Mad'
1380-1422

JOHN 'The Fearless'
Duke of Burgundy
d.1419

CHARLES VII
1422-1461

LOUIS
Duke of Orleans
d.1407

PHILIP 'The Good'
Duke of Burgundy
d.1467

LOUIS XI
1461-1483

CHARLES
Duke of Orleans =
1. Isabelle of Valois
2. Bonne d. of Bernard VII
Count of Armagnac

Charles = Margaret
Plantagenet

ARMAGNAC

BURGUNDIAN

CROWN
IN
CANDLELIGHT

CROWN
IN
CANDLELIGHT

Rosemary
Hawley
Jarman

BOOK-OF-THE-MONTH CLUB
NEW YORK

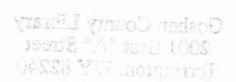

FOR ROY T. PLUMB
With my love

I should like to express my sincere appreciation to
Dr Eurfyl Richards for his invaluable help with the
Welsh translations in this book.

R.H.J.

Contents

Part One

THE MURDERERS

France, 1405–10

The Queen: Yet again, methinks,
Some unborn sorrow, ripe in fortune's womb,
Is coming towards me; and my inward soul
With nothing trembles: at something it grieves
More than with parting from my lord the king.

Shakespeare: *Richard II*, ACT II, SC. II

The seabird was flying east, warned inland by the storm in his cool, hasty blood. From the mouth of the Seine he had come, over the plain of Normandy and the spires of Elbeuf and Evreux. He had dipped in salute to the convent tower at Poissy; he had wheeled briefly southwards towards the distant glitter of Chartres. Now his flight brought him to Paris, over the pepper-pot turrets of the inner and outer walls and down to the Cité for a brief landing at La Grève, where the fishermen were berthed from a trip between Mantes and Corbeil, and on the little strand he filched a beakful of the catch. Feathers luminous in the watery sun, he rose again to fly on inland over the Île Notre Dame and the Île aux Vaches, dropping lower over the Porte au Blé. Below he saw a cone-shaped turret and an alcove with a wide stone sill, a temporary resting place. He swept down in one final arc and landed at an east window of the Hôtel de St Paul. Through the glass the tearful eyes of a princess regarded him.

She had been weeping for most of the day, but at four years old was young enough to be distracted by the bird's appearance. Katherine, youngest daughter of the House of Valois, peered closely at the blanched feathers, the small topaz eye. She edged along the stone window-seat and saw him through coloured panes in a pattern of lozenges and scrolls. He was a blue bird, a green-red bird and, where a pane was broken, white again, under a breeze that ruffled his breast and dried a tear on her cheek. She cried because she was hungry. Yesterday had been a sickening void making her dream of food – hot soup, honey pears, the costly white sugar bonbons eaten somewhere long ago – an unforgettable sweetness linked with a name, a face, a perfumed presence too long unfelt. She was cold too; she tucked her dirty bare feet beneath her and the breeze nipped her through her ragged dress. She wondered whether it would be possible to catch and tame the big bird, put a jewelled bonnet on its head, like the bird that Belle had carried when they were last together. Isabelle. Belle. Hers was the name of all sweetness. 'God keep you, little sister,' she had said. To Katherine, the six months of their separation was a lifetime, infected with constant hunger and fear. Because fear lodged in this palace, in the dark place at the bottom of the stairs where the stone monster leaned from his niche; in every crevice of the unswept rooms and galleries; in the little towers and the places beneath the fortress. And even if one were allowed outside, there was the ambience of past terrors, mysterious ones.

Looking east she could see the Bastille, its gate set in the Enciente Philip-Augustus, the outer wall erected two hundred years earlier to strengthen Paris. Below it the carved and pinnacled Porte St Antoine looked almost insignificant, not to be compared with the town's royal gateway with its reminder of St Denis's martyrdom. Once, passing from Troyes into Paris, she had looked up at the headless saint between his escort of bishops. Denis had walked from the place of his execution on the hill of Montmartre carrying his severed head in his hands, all the way to Catulliacum. Belle had told her: 'Little sister, wherever he trod, a flower sprang up!'

Near the Bastille, beyond the spires of the Temple, was the scaffold of Montfaucon, decked daily with the forms of felons hanging in the wind. Below those gallows Philip-Augustus had watched his heretics burn in the red flame, long before Katherine's birth. This, she had been told, was all part of life, as she opened the proffered breviary illuminated by representations of the fire, the knife, the rope. These images had faded however, leaving wariness. The real terror was here, in the palace, in the next turret, an unspeakable pit of despair.

The seabird stood still outside the window, with its implacable sideways stare. Katherine knelt upright, a tall child with great dark eyes and the long strong nose of Valois. Beneath a dingy kerchief her fine dark hair was clotted with filth. The bird turned to launch itself in flight. She whispered: 'Don't go . . .' while the moment's pleasure equated with lost joy and again she remembered Belle. Even in the far misty days when Belle had wept constantly there had been a place for Katherine on Belle's lap. She gazed at the bird fervently, while behind her shadows fanned into the room and the sun's last warmth departed.

Through the early autumn sky she heard the Célestins bell across the square, calling the nuns to Vespers. All over Paris people would be sitting down to table; the bourgeoisie of La Ville to the north, the nobles and merchants of La Cité within the inner wall, the students of L'Université in the south. Beyond the outer *enceinte* the harvesters would be coming back from the vineyards, already gnawing a wheel of cheese or a crust. Katherine clasped her empty belly. Life had not always been like this. She had dim recollections of a table gleaming with silver, of hot food, of Belle's brocade sleeve under her forehead. And a jongleur singing, laughing because she yawned. That had not been in this place, perhaps not even in Paris. Her father had been there, his hands smelling of lemon flowers and jasmine. Her sisters Marie, Michelle, Joanna, and her brothers Louis, Charles and Jean – had been there too. The feast of St Denis. And her mother . . . here fear closed up her mind.

The door behind her opened with a groan of damp and neglect. A figure came listlessly in and joined her at the window. This princess was six years old, as pinched and pale as her sister. She was naked under a worn woollen gown. Katherine pointed, smiling eagerly, to the window.

'Look at the big bird, Michelle!'

When Katherine smiled all her defects vanished. Her dark eyes gleamed like washed fruit; two dimples appeared as if loving fingers squeezed her chin, and the prominent nose diminished. She was beautiful.

'I see nothing,' said Michelle.

The sill was empty. There were only grey pinnacled towers and the gibbet etched against the dusky sky. In the shadows of the room something swift moved and vanished.

'A rat!'

'Yes. Louis caught one this morning. He's going to teach it tricks.'

They sat silently together then, the familiars of fear and penury, two of the five female heirs of the House of Valois, that great dynasty stretching beyond Charles the Count, son of Saint Louis, through Philip the Sixth, down from John the Good to Charles the Fifth, who had secured Paris by building an inner wall about the city. Charles, brother to three powerful Dukes; Louis of Anjou, John of Berry, Philip of Burgundy. The children sat shivering, close, while lice crept in their hair and under their garments; the daughters of Charles the Sixth, King of France. Charles *le Fou*! Dirty, cold and hungry, these were the offspring of a lunatic's marriage with Queen Isabeau of Bavaria, who last night had lain at the Louvre Palace and who now rode through Paris towards them, full of her customary spleen and mischief. And Michelle had her own premonitory thoughts.

'There was a strange man in the kitchen, and a horse in the yard. The man was kissing Jeanette. She was pleased. She gave me an apple. Here's your half.' She produced a brown object from her pocket. 'I'm sorry, Kéti. It's not very nice.'

Queen Isabeau had sent this amorous courier on beforehand to ensure that there was some wine in St Paul, for life for her without wine was unthinkable. It was three months since she had ridden off on one of her periodic scheming forays.

'They were talking about Madame our mother,' said Michelle uneasily. Katherine's eyes dilated, and she dropped the half-eaten fruit on the dirty floor.

'I wish we were with Marie at Poissy,' said Michelle, trembling. 'The nuns there are kind. Dame Alphonse said I had an angel's face, and that she would pray for our safety.'

'Why?' said Katherine.

'I'm not sure . . . and she promised a novena for our poor father's malady.' She began to cry. 'I wish he were well again!' Katherine wept too. They were greeted suddenly by the Dauphin Louis, who thrust into the room with all the swagger of his eight years.

'Ho!' he cried. 'Why are you grizzling? Look! He's almost tamed!' From his threadbare bosom he hauled a small brown rat, holding it expertly by the tail. Fascinated, the little girls stopped crying. The rat arched and snapped impotently.

'I shall call him Bosredon,' Louis announced. 'After mother's paramour.' His pointed face with its small stubborn mouth and Valois nose was bland with hatred. 'And I shall train him to go for people's throats. And when I am king I shall have Bosredon – and my uncle of Orléans – strangled. Up there!' He waved to where the scaffold of Montfaucon showed black against the dying day. Katherine sidled close and touched the rat's back, jumping back as the animal writhed.

'He's soft, like Beppo.' The fluffy white dog had lain beside her gilded chestnut-wood cradle, long since broken for kindling against the chill of St Paul. He was dead or abandoned, gone anyway like all beautiful things. Like Belle, who had returned from England what seemed so long ago, who had adored her and disappeared again. Joanna was married and in Brittany, Marie a postulant nun. But Belle, wherever she now was, seemed to have existed only in Katherine's heart.

Louis gathered the rat up and thrust it back inside his shirt. He was in good spirits. He had been in the stables, learning new swear words, and in the kitchen, where Jeanette, the pantry-maid whose sometime favourite he was, turned a blind eye to his pilfering. Not that there was much to pilfer; the palace was as bereft as a long-beseiged castle, its few servants as thin and threadbare as the royal children.

'There, Monsieur Bosredon!' Louis patted the writhing bulge. 'You shall tear out their throats . . . when I am king! Aiee! he has sharp teeth! Shall I cut off his head? For his great treachery?'

The sisters were silent as the small figure, warlike, mouthed oaths and accusations, legacy of the ear at the door, the witness of awful scenes between his elders. He swore, spat on the floor, declaimed the fate of whoremongers and traitors. Once I am king, when I am king. All kings raved; he roared louder until Michelle put her hands to her ears.

'Oh, Louis! what if you are never king?'

She had broken the spell. The Dauphin paled.

'I say you will never be king,' Michelle said.

Louis moved forward and struck his sister in her meagre chest. She fell back; he wrenched the rat from his bosom and held it, chittering and squirming, near her face. He cursed her, often-heard and barely-understood words. Whore, wanton, thief, beggar. She slapped his mouth and he screamed in temper. Weirdly answering from the adjoining turret came a dreadful gurgling groan of terror and grief. Louis's face looked suddenly like that of a little old man. The rat jumped from his hand and skittered to safety. Michelle covered her face. And Katherine began to run dementedly about the room. The quarrel might never have been; Michelle and Louis crept close.

'Will they come for us?'

'It is only our poor father,' said Louis bravely.

Katherine reached the door, which opened suddenly. She fell against the greasy apron of a servant; a woman whose lustreless eyes looked at her disagreeably.

'You must come, it's time.' Roughly uncaring that she addressed the Valois blood royal, and truculent from the lack of wages for the past three months. She thought: Mad Charles's litter, all of them, his and that bitch's whose capers leave me with scarcely a crust or a thread. Rancour sharpened her voice.

'Come, all of you! To say goodnight!'

She chivvied them into the passage outside. Louis went bravely ahead, whispering: 'Only to say goodnight . . .' like a charm to ward off devils. They went in dusk through a stone bay, past pillars warted with treacherously smiling gargoyles to the turret of despair. There were two columns built into an ogee-shaped arch surrounding the great oak door, and these were decorated with stone carvings: fish, fruit, a hippopotamus devouring grapes. From a column's lowest abutment a stone eagle jutted, with spread wings. As another frightful groan shuddered through the closed door, Katherine darted from the woman's side. She threw her arms about the cold stone bird, and clung.

'Come!' Hands, hurting, prised at her fingers. Katherine gripped fast, while the woman's impatience became wrath.

'God's life, Amélie! Can't you see she's terrified?'

From shadows a figure stepped, a tall woman with a round peasant face unskilfully painted. Beneath plucked brows her light eyes were dispassionate. She had attempted finery; full breasts swelled the bodice of a worn red velvet gown. A tawdry necklace of amber was wound about her short neck. Odette de Champdivers had been the King's mistress longer than she could remember, his consort both in splendour and present grief. Like all the others at St Paul, she was depleted and downcast, yet she remained with him, resigned, sometimes hopeful. She came between Katherine and the raging servant.

'Leave her,' she said. 'Come, *princesse*, it's your duty.'

She did not speak kindly but her nonchalance was reassuring. Katherine let go the pillar.

'Only for a moment,' said Odette. 'Seeing you may do your father good.'

As she spoke, four men, ragged, bearded, came running along the passage. On their heads they bore a large tin tub. They were grinning. 'Bath night!' they cried, and rushed at the great oak door. They went in, the last remaining body-servants of King Charles, picked and paid for by the malice of Queen Isabeau, men for whom torment of others was sport. Odette said reflectively: 'We have chosen a bad moment!' and looked down at Katherine, without tenderness but as one might contemplate the last chattel of value in a ransacked town.

'The Devil have my soul if I'm not sick of all this,' said the serving-woman.

'Leave here, then,' said Odette.

'And you, Demoiselle? Will you do likewise?'

'Perhaps.' And perhaps not, she thought, for he has been cured before, by bleeding, by clysters. Why not again? And should that monstrous Queen return and find him well . . . I would stay if only to witness that!

'Go on,' she said, and followed the children into the King's chamber. A choking stench assailed them, the product of a body and mind vilely sick. On a decrepit bed in the centre of the bare room the King clutched a filthy sheet to his naked body. He had not been shaved for days and the stubble on his pale face looked like grime. His large dark eyes were filled with unspeakable horrors. Yet there was still the evanescent youthful beauty that had been wildly squandered during his life with Isabeau and their shared debaucheries. Charles had been instilled with the *credo* that he came of a line of saints. Depravity made a bad bedfellow to these maxims. Sinner and saint battled in him; the price was paid with madness. The serving-men gathered about his bed. Rearing wildly, the King cried out and soiled himself. He saw their broken-toothed faces, the bath, now brimming. The water looked cold, sinister, like his wife's last smile before she rode away leaving him raving and weeping. He saw in the doorway Odette and Amélie and the children, all elongated, wavering, as if he saw them through a mullion pane. He began to shiver; with difficulty he raised his hands close to his eyes. It was as he had feared; they were crystal, the long curved fingernails fragile mirrors, and his limbs . . . *Sacré Dieu!* the same . . . He shrank from the men.

'Do not touch me! I am made of glass!'

'Come on, monsieur,' they said, winking at one another. 'We must make you pretty again. Your lady wife commands it.'

'I have no wife! I am Georges Dubois! He has neither wife nor children!'

Georges Dubois, long dead, was a sin remembered; the young gypsy brought by Isabeau to seduce him. How she had laughed, watching them together! Georges's identity remained, a fitting token of guilt, of remorse.

One of the men took his arm, and he screamed. Into his vision, small and apparently menacing, came his youngest daughter.

'Kiss your father,' someone said.

Katherine was held aloft in air thick with the reek of ordure and agony. She slid downward towards the pallor and the staring eyes. She took the glacial hand with its talons and set her lips to it. Unknowingly she drew upon her all his sorrows; they merged with her own unaccomplished years. Then in Odette's arms she was borne away, while Louis and Michelle knelt before the King. The servants were handling him. Over and over he cried: 'I am made of glass!'

The stolen revenues of France clothed her. Her throat wore a diamond serpent, her fingers flashed with jewels. Isabeau of Bavaria was proud, greedy and reckless, and completely without scruple. She laughed at life and sneered at death. She wore expensive Holland cloth. Two torch-bearers accompanied her and a diadem sparkled blue and green on her dark hair. She had dined well at the Louvre; her steps had an extra flaunt and her face was flushed. On her right came her brother, Louis of Bavaria, strong and swarthy. At her left was a man fair as a Rhineland maiden with a weak gentle mouth, and bringing up the rear was a small tousled man. As the quartet entered, Odette remained standing passively by the King's bed. Isabeau spoke, laughing.

'This, gentlemen, is the pigsty! Is it not the finest? My dear Orléans, what do you say?'

The fair man drew a muskball from his sleeve and held it to his nose.

'My queen, I'm impressed. And this is the pig?'

He extended a slim hand as if to prod, and Charles cringed.

'I see there's a sow here also,' said Louis of Bavaria with stolid wit. 'Do they mate, I wonder?'

Odette's eyes stared past them all.

'Not any more,' said Isabeau. 'The poor pig is past his prime.'

'Bah! he stinks!' observed her brother.

'I had ordered him cleansed. Perhaps we should wash him now . . . Monsieur de Laon!'

The small man came forward. He held an unstoppered leather flask.

'Excellent,' said Isabeau. 'The red wine of Champagne . . . I bathe all my swine in it. Monsieur de Laon! Will you paint a pretty pattern on the King of France?'

The King whimpered. His eyes rolled.

'Charles!' said Isabeau. 'Attend me! See, here's my dear brother' (Louis of Bavaria bowed, a jerky insult) 'and your own brother' (Louis of Orléans smiled his depraved maiden's smile). 'And Monsieur Colard de Laon. My protégé. He paints *à l'italienne*. Receive us, Charles!'

'I am not Charles. Leave me in peace.'

She turned in rage to Colard de Laon. 'Anoint him! Mock him! Paint him!'

Shrugging, the artist stepped up to the bed. He poured wine over the King's head.

Charles said faintly: 'Bless me, Father, for I have sinned. *In nomine Patris . . .*'

21

The Queen was irritated. The object of her torment was immune, far away. She leaned forward, her jewels irradiating the King's wan face.

'Charles! Don't you know me?'

'No,' he said sadly. 'You are fair, and cruel, but I do not know you.'

She stepped back. Louis of Orléans said softly: 'He looks on the point of death.'

'He will not die.' Odette's voice drifted to them, almost sepulchral. 'He will recover, and be avenged.'

Isabeau whirled on her. 'Silence! Beggar! Harlot!' And Odette's mouth curved and she looked down at her feet.

'Enough,' said Isabeau. Her malicious gaiety had given way to temper. 'Come, messires. I will see my children now.' Her fury found a target in Orléans. She glared at him. '*You* know all about my children, seigneur! My boys. Charles, Jean are still in your household!'

'At your request,' said the Duke. He saw she was feeling the effects of wine and was becoming irrational.

'And what of my eldest daughter – where is Isabelle?'

'Probably with my son.' He smiled.

'I fear,' said Isabeau dangerously, 'that my children grow away from me. My sons . . .'

'Two of them are safe at Blois,' he said carefully. 'But the Dauphin Louis . . . he is here, I assume?'

He despised her, his sister-in-law, feared her, and lusted for her constantly. She was devious. Often he suspected her collusion with his rivals, the powerful Dukes of Burgundy. For Burgundy and Orléans were the two swords of unrest fixed over the throne of France. Isabeau was the spider at the nucleus of a web; her threads stretched God knew where. To the hands of Burgundy's mightiest peer, John the Fearless? Jean sans Peur was the King's cousin, and his sole aim was to hold the regency of France, just as Louis of Orléans did now. He turned placatingly to Isabeau, taking her hand. 'Come below, let us drink and play a little, my queen!'

'Yes,' she said, her mouth slackening, so that for a moment the years peeped through the jewels and cosmetics. 'And we'll talk more of Isabelle . . . she shall marry Henry of England.

According to England's wish and mine.'

Louis of Bavaria spoke gruffly. 'That I doubt, sister . . .'

She was looking scornfully again at the figure on the bed. Charles was quiet. Beside him Odette rested her fingers lightly on his bare shoulder.

'Farewell, my lord,' said the Queen. She blessed him, blaspheming, hateful. 'God and St Denis protect my pig!'

For a blind instant the air between them shivered with strange intent. Then Charles sat up suddenly. A Lazarus-figure, clear-eyed and composed.

'Farewell, Queen Isabeau,' he said, in a completely rational way. 'I thank you for your blessing.'

Odette drew in her breath. Her fingers tightened on the King's shoulder, and his own came up to cover them.

'I feel so weak,' he said to her, ignoring the others. 'I must eat. I feel so dirty. Help me, my dear . . .'

She bent close to hide excitement. She prayed: Let this not be one of those freakish miracles, seen before and defeated by the recurrence of his delirium. The Queen and her chevaliers were withdrawing, their apprehension far from concealed. Odette's heart skipped with joy as Charles whispered calmly to her, speaking of Jean sans Peur, Duke of Burgundy, bidding her follow his enemies and listen and be vigilant, calling her his good girl, as in the old days when she had first given him her body and her heart.

The stable was one of the warmest places in the palace precincts. Low strips of beam crossed its vault; straw and hay were piled in drifts. There was the rustle of feeding horses. Odette bent to the youth who slept half-buried in hay.

'Gaspard!'

He stretched, groaning, knuckled his eyes.

She sank to sit beside him, warning him with a pressure of her hand. His eyes were a dim spark in the gloom. He was her bastard brother, and the horsekeeper, often unpaid, resigned like herself to wait for better days. He could be trusted.

'Listen,' she said. 'The King has recovered.' He sat up

sharply. A horse, startled, whickered through a mouthful of hay.

'What time is it? Is that she-wolf still here?'

'Isn't that her horse, stupid? It's late. They're talking in the Hall. Be soft. The noise carries. I've often heard you from above, singing and swearing.'

'Is he really well again?'

'He is very fatigued,' said Odette quietly. 'He had me find him food, and a clean bedgown. But he's himself again.'

'So now . . .' Gaspard stood up, drew Odette to her feet. 'He will confront her, demand back the jewels, money, honours she's drained off . . . thank God. I'll go to him. I've stayed obedient, without a sou . . .'

'Wait.' She disengaged her hands. 'It's not over yet. He's very weak, capable of little, vengeance or anything else. But they are warned and afraid, and about to take action.'

She had stood for an hour at the lowest curve of the stairs leading to the Hall. She had heard Isabeau cursing everyone, the ragged pages, her brother of Bavaria and Louis of Orléans, in a drunken fury like the first autumn wind battering the walls and spinning the bodies on Montfaucon gibbet. The three children, sick with sleep, had been brought from their beds. Louis had kicked his uncle of Orléans on the shins, earning himself a smack across the cheek.

'They plan to abduct the children, and take the treasure from the Louvre Palace. Listen well. Ride to the Duke of Burgundy's emissary. He lies at the Palais.'

'Jean sans Peur's man?'

'Yes. Tell him they plan to take the children, if not tonight, tomorrow for sure.'

'Where?' he asked. 'To Tours?' For Isabeau had a court of her own there, a Babylon of pleasure and plots.

'To Milan.'

'Milan!'

'Ask no more.' She was impatient. 'Ride now. I've promised the earth to the gateward, he'll let you through.'

'And what shall I ride, dear sister?' he mocked.

'Take a horse, any horse.' She pointed to a tall bulk placidly feeding. 'Louis of Bavaria rode in on that . . . take it.'

'And be hanged.'

'It's a risk. Take it.'

He peered at her. 'Do the children mean so much to you that you risk your own brother's life?'

'I don't love them. They came from the Queen, that murdering bitch. But I love their father . . . Name of God! Why these questions? By now you should be kneeling before Burgundy's man.'

'I'll go.' Lifting down a saddle, he said: 'I'll need good payment.'

Odette sighed. She unclasped the amber necklet.

'You are as greedy as an Englishman. Sell this to the Jew on the Grand Pont. Do your work first.'

He led the saddled horse to the door.

'One more thing: leave word for Madame at the convent at Poissy.'

'Madame?'

'You grow more imbecile daily. The Princess Isabelle is *always* called "Madame" since she was Queen of England, and has captured the heart of Orléans's son. All his verses are written to "Madame".'

Gaspard opened the door. The rising wind hurled a crowd of leaves across the yard.

'Not one more word. Ride this instant.'

The horse's hooves sounded very loud across the cobbles. Odette's heart was racing; the wind moaned in wonder at her rashness.

As the royal party crossed the square towards the Porte St Antoine, men were taking down the corpses from the gibbet. They laid the cadavers on the ground and with axes proceeded to dismember them. Heads and limbs would be spiked on the twelve gates of Paris. Katherine peeped out through the window of the moving *charrette*. She saw a severed head swinging in a butcher's casual grip. She thought vaguely: St Denis! The small Dauphin Louis gave a raucous shriek.

'It's the stableman! He was my friend!' He began to leap about in the confined space where the three children were

25

cramped by a vast jewel-coffer brought by Isabeau from the Tour du Louvre. The carriage swayed as he jumped about, and the Queen, riding a dark stallion, looked down angrily.

'My son needs discipline,' she said to the Duke of Orléans who rode with her. He was looking rather aghast. The arbitrary execution of Gaspard, apprehended in the early dawn, had increased both his respect for Isabeau and his trepidation.

'You were hasty, my lady. I would like to have learned where that knave had been, riding your brother's horse.'

Isabeau's beauty showed dark against the silvery mass of the Célestins church. She looked at her best in the morning, before the day's wine had flushed her and clouded her eyes.

'He offended,' she said simply. 'Had it been you, I would have done the same.'

And by St Marie, you would, he thought ruefully. You're a despot as dreaded as any barbarian. They rode through the portal of St Antoine. Although the wind had dropped a little, the sky was dark as armour, and above birds wheeled, thrown up like chaff from a hopper. He felt himself likewise tossed and urged. He must go where Isabeau blew him. He shuddered, feeling pressed by danger. There had been genuine sanity in that one look from King Charles's eyes. He thought: my only wish is to live secure with Isabeau in Milan, where at last she will surely grant me her favours, long withheld. He looked at the brilliant ruthless face. Isabeau, my incubus, my storm.

Katherine had cut her foot on the clasp of the heavy coffer. Beads of blood ran down. Leaning wearily against Michelle, she had no idea where they were all going. In her mouth was the accustomed taste of fear. A cup of spiced wine had been forced on her at daybreak by the Queen. It was twenty hours since she had had solid nourishment. Her vision was blurred, her bones seemed disjointed, as if there was not enough flesh to hold them in place, and she was very cold.

Louis of Bavaria rode behind the others and six mounted armed men brought up the rear, weighed down by paniers of gold and more jewels. Colard de Laon rode with them, his face worried and his pack filled with priceless paintings.

'My lord.' Isabeau turned her head, with its purple veil, towards Orléans. 'We shall ride by Melun and make for Sens.'

26

She turned her horse's head east of the Seine.

'I would have thought it better to go by river.'

'Too slow. I'd rather risk an ambush.' She yelped with laughter. 'And who will ambush us? My Bayard is fleet!' She spurred, the horse sprang forward. 'Prick your old nag, brother-in-law.'

He said as they rode: 'Tell me, my queen, of your design for Isabelle. I'm anxious to know.' He tried to disguise his anxiety. His own son Charles's love for the princess was a thorn in Isabeau's flesh. The Queen gave him a malicious look and pinched his thigh, as if their sexes were reversed.

'She will marry Henry of Lancaster's son, the Prince of Wales. I will see some recompense for the dowry she left behind when King Richard died. Twenty thousand crowns should see her safe on England's throne again.'

'She'll not hear of it. She is full of hate.'

'Indeed!' The Queen laughed, to cover annoyance. 'Be this so, England shall buy another of my daughters. Michelle or Katherine shall marry the Prince.'

'What does the King think about this?'

'Since when was he capable of thought?' she sneered. 'He was not against the match, the last time he was coherent. And Henry of Lancaster, they say, is leprous and has few years left. His son will soon be king.'

They rode fast. The road to Melun across a plain gave way to uplands on either side. There were vineyards, terraces of leaves browning in the fall, the tendrils stripped of all but the most wizened grapes. Looking out, jolted and sick, Katherine could see her mother's foot and the sprayed blood from the stallion's spurred hide, mirroring the red drops on her own foot. They skirted the walls of Melun and entered the county of Blois where to the south-east rose the hills of Troyes and church spires like swords against the heavy sky. Katherine dozed, waking to a raging thirst and the sound of water. They had come to a rickety bridge where the Seine, swollen by recent rain, whirled to its confluence with the Yonne. Her mouth was parched; her bladder pressed agonizingly. The Queen, like one without human need, had not drawn rein for hours.

'I dare not ask her to stop,' muttered Michelle. 'Louis . . .'

The Dauphin pushed his fingers through the window. He touched the leg of Orléans who rode close to the carriage.

'Uncle,' he said with hatred, 'my sisters are thirsty.'

A flask was slid through to them. Katherine sucked at it, choked, cried. Wine again. The carriage swayed on to the bridge, she was pitched about, and involuntarily voided her bladder. They were over the river safely, although Colard de Laon's horse almost slipped on the far bank. Approaching the Archbishopric of Sens, their pace was slowed by close forest. Ahead, rearing oak-clad, were the hills of Burgundy. The Duke of Orléans squinted uneasily and Isabeau laughed.

'Not to fear, sweet lord, Jean sans Peur is far from home. And who are we but a parcel of poor merchants?'

He looked back at the paniers of gold and tried to smile. A huge drop of rain splashed his head, trickling over the edge of his chaperon and running down his nose. What a journey! He had changed horses twice already and the third was almost done. About ten miles from Sens Isabeau impatiently ordered the spent mounts to be abandoned, and he watched his favourite mare dragging off wearily into the forest with Louis of Bavaria's horse which Gaspard had been hanged for riding. More rain fell. He looked into the carriage. Katherine and Michelle sat bunched together frozenly and the Dauphin, pale, was swearing to himself like an old trooper.

'For God's love, highness!' His own voice startled him. 'The children must rest. We'll have them sick before Milan.'

She looked at him coldly. 'We shall ride through the night.'

The sky opened. Ahead in a forest-choked ravine lay the town of Tonnerre, celebrated for its storms. The surrounding hills caught the tempest and boiled it in the valley. Lightning glared and thunder bounced off the uplands. Louis of Bavaria rode up.

'We must shelter,' he yelled over the tumult. 'This is madness.'

Isabeau shouted: 'We'll rest an hour at Sens. Then on to Italy.'

Orléans said: 'No, my queen.' She turned to him, haloed by storm. 'You yourself will fall ill, and you are our all, our might, our mother.' (Likewise mother to those wretched brats, he thought, surprising himself with compassion.) 'Let's rest the night at Sens.'

'If we don't, the horses will founder.' Louis of Bavaria spat rain from his lips.

'Name of God! Very well!' She set off at a manic pace, through the spearing water and light and thunder. The gates of Sens were closed. By now a premature night was lit by snakes of lightning and washed by cold rain that beat down the vines and shattered on the trees in the gorge. From Tonnerre the storm lashed back; lightning jumped the miles. The warden had covered fire and gone to bed, and nothing would stir him. Nearby there was a low crumbling inn.

'A godless place, but it must do,' said Isabeau. They dismounted into mud. The children were released from the carriage into torrential rain. The inn had one windowless room and was blue with peat-smoke from a sulky fire-basket. A sow with six piglets snored under a table strewn with dirty pots. A line of hens roosted on the beam of a straw-filled gallery, from which peeped the sleepy faces of children. The landlord had been dozing and creaked upright. In the corner his wife squealed at sight of the armed men.

'Be easy, mother,' said one with a grin. 'Tapster! your best wine for my lieges.' The landlord scuttled to obey, falling over the sow and piglets.

'And food,' said Louis of Orléans.

'Cheese?' trembled the alewife. She watched the Queen warming her wet hands and skirt at the brazier. She had made up her mind who they all were; demons, descended out of the frantic night. Soon she and her husband would be changed into hares, to run wailing on the hills for ever.

'Damn your cheese,' said Louis of Bavaria, throwing himself on a bench and pointing to the piglets. 'Roast a few of those in wine and rosemary, and be sharp about it.'

The inn-keeper's eyes screwed up. 'I was fattening them for market . . .'

A knife pricked his greasy jerkin; he saw the dour faces of the henchmen. Devils. Every time Tonnerre spoke it meant trouble. Last time his eldest son had fallen down the well.

He sighed and set off in pursuit of the devils' supper.

'In God's name, where shall we sleep?' The Duke of Orléans looked hopelessly at the foul straw. Isabeau smiled at him through the steam from her garments, like something beautiful risen from Hell. 'Together?' she mocked. His heart raced. A splitting roar of thunder bombarded the inn, the pots danced on the table. He looked at the children, crouched together on a bench beneath the line of drowsy hens. All three were soaked from crossing from the carriage to the inn. Katherine's face was scarlet. Her eyes were closed. Her breathing was agony. Again surprised at himself, he rose and picked her up; she lay inert against him. Carefully he mounted the ladder to the loft where, in straw, the inn-keeper's brood nestled wide-eyed. He laid her down. To one of the boys he said:

'Give me something to wrap her – sacking? It will do. Look after her. I fear she's very ill.'

He descended to meet Isabeau's twisted smile.

'So, my lord, you play wetnurse now.'

'Someone must care for them.' He frowned.

'They're hardy, like me. In Milan, dear Louis, I shall want swords, not lilies. Do you take after Mad Charles, your brother?'

'Compassion isn't weakness.' He flushed.

'You will serve me in Milan.' Her eyes held him, full of half-promises, taunting love. A prescience of doom struck him. As if one day she might, even unwittingly, encompass his ruin.

'Dear God, I'm cold!' He stripped off his sodden cloak and chaperon. The piglets squealed as their throats were cut. Katherine's tortured breath went on and on.

Isabeau dealt a final hand of cards swiftly on to the table. He watched her, his desire and unease tempered with dislike. Getting up, he said quietly:

'If Katherine dies, there will be one less pawn for you to move on England. The Prince cannot marry a corpse.'

'Sit down, my lord.'

He left the table and mounted the loft-ladder. From the straw the inn-keeper's son looked nervously at him. Dark eyes, olive face, handsome, very thin. Louis felt a stir; once, long ago he had loved a boy like this.

'How is she?'

'I don't know, seigneur.'

He smiled at the boy, from whose clothing a stench of dung and garlic emanated.

'It's not your fault.'

He lowered himself down and took Katherine on his lap. Years since he had handled an infant. Oddly she reminded him of his own son, Charles, as a baby, Charles who now, fifteen, composed songs to Isabelle, widow of King Richard, sister to this wretched waif. He decided in that moment: Isabelle and Charles should marry, and safeguard the interests of Orléans against Burgundy. Katherine opened her eyes. They were full of torment.

'Is she better, seigneur?'

'I think she's dying.' Orléans put out his free hand and patted the boy's slim neck. The straw was gleaming as dawn entered through the loft's broken walls. The storm had gone. There was the sweet rotten smell of autumn washed by rain. He leaned to listen to Katherine's faint heart, her hoarse, ragged breath. More light surged in through the open inn door. The henchmen were standing to attention. Isabeau stood brushing at her gown. Colard de Laon gnawed a cob of bread. Louis of Bavaria was listening to the patois of the inn-keeper who, with great temerity, was demanding payment for the piglets. Laughing, the Queen's brother scattered gold pieces, enough to keep the family for a year, and the man's truculence changed to fawning gratitude.

Isabeau came to stand beneath the loft, eyes bright and unwearied. The henchmen were shepherding Michelle and Louis out through the door.

'Come, my lord!'

Under his hands, Orléans felt Katherine's dry fiery face.

'We must be off,' said the Queen. She peered up through the bars. 'Are you sleeping? Come, we've delayed too long.'

He did not answer.

'My lord?' The voice sharpened.

'The princess cannot stand,' he heard himself reply. 'She

31

can scarcely breathe. She needs a physician.'

'You disobey me?'

He sat, cradling Katherine. To the inn-keeper's son he said softly: 'Go, run into town and bring a doctor,' and the boy slid from the loft on quick bare feet, and, skirting the Queen warily, ran from the inn.

'You'll anger me, my lord.' She laughed uneasily. Louis of Bavaria came to stand beside her.

'We appear to have a brave man in our company,' he said.

Orléans knew himself anything but brave, but a new man, full of strange morality, had got inside his skin.

'I'll punish you, never fear,' said Isabeau.

'No, my liege,' answered the strange new man. 'You need my loyalty. You need your daughter – alive. I'll serve you in Milan, but I'll not ride there with a dead child. Not for all my estate or your esteem.'

'One hour, then.' She stalked back to the table. The doctor entered, a tall cloaked Jew, and ascended to the loft, bringing out almanac and herbs and vials, sending the landlord's son for water and cloths.

'One hour!' the Queen repeated viciously. She sat, they all waited, the henchmen in the doorway, yawning but vigilant of the jewels and the paniers of gold, the small Louis and Michelle asleep again on a bench. The doctor examined Katherine. The evil humours were strong in the ascendancy, he said, shaking his head. The sobbing rasping breath continued. In the town a church bell sounded and Isabeau said: 'Your time is nearly up, my lord of Orléans.'

He raised his head to reply and heard the first trumpet. An acrid bray muted by the trees, but near; lilting as if sounded by someone riding hard, and the sound of many horses, the noise of harness and wheels. The orchestration of swift approach grew and voices drifted, shouts breathless with intent. One of the men-at-arms ran out of the door and scanned the dawn-lit trees. And the Dauphin, awakened, ran out to the edge of the glade to peer down the tree-lined slope. He saw the cavalcade, the mud-soaked finery, the carriages, the arms and colours of the leaders. With a shriek of glee, he bounded back into the inn.

'Burgundy!' he cried. 'It's my uncle of Burgundy!'

Isabeau whirled and drove an evil look at Orléans. Your accursed dalliance has brought us to this, what I most dreaded. Outside the sounds of hoof and wheel merged with the slither of steel. There were more shouts, as the Queen's horse was recognized. And then the inn was filled with men and arms. In the centre, cynically smiling and splendidly clad in a habit of fleurs-de-lys, stood Jean sans Peur.

He was a strong stoutish man with a merry eye. Beneath a tall fur hat the cumbrous Valois nose swooped powerfully. He had owned the dukedom of Burgundy for little more than a year since his father Philip had died, but it sat on him like a treasure. He was amused by the whole denouement, at apprehending Isabeau like this. He crooked his knee and kissed her rigid knuckles, appraising her decadent beauty, her dismay.

'God greet you, Madame. Are you going far?' rising to kiss her on both cheeks. 'To think I might have missed your company!'

Her eyes slid past him to the grim figure of Odette, at whom the Duke turned to smile.

'This lady,' he said, 'is very loyal to the crown of France. So, God rest him, was her brother. A swift rider, Gaspard, eh, Demoiselle Odette?'

'He accomplished his duty.' Odette's eyes moved upon the Queen, speaking of murder.

At sight of the jewels and gold, Jean sans Peur's little smile spread. Over Louis of Bavaria his glance passed without a sign. To Colard de Laon he nodded; he was an artist, immune. Then he saw Michelle and the Dauphin, bursting to be noticed, and went swiftly towards them.

'My lord prince; princess.' He saw the fatigue, stress, hunger in them. His smile grew tight. I have not come before my time; these children are shamefully used. He kissed the Dauphin's hand.

'Where are you bound, my prince?'

'My mother is taking us to Milan.'

'Against your wish?' Jean sans Peur said softly. 'Would you rather return to Paris, to your father?'

33

'My father's sick.'

'No, he's well, he's very well,' said Odette, and the Duke of Burgundy nodded.

'Then it is my royal wish to return to my father in Paris,' Louis said grandly, and burst into tears.

'*Zut!*' said Burgundy, abashed. 'So you shall. Where is Madame? Her coach was not far behind . . .'

'Madame is here,' said a voice in the doorway.

Isabelle of Valois delicately lifted the hem of her gown and stepped into the inn. Tall and fair, she wore blue velvet embossed with pearl roses. Her features, unlike those of the other Valois children, were perfect, and now anger made them shimmer. This was widowed Isabelle of England and France, Isabelle who at eight years old had told the Earl Marshal: 'Sir, if it please my God and my lord and father that I be Queen of England I shall be well pleased, for I have been told that I shall be a great lady.' Now, ten years later, this is what she looked, and what she was.

Michelle ran and flung her arms about the velvet waist. The Dauphin's face shone.

'I was at Poissy when the message came.' She looked steadily at the Queen. 'I was praying for my father. It seems that God has been moved to succour him.'

Inwardly she sighed, for a permanent sorrow weighed her and now mingled with fresh griefs at sight of her brother and sister. She knew they were the tools of frantic power, in a situation all too familiar to herself, fresh from the tragic ravaged throne of England. She thought: Michelle is but a little younger than I was at the start of my griefs, after that small poignant joy. She shall not suffer thus, nor Marie, now with the good nuns, nor Joanna with her own Breton court. Nor . . . Suddenly alarmed, she cried: 'Where's Katherine?'

From the loft came a rustle and Orléans's head appeared, clownishly festooned with straw. Jean sans Peur gave a savage guffaw at the sight. Isabelle quickly went and placed her foot on the ladder. The Duke's face hung in a gold-lit cloud of fleas and dust.

'Madame!' he said. Isabelle half-angrily guessed his part in this affair, but there were old debts owed him and she smiled.

He was relieved. She was not vexed with him. His furious letters to Henry of England, demanding her return to France, had not been in vain. If only he could have secured her dowry-jewels also! Had it not been for him, she might still be imprisoned at Havering-atte-Bower, or Sunning Hill, or murdered like her husband Richard. He deluded himself; Henry Bolingbroke had returned her out of free will, being at no time intimidated by the histrionics of Orléans.

'Your beauty still excels,' he said foolishly. 'How fine you are!' He tried to rise without disturbing Katherine, who was in a heavy, trembling sleep.

Isabelle said, with a twisted smile: 'This is the one good gown I was able to save. Most of my chattels have gone to the murderer's son . . . to Mad Harry, who doubtless adorns his catamites with them at Cheylesmore.'

Somewhere in the depths of fever Katherine heard her voice and gave a mewing cry.

'*Sainte Vierge!*' said Isabelle. 'Is that my sister?'

She mounted swiftly, careless of the rich gown. She pushed aside the doctor and knelt, kissing Katherine's burning face, whispering to her like a south wind, and the strong breeze of love made itself known, pushing back pain, terror, the seductive beckoning of death.

'Kéti, Katherine. Open your eyes.'

'Madame, I tried to care for her,' said Louis of Orléans. The brave inner man had departed and he feared everyone. He could see Jean sans Peur with his terrible knowing smile, epitomizing retribution. Burgundy! again the feeling of unknown doom touched him.

'Your son Charles told me that you would do your best,' said Isabelle. 'Open your eyes, my little one.' The child's lashes quivered; a deep cough rattled in her chest.

'Again!' said Isabelle. 'Look at me!'

Katherine's fingers feebly touched the miniver fur on Isabelle's sleeve. She said clearly: 'Beppo.'

'No, Beppo's gone, my sweet! I have another dog for you at home, one who will love you even better. Open your eyes, little sister.'

Lucent with fever, the great black eyes were revealed.

35

'Belle.'

'Yes. Belle has you now.'

A thick dew began to appear on Katherine's brow and limbs. The doctor exclaimed in pleasure.

'The evil humours are discharged!'

They carried her from the inn and placed her in Isabelle's *charrette*. Odette came with them on the long steady ride back to Paris, then to the convent of Poissy with its sacred relics; the heart of Philip the Fair and the great jewelled Cross of the Templars; and its kind, skilled community of Dominican nuns. And because at four years old tomorrow was a year away and six months a lifetime, Katherine felt safe for ever. Belle had assured her, many times on the journey:

'I shall never leave you again, little one. Not while life lasts.'

'She looks so well,' said Odette in her soft flat voice. 'Madame has wrought wonders.'

Isabelle glanced down at Katherine, riding a pony. She gripped the reins firmly, spurning the protective arms of an attendant groom. Across her saddle-bow was balanced a fluffy white dog.

'The nuns saved her, really,' Isabelle said. 'They watch her carefully for lung-fever. She must stay at Poissy until she is grown.'

'How old is grown?' Odette smoothed her robette over the sidesaddle. 'Eight years? Ten?'

Odette was happy since the King's recovery. He had made fresh provision for her. She was glad to keep gifts and messages flowing to Poissy when Isabelle herself could not visit there, although she did this as often as she could, bringing the irreplaceable gift of herself.

'Maturity comes too soon,' said Isabelle. Again she saw herself, her head almost level with the Earl Marshal of England's sword-hilt, promising to marry the English king.

'They thought I was too young to love him!' she said aloud.

'Madame?' Odette's question went unanswered.

They rode on together over the cobbles. The sun made

a cobweb of Isabelle's white horned coif. Spring with its scents had come to Paris; green vegetables and fresh meat from the Champeaux market at Les Halles; drifting down narrow alleys knit together by the towers and spires of churches. St Eustache, St Germain l'Auxerrois in the north and, towering further north in the city, St Martin-des-Champs. At the west inner wall stood St Honoré and by the Seine the Louvre with its delicate towers from which the King's standard now flew serenely. The river was white and blue with reflected sky, burnished in places by the influx of spring tides. Upon the south bank was the Petit Châtelet, and over the river the Grand Châtelet, prison and treasurehouse. On the Île Notre Dame stood the cathedral and the crenellations of the Hôtel Dieu.

Paris was a heart of piety whose cobbled veins were set with leaning houses. Yet cuddled together on the Grand Pont were dwellings haunted by the assassin and the whore, the usurer and the thief. It was a city of holiness and intrigue, of paradox, of secrets. The morning sun shone on the river, while bells struck the hour in sweet cracked sounds and sombre notes, out-tongued always by Notre Dame. Paris quickened with the morning, the boatmen plying up and down to La Grève with wood and charcoal; in the little streets between the Palais and the cathedral apothecaries and booksellers, drapers and furriers and goldsmiths widened their shutters and looked for trade. There was the scent of flax and dye, fuller's earth and tanning hide. From the north-east quarter came the hammer of armourers, and cheese-hawkers cried in the streets of fine Brie and Champagne. In the Cité, the artists and illuminators and parchment-sellers went about laden with rainbow scrolls.

So Paris came to life in its three divisions: the food markets of La Ville to the north; the artists and scholars in the Cité mingling with lords and dukes; and in the south, L'Université. Some students were in the street where Isabelle rode and gazed at her admiringly, dispersing under the warning looks of her escort. She rode on, greeting people, courteous and correct.

To a priest she bowed. '*Dieu vous gart.*'

To a workman struggling with a ladder in her path: '*Dieu vous ait, mon amy.*'

And to the young Charles of Orléans, who came on her as if by chance:

'*Dieu vous donne bone matin et bonne aventure!*'

'May I accompany you?' His eyes drank her up, from her cobweb coif to her little shoes of Cordovan morocco. He was tall and fair like his father, but without Louis's vacillating eyes; his own were steady and clear. In his pocket he carried yet another excellent poem to 'Madame'.

'Not this day, my lord.' She shook her horse's belled bridle. 'We go to the Sainte-Chapelle to pray, my sister and I.'

She smiled, leaving him; she knew him to be kind and unspoiled at fifteen years old, and how ardently he desired her. She recognized that his father was in thrall to Isabeau, but she remembered that while she, Isabelle, was a hostage in England, Louis had offered to meet the English king in single combat for her sake. And on her return three years earlier he had loaded her with presents, just as Jean sans Peur had ordered great celebrations which she, bereft and heartsick, could not enjoy. She trusted neither Burgundy nor Orléans. Her father she thought of with uneasy affection and pity, her mother with loathing. The one she could both love and trust was gone, his starved body smashed by Bolingbroke's assassins in the dark of Pontefract, then lapped in lead so that his wounds were hidden, his heart rotting in England's earth.

Now, dismounted, they were entering the Palais precincts under delicate ribbed arches, crossing the court to where the twin chapels of the Sainte-Chapelle rose one above the other like a stone flower stretching to heaven. The great upper window was dark, and gave no intimation of the beauty within. She thought: so is a soul concealed under flesh. Only when the flesh is shattered can the soul be seen. Dead, he must have been fairer even than in life.

Into her mind, clear as ever, came the face of King Richard of England, seen for the last time in the precinct of Windsor before his departure for Ireland. He was tall and, sitting on the roan Barbary, his head seemed to touch the sky. He had turned his face to her with a threefold look of love, father and priest and lover in one. They had made their farewells yet he had dismounted, like some royal and gentle bird, and come back to her, lifting her small figure against his breast.

'Adieu, Madame! Adieu, until we meet again!'

She would have shed tears as he kissed her again and again, yet even at twelve years old, something told her: you are a woman, a wife and a queen. It was he who had wept. But now grief dragged at her, killing the sunlit grace of the Sainte-Chapelle; and because she was still and for ever 'Madame', with the vein of adamantine which had sustained her over the years, she composed herself; ascending the Palais staircase with Katherine, passing by the royal apartments. She could hear her father's voice; he was conferring with his ministers, sounding entirely rational, strong. For how long would it last? She dared not think about it. The royal chapel was designed exclusively for those of the blood; Odette drew back. Two large figures, male and female, flanked the chapel door; above them was a formidable angel with a book.

'Who are they?' said Katherine.

'Adam and Eve, before their fall. Now, walk as the nuns taught you. Head held up, eyes downcast. My good girl!' she said lovingly.

Doux Jésus, the English shall not have her! Sooner my own heart's blood . . . Fury stung her. Wrong to come to this most holy place with wrath and vengeance. She stood, letting the hatred burn and cleanse and evaporate.

Emissaries had come from England to Compiègne, daring to ask for her hand in marriage with the Prince of Wales, Bolingbroke's son, and some of the French councillors had acceded, swayed by the thought of the lost dowry, but she had sworn in their hearing to destroy herself, for better the ultimate heresy than a union with the son of Richard's murderer. And now it was Katherine whose life and fortunes were weighed in this alliance, whose destiny could be dictated . . . God send my father well for ever, for when he is himself, he must be totally against this vile design . . .

'Belle, why can't Jacquot come with us?'

The little dog was sitting at the foot of the monumental staircase.

'Call him, then.'

39

Katherine clapped her hands and Jacquot came, scrambling, slipping upwards, like a ball of flax.

'Dogs have souls,' said Isabelle.

Mathe. She remembered him well; a stern wolfhound as big as a yearling calf. She and Richard had ridden in the forests of Windsor and Eltham with Mathe loping beside them. At night he would lie by the bed, watchful (although there was nothing to watch but affection), ready to tear the life from intruders. Would that Mathe had been at Pontefract! But then he was already forsworn.

'Henry of Lancaster came into the chamber and desired the king's abdication. Richard gave up the crown and took it back again, only to relinquish it again. You recall how the dog was wont to place his paws about King Richard's neck, then roll and bare his belly in subservience to the sovereign? When Bolingbroke came that last time, the dog rose and embraced *his* neck and abased himself. He knew.'

She had forgotten who had told her.

They thought I was too young to love him! they said he married me, a child, so that his body could ever be faithful to the beloved dead Anne of Bohemia. But my childish love encompassed Anne's and drowned it as the sea drowns a river. No, my Dickon. Your murderers shall never have my sweet sister, not while I live.

Like its lower counterpart, the royal chapel comprised a single nave of four bays and a seven-sided apse. Light streamed through the rose window, striking the free-standing clusters of colonnettes with their statues of saints and the low wall with its three-cusped blind arcades. The figures of St Louis and Jeanne de Bourbon were frozenly forbidding, he with his orb and sceptre, she with stone blossoms on her marble gown. Yet when the light poured in they were redeemed by breathtaking colour that lay equally upon their rigid forms and those of Isabelle and Katherine; the brilliant apple-green of chrysoprase, the sober milk of chalcedony, the rich dried blood of sardonyx flushing to cardinal red, then mellowing to garnet and rose, and brightening in the crown of Christ to gold. As a cloud darkened the window, red dominated: blood, wine, cerise, filling the shapes of the robe, the crown, all the men and beasts lovingly limned within the glass. Then the sun came again to light not only the pigeon's-breast texture of the opaline Caen stone but the primary colour of window and chapel in a final glory. Red, the red of sunsets and claret, a comforting, loving red, as if one stood inside a ruby. The upraised faces of the two princesses were rosy under it and the little dog's fur warmed like a peach.

Isabelle pointed to the altar, where candles burned, lighting the gems on a square reliquary.

'Look! The most holy things are here.'

The relics of the Passion, pledged to St Louis by Baldwin of Constantinople.

Katherine, totally happy, cuddled Jacquot under her arm. The chapel was almost deserted. Suddenly from the shadowed apse a voice arose, almost inhuman in its purity, joined by another, crisp as a tenor reed, followed by the fauxbourdon of deeper voices weaving a skein of praise.

Magnificat anima mea Dominum
Et exultavit spiritus meus in Deo salutari meo . . .

King Charles's singing-boys, thanking God for his sustained deliverance. Isabelle shivered under memory. At Windsor before that ill-starred Irish expedition, she and Richard had heard Mass together. The voices coiled and soared, a fount of pain and beauty. Adieu, Madame! Adieu, until we meet again!

She bent her head and wept, while a single treble wound upwards, seeking the apogee of glory. Again, memory racked her. Master Maudelyn, the chaplain who had so resembled Richard (some said he was a bastard son of the House), had been brought to her in the midst of her grief, dressed like Richard, a spur for a doomed rebellion. He had stood, his back to a sunlit window and she had run to him, finding a counterfeit Richard, strange flesh, an alien scent. Perhaps poor Mathe had been likewise confused when he embraced the murderer.

Weeping, she went to where the candles burned. She took the largest of the unlit candles and dipped it in the flame of another and set it burning with the rest. She knelt, and Katherine pressed against her. From a stall behind, Charles of

Orléans watched them. Disobedient, he had followed, now suffered and could not keep silent. Quietly he came to kneel beside Isabelle.

He said with difficulty: 'There is still love, Madame.'

'Is there?' she whispered violently. 'Do you love me, Charles of Orléans? Or do you merely follow your father's grand design, that step nearer the throne of France?'

She had hurt him desperately, but he answered calmly enough.

'If you only knew. My heart could swallow yours up.' He caught her hand, holding it hard on his velvet doublet. 'Feel it beat! For your peace I would have that heart brought bleeding from my body and laid before you.'

He had his arm about Katherine and the dog was licking his hand. Isabelle said suddenly: 'Charles . . . I'm in your father's debt.' She looked at Katherine. 'Louis of Orléans, for all his faults, saved my sister's life.'

'He's loyal to you.'

She smiled bitterly. 'Did you know that he is with my mother again at Tours?'

He bowed his head, and she rose, drying her cheeks. 'Come, Kéti. I cannot pray today.'

'Is there hope?' he said desperately, following her down the nave. She was encircled by the rosy light and he thought: I would pursue her to the earth's end, even if it were not my father's wish. For her I would give up all hope of heaven save that of being with her. He felt the male pride of his own flesh, little dreaming that that same flesh had power to wound and kill the most beloved. He looked at her sleek unbound maiden's hair, and secretly praised King Richard's death.

'Come, Katherine,' said Isabelle. 'Bring Jacquot. He's thirsty.'

'Oh, Belle!' said Katherine suddenly. 'I love you!' Isabelle bent to hold her close.

'Then love me, little one. For love is the only candle in this dark old world.'

She glanced up at Charles, who stood silent, daring to hope, while behind them the sunlit window made an endless permutation of colour, the blood-red, the garnet and the gold, and the sobbing anthem rose to find an end in peace.

Isabeau, at Tours, was uneasy. During the past two years her court had been much depleted; her finest hangings, plate and jewels had been removed to Paris at the King's command. Even Colard de Laon's paintings were now closely guarded in the Louvre, and the little artist had, most disloyally she thought, attached himself to the household of Jean sans Peur, and lived there in great estate.

Two of her adherents, however, were unfaltering. Louis of Orléans knelt beside her now with the flagon of Gascon wine ready and a familiar expression on his face that was compounded of disdain, lust, and abject loyalty that he was powerless to betray. She kept him dangling still, giving him half-promises of favours physical and political, allowing him a sight of her body when he came to bid goodnight, but as often taunting him, calling him weak, mad, like his brother – although Charles, to her chagrin, remained whole, with the kingdom firmly under his hand.

The other blood-servant she owned was Louis Bosredon, after whom the Dauphin had once named a rat. Bosredon's love-making had a brutality that stirred her jaded palate, and she used him to drive the gentler Louis wild with jealousy. Once in mischief she had invited both of them to her bed. She and her brother had spied on them from behind a screen. Keen sport; for she knew the predilection of Louis of Orléans. A little womanly, a little warped. Louis Bosredon was entirely man and tempered like one. His fury had excelled at Louis's timid overtures. Only barely had she and her brother prevented outright murder that night.

It was useful to have them at one another's throats. Each striving to outdo the other to her will. She pictured Bosredon's sensual face, his wicked laughing eyes. Only he dared mock her with impunity. And now he had not returned from Paris. She had sent him there to learn what he could of the King's affairs, and had expected him back at Tours days ago. She began angrily to think in terms of his disaffection. Also, she missed him. She took the refilled goblet impatiently from Orléans.

'*You* would not care if he never returned!'

'Who, highness?' he said, too innocently.

She sighed furiously and rose to pace about, more anxious than she cared to reveal.

'I would have trusted him with my life,' she murmured. 'Louis. Louis,' striking her fists against the sides of her gown.

'My queen?'

'Ah, fool!' She spoke so viciously that he wondered: why do I, a royal Duke, stay to suffer this abuse? Why did I rejoice when she finally forgave me for ruining her schemes for Milan and for condoning the match between Charles and Isabelle? Why do I neglect my own wife, my quiet Violante? In the hope that one day this wicked woman will be kind to me? His heart stirred, and with that unholy passion came again the old reasonless precognition of disaster.

'It's late,' he said.

'I shall not retire,' she answered, still treading the tiles. 'None of us will sleep tonight. He *will* come!'

She does the upstart honour. He bit his thumbnail savagely. Isabeau seated herself again.

'Entertain me.'

A page brought Louis a gittern and he drew an elegant thread of music from the strings.

> '*La plus belle et doulce figure,*
> *La plus noble gente faiture,*
> *C'est ma chiere dame et mestresse,*
> *Bon an, bon jour, joye et liesse,*
> *Li doinst dieux et bone aventure!*'

Moved by the music, he believed that his lady was all that the song said: soft and kind. Only when he looked up at her did he know himself deluded.

'That's Grenon's work!' She scowled. 'I would rather not hear the songs of Burgundy.'

She was on her feet again, murmuring and frowning. Louis sang an Italian ditty and the servants dozed on their feet, like horses. Twice Isabeau sent to ask if there had been messages from Bosredon, and her frown grew tighter. The hours hobbled by. In the last shred of night Louis slept, to be awakened by the Queen kicking at his leg with her spurred boot.

'We ride to Paris! If Bosredon has forgotten his duty to me, I shall take pleasure in reminding him.'

Within minutes horses and an escort were ready. Stiff with weariness, Louis mounted and followed the Queen. Four days' ride! and if he knew Isabeau, she would do it in three. He was not looking forward to meeting King Charles and he wondered how much he remembered of the cruel baiting in which he, Louis, had taken part. Skirting Orléans, he saw distantly his own manor, castles, churches, farms, his own fief with peasants toiling there. Somewhere in one of those misted towers was his wife, the patient pale Violante. Bearing and raising his children, uncomplaining of his adventures and thus enhancing his guilt. He thought of her with sudden sad regret, and rode fast through the county of Blois, trying not to look behind.

Charles of France was well at ease. Nothing could alarm him now. He felt as if all his dormant wits had renewed themselves, bright, like fine old armour carefully stored. Standing firm amid a swirl of diminished anxieties, he was a worthy successor to St Louis, to Philip-Augustus. His dangerous calm was ruthless. He knew through his agents that Isabeau would come to Paris. He could anticipate her every scheme. From his high plane of megalomania he saw her powerless beneath his will. He did not recognize his grand euphoria as the fragile thing it was. Thoughts of revenge made him grin like a schoolboy and kick his heels against the silk step of his dais.

He moved between palace and *château-fort*, and had again taken up his quarters in the Palais. From his raised throne he could see through a window the mast-tips of river craft and the bastions of the Grand Châtelet, crammed with treasure and prisoners, most of them Isabeau's adherents, victims of his recent purge. From above he could hear the sound of choristers in the royal chapel. Jean sans Peur was in there, listening, praying. Yes, Burgundy was under the King's roof, cousinly and subservient, daring no harm. Charles sighed contentedly, as he sat beneath the banners of Damascus cloth embroidered with lifesize birds and beasts. His amiable gaze moved over the three young people kneeling before him.

'Be pleased to rise, my dears,' he said.

Isabelle got up, her hand still firmly held by Charles of Orléans.

'And you, my prince, come closer to me.'

The Dauphin Louis mounted the dais. His robe was heavily embossed with gems and his pointed ermine-trimmed sleeves dragged on the ground. Lately he had cultivated a certain smile – more of a sneer; it sat on his soft mouth like that of a wicked old man.

'Isabelle,' said the King, 'soon you will marry.'

'Sire.'

'You will bear fine princes.'

'And,' burst out the Dauphin, 'I will make every one a chevalier of honour . . . when I am king!'

Charles continued to smile. 'Yes, but not for many years. And you, my lord of Orléans, will you cherish our jewel?'

The youth said fervently: 'I shall love her as Our Lord loved the world.'

His fingers clenched tighter on Isabelle's and she gave a hiss of pain. The King looked up at the sparkling banners. On one of them was a pelican, blood on its breast, from which its young fed.

'They drink their mother's life,' said the King, and for an instant his eyes became opaque. Then he shook himself like a dog from a river, saying forcefully:

'Yes, you will be happy. I'll give you great estate. Better, eh, Belle, than marrying the English prince?'

'Rather death,' said Isabelle softly.

'Did you know that Henry of Lancaster sent word that he was willing to abdicate the English throne should you wed his son, so think of that, Belle! You can sway kingdoms!' He laughed a little too high, too long.

'Sire,' said Charles of Orléans, 'is it true that Henry seeks to invade us, being so thwarted?'

'All threats and wind. Henry Bolingbroke is sickly, leprous, finished. As for Harry his son . . .'

'A coxcomb,' said Isabelle viciously. 'Who leches with men and women both. Who chases the matchless spirit of Glyn Dŵr through Wales and calls it war! Yet who dares to aspire to my hand and my sisters' . . . even Marie, a bride of Christ! Michelle, Katherine . . . I know all about him – brawling with his brothers in the London stews . . .'

'But surely, Madame,' said Charles of Orléans, still holding her hand, 'he was with King Richard in Ireland.'

She nodded and swallowed her anger. That morning she had made confession, revealing matters which took aback even the royal chaplain, inured to sin.

'Father, when the usurper Bolingbroke was at Windsor, I ordered that a spiked poisoned instrument be placed in his bed. It was discovered before he was harmed. I confess this because I am weary and sick of murder and would lead a good life. I am to marry again. I must go to my marriage clean.'

She wept, and the chaplain, hating the sound of her grief, said: 'Go then, and renounce your hatred. Wish ill to none. Sin no more. Be penitent.'

But, she still thought, there had been such dangerous glory in it! Such disappointment when the chamberers announced their find with cries of horror. Already she had bidden her retinue tear off Bolingbroke's badge and replace it with Richard's White Hart. The glory was gone. Murder brought only madness. She returned the anxious pressure of Charles's hand.

'Yes,' she admitted. 'King Richard liked Prince Harry well.'

Jean sans Peur entered, full of bonhomie, with a large entourage, including Colard de Laon, merry, with a gout of red paint on his pointed shoe.

'*Ma foi!* God Himself dwells in that chapel aloft! I feel the presence of our mighty ancestors!'

'Yes,' agreed the King. 'And were they not swift to root out the ills from our house?'

Jean sans Peur nodded. His long Valois nose had already snuffed out the King's mood and his heavy eyes glinted. Gladly he anticipated whatever gave the King this gay brittle confidence. There was not long to wait. The outer door shuddered under a violent knocking.

Isabeau, followed by the Duke of Orléans, marched up the Hall. The King, sitting erect, extended his hand, palm down.

'An honour, my dear Isabeau,' he said, as she snatched angrily at his fingers and brushed them with her lips. 'And how is Tours? Our court is bereft without you. Will you not admire my new Italian tapestries? All beauty comes from Italy. Your little painter will know this. But I was forgetting that Monsieur de Laon is no longer in your service. A pity, he is so skilled in the new *grisaille* . . .' He half-turned, almost winked at Jean sans Peur.

It was a puny gibe, but enough. Isabeau mounted the two steps of the dais and put her mouth close to the King's ear.

'Have a care, Charles. Remember when you were Georges Dubois!'

'Dubois?' he said pleasantly, so that everyone heard. 'A paramour of yours? Dead, as I recall.'

The King was ahead of her in taunts and strategy. No longer could she raise his nightmares. Like a vicious child, he ordered wine and sweets, bidding her admire the gold goblets and plate that once had graced her own table at Tours.

She took a long draught of wine and said roughly: 'I did not come here to parry insults. Where is Louis Bosredon?'

He said seriously: 'If he is not with you, then . . . God help us, is there no loyalty? He must have deserted your household. Come, let me console you!' He stretched out his hands. She saw with fury the wry amusement of Jean sans Peur; and the lips of her own son the Dauphin parting in a chuckle. This was a game he understood.

'I demand you bring Bosredon to me. Let me know the nature of his disaffection. Its instigator I need not ask.'

'Why should he be within my court?'

'I sent him – ' She bit her lip. 'I sent him here to Paris.'

Charles laughed. 'Paris! It's full of taverns and rogues who play with cogged dice. Perhaps even now he lies in drink with his pockets cut, tattling of his high associations . . .'

'No,' she said tightly. 'He's here.'

'Maybe.' The King's whole mood changed suddenly. 'You are weary from your journey. You must rest, change your clothes.' He clapped his hands, and Odette came forward. 'My little one, attend the Queen.'

'I have my own servants,' said Isabeau.

'I've ordered a special banquet,' he went on. 'A rare, unequalled catch was taken from the Seine today. I impounded it for my table. You must share the feast.'

She looked back angrily on her way from the Hall, but she was hungry and there seemed little merit in argument.

'You will join us?' He was almost pleading. 'Then we will talk further of Bosredon.'

Servants set damask-covered trestles in a rectangle to the dais. Plates rimmed with gems were brought, and multi-coloured goblets of Venetian glass. A place was laid for Isabeau on the King's right, and for Louis of Orléans on his left. The Dauphin sat next to Jean sans Peur, and Isabelle and Charles of Orléans lower down. Minstrels arrived and began to play a rondel. The King skipped from the dais to greet Isabeau's return, showing such amity that she almost wondered whether secretly he desired a reconciliation. It was only six years since she had borne a child of his.

'How is Katherine?' she said, following her own thoughts.

'She is well, at Poissy,' said Isabelle instantly.

'Broth, my lady?' said the King.

Steaming bowls of venison from the Loire, the meat crushed and blended with eggs, cream and wine. Isabeau ate greedily, while the King watched with solicitous approval. The minstrels played; a youth sang a *chansonette*. Isabeau, her confidence swelling with her stomach, thought: he *is* ready to be reconciled; the idiot is as weak as ever. After supper I shall demand some of my treasures back. Charles kept her cup filled with the cornelian yield from Jean sans Peur's vineyards which tasted, to her, none the worse for that. After a time her reasoning grew muddled and her head hot. She said:

'You keep a good table, my liege. Once we were great and powerful together, and could be so again.' Louis of Orléans heard this and bit his lips in dismay. The King smiled warmly.

'Agreed, why should we not all be friends? You and I, my

49

lords of Burgundy and Orléans, and your chevalier, Monsieur Bosredon . . .'

Fuddled by wine and food, she had almost forgotten.

'So he is here! Charles . . .' almost wheedling: 'Tell me.'

'He'll be with us, soon.' Flambeaux had been lit all round the hall, shining on the tapestries and the goblets' jewelled eyes. At Charles's signal, the minstrels played a fanfare. From the buttery twelve men bore in a vast covered dish.

'Fresh!' said the King. 'The bounty of Mother Seine!'

Isabeau leaned forward. 'Is it salmon?'

'No, but a big fish.' The butlers lifted the cover of the dish. Neatly lying in the middle of a bed of green herbs lay the naked, cyanosed body of Louis Bosredon. Before drowning he had been half-strangled, and the marks were livid on his neck.

Even the butlers had not been told, having been forbidden to lift the dish's cover earlier. One of them reeled into a corner to vomit. For a moment his retching was the only sound. Then the Dauphin Louis, jumping up, ran round the table to peer closer into the dish. He let out a shriek of laughter, while the King watched Isabeau greedily; the wine-flush faded to chalk and her hand snapped the stem of her goblet so that Burgundy wine ran softly over the table edge. Then the child's laughter died away and there was only the drip of the wine on the tiles.

The Princess Isabelle sat very still, her head filled with rolling waves of faintness. She saw her father's terrible triumphant eyes, the gleeful face of the Dauphin, the barely concealed satisfaction of the Duke of Orléans. She felt herself surrounded by monsters from some lavish portrait of Hell. A voice beat at her silently: you too inherit Charles's madness, Isabeau's evil. All the intercessions in the world cannot temper this devil of Valois. She would have cried out, then felt an arm about her. Charles of Orléans was beside her, pulling her up and through a side exit between the ranks of stunned servants, just as the storm broke.

'Your doing, my lord!' Her mother's voice.

'Yes, mine! And so shall I do to all your mountebanks and spies that fill your lust, that weasel into my Council chamber . . .'

There was a scream, the crash of glass, wild weeping.

Isabelle and Charles went, as urgently as if heaven itself were about to close, up the stairs to the chapel.

'Sometimes,' she said faintly, 'I would gladly die!'

He swathed her in his cloak. 'And take my own life away? Madame, sweet Madame . . .'

She clasped him tightly about the waist. I told Katherine . . . love is the only candle . . .

'The world seems darker still today,' she said.

They reached the chapel. The door was open and the scent of flowers and wax wreathed about the high altar with its burning golden Christ.

'Stay by me,' said Charles of Orléans, 'and I will be your light.'

'Murder,' said Jean sans Peur, stretching his long legs in the hearth, 'is not the royal prerogative.'

It was November, sickly with fog and the stench of wet withered fruit left on the bough. A grave-cold mist clung about the fortress at Bapaume where the Duke had installed himself to meditate, to assess, and to worry more than a little. Tense and sober, a small ring of followers deployed themselves quietly about his presence.

Three things fretted Jean's cool mind, and two of them concerned the House of Orléans. Isabelle's forthcoming marriage with the young Charles solidified the rival claim to Valois. Bosredon's assassination two months earlier had proved fortunate for Duke Louis. Lastly and most important, the King's health, when last assessed, had given Jean sans Peur some disturbing moments. He could only hope he had imagined that clouding of the eyes, those non-sequiturs in the royal conversation. The King had studied his own fingernails intently; always a bad sign. His calm was precarious. Any shock could overset him. Jean sans Peur spoke quietly to a man in the forefront of the circle about his chair.

'And where was the Queen yesterday?'

'At Troyes, my lord. Orléans was with her. They are preparing to leave for winter quarters.'

'Where?'

'Paris. The Palais again.'

Jean sans Peur lowered his head, smiling ruefully, his heavy nose like a preying bird's beak.

'She's confident, then.'

'Yes, lord. So is he. Very light of heart.'

'She would not go to Paris,' he said, raising his head and addressing the listeners directly, 'were she not sure of some calamity to follow that will render her immune. After the Bosredon affair she swore never to return while Charles held power. Are there physicians with the King?'

Anxiety cooled his brain further; his thoughts, like swordsmen in dark places, moved deliberately on. He weighed the whole structure of events, intuitively seeing France in the round, a globe balanced precariously on the fragile thread of her sovereign's spirit, a globe about which rats crept and gnawed. Also he foresaw the danger from beyond that sphere, from Henry of Lancaster, who even though sick was capable, through his heir, of further ruthless demands. Henry had been willing to compromise for a French princess but would soon be willing no longer. Jean sans Peur thought, suddenly appalled: Valois has behaved like a true imbecile. Diplomacy is dead. Were I in my cousin's shoes, I would by now have averted disaster. Should that cousin's reason fail, what then?

Isabeau, allied to Orléans, will see the country damned. So long as she can have her pleasure, rape the treasury before Henry of England gets to it, and doubtless flee with her favourites across the nearest frontier . . . just as I caught her once before, on the road to Milan. Milan.

The name came like a flash of flame. Violante of Milan was wife to Louis of Orléans. A poor neglected wife for sure, but Louis had a certain sense of responsibility, a basic tenderness. Had not Jean himself seen him, refusing to travel on because of a sick child? Was this the answer, or part of it? The way to weaken by elimination, at least some of the dangerous power of the Queen?

There was a trick to which lovely sinful Paris would lend her darkness. He beckoned his agent closer.

'All others may go,' he said.

Murder is not the king's prerogative, he told himself again.

Had I been king, France would be safer than she is today. It is not too late.

At seven years old, Katherine had grown tall but was still very thin. She had a trick of holding herself tight, arms crossed over her waist. Her appetite was hearty but she remained pale, and the nuns, surveying her like some jewel, worried in whispers. Daily they enveloped her in prayer.

She found Poissy safe and boring. She watched her sister Marie take her final vows; she played with Jacquot, who had outgrown puppyhood and guarded her with dignity. She wove small coloured tapestries of St Denis and St Antoine. She rose obediently to the night offices and yawned through the long services of the day, and all the time she waited for visits from Belle. She marked the days off on tally-sticks, she cut them from candles and watched them waste to bring Belle nearer. Sometimes there was an unexpected visit, which threw her whole calendar into joyful chaos. On a foul November day, Dame Alphonse bustled into the parlour where Katherine sat coughing from the fog which seeped even through the lead-lined windows.

'My princess!' She stopped mid-stride, keys and rosary swinging. 'Have you *la grippe*? Here . . .' She fumbled in her pouch. 'Wear this. It will cure you quicker than anything I know.'

It was a suckered frond of sweetbriar, noduled with a warty growth.

'*L'églantine*,' breathed Dame Alphonse. 'The bush from which this came was planted in our garth during the time of Philip-Augustus. When the canker shows on the briar, it cures the cough. Permit . . .'

The princess bent her long neck to receive the garland. From his corner Jacquot watched sternly, then seeing that the nun meant no harm, went to sleep again, waking the next instant to leap and fawn round Isabelle, who entered with a smile.

'Oh, Kétil!' Isabelle cried after a moment, half-strangled. 'How strong you've grown! Wait, I can't breathe. I want to give you a present.'

It was a miniature painting by Colard de Laon mounted in blue enamel. It was a good likeness; the little artist had caught Isabelle's courage and much of her beauty. She sat down on a high-backed chair and drew her sister on to her lap.

'You're too old for that, Princess,' said Dame Alphonse, hovering near the door. 'You are nearly grown up. Nursing is for babes.'

'Then I'll be a babe for ever,' said Katherine.

'Madame.' The nun was red with importance under her wimple. 'All the community offer you felicitations on your betrothal. When is the marriage to take place?'

'Very soon,' said Isabelle absently. She took between thumb and finger the sweetbriar garland round Katherine's neck. 'What's this nonsense?'

'The princess was coughing,' said Dame Alphonse, redder than ever.

'Then she must have a physician.' Isabelle looked gravely down at Katherine. She removed the prickly trophy and held it out in silence to Dame Alphonse. Defeated, the nun withdrew.

'Belle,' said Katherine in the peace that followed, 'are you really to be married soon?'

'Yes, my love.'

'Will you be very unhappy?'

'I trust not.' Isabelle laughed. 'Why?'

'When you were married before . . .' She slid from her sister's lap and knelt. 'I remember, Belle, how you wept.'

'That was afterwards.' She looked down tenderly at Katherine. 'I was only a year older than you when I married Richard . . . he said to my father: "I would not have her any older. I am young enough to wait for her. We shall be so strongly united that no king in Christendom can in any way . . . hurt us." '

'Oh, sweet Belle!' cried Katherine. 'You're weeping now!'

Unheeding, Isabelle went on. 'And when I was conveyed in state from Lambeth to the Tower, soon after we came to England, nine people were crushed to death in their effort to see me – the little queen! It was a bad augury which was fulfilled worse than either of us had dreamed . . .' She brushed her tears away. 'It's finished. Charles loves me and I am fond of him. His father was kind to you. I shall be saved from Henry Bolingbroke and his knavish son. You also, and Michelle. You will make good marriages and be happy. When I'm married I shall live at Blois. Or Charles will take me to Angoulême, where he is Count. It's lovely there in spring . . .'

Katherine's dark eyes were suddenly wild.

'You swore you'd never leave me, Belle! Never while life lasts!' She began to sob, and Isabelle took her close again.

'I swore it. I swear it now. We shall not be parted for long.' She shivered. A ghost-voice whispered in her head: *Adieu, Madame! Adieu! until we meet again!*

'I want to be with you. Take me with you to Blois, to Angoulême!'

'Katherine,' said Belle sternly, 'you must trust me. It's safer for you here at Poissy, until such time as you marry. Oh, Katherine! as if I should ever desert you! I'll come to see you often, do you think I don't miss you? Care for you constantly, pray for you every day? I've told you, Kéti, this is a dark, evil world. Stay a while longer here. Dame Alphonse is loyal and this place is so holy none dare meddle with it. Here, dry your eyes. Bring your lute and sing to me. We'll have a lovely time together.'

While they played and sang and told one another stories, the day shortened and the fog thickened, becoming a noxious brew like that which had covered Paris the previous evening as if obedient to some powerful will. Death-cold and filled with the stench of sewers and river, it seemed elemental and gorged with sin.

As Katherine played and Isabelle tapped her foot and smiled, there came a hammering on the outer door of the convent. A hammering that might have come from the sword-hilt of one seeking sanctuary, so desperate and violent were the blows. They heard the porteress's raised voice, and feet running down the cloister to where the sisters sat. A man's voice cried: 'Madame! I must see Madame!'

It was a henchman of Charles of Orléans, one who loved the family well and who consequently wept and whose white disastrous face made Isabelle spring up with a cry. When he could speak he told a dreadful tale. The secret premonitions of Louis of Orléans had come to their full.

For him, triumph and consummation had been all he had ever hoped for. After the evening of Bosredon's murder had ended in chaos, the Queen shrieking with rage and grief, the King laughing wildly and eventually becoming pale and silent, Isabeau had almost collapsed. Leaving the table with its overflung goblets and skirting the gruesome corpse, Louis had followed her from the hall, offering her his arm, expecting it to be struck away with a malediction. But she had turned to him, her face patched scarlet and white, her eyes sunken with shock.

'For God's love, Louis, take me from this place.'

He summoned all his resources to find a lodging fit for her and not too far away, for her strength seemed on the wane. An unfamiliar sense of power possessed him; he blessed Bosredon's demise and found it possible in his mind to congratulate the King. It seemed a long time since he and Isabeau and Louis of Bavaria had wandered into the Hôtel de St Paul to taunt the filthy and raving Charles. St Paul was where he took Isabeau. The place had recently been re-furbished; fires were kept burning and chambers sweet. There they lay that night, Isabeau tossing in a great bed, Louis watching from the foot and soothing her with eloquence he had not known lay in him. On the following day they returned to Tours, and there the Queen rewarded him at last. No longer did she flaunt her person before him only to send him off next minute with an oath. She scarcely let him out of her sight, accepting his embraces voluptuously, sharing with him the days and nights, her cup, her bed. After a few days they left Tours and moved to Troyes, within sight of the Seine and easy access to Paris. There she breathed her poisonous ambition in his ears.

'I have the King watched day and night. Yesterday he dropped his cup, his hand was shaking. The day before he wept for no reason. He is failing again, and soon we'll show him no mercy, you and I!'

She was confident. It would have surprised her to learn that the agents of Jean sans Peur also watched the King just as avidly, and bore back to their master the disconcerting evidence of their eyes. It was as if the whole of France reverberated with the beat of hooves and whispers. And at Blois, Violante of Milan watched sadly from her château-tower, watched the empty courtyard and the barren vineyards and wondered when, if ever, her husband would come home. Sometimes, Louis still thought of her, but he was enwrapped in Isabeau, feeling, ecstatic and afraid, as if he rode a wild horse down an avenue of darkness. By the time they left Troyes and took up residence at the Palais, joy had vanquished his fear. He grew bold and more assertive. He was in bed with the Queen, late at night, when the message came, voiced in ancient squeaky tones outside the door.

Isabeau said: 'Call out. Say we have retired, and that tomorrow I'll punish whoever has disturbed us.'

The scratching on the door continued with the urgent summons.

'Make a light.' Louis fumbled for flint and tinder. The Queen raised herself on her elbow. The light rippled on her heavy white breasts; her face was puffy with sleep. Louis slid from bed, threw on a robe and opened the door. The servant confronting him was unfamiliar but there were many such in Isabeau's entourage; distant relatives, hangers-on.

'Seigneur, you must come. Your wife, the Duchess Violante.'

'She is at Blois,' he said curtly.

'No, she is in Paris here, at the Louvre, mortally ill. She was brought this evening so that the King's physicians might save her life, but it is hopeless. She is asking for you.'

'Wait.' He went back into the chamber and began quickly to dress. Isabeau had overheard the conversation. She watched him cynically.

'You still have a tender heart,' she mocked.

'She's my wife,' said Louis, and threw on his chaperon and mantle. He picked up sword and belt and buckled them on.

'But you, my queen,' he said gallantly, 'are my life!'

The old page, agitated, was waiting, and went ahead down

the stairs and out through the great gate into the foggy street where horses and an escort of five men waited. We must hurry, they said, and took Louis at a fierce pace through the deserted city. He rode in the midst of the escort, the man at its head going so fast through alleys and courts that the lantern he carried swung up and down, its rays like pale steam against the fog. Louis thought of Violante: I could have treated her better, though I was never cruel . . . They turned over cobbles glossy with fog, into the Rue Barbette, narrow and dark, in the meanest quarter of Paris. A short cut, seigneur, said the leading rider, slowing his horse and turning to smile with unpleasantly black teeth and unshaven jaw poking from his hood. What a devil, thought Louis; why does Isabeau employ such villains, but then doubtless he is good with his fists. It was his last conclusive thought. From a darkened house on the left four men rushed out. Louis turned with a cry to the escort, just as the first blade drove into his side, doubling him in agony. He raised his head appealingly and was instantly almost blinded by blood from a slash to his brow, yet saw the unshaven man steadying the light and smiling. Louis slipped from his horse. His left hand clawed upward and clutched at the saddle-horn. One of the assailants raised a short sword and the Duke felt a searing pain. He looked up through blood, saw his own severed hand still clinging to the saddle, and fell below it to the ground. There nine men hacked at him and he died.

Nearby a window was flung open, a light bloomed and a voice called sleepily. Quickly the leader doused his lantern and shouted through the murk.

'The Watch here! All shut, blow out your candles!' and the window went dark again. Nine red blades were sheathed. Nine riders set spurs and were gone. Louis lay still in his blood. A little runnel of it was moving, coming to rest beside the severed hand on the other side of the street.

By a strange irony, Violante of Milan had indeed been ill at Blois, and now in Paris she had a deathly appearance. With the Princess Isabelle she sat in the foremost carriage of a long mourning procession which wound north-easterly to the Hôtel de St Paul, where the King now resided. Isabelle had designed the cortège with as much care as her resources could muster. Seven black *charrettes*, each drawn by a pair of white horses, slowly moved, a magpie chain of grief, from the Porte St Jacques where at the south outer wall she had received Violante with tears. In the second of these carriages lay the black-clad body of Louis of Orléans, wearing his orders and jewels, with his left hand wrapped in cloth of gold and placed by his head. Following the corpse came the young Charles, his sword drawn and carried before his face. Behind him in the remaining wagons sat Isabelle's retainers and those who were prominent in the household of Orléans. Word of the procession's approach had leaped ahead and the streets filled with citizens craning for a long look at the murdered Duke. From the Abbey of St Victor, from St Geneviève and St Etienne the students and tutors came hurrying and followed the cortège into the Cité. As the slow black-and-white river moved over the bridge at the Petit Châtelet and into the shadow of Notre Dame, the crowd swelled. The bell was sounding, mingling with the rattle and ring of hooves and wheels. The train passed through the Porte au Blé into the precinct of St Paul where the Célestins bell joined that of the cathedral. Men bared their heads, looking awestruck on tiptoe at the Duke's remains. A voice said loudly: 'Whose evil work was this?'

Isabelle had no need to wonder; she was sure. The King's words to Isabeau still haunted her. '*So shall I do to all your mountebanks, who fill your lust . . .*' She sorrowed for her uncle but her prime emotions were rage and revulsion. Bosredon's killing had been bad enough, for all that he had only been an adventurer and a spy. Now this ambush in the dark brought to her the sick reminder of another dearer death. So had Exton's assassins, on Bolingbroke's orders, struck down Richard in the night at Pontefract. There were still the marks of cudgel and sword on the pillar in that dungeon in England's north. Richard had managed to kill at least two of them, but had been defeated by numbers, the coward's method. What despair for him, in the dark! Beside Isabelle, Violante sobbed, pressing a linen square to her eyes.

'Do not weep, my lady,' said Isabelle grimly. 'I will be your champion. You shall see my father's shame!'

At the gate of the Hôtel de St Paul the cortège halted. At the foot of the steps she turned to Charles, who shook his head, still holding his sword. 'I must stay to guard my father.' So she assisted the widowed Duchess upwards to the Hall, through the columns decorated with weird howling faces, into the presence of a large assembly. The King stood by his dais, Odette behind him. The Dauphin Louis, now tall at eleven years old, his younger brothers Charles and Jean, and Michelle were there, standing quietly. And there was Katherine, with the King's hand resting on her shoulder. When she saw Isabelle she made to run forward, but halted at the expression on her sister's face. Why in heaven has he taken her from Poissy? thought Isabelle. God knows I would not have had her witness what I shall say, but it's too late. Supporting Violante, she walked between the bowing courtiers and faced her father. He smiled at her tremulously; his eyes were black-ringed and a vein flickered in his temple. She thought: once I pitied him, sorrowed for him. But now his barbarism has cast out all my compassion.

'Madame,' he said softly, 'and my lady of Orléans. God be with you both.'

He stretched out his hands, the fingernails grown long, for his daughter and sister-in-law to kiss. The Duchess Violante sank to her knees; the princess stood still.

'Belle?' said the King in a high voice. 'Come, greet me. This is a sad day.'

'Your day! Your doing!' said Isabelle with great violence.

'Madame?' he said uncertainly.

Dimly she heard herself begin a planned tirade that outgrew its intent and overwhelmed her, bringing the sweat on to her face and shaking her whole body. From somewhere outside she looked amazed at this crying, ranting self, then seeing, as through mist, the faces of the company, nervous and appalled, the small princes drawing closer to Michelle, the Dauphin forgetting to smile. And the King's eyes ringed with deeper black in new pallor, his speechless immobility. Everyone still as stone except for Odette, who came with a quick fluttering step to stand beside King Charles.

'You are my shame,' Isabelle said on a harsh breath, and lapsed into the formal third person singular. 'For my father has murdered his own brother. He has become as barbaric, as gross in villainy as . . . as the English! As vile as Henry Bolingbroke!' And in that instant it was Bolingbroke whom she wildly confronted.

'My daughter,' said the King very faintly, 'you are wrong. I am guiltless.'

'Assassin!' she cried. She drew Violante up, holding her in her arms. 'See your handiwork! For God's sake!' Her voice wailed about the pillared Hall; it might have come from the carved mouths of the wild men. 'Has Valois come to this? Butchering its own flesh in stealth, by night? Louis of Orléans would have been my father on my marriage, so you have robbed me of two fathers. For from this day I count you none of mine!'

She finished, almost fainting. Even Violante, her own sorrow momentarily eclipsed, was looking at her aghast, like the whole court. Then the King gave a groan. Forty pairs of eyes swivelled to the dais. He had sunk to the floor, his arms waving wildly. He had knocked off his diadem. It fell and rotated like a glittering coin. The King clutched at his head and Odette bent to him. Katherine crept nearer and laid a timid hand upon his neck.

'Do not touch me! I shall shatter!' He held out his taloned fingers. 'Look!' he cried into the frightened child's face. 'I am made of glass . . .' Then he buried his head in the skirt of his mantle and rolled about against the steps of the dais. Doctors ran and milled about him as the dreadful silence began to break up into whispered oaths and little prayers.

Odette left the King's side. She came down to where Isabelle, horrified, stood staring at her father.

'I trust you're satisfied, Madame!' She looked sadly back at the writhing figure. 'I would have given my heart's blood to spare him this. Orléans was of no account beside Charles of Valois, for whom I would gladly die. A hundred lives would be small price to keep him well. And now . . .' For the first

61

time in memory Isabelle saw tears in Odette's eyes. 'He will not recover easily from this storm. Why, Madame? Why did you do it? He had enough on his soul without false accusation! You should have saved your spleen for Jean sans Peur!'

Isabelle covered her face with her hands, but Odette pulled them away.

'Look, Madame! Look well! There's the beginning of France's ruin!'

Haggardly Isabelle looked. The Dauphin Louis had picked up the fallen diadem, and was surveying it with a reckless infantile greed. And on the steps, unnoticed by the distraught throng, sat Katherine, shivering and crying like a little old woman gone mad.

In the cloister garth at Poissy, between the troutstream and the house, a willow grew. Each autumn Katherine watched the leaves changing from silver-green to grey, and listened to the shivering branches. It was now the third autumn since that dreadful day at court, from which she had returned weeping, fevered and coughing. Dame Alphonse had nursed her back to serenity; now she was cherished and cloistered and knew little of the world outside. She was denied nothing, hence the private chamber overlooking the garden, the bounty of silver toilette appointments and fine gowns sent by Charles of Orléans, now married to Isabelle at last.

She did not know that her father lay in the worst madness of his life nor that the thirteen-year-old Dauphine Louis feebly held government under the regency of Jean sans Peur. She did not know that Louis of Orléans had been buried with honours in the royal vault at the Célestins, where, less than a year later, Violante had joined him. Neither did she know that Jean sans Peur, emboldened by his new supremacy, had sent an army to besiege, albeit abortively, the English stronghold of Calais. Henry Bolingbroke had viewed this impertinence gravely from London, sending Prince Harry, as Captain of Calais, to keep the tenure under arms.

She sat holding the silver mirror close to her face. Outside the willow waved and mourned and Jacquot lay on the bed, watching her. She looked deeply in the polished metal; her eyes were immense, black as autumn fruit. Her dark hair fell thick and shining to her waist. But, inescapably, her nose was too long. Frowning, she smoothed and pressed it, grimaced and dropped her hand. Beside her lay the portrait of Belle. She slept with it beneath her bolster; she took it out to fix her eyes on it before she extinguished her candle. That face must be the last thing she saw before sleep, or ill-luck would come in the morning. Now she compared it with her own mirrored image, staring alternatively at Belle's perfect features, the bright determined eyes with their essential sadness, the enchanting half-smile. She glanced at the September candle she had marked and burned in anticipation of Isabelle's next visit. It was nearly down. A smile touched her face, completely translating its sombre curves. The unwatched mirror reflected a loveliness that far outshone the envied portrait.

The days of sitting on Belle's lap were over. Indeed now it would be impossible. Isabelle was near her time, rounded with a mystery that looked almost comical against her slenderness. Charles of Orléans, more worshipping than ever, had accompanied her on that last occasion. He had been kind and solicitous, but Katherine was jealous. He had not allowed Belle to stay long, saying that she was tired and Katherine must have patience. Now surely the child was born and they would meet again; very soon, if the candle did not lie.

'Princess, if you look too long in the mirror, you will see the Devil,' said Dame Alphonse, entering with a swish and jangle.

'He can't be as ugly as I am,' said Katherine. 'Oh, sweet Dame! I'm very bored.'

Two sins in one breath, thought the nun. Heresy and worse, *accidie*, kin of sloth and father of mischief. But I'll not reproach the child. Dame Alphonse had her finger on the pulse of the world outside. The King's malady was worse, and, incredibly, Queen Isabeau had made a new conquest. Jean sans Peur had spent some weeks with her at Tours. What a world! thought Dame Alphonse, and blessed her own vocation.

'How I wish I could see Madame!' said Katherine. 'Is there any news?'

She looked at the portrait longingly and the watching nun began to tell her beads mechanically. After a moment, she said:

'Don't love so much, Princess. It is unfitting.'

'Unfitting!' Katherine looked up sharply. 'To love my Belle, when there is none other in this world . . .'

I can't blame her, thought the nun. Yet she said:

'Princess, it's good and right that you love your sister. But Madame is as sinful as you and I, as any mortal creature. There's One above all princes, exempt from sin, eternal. It is He whom you must love . . .'

'Oh, I do,' said Katherine quickly. Into her mind came an old picture from the breviary with the burning heretics. God had been there, gravely judging from the clouds above the smoke and flame. Her eyes returned to the portrait, the face with its certain pledge of love. Her choice was already made, but it would not do to acquaint Dame Alphonse with it. Better anyway not to pursue the argument, for Dame Alphonse had recently returned from a rare expedition to Calais and Katherine was longing to hear about it all. She rose and laid her long white hand on the nun's capacious sleeve.

'Did you enjoy your journey?'

'Too swift at my age. My joints are still aching.'

'Did you see many people?'

'I visited the Dominicans. Their house can't hold a candle to ours' (with a smirk that embraced the sin of vanity). 'Their discipline comes and goes like April weather. But then, they're in English territory and doubtless infected by that wayward environment. They've a fine image of St Catherine. I asked intercession for you, and I swear she smiled at me.'

'What else?' said Katherine eagerly.

'Isn't that enough?' Dame Alphonse was hurt.

'Did you see the English? Belle told me that some are more fiends than the Fiend himself. Did you attend any banquets?'

'Banquets? Me? I stayed in cloister, of course. By courtesy of the Abbess. I saw no fiends!' A little alarmed, she glanced at Katherine. Madame had put some wild notions into the child's mind. The princess was looking so disappointed that Dame Alphonse relented.

'I did see Prince Harry, though. He rode by with a great train, very fine, on the way to the harbour. They say his father's likely to die in England, but it seems he takes his time over it. And Harry badly wants the crown . . .'

Just as your own young brother Louis lusts to rule France unhampered by regency, she thought. Already Louis was grotesquely playing at manhood – eyeing the women at court, and more than once drinking himself insensible.

'How does Prince Harry look?'

'I only had a glimpse.' The nun hurriedly collected her thoughts. 'His head was bare, his cheek florid. He has a scar on his face. Aged about twenty-three. He looks . . . clever.'

Katherine felt, in loyalty to Belle, that he should at least have ridden in a haze of fire and brimstone. But then Dame Alphonse often confessed she needed spectacles. Strange to think that she, Katherine, could have been his bride. A wicked thought popped up: it couldn't be more boring than Poissy!

To counteract her instant guilt, she said loudly: 'They wanted me to marry him. But I would first have put an end to myself!'

'Now there's real heresy!' said Dame Alphonse grimly. 'Pray for pardon. This minute.' She slid stiffly on to a prie-dieu and pulled the princess down beside her. Together they murmured quietly to the little flame above, while a willow branch tapped at the window as if afraid of approaching winter and begging entry. Its tapping was echoed from outside the chamber door. Dame Alphonse prayed on steadily for a few moments, then rose, and opened the door. Katherine remained kneeling. Just outside the door the nun saw the house chaplain and a young man, mud on his mantle. She recognized him after a moment; Antoine l'Astisan, secretary to Charles of Orléans. Katherine, pretending to pray, listened hard. She caught only a stray word or phrase.

'God save us!'

'Amen. Do your best.'

'Michelle . . . attends the Dauphin, and he is loath to leave Paris.'

Marie was mentioned. '. . . in seclusion. The little one . . .'

'Of course, the favourite. God, sir, be hasty!'

Katherine got up just as the nun returned, her eyes bright, wearing an odd little smile.

'Princess, make ready. You are going to Blois. Madame has been delivered of her child.'

Joy and with it beauty flooded Katherine's face.

'They're waiting.' Dame Alphonse turned from Katherine, fixing her eyes upon the flame beneath the image of Christ, while Katherine ran about, collecting clothes in an untidy bundle. She did not offer to help, for she did not trust herself. 'God go with you, child,' was all she said, as the light feet left the room and the door slammed shut. After some little time, she heard the rattle of wheels and hooves departing from the courtyard outside. Then she knelt once more, and very soberly resumed her prayer.

It was the worst journey of Antoine l'Astisan's life. He was so saddle-weary from the swift ride north that he shared the princess's litter on the return journey. He had rested for only an hour, and now there were fifty miles to cover again. So he sat with Katherine and tried to avoid her eyes. He feigned occupation with documents carried in his satchel, letters half-drafted, meaningless and blurred to his eyes, one or two of his lord's poems awaiting fair copying. Yet Katherine, sitting very straight and important, demanded his attention. He shuffled the parchments away and looked out of the narrow window, at the trees sparkling with September colour, orange and ochre and gold, and heard her asking him questions.

'Where are we now? Shall we be much longer?'

'This is Chartres, my lady. And it depends on the road how long we take. Look out, Princess, and you'll see the cathedral. When one goes in, it's like standing inside a sapphire.'

She looked and saw massed spires, silver arches, the diamond of windows, all this beauty nesting in a maze of trees, their leaves splendid in death. The sun was already beginning to decline, its light mellow and lovely. There was the merest breath of frost.

'The weather is drier today,' said Antoine l'Astisan, for safety.

'Tell me – ' the diversion of the cathedral was over – 'is the child pretty? Shall I be able to hold it? What is its name?'

'The little maid is very pretty,' said l'Astisan, fidgeting with his satchel. 'She is not named yet.'

'I'm longing to see her, and Madame!' At this, the secretary leaped to his feet in the swaying litter and, through the window, rapped on the panels outside. The carriage slowed; an outrider bent to look through at him.

'Can we go no faster?'

'The horses are tired. We must rest them at Bretigny.'

Antoine l'Astisan cried: 'Make all speed!' and then to Katherine: 'We must stop at Bretigny but . . .' He passed a hand over his eyes. He heard her say gently: 'Do they hurt you?' and in a voice so like Isabelle's, a voice loved by all: 'I think my brother-in-law works you too hard!' He could not answer. He shook his head and delved about in his documents.

'Where do we go after Bretigny?'

'We cross the northern Loire near Orléans . . . then we're almost there . . .'

He heard her say wistfully: 'If we had wings!' and answered, his mind made up as if to propitiate whatever gods worked on this journey: 'Very well. We'll ride through the night.'

We will ride through the night. An old memory awoke. She fancied she saw, through the moving window, her mother's spur spraying red from the horse's side, beads of her own blood running from a wounded foot. She fancied she felt the ache in her lungs, the burning of thirst, the plunging of the horses as the Loire met the Yonne, the pain and terror of the night in Tonnerre. Fears laid away during the shady time at Poissy renewed themselves. But Belle had come . . . she reached out and touched l'Astisan's knee.

'How is my sweet sister?'

'She is very tired, Princess,' he said, reading a letter and making nonsense of it. 'She had a difficult accouchement.' Then he closed his eyes as if to doze, and secretly began to pray. If there is any mercy, great God, give it now. Give us one little hour.

Leaving the plains of Normandy, they entered the county of Blois and the Loire valley. With fresh horses entrained at

Bretigny they came just before dawn to their destination. It was to be another fine day, and the sun's gleam climbed in mist up the château of Blois, piercing the vapours on the river-moat, highlighting the flamboyant architecture and the candle-snuffer turrets. The standards flew; the peacock feathers and broom, the fleurs-de-lys. The sun touched their misty colours to jewels.

Katherine was out of the carriage almost before it had stopped, running over the drawbridge and under the portcullis, diminished by its great height. Into the hall she ran, and Charles of Orléans moved slowly to greet her. His hands were cold; he looked over her head, mutely seeking the face of Antoine l'Astisan. Very softly their voices drifted, the secretary speaking first.

'We are too late . . .'

'By half an hour.'

Antoine l'Astisan fell to his knees, his hand on Katherine's shoulder pulling her down beside him. He crossed his breast.

'Madame is dead,' she heard Charles say. 'My wife. My life. My lovely princess. Ah, Death! what made thee so bold!'

There was no reality. The hall was a place in a dream, the weeping servants half-seen ghosts. Even the distant mew of the new-born infant the wail of an imaginary fiend. She allowed Charles to take her hand once more and lead her into a great chamber. There, colourless, almost translucent, lay her sister, made traitor by death.

She spoke to Belle softly, and the carved lips kept their distant secret smile under the ranked candles about the bier. As surely as if the knowledge had been laid before her, a signed and sealed decree, she knew that her childhood was over. It left the windows of her mind as swiftly as the white bird, flying inland from the storms of the sea.

Part Two

THE PROPHECY

Wales, 1414

I did not refuse the collar which bound me,
The poet's peer, for her arms around me
Were white as the chalk or a circlet of snow –
How gay the gift a man's throat will know . . .

Dafydd ap Gwilym, 1325–80

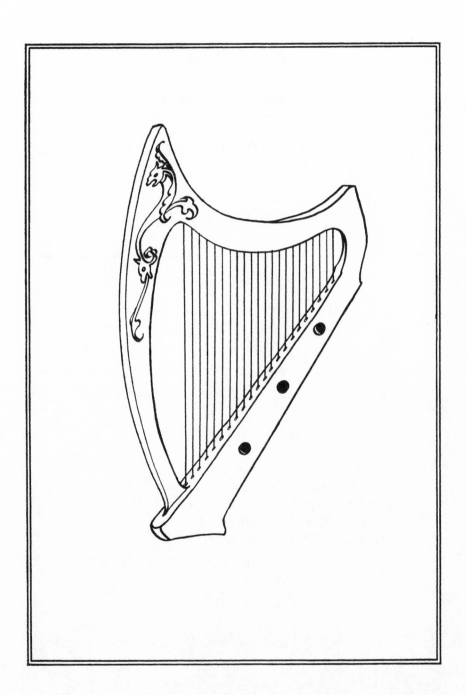

Hywelis was watching the vixen and her cubs. She lay upwind of them, pressed deep into the bracken and heather that spread over the whole of Llangollen Vale. Looking through a tunnel of green fronds, each tipped with a tiny perfect bishop's crozier, she was quite still, save for the rippling of her long red hair moved by the wind from Eglwyseg Mountain. She had known the cubs from their conception, had watched the mating one night under a tremulous moon. Now they played two yards from her hiding-place where the June sun warmed her back and the past night's dew dampened her breast. She saw how quietly and intensely they played, biting one another. The largest was exactly like his father. Hywelis whispered: 'Madog. Madog, old Reynold's heir.' Bronwen, the vixen, lay nose between paws, stern eyes on them all. It was rare for them to appear in daylight.

Hywelis played with them in her mind, running with them until they were silhouetted against snowy cumulus at the top of a bank, then sporting down again with fierce embraces. They were fed; on the ground was a tossed chewing of fur, stripped small bones. In thought, too, Hywelis had shared the feast, tasting the warm blood, cracking the carcass between her own sharp teeth. For today she felt three-quarters vixen, and anyone seeing her might have fancied her face more pointed, her hair shining redder, the tilt of her eyes more evident. She came and went as she pleased within the vale, moving through it even in darkness since she was a small child, seeking completion in the wild, and learning, and although there were boar and wolf roaming her domain, she had never been harmed.

Once long ago, the Lord of Sycharth and Glyndyfrdwy had sent a search-party with torches for her; the night was perilous with storm. She had been beaten. Not a hard beating, for the Lord, above all others, understood her craving. Still she came and went at will and now, at eighteen, she had seen things at

71

dusk, in moonlight, at dawning, beyond the comprehension of the world. Things not only of nature (the fight to the death between badgers, the mourning of a swan for its mate), but of supernature, like the procession of men and women, none of them over two feet tall, who sang as they vanished into a cleft in the hill; the ring-ouzel who, playing in a tributary of the Dee, had looked at her with human eyes; the speckled grouse that had once, clearly, spoken her name. Hywelis had the lore, the knowledge, the sight. The Lord of Sycharth's blood beat in her veins. He who could whisk up a storm, darken the moon with a wink, and whose plumed horses rode the air with grace. Upon this heritage she had built her power.

The sight and knowledge that was hers had been put to use on the day of her earliest memory in the time of Sycharth's long-gone splendour; the Lord ensconced in his wolfshead armchair, she wandering among the hall-floor rushes. She had been two years old. All Sycharth was awaiting the return of Iolo Goch. Iolo the Red was the Lord's prized bard, himself a lord and seer. His place was far above the three guild categories of the hierarchy of music: the *pencerdd*, chief of song, the *teuluwr*, or household bard, and the *cerddar*, head minstrel. Iolo had gone to Coed y Pantwn to commune with spirits and establish his prophecy.

The summer dusk was haunted by owls. Impatient, the Lord had risen, lifting Hywelis to his shoulder and striding up to the battlements for a sign of Iolo's return. He had worn a fur cloak with a great emerald clasp and Hywelis had hooked her fingers round the stone. Bats streamed in rays up from the tower and, mere flashes of black in the torchlight held by a sentry, danced above. Together lord and child looked out. To the west were the Berwyn peaks, fast losing shape as night fell, as did Llanrhaedar and further south, Llangedwyn in its bower of curving hills. Far behind the castle were the mountains of Llantysilio and Eglwyseg and behind them other ranges, their unseen tips disappearing in darkness and dewfall, great Mynydd Hiraethog among them. The last light was dying from the moat about Sycharth; sounds were enhanced – the squeak of the bats, the plash of the river and stream and the noises of creatures fishing at the dam. Over the stream in gloom Pont

Sycharth lay, and this Iolo would cross to reach home. A water fairy lived there, but she was harmless. They had burned a coracle in her honour for many years, pushing it downstream with offerings of bread and ale aboard.

Hywelis pressed close to the Lord's handsome head and gripped the emerald brooch tighter. She looked across the darkened moat to the bridge. 'Iolo's coming,' she said. 'Not alone.'

The Lord shifted her weight from his shoulder and placed her feet on the battlements. Holding her fast, he said: 'Are you sure? And who comes with him, friend or enemy?' glancing, always wary, east to where the distant invisible border of the marches yielded to England.

'It's Iolo, my Red Iolo!' said Hywelis. 'With many lanterns.'

'No, child!' said the Lord, almost pleadingly.

'Yes!' She was excited. 'All about him, dancing, pretty lights.' A voice, old yet strong, called out:

'Merfyn! Take my horse. *Diawl!* I've dropped my lantern in the stream. It grows dark quickly.'

'You see,' said the deep voice in Hywelis's ear. 'You were mistaken. Iolo came from the bridge without light. Do you see him now?' She leaned against his arm, out over the drop and looked where the bard was giving his reins to Merfyn at the stable-door. The lights were all around Iolo Goch, brightly playing, a steady shower of fire, each almost in the shape of a small slim man. She felt the Lord's hand close over her eyes.

'I see them, too,' he said softly. 'But yours is the clearer vision. To me, he walks only in a gleaming haze. What see you? Truly?' He withdrew his hand.

'Like many candles,' she struggled down. 'Burning bright. Iolo is back . . .' and she ran down the dipping spiral to where the bard, looking weary, doffed his mantle in the hall. The Lord followed slowly, thoughtful, sad, yet unsurprised, for the child was of his flesh, conceived of a dead concubine, a faery-woman. Her eyes were those of a seer. He thought: she will be greater than I in that respect. She is purer than I, pure enough to be cursed with the spirit-sight. She has power to frighten her enemies and alas, her friends, even unto death.

He watched Red Iolo greet her with a kiss. The Lord clapped his hands and servers ran forward with mead. Iolo held up his drinking-horn appreciatively.

'Blue mead,' he said. 'My journey ends in sweetness.' He took a long pull from the silver-chased horn, and extemporized:

'We have drunk blue mead from the fountain of triumph,
We have drunk red mead from the veins of a foe,
Those that are princes are now our bondmen,
Our rivers run with the mead of their woe.'

The Lord sat down opposite him.

'You have learned?'

'Lord, I am full of learning, from Coed y Pantwn and my lordship of Llechryd; and I stood before the true cross of Eliseg and heard his bones speak through fathoms of granite. Lord, your day begins. In my heart's sight were four springs, four winters. When the fourth winter is done, there will be the sign of your greatness. I spoke with the Abbot of Valle Crucis. A hundred years seemed to pass in his words. He said: "The Lord has risen early." When the sign appears, you will rise to heights undreamed in the annals of Gwynedd, Powys, Deheubarth . . .'

'I shall be Lord of all Wales.'

'Supreme. Wait for the sign. A tail of fire in heaven and whirlwinds to crush the mountain tops. You will rise early, Lord, and you will defeat for ever *Y Sarff Cadwinog*: the chained serpent of whom Taliesin sang: the English!'

'*Diolch i Dduw!*' The Lord bowed, giving thanks to God. Then, raising his face, he cried: '*Menestr!*' to the cup-bearer who came to replenish the horns. Hywelis leaned on his knee, studying Iolo Goch with intent, unchildish eyes.

'I saw lights about you as you entered Sycharth,' she said softly. 'Like candles, they followed your steps.'

Iolo Goch slackened his grip on the drinking-horn and it rolled to the floor. He closed his eyes and did not speak. After a time the Lord said sorrowfully: 'It's true.'

The bard opened his eyes, smiled, sighed.

'Do you know, girl, what you have said?'

She came and placed her arms about his neck.

74

'The candles were pretty. Now they're gone.'

'Were they many?'

'Many, at least a hundred.'

He released her and raised his vessel to his Lord, who sat with tender, troubled face.

'Then so be it. I have at least a hundred days of life left to me. I may put my affairs in order, compose my soul. I shall return home to die, to Coed y Pantwn. I shall be buried at Valle Crucis, where Eliseg died, fighting *Y Sarff Cadwinog*. My one regret is that I shall not see your glory. Your triumph riding on a tail of fire – your victory against the English, *Prince Owain Glyn Dŵr!*'

Why was she remembering Sycharth now? Where was the merit in craving the old days, when Sycharth was a prince's palace of unparalleled splendour? Every goblet shone with beryl and emerald. Every draught was kept fangless by heavy wolfskin, deerskin, hanging from loft to floor. Every man a fighting man. Unencumbered by the full armour that the *Saeson* (Glyn Dŵr's contemptuous name for the English) wore, they were clad in skins and leather with steel protecting only their vitals. They carried bows of polished elm, far superior to the *Saeson* yew. The Lord's men were pure, they would go into Hell for him and love the going.

Yet she thought on, staring unseeingly now at the playing fox-cubs. From the night she had seen the corpse-candles, Iolo Goch had begun to decline in the gentle fading of a life well spent in song and story and comfort of his Lord. How fair Sycharth had been! When poets from all Wales had come on *clera*, the bardic circuit which by guild law they were bound to travel, they had been enthralled. The eulogies rang out in praise of the Lord and his ancestors, the legendary Cadwallader, synonymous with Owain himself, who was deemed the reincarnation of the earlier, mystical Owain, blood-kin to Arthur. They hymned Sycharth as none other had done; not Iolo, or Llewellyn Goch, or Gruffydd Llwyd of Powys, or Sion Cent, with his terse-metred verses. Or even the sublime, revolutionary Dafydd ap Gwilym, the Nightingale of Dyfed,

75

the merry one who in his rhymes equated God with human love.

They had praised the Lord Glyn Dŵr, not only in their own tropes and similes but in the songs of Taliesin, who, two hundred years earlier had made pæans to three kings: Rhydderch the Old, Nudd, and Mordaf, who fought against Hussa. In turn Taliesin had likened these three to their own mighty ancestors; to Urien of Rheged and his son Owain ap Urien, who vanquished Deodric the Flame-Bearer. Urien the land's anchor, whose son's javelin drew blood from the wind. Those who came to Sycharth all those years ago were the Gogynfeirdd, the poets of the princes, speaking through genius loosed by Iolo Goch, and the Lord and his lieutenants had listened to them. Not as past princes had listened, inattentive, for the long eulogies were as familiar as the Mass, but sternly, with a growing tremor of excitement and eyes always aloft for the coming of the comet.

> *'There will be weeping and widows and tearing of raiment,*
> *There will be blood in the stream and bowels on the thorns,*
> *Owain the seed of Owain has said farewell to mercy.*
> *Riding on clouds with the fire in his fist,*
> *He will whirl the bones of the Saeson about his head,*
> *He will rise in starshine and raise a new mountain,*
> *A mountain of piled red corpses.'*

Hywelis's early childhood rang with these fierce hymns. Glyn Dŵr had many wards, children of friends and kinsmen, but from the night of Iolo Goch's return he favoured Hywelis, and kept her by him. She remembered the nights, drowsing at his side, half-listening to the poets, and the lieutenants drunk with forecasts of indisputable victory. Perhaps even then her sense warned her that the hubris all about her was bad. But what she felt was formless; she could have spoken of it to none, even Owain's own children: Cathryn, who later married the hostage Mortimer, or Alice, later the wife of John Scudamore, who, though English, loved the Welsh better; or Meredyth, now the last survivor, or Gruffydd, or Owain's lady, Margaret of Maelor – beautiful, kind and now, like nearly all the Lord's immediate family, dead.

Even his grandchildren dead before him, and Sycharth a

ruin, its timbers corroded by fire, its great tower fallen.

There was an ancient song, the lament of Queen Heledd, surveying the waste of Eglwysau Basa; Heledd, who knew that to rejoice too soon is death.

> *'The Hall of Cynddylan, it is dark tonight,*
> *Without flame, without bed,*
> *All from the serpent of my tongue's boast.*
> *I live; my lord is dead,*
> *I will weep awhile, and then be silent.'*

Hywelis closed her eyes, and dreamed that when she looked again she would see other mountains in southerly Tanat Vale, and there the golden manor, ringed with bright water, its tiled roofs glowing between stout battlements. The door, which by tradition was never locked. Merfyn grooming the horses, whistling. And the lady Margaret of Maelor coming to welcome guests down the three bowed stone steps, and scolding Hywelis sweetly: where were you, girl? Wandering again? Come, bring the best Shrewsbury ale for our company! The white bread, the wine, the roast meat. Strike the harp! Help me! Bad one, pretty one! *Lili'r môr!* Lily of the sea – it was the Lord's name for her, it honoured the peculiar whiteness of her skin, made whiter by her red hair. The guests streamed in, singing the eternal theme that Sycharth was blessed, without shame, without famine, dearth or thirst, a haven. Now, within its fire-darkened walls, the forest celebrated its own subtle victory; ivy and lichen and moss filled the wounds. Squirrels ran among the bones of Sycharth, and at night the owls lamented or mocked its ruin.

All through the Lord's impatience. The comet had set his mind on fire. Had he only waited a mere two years longer! Then the comet would have honoured him and not the Saeson. Owain Glyn Dŵr and not Prince Henry would have been true Prince of Wales. Henry, a sixteen-year-old boy, had burned Sycharth, had outmatched the great Welsh lord. Men had argued, over the years, that matters might have gone differently if Owain had done this or that, had favoured one marcher lord or ambushed another; had employed trustier lieutenants. If only his French allies had not proved cowards and traitors. Wise and foolish men had talked: of the victories given to him – at Plinlymmon on the slopes of Mynydd Hedgant, at Bryn Glas, at Craig-y-Dorth, on the border of Shropshire; of the frustration, near Worcester, when his hardwon French allies withdrew their support; and of the defeats, at Welshpool, at Carmarthen, at Pwll Melyn of Usk, at Grosmont, from which Glyn Dŵr's spirit never recovered. And throughout, Prince Henry had been at the forefront of the harrying, young and bold, already a legend as the Lord once had been.

Glyn Dŵr had waited only two years after Iolo's prophecy. He had descended, blood-mad, with troops, upon Ruthyn Fair in the manor of Lord Grey. He had spared none that September day in 1400; killing the English merchants as they tried to protect their fair-booths, he had sought vengeance on Grey's tenants as if Grey were the Chained Serpent himself. The annexation by Grey of Glyn Dŵr's manor at Dyffryn Clwyd had unleashed the war, and it was not so much the loss of property that had enraged the Lord; it was the instinct that Grey had treated him, a great Welsh prince, as inferior. And now the Lord kept himself bitterly at Glyndyfrdwy, wronged and brooding and defeated.

Yet he had once been part of the English, had been educated in the London Inns of Court, spending many months at the court of Richard the Second, and he had married a daughter of the English holding of Saeson Maelor. King Richard he had loved; Henry Bolingbroke he hated. As for Prince Henry, now King of England, had it not been for his styling of Prince of Wales, the Lord would have honoured his valour. But Glyn Dŵr had taken his stance as a pure Welshman, the son of Gruffydd Vychan of Powys Fadog and Helen of the royal House of Deheubarth. And now Hywelis, his natural daughter, thought of him with love and sadness.

The foxes had run into a mossy clearing white with stars of campion and patched blue with speedwells. Down to it a rough track led from the distant mountains, a trail veined with a thousand tiny streams from the great white fall above. Flies sang over wet stones. A toad sat waiting to feed, its claret eyes rimmed with gold, one hand furled and knuckled, the fingers of the other splayed and transparent. Hywelis watched its cunning beauty avidly. She did not see the rider on the ridge above her, or the great bird circling overhead.

The golden eagle, gliding high on a cushion of light wind, had been watching the cubs for some time. Its talons were like shears, its look regal and terrible. Earlier it had chased a feral goat over a cliff edge, but the prey had fallen into a stream and been swept away into a mountain crevasse. The eagle dropped suddenly and Bronwen, the vixen, looked up as the shadow fell on her and her family. She gave a shrill gibber of fright and rage. The talons closed on Madog's back. The other cubs fled, but Bronwen stayed bravely crouching in menace at the great bird that clutched the cub and made to rise from the ground. It stood half as high as a man and its wingspread measured a man's length and more. Deep in its throat it growled, the growl echoed by Bronwen and by Hywelis's cry as she leaped up and ran towards the bird. She knew an eagle would attack a human; yet Madog was her cub as much as Bronwen's. He struggled in the talons, his downy white waistcoat catching the sun. Hywelis, seizing a fallen branch, ran at the eagle, half-tripping on her ragged dress.

The rider spurred his pony down the hill and drew rein. He was young, just on manhood, with a strong wild face and thick tawny-gold hair. He had extraordinary eyes, flecked and ringed with gold but essentially a brilliant blue, flawless and penetrating. Strong light or certain moods could turn his eyes from blue to gold, and now the sun coloured them an amber honey. He carried a small springald loaded with an arrow, and, steadying his mount with his knees, he stood in his stirrups and fired. The arrow sped; he bit his lip, there was not as much time as he would have wished, and even with this beautiful springald which he had made himself, there was the chance of error. The barb curved as intended and pierced the eagle's throat. A white membrane veiled the bird's eyes, the talons unclenched and Madog rolled crying away, his back cut to the bone, his forehead bleeding. The eagle died, wings shuddering, flexed open. Hywelis bent over Madog; he was too badly injured to run. Bronwen was watching, frantic, from some close hide. Hywelis gathered the cub into her skirt, while the rider dismounted and came near. She looked up, and knew him.

He said: 'Is it badly hurt?'

She shook her head.

'I shall nurse him. Look, he trusts me.' The cub, shivering with fright and pain, had turned blindly to Hywelis, pressing its mask against her, bloodying her dress.

'I shot well,' he said, though not boastfully.

'You did indeed. Owen ap Meredyth ap Tydier, my thanks.'

'A brave weapon, this,' he said, and patted the *baga* at his saddle-horn. It was filled with dead rabbit and pheasant and grouse. He surveyed Hywelis. He had known her always; they had been brought up together at Sycharth and Glyn-dyfrdwy. To him she was merely one of the wilder elements of the courts, along with the poets and doom-bringers. Always fey, always solitary. Never elegant. Today, he saw her ankles scratched bloody by thorns, her neck splashed with mud from a peat-hag, her hair uncombed. He himself was fastidious to a degree, and his own jerkin, although patched, was good wool and deerskin and carefully preserved. Yet he realized that Hywelis here in the valley was perfect. Her torn green gown merged with the bracken, her white skin was like the clouds over Eglwyseg and her hair was as rich as the fox's pelt. She was smiling at him.

She was almost three years his senior. He had a vague memory of her being put in charge of him when he was small and dreaming off while he got into mischief, leaning down the well-shaft to see his reflection, opening the stable-door and nearly being trampled by the Lord's big stallion . . . long ago. He, Owen ap Meredyth ap Tydier, was now a man, nearly the age of Prince Henry when he burned Sycharth. Owen was related to Glyn Dŵr through a cousin of the Vychan line; he was also his godson. His father, Meredyth ap Tydier, outside the law for killing a man while in service to the Bishop of Bangor, had left his infant son with the Lord for safety, and had departed for ever.

Hywelis continued to look at him, gratefully, at the strange iridescent eyes, the bright hair and tanned face, and something moved without warning in her mind, a mystery. Without form but carrying sure consequence, it was the same feeling of significance as on the night of Iolo Goch's return. Feelings of climax yet of expectancy, maddeningly obscure; the end or the beginning of something unknown. It flowed within her head, it faded to stillness; she was changed by it. Rising, she folded her sleeves tenderly over the wounded cub. She looked at the great sprawled body of the eagle. Its glory was gone.

'Something must always die.'

She looked up, startled, for he had voiced her thought.

'Yes. A sacrifice.'

'But to what?' he asked, and they looked at one another inconclusively. Then he said: 'What shall you do with the fox?'

'I told you. I'll nurse him and he will love me for ever.'

Owen laughed. He had a firm mouth that curled as if always on the edge of laughter. Somehow his mouth looked wise and self-mocking, as if it were older than the rest of him.

'When he's strong again, he'll leave you, Hywelis. A fox isn't a dog; he will be bondman to none.'

She said: 'Will you take me back with you, Owen?' He nodded. 'Yes. The Lord is asking for you.' He held the springald out, admiring it. 'I have made a lovely weapon here. With this I could pick out the eyes of the French.'

Hywelis was on her knees again, searching among the grass by a stream. She came up with a handful of rough hairy leaves and a few purple and cream flowers. The cream ones she discarded.

'Comfrey plant,' she said. 'The Saeson call it Yalluc, or Asses-Ear!'

'Never let the Lord hear you name it so then. I slipped an English oath yesterday and he hurled his cup at me.'

'The purple flowers for Madog, he is a male.' She wasn't listening. 'I'll boil them in milk and his back will heal soon. And his poor head!' She touched the cub gently between its ears. She got up. 'Are we ready?'

He stretched a foot out from the stirrup and she put her own on it. The pony started up the heathery hill, putting its neck down for the climb. Hywelis said, as her hair blew back and tickled Owen's face, 'Why did you talk about shooting at the French, when it's the English who are our enemy?'

He chuckled. That was part of a glorious secret, so far a daydream.

'I don't know,' he lied. 'Is your fox easy? We must be home soon, the Lord is restless today.'

'I haven't seen him since last night; I was away before dawn.'

'With the dew on the grass?' He clipped the pony's sides with his strong slim legs. 'You are strange, Hywelis.'

She slewed to look at him and she was indeed strange, with her milk-white face and her tilted eyes in which the lingering mysticism of her thoughts still moved. He held her tighter and they rode on over the rise of the hill, where the bracken yielded to sparse sunstroked grass and hawthorn bushes cast round shadows, each like a crouching spider. Below the hillside grew mile on mile of great trees, oak and ash and elm, a city of birds, roaring with song, the lark taking the highest stave over the croak of the starling and the jay's erratic scream, while thrush and blackbird cried alarm and sweetness. Riding, they passed through a droning mist of insects, and a dragonfly settled for an eyeblink on Hywelis's hair.

'The Lord's restless, you say?' She shifted against Owen. Her back was dry, the dew of her early wandering had vanished into his warmth. She stroked Madog's quiet feverish head. Owen was easing her earlier melancholy, merely by holding her, by talking in his casual voice. This was no longer the naughty boy she had once been put to guard. This was someone capable, healing, worthy. Dead creatures, her friends, lay in his saddle-bag, but he had slain an enemy . . . She lifted her face to the sun as they came down the hill to Glyndyfrdwy. It was a small manor, unkempt, its outlying lands lonely, its very stance spelling retirement and defeat. Sad again, she leaned against Owen, her face pressing his neck, the cub still lying like a baby in her arms.

He felt curious about her. They had grown up together, but now, pressing her, smelling the heather-scent in her hair, he thought: were she only dressed properly, her body groomed . . . but then, she would not be Hywelis. His contemporaries had had their *amours*, and the bards sang constantly of man and maid when they were not chanting of war. In theory Owen knew all about love. Dafydd ap Gwilym, the Nightingale of Dyfed, had been a famous lover and had found himself in trouble on more than one occasion. One moonless starless night on the way to keep tryst with someone's wife, Dafydd's horse and he had fallen into a peat-hag. The song ended with a curse on whoever had wielded the spade . . . love made apes of men. Owen smiled.

Hywelis said: 'Hangman's Hill looks dark today!' She pointed to where a mound, topped with a spreading oak, glowered over the valley. There were tufts of white bog-cotton growing at the marshy hill-foot, and squirrels leaping in the branches of the oak.

'I remember,' he said. 'We hanged the Saeson there, after Bryn Glas.'

'We!' She turned to laugh at him. 'We were children!'

'Yes. And we are children no longer.'

Near Glyndyfrdwy an offshoot of the Clwyd rushed down from the mountains, and in it choughs and dippers played, taking off with a clap of wings as the burdened pony approached. To the east on an eminence stood the castle of Dinas Bran, another of Glyn Dŵr's possessions, and north-easterly between Llantysilio and Eglwyseg a narrow fissure marked the pass to Ruthyn plain and the territory of the Lord's old enemy. With these grim landmarks in sight they came home, passed through the desolate courtyard and entered the manor. There Hywelis carried the cub up to her chamber and anointed his wounds, leaving him to sleep on sheepskin in a chest. She rejoined Owen at the door of the meadhall and they went in to where the Lord sat, fretful and rigid, before a smoky fire.

Owain Glyn Dŵr was over sixty years old, spare and straight, his hair and moustaches thick, his face still unerringly handsome. Only his deep eyes were fenced in by regret and dreaming, as if by looking into a time past they might by will cause reversal and change, or command a second chance. The mind behind those eyes was peopled by the dead. Often they emerged to keep him company, with sweet smiles and warnings and battle-cries from lips long rotten. Today had been one of profound phantasms and silent oaths. Faces had fled before him like hawthorn-blossom in the wind. He could swear that his dead wife had passed her hand over his face, and that

Gethin the Terrible, his favourite lieutenant, had once more raised the Dragon banner on Craig-y-Dorth. The Lord sat, his long jewelled hands hanging limply over his knees, and in the draught from the opening door the smoke whirled about him so that he sat in a cloud. The fire was unnecessary, but this was his hearthstone and must be kept warm at all costs, or everything was ended. A dog lay on the edge of his mantle, in dog-years twice its master's age. It raised its old blind head and growled, then, catching Hywelis's scent, thumped the floor with a bald tail.

'Quiet, Cafall,' said Owain Glyn Dŵr.

Hywelis went forward and knelt. The dog probed her skirts, smelling fox-blood, then sighed and dropped its nose. The Lord looked at Hywelis and she knew he saw her well, was examining every pore of her skin, every thread of her hair, and her every thought.

'How is my lord and father?' she said tenderly. The meadhall in which she knelt was sparsely furnished and its Lord the captain of a broken ship, but she felt strong, able to shoulder the trouble of others, give comfort.

'There's blood on you, girl,' he said. 'Are you hurt?'

She laughed and stroked his hand, feeling the little scars from years of handling steel and leather, and the tender veins, engorged with age.

'No.' She half-turned. 'Tell, Owen.'

Owen stripped the *baga* with its booty from his shoulder and threw it down in tribute.

'We shall eat well today,' was all he said.

'You've tried your new weapon?'

'Yes, and it's sweet. It gives death – and life!' – with a winking smile at Hywelis. She caught the light in his eyes, it made her shiver. She did not know him at all; or if she had ever known him, the time had come to learn him truly. He was young, and it was as if his very youth made him dangerous, ready to play with life as if it were weightless . . . and she remembered suddenly how well he could sing, and wanted to hear him sing now, this minute. But his glow, his arrogant stance, gave extra years to the Lord, whose face seemed greyer as if Owen had drained off all the light.

'Is my lord sad today?' she asked.

'Sad? Since when need you ask my mood? Owen, feed the fire. This hall is full of ghosts, they chill me through.'

Owen bent as bidden with a branch. The fire coughed out more smoke. In the whirling greyness Hywelis saw a face, gone in a blink but unmistakable. As Owen straightened she whispered in his ear: 'Cheer him!'

He answered merrily: 'I'll set a feast for my lord! Fine plump birds, if only Megan troubles to roast them right!'

'And Hywelis shall wear a fine gown,' said Glyn Dŵr, brightening a trifle.

'And I'll be your cup-bearer!' cried Owen, 'and serve you even though you keep me on my feet all night!'

The branch caught as he spoke, burning hotly. The Lord smiled at last. 'Your father bred a fine boy, Owen. What say you, Hywelis?'

'Not a boy.' She raised her face. 'A man.'

'I'll go and tell the bard,' said Owen. He left with the dead birds over his shoulder, their beaks dropping blood the length of the hall.

'Your face is red, Hywelis,' said Glyn Dŵr.

'It's the fire.'

'Is it?' The Lord examined his own hands, watching them tremble slightly. They had been steady at Craig-y-Dorth. They had shaken after Grosmont.

'I saw Gruffydd today,' he whispered.

'So did I.' Hywelis dropped her head on his knee. 'Not a moment ago, in the smoke.'

'All my sons . . . save one. And Gruffydd was the dearest, my edling, my heir. And Meredyth seldom comes, though he upholds my name in Deheubarth. We are still rebels, Hywelis.'

The trembling extended throughout his body. The old dog awoke and whined.

'Margaret came to me, so sorrowful. And Cathryn, and Alice, and Rhys ap Gethin, and I knew not who was dead and who was wandered away.'

'I have wandered from you myself,' she said sadly.

'But you always return. *Diolch i Dduw!*'

'From today I promise to stay in hall,' she said, wild

regret striking with her words. She did not give promises lightly. Now she surrendered delight; the dawnlit stealthy ramblings, the stroking of young rabbits too trusting to run, the sight of eagles at play, throwing a heather-root to one another in mid-air. But Glyn Dŵr shook his head.

'I would not have you other than you are. Your mother was a hill-woman, a faery-woman, and her spirit became yours at her death. It is not for me to imprison you for loving your wild kingdom.'

'Father, my heart and love is yours, you know it.'

'For ever,' he said in a queer harsh voice. 'To be given to none other. Pure as light you are, Hywelis, and your eyes will see what is hidden, so long as you cleave only to me. You are rare. Gentle. Fierce. Though you are not like the women of my generation, who became wild beasts after Bryn Glas, when Mortimer and his army were captured. You were too young to see what they did . . .'

'They castrated the Saeson prisoners,' said Hywelis flatly. 'I remember Megan coming home, blood to the elbows, and laughing.'

'We were desperately provoked. Had I been crowned Prince of Wales and recognized in Westminster; had Grey, God's curse on him, not – '

'Father, my lord, leave it. It's done.'

'It is never done!' he said wildly. 'And some day, girl, you will point me to another comet. Your sight will show me new victory. So long as you are pure and love me only. For the giant must die when his daughter marries . . .'

Suddenly her heart contracted. She said: 'That's a legend I do not know.'

'Then,' said Glyn Dŵr, rising, suddenly tall and terrible, 'we will have Owen ap Meredyth ap Tydier tell it to us both.' The old dog staggered on to its legs. She knew then that the Lord was jealous; it was more than a father's jealousy, it was a warning, and she was lost in it. 'I'll change my clothes,' he said. 'This night we'll be merry. We'll damn the Saeson, and tell the old tales, and drink to our lovers. I'll call their souls from Hell to our hearthstone. Girl, tend the fire!'

*

Megan, who with her countrywomen had tortured the English prisoners twelve years earlier, now helped Hywelis dress for the Lord's impromptu revel. Megan was black of hair and eye, stern and wiry, She had been body-servant to the lady Margaret and now acted as chatelaine and cook, servant and hostess. She was changed, like all others in Glyn Dŵr's meinie, from the sentry on the gate that once welcomed all to the rough ponies in the stable built for the destriers of war. She stripped Hywelis of the bloodstained rags and plunged her into a tub of hot water redolent of gillyflower essence. Hywelis sat fretfully watching her whiteness redden, wrinkling her nose. Megan washed her hair, rubbing it dry as Hywelis stood naked, shivering in the air that blew though the arrow-slits.

'Here.' Megan tugged with a horn comb. 'You do it. I've not the patience.'

Hywelis caught their reflections in the burnished silver mirror. She fancied Megan looked sour and sneering, and remembered that she had once loved the Lord with a desperate passion and likely still did.

'Your father says you are to be royally robed tonight,' said Megan.

The giant must die when his daughter marries. Was she then to be always the precious vessel of his power? Was there more to it than she knew? She met Megan's eyes in the silver. Then the woman laughed, the tension fading from her face.

'It's nothing,' she said. 'I was only thinking . . . how young you are, how beautiful your body. Repining that age has me now, and I kick against it.'

'I'm still the same,' said Hywelis. 'Just a dirty, wild, wood-land girl.'

'Not dirty now!' said Megan with emphasis. 'Here, I'll find you a gown.'

A strange spring of excitement started in Hywelis. She looked down at her own body, amazed. Megan, who had no great love for her, had called it beautiful, and she was now determined to make herself as much a thing of beauty as possible. Tonight Owen would sing, and the song would unravel a fresh mystery, plant new signposts. . . .

Silk over Megan's arm, silk the colour of old leaves, laced with tarnished gold. She swirled it into a cave for Hywelis, drew it over her body. Her skin took on amber shadows. There was a narrow gold girdle which snaked twice about her waist and fell in tassels to her knee. Megan lit candles and Hywelis leaned to the mirror. Out of the gloom her face bloomed like a strange milky flower, her eyes reflecting the dress and the dusk. Enormous eyes through which the sad past spoke, yesterday and all the days before it, the mourning of widows, the crying of children, the lament of lovers lost. Even the screams of horses mutilated on the field of battle. The eyes filled and the dolorous images were washed away. All but one; for the hands that now tended her hair were real, and what had those hands once done?

'Did you enjoy it, Megan?' she heard herself say. 'Did your blade give glory? They were men . . .'

'They were our enemy,' said Megan briskly. 'And it was long ago. Are you ready?'

Hywelis stood up, slender as a knife, the gold tassels swaying on her thigh.

'Who wore this dress last?'

'The Lord's daughter Cathryn. She'll not need it where she is.' Hywelis bowed before the mirror in mourning and in gratitude; then, casting one last look she saw sadness changed to recklessness, and the dream in bud.

The Lord was talking with a neighbour on his dais. Another departure, for he seldom invited guests these days. His hair and moustaches were sleek and he wore a gown of soft green wool with a gold collar set with beryls. His bard stood nearby. The bard, whose title was Gruffydd Llwyd ap Dafydd ap Einion Lygliw was neither old nor young, but as he had never in his life had his beard trimmed, it hung unclean and sandy-grey to his waist where it was tucked into the girdle of a soiled purple mantle, and gave him the appearance of great age. He was at present offended, for the Lord had been recalling the art of the late Iolo Goch and the Nightingale of Dyfed, lecherous as a sparrow, thought Gruffydd Llwyd sourly; one would think there had never been any other bards but those two, and doubtless they had been wafted to Paradise on sheaves of their peerless couplets and stanzas. Still, this place was a living in hand, with most of the noble households of Wales split or overturned . . . Then Glyn Dŵr turned to him and smiled and before that warmth his rancour fled instantly and he knew he remained at Glyndyfrdwy not for convenience but like all others, through love.

Hywelis entered, and the Lord's eyes brightened with pleasure, for she was the faery-woman reborn, so fine and fair, and he came from his place to take her hands. The bard looked uncertain, wondering for an instant who she was, then saw it was merely Hywelis, scrubbed and bedizened, and taking down his little sycamore harp from its nail, he teased a sweet chord from it in her honour.

'You're beautiful, my daughter,' said the Lord. '*Lili'r môr!*'

And it was so long since he had called her this, his lily of the sea, that she felt her eyes grow hot and controlled herself, for here came Owen, who thought her strange. She would be strange no longer; she was fair and a lady. The Lord was holding something out to her, a coil of gold plaited like the water sliding off the rocks just before it reached the basin beneath Eglwyseg Mountain.

'This is the torque my wife Margaret wore,' he said softly. 'Welsh gold, mined two centuries ago in Tanat Vale. Take it in memory of the power and the blood we share, Hywelis. With this gift I bind you. Lift up your hair.'

She lifted the red fall at the nape of her neck and the Lord fastened the torque about it. He kissed her, and she knew that in truth she was his last link with splendour. Through her eyes which had foreseen honourable death for Iolo Goch, he would live again to ride his horses of the wind. So he put his destiny upon her spirit's sight, and she sighed, feeling the weight of his trust. Then Owen, brilliant of eye and dressed in a sky-blue doublet, fashionable and sleek as a St Valentine's Day bird, was beside them, ready to sing, and now, if he had his way. She stood between the two of them both looking down at her, one burdening her with his intense love, the other curious, stirred by her new glamour and some secret mischief. An irrepressible light seemed to burn around Owen; he began to talk to the Lord, telling him about the eagle.

Glyn Dŵr frowned. 'Then the bird was flying low? That's bad for Wales when the eagles stoop.'

'It was after prey,' Owen said. 'Madog, Hywelis's fox.'

The Lord was intrigued. 'A fox? But Madog is a prince's name. Madog ap Maredudd sired Gwenllian, who became the bride of the mighty Rhys, two hundred years ago . . .' He stopped, saying abruptly: 'Let us begin.'

A *menestr* approached with a tray of flagons, its rim hung with drinking-horns, and behind him two boys rolled a kilderkin of strong drink, setting it upright at the top table. With great ceremonial, the like of which had not been seen since Sycharth days, Owen served the Lord and his company. Hywelis drank: the liquid's surface was luminous with honey, as if a long summer were distilled in it, and the sweetness had an aching bite, like the sting of an angry summer bee.

'*Bragod* mead,' said the bard. 'The best I ever tasted.'

'Megan brewed it,' said Glyn Dŵr, with a bow towards her where she sat at the far end of the table. He raised his horn. '*Iechyd da, Megan!* All cheer, my jewel!' and her dark face flamed. They ate a vast rabbit pie, savoury roast fowl. Owen stood behind the Lord's chair, replenishing the horns with a dipper from the barrel, so that Hywelis's cheeks burned and she found beauty in the sight of her own long fingers clasped about her knife and in the dying sunset as it painted the window recesses with rose. The Lord charmed her with conversation. Not for months had she seen him so uplifted. Then Owen, leaning between them to serve, pressed her thigh lightly but deliberately with his and she jerked upright. His face, the heavy-lidded eyes seriously downcast as he poured the drink, came between her and the Lord's stark profile. The honey of his touch ran through her. She smiled at the Lord, and longed to say: 'Father, let Owen sing!'

Instead, Gruffydd Llwyd rose, and with his little harp wandered to the stool placed in the centre of the hall. Cafall, under the table, growled; he hated music in all forms and would have been pleased to bite the bard. But then, as he could no longer even bite the bone between his paws, he sighed deeply and went to sleep.

'I shall sing extempore,' announced Gruffydd Llwyd,

looking severely in the direction of the growl. 'About that animal's wonderful ancestor, King Arthur's own dog Cafall. There is a mountain in Llanfair-ym-Muallt in Brecon, where Cafall and the king went hunting . . . there was never such a dog before or since.'

Hywelis felt so sorry for the ancient descendant that she woke him and fed him a soppet of bread soaked in mead, and he laid his heavy head on her foot in gratitude.

'The dog was so strong that when he touched the mountain top his paw left a deep hollow. King Arthur, in homage, built a cairn over the hollow and placed a stone on top. He named the mountain Cefn Carn Cafall, the ridge of Cafall's stone. If the stone is moved away, it will always return, and of this I shall sing.'

And he did.

The Lord, tapping his old bright hands on the board, gave unaccustomed attention to the bard's long-drawn phrases with the spills of melody in between. Encouraged, Gruffydd Llwyd prolonged the song-story for an hour, wrenching metaphors from the tale as a thrush drags a worm from the ground. Miraculously the lines scanned and held an undisciplined beauty. He sang of forest and valley, of a ring-dove half-awake on its bough, its hunched wings like the cowl of a monk; of the woodcock like a black Dominican friar; of blackbird and nightingale singing together like two priests. He was proper in his similes and orientated to God, though, carried away towards the end, he did tell of the trees and May-bright payment to lovers, florins of green and silver leaves. There was much applause.

These were the things Hywelis knew best, but in the mead-hall they were only words, coloured by the bard's reedy voice. Her attention wandered to where Megan sat, a look of unutterable sadness on her face. Megan wished for youth again, for beauty and bloodless innocence. Hywelis felt the vibrations of regret, of stifled shame. For to the conqueror, past deeds, however bloody, give glory; to the defeated they are added burdens. The spoiled corpses mount up, saying sadly: We were doubly wasted! You were unworthy, and it was all for nothing!

She shivered, and just then Owen came to fill her cup.

He leaned close, so close that she could see the gold rings of his eyes, and he whispered, his cheeks cleft with a wicked smile: 'Praise God that's over! a heron makes a prettier noise, and knows when to stop!' And he drew his fingers over the nape of her neck under her hair, and whispered again: 'Hywelis . . . Hywelis . . .' moving on to fill her neighbour's vessel in the same breath. Only her name but enough to bring heat where there was shivering, and then a void as he went away. Graceful and tall and young, he went behind the trestle, ministering with his pitcher of enchantment. Then she felt Glyn Dŵr's eyes upon her. She met them nervously. He smiled, and then began talking with his neighbour, a white-haired marcher lord, going over old terrain.

'I thought when the tripartite indenture was signed, our troubles would be ended and I could stand in Wales as true king. My Cathryn brought over Mortimer to that end; a worthy enemy and a better son-in-law. Henry Percy too – all was set fair with his allegiance, but the spears of Shrewsbury field had him . . .'

'All dead,' said the old marcher lord. 'It's one gate that a man goes through with no returning. No bolts or bars; the gate has vanished, and he with it.'

'Where did we go wrong?'

'Blame the French, who betrayed you, who ran home eight years ago, for all the gold and honours you pledged them to fight against the Saeson. Every one a *milain*!' He spat over the trestle.

'What can one expect, with a madman at their head?' Just then the bard came from refreshing himself, combing bits of meat from his beard.

'Shall I give you more entertainment, Lord?'

In the same breath the neighbour said, leaning kindly: 'Your girl is lovely tonight, Owain!'

The Lord's deep eyes surveyed her again. Yes, he knew her mind.

'And she would rather have Owen ap Meredyth sing, which he does well,' he said. Instantly Owen came before him, standing beside the bard, who seemed much put out.

'Did I not please?' said Gruffydd Llwyd, and Owen answered

instead of the Lord; so sweetly that the taunt was almost hidden. 'It was like some wonderful bird, sir . . . like the Nightingale of Dyfed . . .'

The bard was enraged. 'Dafydd ap Gwilym was carnal,' he said. 'Even I recall the disgrace of his in an English inn – wooing the tapwenches, falling over stools at midnight, leaping through windows in only his shirt . . .'

Owen chuckled, and the Lord held up his hand. 'You did well, Sir Gruffydd Llwyd, and we love you. As for Dafydd, he sleeps easy at Strata Florida, under the yew tree. You live on. This youth can learn from you. Let him sing. Owen, a tale of the Mabinogion . . .'

The bard was appeased. 'One of the Four Branches, Lord? He could tell of Bran and Branwen.'

'No,' said the Lord. 'We will hear of Culhwch and Olwen.'

Owen took the harp and sat on the little stool directly below Hywelis. His eyes seemed to gather up all the light from the torches and candles, channelling it directly into hers. He struck the first phrase, and Hywelis felt her spirit drawn towards him on the shining ray that linked them and on the thread of his singing.

He had a peculiar sweet voice with a keen edge, lacking the formal cadences of the bards, and his hands on the harp were sure. There was drama in him, and he limned his characters with care so that they rose from word and note and moved through shadows into the sight of the silent audience.

'Ysbaddaden Chief-Giant was as tall as a tower, as thick round the middle as the boles of twelve oak trees. When he stood upright he blotted out the sun from three counties. His outspread arms would reach to London on the one hand, while with the other he could stir the sea around Ireland. Where he kicked the ground, mountains arose. If he spat in the sea, the water boiled. His hair was like the mane of forty lions, and hung, ungovernable, to his waist; none could dress it. No armies could defeat him; steel crumpled, fire lost heart, kings went mad at sight of his eyes. Ysbaddaden! you were greater than God!

'Then one day came Culhwch, cousin to Arthur. Culhwch was without sin, his armour bright as starlight; he was chaste and noble as a singing mountain. He was fleeter of foot than the magic deer of Powys Fadog, and handsome as the dawn.

'When he was born, a witch prophesied that he would never marry unless he could win the hand of the giant's daughter. He rode to the court of his cousin the king. His horse was the colour of mother-of-pearl, its head was graceful as the serpent's. It had hooves like pale-pink shells and wore a gold saddle and bridle. In one hand Culhwch bore two silver spears and in the other a battle-axe, whose blade was the length of a grown man from edge to edge. And he wore the gold sword with a jewelled blade, every jewel mined from a sacred mountain. His weapons could draw blood from the breeze. Not a hair stirred on him as he rode, so light was his horse's step.'

Owen looked at Hywelis, a little smile on his mouth, his face and hair all brightness.

'At Arthur's gate was Glewlwyd Mighty-Grasp, whom no man had ever passed alive. But Culhwch evaded him and came to the throne of Arthur, who listened to his quest. The king appointed six of his mightiest warriors to accompany him. There was Cei, who could make fire from his own belly; Bedwyr the One-Handed, dangerous as three men in battle; Cynddylig the Waymaker, who knew every pass over every mountain on earth; Gwalchmei, the best horseman in the world; Gwrhyr the Translator who could speak every tongue known to man, and Menw, who could make them all invisible.'

The bard frowned. Much was being omitted. Even the careful rhythm of the music seemed hurried, as Culhwch and his company roamed, meeting monsters, seers, hermits, conquering, listening, learning. Now they were at the castle of Ysbaddaden. Worst of all, Owen had left out King Arthur, who should have accompanied them, whose feat brought victory . . .

'Ysbaddaden received them with taunts, and spoke the only conditions that could win his daughter in marriage: the thirteen treasures of the world. And the last and greatest, the head of the Twrch Trwyth.

'This was the fiercest boar, standing as high as a castle. Between its ears it carried a magic comb and scissors, and only with these could the giant's hair be dressed for his daughter's wedding. Ysbaddaden cried:

> *"No mortal man shall mount my daughter!*
> *For when she marries I must die,*
> *White she'll remain, although you strain*
> *Through earth and water, fire and sky,*
> *Only the Twrch Trwyth's mystic comb*
> *Shall loose my nestling from her home."*

'. . . and after the penultimate task was completed, Culhwch set out to find the savage dogs needed to hunt down the Boar. He consulted the five wisest creatures – the ouzel-cock, the stag, the owl, the eagle, and the salmon. . . .

'. . . in the fight with the boar many of the knights were torn to pieces. Yet Culhwch pursued the Twrch Trwyth for forty days and nights, even to the land of the Chained Serpent and to Cornwall. There the Boar was driven over the cliffs into the sea. As it died, Culhwch tore the comb and scissors from its head.'

'*Arthur* did,' muttered the bard.

'And then the giant's power was as a little child, as soon as his hair was dressed. And they cut off his monstrous head and speared it high. Then they sought his daughter, the fairest woman ever born.

'And she came, with a gown of fire-coloured silk about her and a heavy torque of ruddy gold about her neck, set with rubies and a precious pearl. Her head was yellower than the broom blossom and her skin whiter than the horses of the sea. Her hands were as the bog-cotton where it grows beside a river. And her eyes! Their look was lovelier than that of the thrice-mewed hawk, and her breast, uncovered for her lover's eyes, softer than the sun. Wherever she trod, four white clover flowers grew behind her feet. Whoever beheld her was filled with longing. And therefore she was called . . .'

There was such a long pause that Gruffydd Llwyd clutched at his beard in rage. The youth had bastardized the entire *awdl*, and here he was at the climax, hanging on words while the meadhall waited and Hywelis, who should know better, looking at him like one moonstruck.

'. . . therefore she was called Olwen.' The name drifted away under the sweetest chord of all. The Lord struck the table with the tail of his drinking-horn, and the applause rose, little cries, the tapping of feet and hands.

Hywelis sat still, her thoughts pouring out across the ray of light between her and Owen, thoughts so tangibly defined that she could not believe they did not pierce him. He gave no sign, however, but beside her, the Lord, whose mind and blood were hers, stiffened and turned his eyes on her for one more questing, warning look, like that of the eagle the moment before it died.

Owen. The singing, fading ray carried it straight and true. You are Culhwch and I am Olwen. Yes. You are mine.

Summer rain was drying in the sun. The puddles in the courtyard where Hywelis stood reflected white clouds. The wet granite of the curtain wall shone like a jewel, and crystal drops rimmed the lintel of the bakehouse door whence came warm fragrance and Megan's cross, calling voice. Hywelis remained standing, staring at the outer gate, then slowly turning to keep the inner door in view. Her forearms gleamed with wheat flour, she had already been helping Megan with the day's bread and had escaped, driven by a melancholy need. Her excuse had been that she must fetch Madog down from her chamber before he soiled or chewed anything. She had already stretched the promised five minutes into half an hour. Bored, the fox slept on the cobbles at her feet.

After a month's nursing his wound was completely healed. The hair over the scar between his ears and withers had grown back in a broad white stripe like a badger's blaze. He was docile but far from tame, and now uneasily wore a collar and lead of plaited rushes, which Hywelis held as she palely watched the gate and then the door. She was watching for Owen.

There had been no more revelling since that night a month ago when she had seen into her own desires and, so she fancied, into his. She had fashioned a part for him to play and words for him to say, and was amazed to find a bare and silent stage. He knew, and he cared, she told herself as the first day wore on. She knew that he had gone hunting with other young men of the manor, he was waiting till nightfall to seek her out. But she deluded herself, then and during the following month. She saw him at mealtimes, she put herself in his way. He examined Madog and admired her nursing skill. But she could never hinder him for more than a moment.

She had never troubled before over what he did. Now he was precious to her and his every absence was a target for jealous longing or anxiety. She feared for him; there could be the eagle's mate, waiting to strike out his eyes. She wandered the valley as before, her wild spirit diminished. She no longer wore her careless gowns, but sought conformity in the wardrobe of Cathryn, the Lord's dead daughter, as if looking for a clue to bring Owen near. The summer was in full, the grasses bleached, and at night tides of moonlight drenched the valley. Everywhere were meadow-scents and the shout of birds, and she felt that such a summer would never come again. She set to feeble ploys to gain Owen's notice, polishing the yet unused half-armour which the Lord had given him. She spent hours alone in the clearing where they had met the eagle. He seemed more distant daily, riding out armed with springald and dagger, returning late with a bounty of game.

She sought the help of powerful deities, particularly the love-goddess, Drwynwen of Anglesey, Owen's birthplace. Come to her he must, for she had not imagined that swordlike look of light, the night of his singing. Yesterday she had gone to the banks of the Dee in a vague hope of invoking Aerfen, although she was primarily a martial spirit, demanding three yearly human sacrifices so that Wales should conquer England. Hywelis was not confident, for the Lord had been heard to remark that sacrifices or no sacrifices, the goddess was dead. She stepped through the reeds and saw the bard standing among the kingcups. He had been washing his beard in the river, a practice he believed gave him inspiration. He looked severely at Hywelis as she came.

'In my young day,' he said, 'women kept within hall and served the hearthstone. They did not moon for things not for them.'

'*Things?*' said Hywelis.

'Persons, then. My sisters walked with eyes down. If they sighed, they were beaten. They had discipline.' He blinked at

97

Hywelis, watching her colour deepen.

'But what have I done?' she cried, half in fury.

'Sighed. Mooned. Looked. Wished. I know you, lady. You pursue that youth, without shame.'

'You know nothing,' said Hywelis tartly. 'I have said nothing to . . . to Owen.' The bard laughed unprettily, combing his beard with his fingers.

'His name heats your blood! You'll have none of him. Maybe he's the last to know. His mind's on other things. He has a pretty voice,' he said with rancour, 'and soon it will be singing a French air, or I'll cut off my whiskers.' He went on combing.

There was that talk of France again with which Owen had himself mystified her. It was hopeless to probe the bard, he was in a maddening, obstructive mood, and full of jealousy both of Owen's prowess as a bard and of herself, so high in the Lord's favour. She sat down. The river foamed and steadied into a broad lake before sliding over a ridge and whitening to a torrent. The water shone like the ray of light from Owen's eyes to hers, and she caught at the only comforting memory: the press of his thigh against hers at the table, his murmuring of her name. I was not mistaken. Our lives are linked. It is as clear and vital as the corpse-candles around Iolo Goch. *He is mine*, and the eagle was a sacrifice to whatever shall be between us.

'Do not displease the Lord,' said Gruffydd Llwyd. 'Remember the legend; it was plain enough.'

'The giant must die? Then am I never to marry?'

'There are marriages and marriages,' he said. 'You will have no marriage from Owen ap Meredyth. Your purpose is designed, and you know it as well as I.'

'I am Glyn Dŵr's prophet. So long as I am pure.'

'You are his breath, his eyes, his hope.'

She pulled brutally at a clump of reeds. 'Did you intend to meet me here?'

'I see you. Full of envy, I am.'

'Because the Lord loves me? I am his daughter.'

'Because,' he said, his voice suddenly tragic, 'you have the power I lack. All these years I have pretended I was like Iolo, or Taliesin, with the foresight of all the great ones who sleep. I am only a rhymer. But you! Had I been born with your might! I would have bored a window in my head to achieve it, as the old seers did. Now you would thrust that power from you, for a moonish whim. Anyone can love, Hywelis. Few can *see*.'

'And my marriage?'

Gentle now, he came and sat and took her hand, his beard spread in hay-coloured wisps over his narrow chest. He looked older than his years, and sad.

'Marriage to God, in your father's name, and in the name of God the Father. Do you recall the words of the anchorite of Llanddewibrefi, who had the vision of Christ? That holy face so pure and radiant as no earthly or heavenly creature could be compared thereto . . .'

'The Lord wants me to become an anchorite! Living lonely in a cave, visited for visions of death? How do conquest and mutilation keep tune with your lovely song? I love Glyn Dŵr, and serve him. I am bound to him – ' she touched the golden torque about her neck – 'but I am likewise bound to Owen.' And then: 'I had hoped you might help me, Gruffydd Llwyd.'

'I?'

'I can't speak to Owen myself. But if – if a message, a poem for preference, could be given in my name, then he would know and could answer me with a fable, next time he sings in hall. Could you . . .?'

The bard fell into a fury.

'You wish me to be a *llatai*? Play Pandarus to your whim? Run like a slave to that ambitious whelp who would like to supersede me in my calling and isn't even a member of the guild? Never! Insult!' He wound his beard about his fingers, tangling it dreadfully.

'I only wanted him to know,' said Hywelis.

'Then tell him yourself!' The bard scrambled up the bank, splashing himself with mud.

'Dafydd ap Gwilym would have done it!' she screamed after him. 'The Nightingale was kind and loved lovers. He had a heart!' It was the most hurting thing she could think of, and whether he heard her or not she was unsure, but he waved

99

both hands in the air and ran dementedly towards the manor. They had not spoken since.

Now, a yap from Madog roused her abruptly. He had sprung up and was looking towards the opening door at the top of the stone stairs. Cafall was growling hoarsely. Three figures appeared; a dark man with a black eye-patch, and, making first for the steps, a taller one, wearing a mantle the folds of which swirled open to reveal the royal arms of England. The Lord and Cafall stood behind them. Glyn Dŵr's arms were folded on his chest. His voice was so cold, so exact, that every word carried across the courtyard. He was addressing the dark man but his eyes were set on the King's courier and the fury in them made him stumble on the stair.

'Kinsman, tell this knight,' said the Lord, 'in his own loathly tongue, that I reject every word!'

The man with the eye-patch turned and spoke in English to the courier, who answered briefly. Hywelis leaned to listen and Megan came from the bakehouse, saying with a smile:

'He is very angry! Glyn Dŵr can speak English, and French, as well as many. Didn't he teach young Owen ap Meredyth . . .?'

Hywelis's heart jumped, but she still listened; the interpreter was speaking again.

'Kinsman, he is only relaying his sovereign's desires. King Henry the Fifth promises pardon to all rebels if you will send young men to join battle in his name. In my view, Owain, it's . . .'

'Davydd ap Llewellyn ap Hywel; Davydd Gam!' said the Lord formally. 'You are my brother-in-law. We are bound. But your view combats my own. I desire no amnesty, I have no interest in battles, save they be between Wales and *Y Sarff Cadwinog*! Has this young king forgotten we are still rebels? Why does he ask for my fledgeling warriors? Are his own armies so puny? Tell him no, and no.'

Cafall still growled. Saliva dripped from his naked jaws.

Davydd Gam said to the courier: 'You are answered.'

'My King will be disappointed. He is good and great, more beloved than his father. Tell the Lord a new era begins. King Hal will make England rich. Wales should share in the booty.'

'Let him depart!' said Glyn Dŵr; bitter with frustration, the old dog groused at his side. The courier pulled his mantle about him and lunged away down the steps. He muttered: 'Madman!' By now others had come into the courtyard from stable and armoury and stillroom and a little hiss of malediction arose. An urchin skimmed a stone towards the courier as he mounted his horse and rode through the outer gate.

The Lord withdrew, crashing the door shut behind him, and Megan chivvied her boys back into the bakehouse. Hywelis turned to speak to someone who had come to stand beside her. It was Owen. He had ridden in not a minute ago. By the gate his pony was at the water trough, and his friends, with their hounds, were unloading a dead deer from muleback. Owen's clothes were damp with rain, his sleeves streaked with grass and foam where his mount had rubbed its head. His hair was tangled and he smelled of summer. His eyes were lit to raw honey flecked with darker gold, as he stood in a shaft of light. Then the sun was covered by a new rain-cloud and they were blue again. Hywelis felt, as if in her own body, the agitation of his heart, pounding so that she could hardly hear his voice, asking her a question.

'Hywelis!' Impatient, amused. 'Are you asleep?' Then: 'Tell me quickly. You saw and heard. I must know . . .'

'Tell you?' she said faintly.

'Duw!' Exasperated now, he moved closer, looking down at her from the little difference in their height. 'The courier – the King's man. We met him riding away, but he didn't stop. How did the Lord decide?'

Owen, you are here, she thought. This time you do not greet me with a pleasantry and go. Ah, Owen, Culhwch, my knight! And in her mind he replied: Hywelis, Olwen, I have come to take you through the world on the shell-hooved horse, with the swords of silver and gold. We are one for ever . . .'

'If you don't tell me, Hywelis, I shall ask Megan,' he said, and the dream-conversation fragmented as she became conscious that his lips were white with annoyance and it was raining again. 'I asked you what dealings the Lord had with the King's man. It's important to me.'

She said, hastily obedient: 'My father declared that King

Henry must have only puny armies if he wished to enlist the untrained donzels of Glyn Dŵr. He refused the offered amnesty, and swore that none of his house should go to France under the English banner. He all but threw the courier down the steps.'

He cried out with an oath. '*Diawl!* Then it's hopeless. I rode back so fast, I thought to find the old days forgotten . . .'

Amazed, she said softly: 'How can they be forgotten?' He did not hear her.

'I am so disappointed,' he said. She peered up at him where the tawny lashes almost met over the brightness, and saw the brightness spilling out in tears. Pain laced itself about her heart. She thought: he must hate me for my witness of this. She looked away to where Megan stood in the bakehouse doorway, then to where the boys were dismembering the slain deer. She said: 'Why are you so mad to lose your life in battle?' and instantly there came to her a true, unassailable vision. Owen, you will live to be a very old man. *And always mine,* now and at the day of your death. You will fight unvanquished, until one day . . . The sight and knowledge surged about her, terrifying. She clutched the solid wall behind her. There were times when the merging of present and future was too much to bear. She felt his arm about her.

'What is it, Hywelis?' His breath was warm on her cheek.

'Only that I love you.'

He showed no surprise. He held her, while the drenched courtyard gleamed again under sunshine, while the wicked past, the treacherous present, the giddy future spun in a whirl of elation, because she had spoken truth to him; and now it seemed they could talk together as she had willed it. He bent to her, listening, answering softly.

'I never knew you were such a warrior,' she said.

'Yes, you did. You must remember how I cursed and cried – a whelp – because I was too young to fight at Bryn Glas, at Grosmont! Because I was too young to attend the Lord's great Parliament at Machynlleth, which was spawned from his ambition . . . How far back *do* you remember, girl?'

Further back than any, she thought. Centuries long-gone; my instinct has eyes that bring me Heledd weeping at the ruined hearth. My blood sees the upthrust of tidal seas, the birth of mountains when this land was pitted with the footfalls of a giant race. My bones ache sometimes from a thousand-year winter. For I *am* Wales, her eagle and her fox, her forest and rill, and every leaf that drops from her trees brushes my heart in passing.

And yet I can remember Owen truly only from the day in the valley when we, born into the same time and place, came together as appointed. So were we born together in earlier times. And now my spirit's sight begins to relinquish the past and looks towards the future . . .

He said: 'Come, walk with me. Bring Madog.' The leashed cub looked up with melancholy eyes and padded beside them as, arms about one another, they made for the gate and the open country beyond. Frowning, Megan watched them, then she wiped her floured hands and went into the manor where, behind closed doors, the Lord sat biting on his new anger.

'You still wear the torque,' said Glyn Dŵr. He touched her neck. His eyes were hard. It was a warm evening but still fire blazed on the hearthstone, and often he motioned for it to be fed so that the flames raged higher. Sweat streamed down Hywelis's sides, and the bard, sitting a little apart on his stool, showed a dewy white face. The three sat alone.

'I do. I cannot remove it,' she answered honestly. 'Nor would I wish to, Father, your gift . . .' Reasonless guilt held her as she tried to read his expression. There was nothing for her to hide and, like a resentful child, she saw in his strange humour the spoiling of her day. She would like to have crept to bed where she could lie, enhancing in recall every word, every touch, every look.

They had strayed only to the river, pausing at a small white rapid that poured over round stones. She had cupped her hands, and he had nuzzled the water from them like a thirsty animal. Laughing through diamond drops, he had laved the coolness over her face and neck, while Madog groped with a slender paw in the river-mud, gloomy and sad and suspicious, as the Lord was now.

Owen had praised her beauty with a skilled affluence of words that had amazed that small corner of her mind that remained unbewitched. He had held her close, she had felt their hearts, hers racing in double time, his calm and strong. His eyes had invaded hers with blue and gold. He had kissed her, brow and cheeks and lips, as if he loved her but had room for other thoughts, and this she accepted as his right. And whereas she had longed for him woman to man, now she craved him as a dying person craves the Host. It was more than love, more poignant, more fated; heavy not only with their twin destinies but with the destinies of kingdoms. For he had given her a commission to fulfil.

She did not know how to begin, not under the Lord's searing stare. In the end it was Glyn Dŵr who broached the matter.

'You saw the emissary from Young Harry?'

He managed to inject venom into the name, although it was half-hearted. For through all that prince's burning conquests, the Lord had watched him as a father, rueful yet secretly proud, surveys a renegade son. There was still anger in him, but it was controlled.

'He offered us the King's peace. I shall die outside the peace. And be buried in a churchyard wall – neither in holy soil nor out of it – to fox the Devil!'

She laughed nervously. 'Don't speak of death.'

'Nor shall I, *until you do*.' His eyes flowed over her in the hot light, probing. Almost whispering, he said: 'Hywelis . . . you'll tell me. Say that you will acquaint me with my day and hour, so that I am not taken at odds, unfinished. So that I, like Red Iolo, may truly choose my burying ground.'

She flinched from the unspeakable task within her power. She looked for guidance towards the bard. He sat soberly stroking his harp. She fidgeted with the golden torque. It felt cool and volatile, a weighty serpent. Madog, who had been sleeping under her chair, got up and stretched, and old Cafall, lying on the Lord's robe-hem, tensed instantly and snuffed about.

'I promise,' she said at last.

'The day and hour?' he said eagerly. 'When you see, you

will share the sight? So that I may prepare my soul's health and the disposition of my estate?'

'I will.' She was emboldened to seek payment for the promise. 'I am exercised in my mind, my lord, about a certain matter. Will you now hear me?'

He was still. His eyes made her shiver. She wondered how to start; useless to dissemble. The Lord shared her blood.

'Concerning Owen ap Meredyth ap Tydier . . .'

The eyes grew fiercer than the fire. Frightened, she half-rose and stepped by accident on Madog's paw. The cub sprang across the flagstones, colliding with Cafall, who gave a rasp of fury. He blundered forward, and felled Madog. Cafall could no longer bite, but he could roll and crush and tear with claws. The bard leaped from his stool and seized Cafall by the jaws, wrestling him to the ground. He lay breathing tersely, his eyes closed. Hywelis dived to take his head on her lap, while Madog skulked behind her chair.

'You laid hands upon a royal dog!' said the Lord, without anger.

'Your pardon, Lord,' said Gruffydd Llwyd.

'He's old, he's ill.' Hywelis did not look up. 'It's no one's fault.'

'He hates the fox,' said Glyn Dŵr. 'The law of nature. Tend him, Hywelis.'

She cradled the great head. Trails of saliva glistened on her gown. What she had begun, she must complete.

'Concerning Owen . . .' She kept her eyes on the dog, heard the Lord's gaunt silence.

'. . . he longs to go to war. Your refusal has broken his heart.' Again silence, until a green branch spat in the fire, and Cafall in his swoon sighed deeply. Above her head she felt the Lord relax a trifle.

'And that is all?' he said slowly.

She bowed lower over Cafall's grizzled brow, silent. Far from it, she could have said, and needlessly. He knew.

'But you'd send him away? Perhaps to death?'

She looked up, full at him. 'He will not die in a French war. But he is linked, somehow, to France.'

The Lord's eyes gleamed, the fine falcon face grew drawn

with intent. 'You've seen? You know his fate also?'

'I have an inclination as to his fate. I still have power.'

It was all he needed; the unassailable testament of her purity. She was still his seer and salvation.

'Get up, girl. Tell me your mind.'

The blaze had gone from his look, even the fire burned less unbearably hot.

'You think I should send my lordlings to fight for Henry?'

'Father, other marcher lords will do so. Even your brother-in-law, Davy Gam, is in favour. In all the valleys men are weary of stagnation, and the young ones are keen to be tried, and I heard the courier say that Wales would be rich, rewarded by the King.'

In his mind a blackened ruin arose, corroded by grief and fire.

'Sycharth,' said the Lord. 'I cannot forget.'

'Do you hate King Harry for what he did?'

'No. I remember the good fighting he gave me. I remember how my brother was killed at Usk, when Harry had lately been made Lieutenant of Wales, but I remember also the friends of his I slaughtered. I taught that young cock all he knows of strategy and siegework, as surely as if I had put him to school in my yard and at my quintain. I respect him truly. But his race is my enemy, and it was under Henry Bolingbroke, not his son, that I learned to hate the Saeson. Hate them in my own right, apart from the old persuasions of Taliesin. All the traditional hurts I took upon me, when Bolingbroke usurped sweet Richard's throne . . .'

The bard began a little doleful tune.

'. . . so that Grey's usurpation of my lands echoed that greater crime. Ay! that's the song I wrote to Richard. I wrote it when the campaign was afoot to prove him living, though we all knew him murdered at Pomfret. And he loved Harry, and nurtured him. Another reason why I cannot hate the King. It's a web, all the threads tied wrongly now, confused and warped. The one clear skein is my desire for the supremacy of Wales, of which you will apprise me, Hywelis, in God's good time.'

He continued: 'I met Richard's little French girl, Isabelle.

For her sake I was pleased to ally myself with her countrymen. When they came to Milford Haven, after my second Parliament at Harlech, they brought me six hundred crossbowmen and twelve thousand armed troops . . .'

'And then they ran away,' said Hywelis. 'Back to France, never to return.'

'Ha!' Savagely amused, he said: 'You've learned your lessons well, girl. You deem this reason then to ride against them? To reclaim, in the King's name, all Aquitaine, all Normandy, the South. Harry's grown greedy. He wants not the riches of France or a bride of France, but both. And if he fights as he fought me, I see no bar to his gains. But what has this to do with Wales? He has drawn our cousins in antiquity, the Irish, to his banner, but he will find Wales, at least my portion of it, a different matter.'

'The marcher lords will agree,' she said stubbornly. 'Davy Gam will go, and the young men, and – '

'And so they do not love Wales as I,' said Glyn Dŵr. His eyes were no longer benign. Hywelis slid to her knees again.

'Father. Let Owen go.' She kissed his hand, the raised tumultuous veins. He laughed, cruel and triumphant, like the growl of the eagle. Gruffydd Llwyd looked up from his harp.

'A strange demonstration of love! Can you no longer brook the sight of him? I thought you were enamoured . . .'

'Deeply. Dearly.' And the bard instantly struck an intricate distressful chord, hoping to cover her words.

'Then he shall not go,' said the Lord, getting up. Painfully, Cafall also struggled to rise. Glyn Dŵr stooped and lifted the great beast in his arms. Standing thus, he said: 'No scion of my house shall ever ride under the English banner. And hearts do not break. At least, not for something as slight as this. Poor Cafall! We are old tonight.' He left the hall, bowed, as if he carried his own soul.

The bard and Hywelis looked at one another. Yesterday's quarrel was forgotten.

'I don't understand,' said he. 'I have never seen him so unkind. And you! Why, if you love Owen so, would you send him away?'

'Why? I cannot bind him. I can only give what I can, and even now I've failed him. Should he leave me, I would still be with him. Even though my body were here in Glyndyfrdwy, my spirit would be with him in the field. How can I show him my love, other than by giving him his heart's desire?'

'Don't weep,' said the bard, disturbed.

'I've failed.' She got up, crying, stumbling to the door with Madog gliding beside her. Outside in the passage the worn stone arches were lit through the embrasures by a moon almost at the full. Light silvered a deep recess and limned a shadow round the figure waiting there. She went to him. Once again his breath was hers, his heartbeat shook her own flesh. She tasted him, drank him, slipped into his mind, saw through his eyes, becoming the moon and the dark that bathed him, becoming his past and his future, his griefs and joys, flowing within him as his own breath. And all this without a touch or a word, for she stood apart while he waited, tense and hopeful.

Madog saw the moon through the slit. He lifted his mask and bayed gruesomely. Owen came forward to Hywelis. He touched her wet cheek.

'So it was hopeless?'

'I tried. Owen, I tried.'

He took her head in his hands and kissed her.

'You must try again.'

'I dare not.' Madog gave another awful howl.

'What ails the fox? You should let him go. Soon it will be too late. He will be estranged from his brothers and they will turn on him.'

'I have never asked the Lord a favour before. I thought he would grant me this,' she said.

'Yes. You were the one. He would not even listen to Davy Gam. But you are closest of all to him.'

'The old dog is sick,' she told him.

'Ay!' said Owen, and laughed almost bitterly. 'But there's still might in him!'

'The Lord is jealous,' she said. 'Of your youth, the sights of blood that await you. He was training you to fight for Wales. Only to that end does he think you should show your strength. And he is jealous' (more softly) 'of what passes between you and me.'

After a moment he pulled her to him, saying: 'You're my true, good girl. You know my needs and hurts. Come . . '

They began to walk along the passage, Madog pulling at his lead to avoid the moon's weird face.

'I must go to bed.'

'In a moment. I still need your help. Though the Lord says no, I say yes. I will have my way, Hywelis.' They were at the stone stair which snaked upwards to the women's apartments and coiled down to the men's quarters below.

'What must I do, my Owen?'

Whispering, his face trellised by moon and shadow, he told her. The King's courier had not yet departed over the border. Even now he was negotiating with Davy Gam and the henchmen of other marcher lords, and all not a mile from Glyndyfrdwy. But secretly, for they were chary of the Lord's displeasure.

'You know this valley, Hywelis.'

'Every blade and stone of it.'

'In day and darkness?'

'Both.' Then, warily: 'Owen! you would disobey the Lord?'

'You must guide me. Without you I'd be lost. Even with the full moon tomorrow . . .'

'Betray the Lord?'

He tipped up her face. The patterns of moon and shadow altered his expression so she could not read it, but for an instant he looked distinctly like Glyn Dŵr himself at his most sardonic and fierce.

'You love me. You gave me the word. I did not even have to woo you.'

'Yes. Oh, yes.'

'And now, when I ask so little, you falter, you fail. *Cariad*,' he said caressingly, 'you would not be culpable. We should be back before dawn, unseen. I need only place my hands between those of the King's proxy and swear loyalty to Henry. Even the Lord would have to acknowledge such an oath, or live in dishonour.'

'I am his bondmaid and his sight,' she said faintly. 'I dare not.'

'No harm will come of it.' He began to kiss her, long and slowly. She stood, passive, dreaming, doubting, lost. In her flaccid hand Madog's collar slackened. The fox raised his paw and thrust off the rushy band, and was gone instantly down the spiral stair.

'Love,' said Owen. 'I need you, girl. Be my eyes and ears tomorrow night.'

'I have lost Madog!' she cried suddenly.

'We'll find him together.' Still kissing, murmuring.

'No, there's a gap in the wall below, he's been watching it for days. He's gone.'

'Then it's an augury.' Owen's voice shook. 'The valley for Madog and France for me. None shall know your part in tomorrow night. Only do this, I beg you, Hywelis.'

She had no choice. He would go from her. No more love-legends, brief joys. Yet he would be closer to her in France, and in her debt, than if he stayed, full of resentment, perhaps hatred, on the manor. Either way she would lose him, but this way his essence would still be hers. Decision gripped her. She nodded.

'Will you return to me from France?' she whispered. 'Will you ever come home to me?'

'My pledge on it.'

'I shall be with you always,' she said softly. 'Owen, though I hate war, every sword-thrust you make will have my arm behind it. If you wake in camp be sure I will be wakeful too. My soul shall be your shield.'

He half-listened, preoccupied with plans.

'After supper, make your excuses. Watch Megan, she has prying eyes. Rhys keeps the gate – we shall have no trouble there. We are brothers in ambition. Ah, *cariad*! my true, good girl!'

His words and touch were like the *bragod* mead, honey-sweet with a biting core. She felt weary. The two men she loved were instruments of her will. One would be deceived, and to the other she would hand the keys of exile. But not of death! Had she not seen the safety in his future, she would not now be here, acquiescent to his eager strategies.

'Sleep well.' His arms held her once more, she felt the

surges of his excited mind. As she climbed soberly upstairs, the torque weighed on her throat, the little pulse beneath it making it shake as if with life.

Half a mile away in the valley, Madog ran. Prison had wasted his fitness; his tongue lolled and his sides heaved as he chased the thread of scent, token of home and kindred. The white night picked out his badger-blaze. Lying still in her bed, Hywelis was with him. Her mind twisted and turned with him in his desperate erratic search, over pebbles and peat, pursuing that ribbon of vague scent, finding the empty earth, the family gone. Hearing, in the deepest chambers of her mind, his wild lament.

Rhys, swarthy and squat with two missing front teeth, let them out through the gate. The immense white moon was high. Rhys was wistful.

'Would that I were coming. All's quiet, *Diolch i Dduw!* The harper was by, singing me a new song, but he's gone to bed. The Lord will have my bowels for this.'

'You know nothing about it,' said Owen. 'We flew over the wall.'

'Get you gone,' said Rhys, and pushed them through the wicket. They stepped out on to the moorland path, moist from the nearness of the Dee and its offspring streams. The road ran downwards and disappeared in the valley. Hywelis raised her head and sniffed like a questing animal. Rain edged the calm night, rain not for tomorrow but the day after. She felt it in the ends of her hair, her fingertips. She set out down the path, striding, anxious to gain the valley and be lost. Owen followed, his eyes fixed on her narrow shape wrapped in a green wool cloak, his steps less sure than hers. Almost at once he found one foot sucked down; the cold of ice-ages seeped into his shoe, and he called softly: 'Hywelis, wait!' She stopped, turning. The moonlight shone on the fine bones of her face. She smiled at him, a look of love and confidence but one which the moon translated into something fateful and weird. He put out his hand for hers. Her touch was warm.

'You must follow me closely,' she said. 'See – here's the

thorn tree, where I freed a rabbit once, and it thanked me in its own tongue. We must skirt the tree . . .' She led him over the friable ground, a nest of warrens, intricate, unseen.

'Now.' She halted again. 'You must tell me where you are to meet the English.'

'That's easy, half a mile west of the place of the eagle.'

He matched her steady gait, clasping the fingers of a moon-kissed witch, feeling with his free hand the baselard tucked into his belt, the sharp blade ready to bite into whatever enemy he would eventually be put to face. The fighting lust was his; it would have sent him to battle under any colours – even under the French themselves. He had no quarrel with any, but the years of old war-talk, coupled with indolence, fermented in his heart.

He was wearing a soft velvet cap which was suddenly terrifyingly torn from his head as a lemon shadow drifted across the moon and dropped with an eldritch yell. A demon with claws, a form from a holy tapestry come alive. He clapped his hand to his head, staggered and almost fell. He heard Hywelis laugh, saw her lithe shape darting, her feet almost weightless on the crust of the westerly bog. She called to the soaring pale shadow in some inhuman tongue and the cap dropped at her feet. She ran back just as lightly, brushing at the muddied velvet.

'*Duw!*' he whispered. 'What was it?'

'Only old Drwyndwn, the Flatnose,' she said, still laughing. 'The hunting owl. He has a nest in the cliff. Here.' She handed him the cap. 'Your gear's not edible, Owen.'

'Drwyndwn,' he said, annoyed to find his heart still pounding heavily. 'Do you call all your creatures by the names of kings?'

'What else are they?' She held out her hand again.

He went with her, still angry and ashamed of his fear. He had never been in the valley by night and resented her immunity. The moon sailed its painted course, a knowing white eye. A thousand dark sounds assaulted him, as if this night were the one in which all loving and fighting and preying must be accomplished. Foxes warbled, gibbered and roared. A dreadful scream rose ululating in almost human syllables and died with a terrible hiss. He crossed himself.

'Badger,' said Hywelis. 'They call like that only once a year.'

Owen thought: when I reach the English camp I shall be an old whitehead, useless for service. Thank God for this woman.

'Careful,' she told him. 'Here we must jump the stream.'

He had not even seen it, but now she showed him its dark diamonds and he heard it fluting over rocks, between willow and alder trees, as he stepped to the brink. Hywelis leaped, landing upon a broad stone midstream. She poised there for a moment, then cleared the remaining strip of water and turned on the far bank. He heard her encouraging voice.

'Jump, my Owen!'

He launched forward and, as if cued to the moment, all hell gave tongue from the grove of trees. A gobbling roar, tormented shrieks and rasping yells mingled with the beat of wings. It was only a flock of young heron going to bed, but shocked, Owen wavered and plunged into the heart of the stream. Luminous eddies curled about him; his hose, new for the expedition, were soaked to the top of his thighs. His oaths, some of them extraordinarily inventive, curdled the air, while he waited in rage and shame for Hywelis's laughter and clammy creatures circled his drowned legs warily. Then she came, far from laughter but distressed, girding up her skirts about her waist, wading to him through the water. He clutched at her hands. The moon-bright eddies danced on her pale thighs. She hauled him out until they both stood on the rock. There, making little concerned noises, she tried to dry his hose with her bunched-up gown, and he himself began suddenly, riotously, to laugh.

'A baptism,' he spluttered. 'Pray God it's not an omen that our ship will founder *en route* to France.'

'No, no!' She patted and rubbed at his clothes. 'It's my fault, we should have brought lanterns.'

'And have the Lord see our departure from the window?'

He caught hold of her suddenly and her hands grew still.

'You've done your best. Leave it now.'

'I have always been your nurse.' Her face was against his shoulder, and he had the odd sensation that when she looked at him again she would be an old woman. So he raised her chin and kissed her, lifted her in his arms, and saying that he was wet already, waded with her through the stream.

After they had been walking for about another half-hour, he found he had caught her instinct and was skirting the hazards before they loomed. He walked a little ahead while the hot white moon judged him, swimming on a toss of cloud the colour of a pigeon's wing. They went lightly along the ridge of ground between the peat-hags, and began to ascend the hill that would eventually become the mountain broken by the pass into England. His spirits lifted; his hose were drying on his legs, and his feet grew warm. Even the sudden hoarse 'Fr-aa-nk!' of a heron disturbed on the nest made him smile instead of shudder. Hawthorn grew at the hill-foot, and its scent blew in the mountain wind. Long-eared owls barked and quacked like dogs on the wing; a flock of curlews, flying upstream, emitted their ghostly whistle. Owen stopped on firm moss and pointed against the moon.

'See! Their lights!'

In the lee of the hill a glow showed, dulled by the canvas of two large tents. Silhouetted figures could be seen and another brighter light swarmed to and fro as a guard with a lantern patrolled the perimeter.

'My prayers are answered.' He squeezed Hywelis's hand so tightly that she winced. 'I feared they might already have left.' He started to run forward up the hill, past a dark oak-grove. She hurried after him, catching up her gown.

'Are they expecting you? Wait . . . they will be armed. Owen . . .'

Another lantern up ahead had joined the first. Voices floated down the hill.

'They've seen us,' she whispered. 'Let's be careful. I've no wish to stop an arrow.'

'We'll show ourselves, by my faith,' he said. 'Hail, Sir Sentry! Hail, Englishmen! Look, Hywelis, it's Glewlwyd Mighty-Grasp himself! Hail, Glewlwyd, I've come to fight for you!'

A big man, sword in hand, raised his light at the boast. As they approached the tents, the flare picked out Owen's bright flushed face. The sentry turned to his companion.

'Another raving-mad Welshman!' Peering closer: 'Do they bring their own camp-followers these days?'

'Maybe it's his wife, come to coddle him,' sneered the other. 'Our discipline may be too stark for these mountain trolls.'

'Have sense,' the big man told him. 'They're demons in fight. My brother was at Grosmont. He still wakes up screaming o' nights. Savages. Come forward!' And Owen strode up so that he was within the unsteady circle of light and could hear the buzz of talk from within the tents.

'Your name?' said the sentry in painful Welsh.

'Owen ap Meredyth ap Tydier.'

'You're a volunteer?'

'Yes. From Glyndyfrdwy.'

The sentry said to his fellow: 'I thought Glyn Dŵr had spat upon the treaty.' He leaned to study Owen. 'Now again, your business! The truth this time.'

Owen said coldly in perfect English: 'I have come to see Davydd Gam and the English envoy.'

'Sent by the old wizard, were you?'

'That,' said Owen, 'is an honourable title in my country. However, the Lord knows nothing of my coming here tonight.'

'You've mastered our tongue,' said the second sentry.

'I speak French even better,' said Owen. 'One day I shall be like Gwrhyr the Translator. I am from the household of a prince and here to offer arms in the service of another, lesser one.'

The guard roared with laughter. The big man said: 'Christ's Wounds! You won't last long in the army, lad, with talk like that! Yet – ' he mocked Owen with a flourishing bow, so that the light in his hand tilted a crazy arc about them all – 'conceit such as this has all our battles won already. Go in, my lord, if our pavilions aren't too rude for you. There are other whelps in there, not quite so hot-tongued as yourself.' Owen stepped forward with Hywelis gliding behind him. The sentries barred her way.

'No women!' Owen turned, saying, 'Wait for me,' and went into the tent. Hywelis retreated a few paces and sat down in the heather. She fixed her eyes upon the tent-flap; a light-chink came through it and the hum of voices was more distinct.

After a few more witticisms about Owen, the big man wandered over to her, his lantern glaring in her calm pale face.

'Quite a beauty!' he observed.

'Are you his woman?' The other man jerked his head towards the tent.

'His soul and his guide,' she answered in Welsh so soft and quick that neither man comprehended. Suddenly the big man crouched. He put out his hand and fumbled her breasts.

'Yes, a beauty,' he said again, breathing heavily.

Hywelis sat on motionless in the heather. Only her eyes stirred; they wandered from the pavilion and fixed upon the sentry's face. There were drops of sweat on it, and his tongue flicked over his lips. And suddenly, frighteningly, she saw his temporal image changed. He was in a different place, a different time, chalk-white, sweating not with lust but from unspeakable torment. Though he still crouched over her, she saw him lying while a priest bent near, she heard his groans, smelled a vile stench. In an eyeblink the pageant of his doom was played out before her. She put out trembling fingers and touched his cheek. The vision faded. He smiled with pleasure and his hand dropped between her thighs.

'I'll have her over in the grove. Keep watch,' he said to the other man.

'What's your name?' said Hywelis, stone-still.

'Why, John Fletcher, my pretty. Come . . .' He was undoing the points of his hose with his free hand.

'John Fletcher, look at me,' said Hywelis in her halting English. 'Do not set foot in France. Your death is there.'

The hand grew still. Her eyes swallowed him. He tried to speak but his tongue became like sand.

'You will die.' She spoke sadly and very clearly so that he should understand. Had she had any doubts before, the proof was coming, the last, ineluctable sign. All about Fletcher's shoulders and close-cropped head, little flames played, danced their pale pavane and melted away.

'Death, in France. In one year and a little more. You will lie in French soil with many others.'

Intrigued, the other man came closer. 'What's to do, Jack? Won't she have you?'

Fletcher got up and backed away from Hywelis, yet her eyes still held him. He said hoarsely: 'You lie.'

She shook her head.

'You're guessing!' said Fletcher wildly. 'I'm a fair fighter and I keep my arms in good order, the French are cowards and Harry will lead us to victory . . .' Blustering: 'Women! if we listened to them we'd all run home. Anyway, I'd be proud to take a French blade in me for Harry, but I shan't, do you hear?'

'No.' She rose fluidly from the ground. 'You will see no fighting. It will be a . . . a belly-rot, great pain, over many days.' She covered her eyes with her cupped hands. 'I'm sorry, Master Fletcher, but it is so.'

They stared at her. John Fletcher's fingers sketched a small cross.

'Your kind have been burned before now,' he said unsteadily.

Hywelis slowly bared her eyes. Both men backed even further away.

'I want to go into the tent,' she said softly.

'You can't.' Fletcher's voice still shook. 'Sir Gilbert Talbot, the King's deputy, will be hearing the oath.'

The men stood close together, staring at her.

'Then let me look through the flap.' Hywelis walked forward and the guard fell back. She rested her face against the cool hidecloth. The tent was lamplit and a trestle-table had been set up. There were parchment rolls and tapers and the smell of new-sealed wax. Standards, furled and tasselled with gold, stood leaning in a corner. Behind the table sat the King's deputy, clean-shaven and with close-cropped hair. One of two men who stood at his elbow addressed him as Sir Gilbert; it was the courier who had been hounded from Glyn Dŵr's manor. The other was Davy Gam. He had removed the black patch from his eye and the barren socket stared warningly out at the dozen or so youths who knelt before Talbot.

Their ages ranged from fourteen to twenty. They were quiet. Their eyes, of a bloodline used to lifting to the mountains for generations past, were tilted at the corners. Sir Gilbert assessed the youths as he talked. This was the last contingent to come to his standard. Wherever he had pitched his pavilion they had come, some like these, secretly by night, disobeying fathers and guardians; from Ruvoniog, Kimmerch, from Dyffryn Clwyd, from Mold in the Alun valley, from Chirk, from Pool, from Powysland and Kerry, from Clun, Wigmore, Radnor, from Talgarth and Blaenllyfni, from Gwenllwg, from the twenty-four minor lordships of Over Went and Nether Went, and from the Honour of Monmouth. He thought they were like beans in a row, many related by blood, and tossing away the old grudges of their forefathers. Chance and youth were theirs, and life would never again be so new.

'I take it you can all speak English?'

There was some fidgeting. Davydd Gam bent to confer with the King's deputy.

'But you can understand, if I speak slowly?' Sir Gilbert asked, and they nodded and composed themselves to listen.

'It is plain you are all anxious to join battle, or you would not be here,' he said. 'But first you should know for what you will be fighting. Our good King Henry the Fifth, sovereign of all England, Prince of Wales, has for some time been negotiating, in chivalry, to reclaim the lands of France which are his by hereditary right. The throne of France descends to his Grace through his great-grandfather of blessed memory, King Edward the Third, whose mother, Isabelle, was daughter to King Philip of France.' He cleared his throat. These were indeed the terms of Henry's claim but spoken thus they sounded somewhat tenuous. To counter this unspeakable internal doubt he continued quickly.

'This same mighty ancestor of the King was in truth sovereign of France.' (Actually Edward III had styled himself thus two years after his invasion and then surrendered the title in exchange for the Duchy of Aquitaine and other prizes. However Sir Gilbert had long ago decided that paraphrase was best, especially in this instance.)

'The French proved traitor,' he went on. 'They fought us for our rightful possessions, for Aquitaine, for Poitou, Limousin, Quercy, Rouergue, Marche, Angoumois and Calais. Today we own but Calais, Bordeaux and Bayonne, and a few Gascon lands. We would have had Guienne province also, but

King Richard the Second, in his unwisdom, signed a truce and surrendered this, among other possessions. It is left to our good King to amend this grievous error and . . .'

'Sir.' A treble voice came from the end of the line. A boy looking no more than twelve had raised his hand. It wavered up and down like a spider on a thread. Sir Gilbert smoothed a parchment and looked at him sternly.

'Speak.'

'Lord, is it true that King Richard is still alive? My father says – '

'It is not!' Scarlet washed the boy's face. More quietly, Sir Gilbert said: 'These are rumours spread by the disloyal to harm our King. Richard is dead. I have seen his corpse. He was exhumed for the purpose of quelling those who doubt, and his body, green from the grave, transported in a great chair from Langley and through the streets of Westminster. I have smelled the corruption of his bones.' The boy, pale now, looked afraid. 'Richard's wives are dead also, both Bohemian and French. Queen Isabelle's widower, Charles of Orléans, has married Bonne of the Armagnacs. They now form one of the factions of Burgundy and Armagnac, which have split France and made her ready for our conquest.'

Most of the boys were by now looking utterly lost.

'So be warned,' said Talbot. 'Whoever sets out to nurture the monstrous tale that Richard lives may look to Sir John Oldcastle for example. He was cursed on Paul's Cross for that very thing, and when captured will be burned alive. For this talk is heresy, and the King sees heresy as more loathsome than a nest of scorpions. When he has taken France and is supreme, he will pit himself against the Infidel and all that is evil. He will unite the world in righteousness and amend the Great Schism, that crime initiated by the French; there will be only one Vicar of Christ . . .'

One of the youths had his eyes closed. His body sagged and a vicious nudge from his neighbour jerked him upright. The boy who had first spoken asked intelligently:

'Sir . . . the Burgundians and the Armagnacs. Which is our friend? Which is our foe?'

'Neither. Two years ago, we fought with Burgundy against

Armagnac. We slaughtered hundreds at St Cloud. Then, not a year later, the Armagnacs came, begging our aid against Burgundy! The French are all turncoats, and the man who rules them an imbecile, his heir the Dauphin Louis a libertine. This time we shall be England fighting for England's dues in France.'

'Thank you, lord,' said the piping voice.

'Our King,' said Gilbert Talbot, 'has demanded two million crowns from the French to recompense him for the rights so far denied. What has he had in answer? Threats and taunts from the libidinous boy styled Dauphin, and from King Charles, mere vapid maunderings. Our King suggested a match with one of the princesses, to unite the two realms. In reply he received obstructions, lies, protests, more taunts. So now the sword will achieve what diplomacy cannot. He will take what is his by right and blood. He will rule France as she should be ruled and exorcize the curse laid on her by the Knights of the Temple a hundred years ago . . .'

Davydd Gam leaned and whispered; many of the boys were looking bewildered again.

'So, to this hour.' Sir Gilbert shortened his peroration. 'I have you gathered here so you should know for whom and for what you are offering yourselves in service. You will serve under a King as strong as Achilles, as brave as Hector, as wise as Solomon, and as righteous as the Archangel Michael. You will be part of the greatest army ever to depart from England. Though you are Welshmen, the glory of England will be yours to share. There will be rewards, triumphs, perquisites. You leave these shores as babes; you will return as men, and tell your grandsons how you went forward with the seal of Heaven upon your cause. Come to me now, those who desire immortal honour.'

Taken all round, it was a good exhortation, and by English standards greatly flamboyant, although a bard would by now have drawn tears and cries of assent from his listeners, and there was still quietness. Yet Hywelis saw Owen affected; he rose with the others, his face pale and attenuated; he trembled and his golden eyes were feverish. The assembly lined up to kneel again and raise their hands to those of the King's proxy. The oath was administered, repeated, never louder than a breath. The night-breeze crept through the tent-flap.

Ardently watched by Hywelis, Owen's turn came. She saw his shape lucent as steel, his arrowed hands following the line of his straight back. In that same moment she saw the quintessence of his greatness. To all the others he was merely another youth, arrogant, restive and suggestible. To her he was the embryo of something immeasurable, greater than the highest martyrdom or the keenest fame, stronger and more obsessive even than love, though love was there in bounty. She could not yet gauge its form, yet the unseen grandeur of his destiny lit him like a torch and diminished all else about it.

Abruptly the ceremony ended. The youths milled at the table, merry with nervous relief; Welsh and laboured English mingled. Someone was asking naïvely about the commanders – would they, the recruits, be riding with the King himself? No, there would be hundreds of captains; if one were fortunate one might march a mile behind the King's brothers or the King's friend, Richard Courtenay, Bishop of Norwich, for the Church was also to join this sacred war. The impressive names were drawn out like jewels from a bag; the Earl of Dorset, Lord Fitzhugh, Sir Thomas Erpingham, Sir Gilbert Umfraville, the Duke of York, the Earl of Oxford . . .

There were to be months of preparation. Every man must have a harness always ready; a jack, the quilted steel-lined coat, a helmet, gloves, sword, dagger and poleaxe, and the matchless longbow and arrows. Every man at muster was to wear the cross of Christ and St George. There was to be no whoring, no camp-followers. Churches were not to be looted on pain of death, and monks and nuns left unmolested.

Those insufficiently trained in arms were to go at once to London where schooling awaited them, and Owen was one of these selected. Hywelis, with a sinking heart, heard him ask: 'Am I to leave tonight?' and the answer: 'No, you will collect what gear you have and say farewell to your mentors. We shall be here another four days.' She knew he would have gone on the moment, but now she had a reprieve, four whole days of him. The Lord would be angry with him but there was nothing he could do. Owen's allegiance was chosen, his oath must be honoured.

When he came from the tent he was subdued and serious. He spoke to the sentries courteously. 'Until our next meeting,' and they nodded, but Fletcher, still plainly uneasy, stepped back as Hywelis went by. He offered Owen a lantern which he refused, for although the moon was declining, its light still washed the valley. Fletcher watched them go, and to him Owen went handclasped with the powers of darkness. It would need many a pot of ale before he could begin to laugh and damn Hywelis's words of that night.

She pressed lightly against Owen as they made the mossy descent, searching with feet and eyes and instinct for the track down into the valley. The heather scents mingled with the bitter-sweetness of campion and meadowsweet, peat and ferns. Somewhere towards the mountain ridge, a vixen bayed of love. Hywelis searched the night for Madog's essence, and knew him far away.

'Did you see that sentry's hands shaking?' said Owen.

'It was my fault, I told his fortune. Now I wish I hadn't.' She forgot that her vision had saved her from an unknown brutality.

Owen stopped and faced her eagerly.

'Tell me mine, Hywelis. If you have the power . . . it would be wonderful to know . . . I'd know what hazards to dare, and when to hold still. Tell me, Hywelis.'

She pulled him on, saying that the night was fading and they must be back before early Mass. Rhys would be watching for them, and Gruffydd Llwyd was a poor sleeper, often rising to play his harp to himself. As for Glyn Dŵr, God send him an unbroken night! Tomorrow would be bad enough. Tomorrow, today, for already the moon's pallor looked weary and clouded by dew. Ahead of them they heard the stream's lonely, small-hours voice. Drwyndwn Flatnose, glutted with prey, floated beside them from crag to crag, riding the air on his great lemon wings.

'Here's the water. Are you ready for the leap?'

'I could do it in one stride. Now I am the King's man, a soldier. I am strong.'

'Come then.' She poised on the lip of the stream. Her voice trembled.

'Hywelis,' he said uncertainly, 'are you weeping?' He peered into her face, at the wet glitter of her eyes. She did not answer, but thought: yes, I weep, because I am moved by the regard you have for yourself, a good thing in truth when there are so many who cringe and doubt and draw back; because of what I saw in you as you took the oath, that destiny that you, all unknowing, wear like cloth of gold. And because you are my other self, and in four days I shall be split, and bleed.

'Girl.' He came close and they stood, their ankles deep in meadowsweet, the noise of the water in their ears. 'Be happy. I have not thanked you for tonight. I've no right to ask more. Let my fortune remain unknown. I'll remember your kindness, not your prophecies.'

She said: 'Remember me. Yes. Remember me, and that I said this: you will be safe, and loved as few have ever been loved.'

'I know. You will always love me.'

'Not I alone,' she said heavily. 'Those of more noble fame, Owen.'

Instantly excited, he said: 'What do you mean? Shall I rise to a height in some great lord's favour? You must tell me now, I didn't press you! For if this is so, I'll fight like ten thousand, and one day I'll meet Glyn Dŵr as an equal, not an orphan nurtured of his charity. Tell me, tell me . . .' He held her shoulders, searching her face. She gave a long sigh, and said:

'I can tell you this. You will be truly great. Your name will live for ever.'

'How? Through my skill in arms? Through my leadership in the field? Through my music?' The moon cast off cloud and gleamed in his eyes. He was breathing rapidly. Hywelis sighed again, almost a groan. Waveringly she let her hand fall to his loins. There she touched him, feeling the springs of his excitement made flesh, the tall hardness that beat like a second hidden heart.

'Through your seed,' she said, and withdrew her hand. As if exhausted, she sank to sit on the ground, and instantly he knelt beside her. Unsure of which had aroused him more, her words or her touch, he took her to him passionately, kissing her mouth, fondling the long wild hair, kissing the sad wild eyes. From a nearby tree came a crystal spill of song, a rapturous torrent wasted on the night.

'The nightingale . . .' he said, muffled and trembling.

'No, a whitethroat,' whispered Hywelis. 'We have awakened him.'

'*Cariad*, let me . . . let me now . . .'

Revealed, her body answered the moon's whiteness. She was a pale pearl, glowing so that the grass where she lay seemed illuminated by her, and for a moment he recoiled from her mystery. Then she drew him to her brilliant arms, enfolding him, the moon, and the clamouring night.

At the zenith of their embrace, the torque became loosened from her neck. A careless upthrown hand nudged it away. It hung for an instant on the edge of the bank then slid without sound into the racing stream.

The Lord stood on the battlements of Glyndyfrdwy. Soon after midnight he had been glad to wake from a dream of terror. He had been poised on the crest of Dyna Mont Owain, the hill named after him where he had often stood to watch his enemies coming from Chester in the east. Yet he had seemed to be shadowed by the tomb of Eliseg, saint and king and inspiration of the Welsh. He had watched a ring of flambeaux coming closer to surround him. Turning to yell a command to his troops, he had found himself deserted. A bluff wind wavered the grass, and the bog-bean flowers swayed, dyed pink by the encroaching flames. Behind him a ring of burial stones rose starkly from the turf. He had rushed down the slope, roaring his challenge, striking out at nothing; the forces evaded him though he lashed and grappled and swore. Then he fancied that Rhys ap Gethin fought beside him with grinning skull-face, and that Margaret of Maelor, made fragile by the wind, wrung her dead hands and whispered: 'Fight, my Owain!' then, sadly: 'Fly, my Owain!' He had heard his own guttural breath, felt the pain of effort in his lungs. Woke streaming with sweat, his wolfskin coverlet tossed aside.

The harsh breathing went on; it was Cafall's. The great dog lay by the bed. He had lost flesh in the past two days, his ribs stood out like a mammoth's skeleton. Glyn Dŵr swung his legs from the couch and bent to him. A burning tongue feebly lapped his hand.

'Some air for you, boy.' He carried the dog up the spiral, feeling the bones, the sadness. I should kill him! he thought, and Cafall laid his head lovingly upon the Lord's upper arm. Your way, not mine, said the touch. Your wisdom is my contentment.

No, he thought. Who am I to quench the spirit of a god? Cafall lay on cool stone, breathing the night under the dewed dimmed moon. While Glyn Dŵr thought once more of the dead, the loved, of the past arrogances, his Parliaments at Machynlleth and Harlech, of his own rising fame and his slow decline. Of Margaret again, as blithe and temperate as the summer of his years; of his brave sons, of Megan, asleep below, who loved him, and of lovely Hywelis, born of the faery-woman and his last anchor and guide. He rested his brow against the embrasure above a declivity built for the discharge of weapons, and heard a shuffling on the stair. For a moment he hoped it was Hywelis, aware of his distress and come from bed to talk away the night. But Hywelis never shuffled, her step was silk. He turned to see Gruffydd Llwyd, holding his syca-more harp like a limb without which he could not function.

'So you're wakeful too,' said Glyn Dŵr. 'Mind the dog.'

The bard stepped carefully over Cafall, and leaned beside the Lord.

'It's late, I mean early,' said Gruffydd Llwyd, and the Lord knew a harsh desire for the voice of Iolo Goch, who had never spoken unless it were sense, and never for speech's sake. Iolo lay at Valle Crucis, under the protection of Eliseg. Yet Gruffydd was a good fellow and doubtless would go down in the annals with talents enhanced once his time was done.

'Lord, are you well?'

'I dreamed,' said Glyn Dŵr. 'The dream misliked me.'

'Did you conquer?' asked the bard, with insight.

The Lord shook his head.

'Only a dream,' said Gruffydd Llwyd. 'Remember your

triumphs! Eagles have devoured the corpses of your slain.'

'My loved and hated, both.'

The bard teased the harp. Its plaint squeezed through the stone machicolations and down into the valley which now looked palely flattened, as if the moon had wearied it.

'Those who have hurt you,' said the bard, 'writhe in the flames, howling that death never slays.'

Glyn Dŵr grimaced. 'I wish them no hell-flames. My own are before me.'

'No, Lord. You are all goodness.'

'Sing,' he demanded. The bard struck strings again, and called, in his nasal reed:

'No 'scathe 'twill be, occasion thus to take,
And May did well, houses of leaves to make,
Long ages there beneath the trees we'll be,
From all secure, I and my sweet with me . . .'

The Lord raised his hand.

'What's this? We are men together. Sell me no lickerish tales of love.'

The bard crashed out a discord.

'There are doings tonight,' he said.

'Ay,' Glyn Dŵr looked out across the valley. 'Of flesh and fowl, of ghoul and memory.'

'And' (rancour drove out discretion) 'of man and maid!'

The Lord was silent for at least a minute. Drwyndwn Flatnose paid a visit to the battlements, cried eerily and soared away. The moon pearled from the shadows of dawn and hung full of the night's history.

'Do you speak of my girl?' said the Lord at last.

'She and Owen ap Meredyth. It was best that I gave it you in verse. It was written by a kinsman of his . . .' Suddenly anguished and afraid, the bard took his harp and went quickly away.

Glyn Dŵr looked down at the very moment. He saw the gate and the little movements around it. Rhys the postern guard, full of an agitation plain even at a distance. Then a straight figure whose triumph all but sang. Lastly, his lily of the sea.

*

She was no longer the white Olwen, daughter of Ysbaddaden the Terrible. She sat locked in the topmost tower of Glyndyfrdwy and contemplated the stone wall with its reflection of raindrops under sunlight. She pictured the valley, starred with cinquefoil and rapt with dragonflies, the stream running down, the bent bruised grass where she had lain with Owen. But now that she was revealed, taken, divided, her mind was bound to earth. It could no longer slide from her flesh and roam, projected as easily as the breeze. Four solid walls surrounded her, an appallingly alien sensation. The inner sight was gone, leaving its meagre proxy, imagination.

The Lord knew everything, without a word of confession: the dissolution of her will, the hurt, the final sharp pleasure. As if he had experienced it through his own senses, he knew how Owen, wildly amorous, had dealt with her a little savagely, clumsily, had made her cry, then kissed her tears. And how afterwards the clarity of moon and night had assailed her in a bleak, foreign way; the shapes and sounds of predators and prey, the pattern of the clouds, had assaulted her so that for the first time in her life she felt vulnerable and on the edge of fear.

The Lord knew everything, not because she had told him but because their blood bound them by brain and spirit and intent, as if they walked with the same shadow.

For a day and a night, since the Lord had given her over to Megan's charge, she had sat in this tower, dress and hands still stained with grass. Far below in the courtyard she heard sounds: hooves, a snatch of singing (quickly hushed as news of the Lord's mood spread abroad), the chink of the anvil from the forge, a dog whining. She sat enthralled by loss. Old songs raged within her; the song of mourning for Angharad: 'ill work for the eyes is long weeping, the bondage of sorrow', and the sadness of old lovers became a comprehension of the sorrows of the world. Owen was not dead, but she was kept from him and already time passed, bringing him nearer to departure. Outside the day clouded and wept, the rain that she had forecast teeming down in the courtyard, pooling in a mosaic of green and brown upon the mossy cobbles. The wall on which her eyes were fixed rippled and dulled. Set into it were niches filled with the effigies of saints: Dewi, Beuno, Collen, Curig, Winifred and Gwen, mother of Cybi; they lost their edge before her gaze and seemed also to shimmer and weep.

Owen would soon be gone and with him the last remains of her knowledge and power. She was blinded by loss. No longer could she probe the destinies of Owen or any other, or point the Lord to a new comet and share his visionary hopes and regrets. She could not even track down the essence of Madog; he ran somewhere outside the gates of her vision. White Olwen was dead, the pure vessel shattered, and her giant father clutched an edgeless sword.

Her fingers fluttered to her neck, the target for the Lord's first look, in that terrible moment when she and Owen stood before him in the breaking dawn, and Rhys had gone to be flogged. Glyn Dŵr's voice had been calm with rage, almost dispassionate.

'So you have cast away the torque of Maelor. Our bond was broken easily.'

Until that moment she had not noticed its loss, and cried out in fear. The rest was nightmare, Glyn Dŵr's voice rising and falling, the smoke from the eternal hearth writhing in concord with his words of shame and heartbreak and rejection. In one corner of the hall the bard sat trembling, and through the dream of despair she noticed Cafall, lying limply, seeming very ill.

The rain harped outside the walls and the wind blew drifts of it in through the slit, dampening her hair. Birds, disturbed by the sudden change in the weather, flew past the embrasure in haste. She was startled by a clap of heavy wings and claws scratching on the sill. For an instant a great white seabird rested there, fixing her with its sidelong yellow stare. A terrible hunger assailed her, as if the seabird's look had implanted it. Then the bird launched itself on its upriver flight, dislodging a tiny hail of stones. The rain continued, bringing the night.

Megan aroused her in the early dawn, bearing a cup of ale, bread and cheese. She entered and locked the door behind her. Hywelis smiled woefully.

'Then I am not to be starved to death.'

'You ate yesterday,' said Megan, her face like those of the stone figures.

'Did I?' She thought: Owen has taken away my mind, with all else. She held out her hand for the food.

Savagely frowning, Megan said: 'First, this.' She uncorked a small vial. A bitter smell filled the room, flowers distilled in pain, to kill whatever tiny hope might be growing. Hywelis knew all Megan's skills.

Obediently she drank. The liquid poured vilely into every corner of her stomach. It makes no difference, she thought. I was never meant to bear his child, I have no part in his greatness . . . greatness. A gleam of remembrance came, like the half-forgotten face of a friend. *Always mine, but not mine alone . . .*

She retched. 'Was this your doing?'

'No. The Lord's will, but I endorse it with my heart. I would not see any living token of your shame.'

'Shame? I have only done what others do!'

'But you were not others,' said Megan heavily.

Hywelis ate a little, and drank the ale to erase the bitterness in her mouth.

'What of Owen?' It had to be asked. Megan's face grew fiercer. 'Is he to be punished? He cannot be gainsaid now. He has a duty.'

'Why do you not ask after the Lord your father?'

'May I see him?'

'In half an hour.'

Why half an hour? The Lord did nothing without reason, and he had had Rhys made a whipping-boy for the sins of the night. What of Owen?

'You must abase yourself.' Megan put the key in the lock. 'And you must be cleansed, made proper. *Duw!* Had I been born in your skin, I would not have used our sweet Lord thus.'

The bath was filled in Megan's chamber, and Megan as efficient as ever, scrubbed and towelled, her face growing blacker as she saw the dried blood on Hywelis's thighs and the marks on her breasts. Hywelis thought of the other bath, the night of Owen's singing. Megan took the dead Cathryn's dress from the closet. Another reminder.

'Not that one,' said Hywelis, and was given a long robe of dusty black, in which, pale and thin and nunly, she descended to the hall. The hearth smoked erratically over its red heart. Cafall, much weaker, lay with his head on Glyn Dŵr's foot. The bard was reading sombrely aloud from a great book bound in hairy hide. The Lord had his head in his hands; she saw the rings and the raised violet veins.

'. . . so Adam, dying, sent Seth to Paradise to fetch the oil of mercy. There the angel gave him three seeds which he put under his dead father's tongue. And from these sprang the Tree from which the Cross was made . . .'

The bard saw Hywelis and closed the book. 'She comes,' he said nervously, and Glyn Dŵr raised his head. His eyes had lost their anger, they were weary and red-rimmed. She longed to fling herself into his arms, to be small again and sit on his shoulder to look for omens over the battlements of ruined Sycharth. But she crept to him on her knees and laid her mouth upon his hands. They were cold, their pulses slow.

'Go,' said Glyn Dŵr to the bard, and with an anguished look at Hywelis, he obeyed. She continued to press her lips on the Lord's skin, her tears running, moving her mouth in the word *Forgive*, so that only his flesh heard it. He said:

'I have a mind that you shall become an anchorite at Valle Crucis. The discipline is rigid and they mortify the flesh.'

She looked at him desperately.

'No, my lord, my place is with you.'

He grimaced, turning his sad tempestuous face away. 'You say me no? What are you to me now? You are blunted and blinded and null . . .'

Cafall, in his dying sleep, whimpered and sighed.

'I can still love you,' said Hywelis.

'But you were more to me than love.' He looked at her again. 'You were my strength, my counsellor. Now I am a small boy wandering in the night. I cannot read you any more. You cannot read me. We are divided.'

His voice was mild, sad now. Courage came to her.

'May I ask?'

'Ask.'

'What has become of him?'

Still not angry, he looked almost satisfied that she had asked. 'He has gone, within the last half-hour. With my blessing; I would not send a man into battle with curses. He will make a fair soldier. But he shall do no more hurt to me and mine.'

There was to be no farewell, and she had lost them both. She crept closer, and laid her head down by Cafall's weeping muzzle.

'Do not grovel, Hywelis,' said the Lord. 'It is unfitting for my daughter.'

'Then let me serve you,' she said, against his foot.

He laughed, loss and contempt within the laugh, and said as if he hoped against hope: 'Very well. Come sit by me. Sit, and look in the fire!'

She followed his instruction eagerly. She blinked, dashed a hand across her eyes as if to strengthen them. The Lord folded his hand about her own.

'Look in the fire, girl. Look in the smoke, and tell me what you see!'

The strong vapour snaked upwards, forming puffs, blowing this way and that, almost purple at the core, diffused into white as its edge thinned. The heart of the fire seemed to diminish as if an invisible hood dampened it. She had never seen it so low, yet while he watched her, he tipped the dregs of a drink into the embers, fostering thicker smoke, a screen upon which she must write her will. She crouched, bent like a harridan, staring through stinging, moistening eyes. Greyness swirled and streamed, the moving dust wherein, countless times before, she had seen the face of Gruffydd Glyn Dŵr, of Margaret and Cathryn, of Rhys ap Gethin, of Iolo Goch and the Nightingale of Dyfed, of Glyn Dŵr himself, horsed and snarling, riding to an unknown war, an unfought battle, every colour and vein of him limned on this insubstantial canvas. Every mood, every sickness, every celebration; his soul and ambition, written in smoke, clearer than truth.

Cafall's stertorous breathing went on and on. Hywelis stared until her eyes were scarlet with smoke and pain. There was only greyness, a suffocating cloud of nothing. She turned and shook her head.

'I had hoped,' he said. 'I was foolish. The fire is dying, Cafall is dying, and my *Lili'r môr* has failed me. Once, by your light, I could tread the black road of tomorrow. By Him who died on Tree! that was sorry work that Owen did!'

His hand left hers, his face closed to her.

'Go from me,' he said.

Outside the hall she began to run, stumbling on the long black gown, no longer attuned to castle or Lord or valley, almost insensible of the world itself. She saw Megan standing grimly by the door to the courtyard and cried out, before the woman could speak: 'I see nothing! I am nothing!'

Megan, turning to open the door for someone who came slowly up the steps, did not answer.

Hywelis reached her room, dizzy from the spiral. Under the bald stone eyes of the saints she threw herself on the floor. Soon they would come and turn the key in the lock until such time as she was taken to the house at Valle Crucis, to live without the breeze or the grasses, or the wild monarchs who flew and scampered between plain and mountain. Without father, without Owen. There were deities who when displeased could take mortal wits away. Then Owen ap Meredyth, his voice and his flesh, was the most powerful of all.

Weeping she lay, and did not hear the scraping outside, or the timid voice, but felt the rush of air from the opening door. She turned her head so that into her vision came a dirty sandalled foot, an ankle fanned by a threadless gown.

'Hywelis,' said the bard's thin voice, 'I have come to beg your pardon.'

Wearily she struggled to her feet and went to the arrow-slit.

'I betrayed you to the Lord . . .'

'He would have known anyway.' The sun was shining. In a far meadow someone was flying a peregrine, it hovered and stooped, brightly bound by a sunbeam.

'I love the Lord,' said Gruffydd Llwyd, 'and was envious of your favour.'

The sun grew brighter.

'I have been to the river,' he said softly. 'I brought you something to make amends.'

'Nothing . . .' she said, then looked round and saw what he carried, half-swathed in his garment. Bright eyes in a thin face, and the white blaze between the ears and down the back. The coat a little rough, and a new wound on one delicate paw.

'Madog, Madog!'

'He has hurt his foot, but you can heal it. When I found him he was embattled, with a feral cat.'

'By the river? Then he was near . . . he was coming home!'

He came to her quite gently, a spark of mischievous affection in the golden eyes. She sat, cradling him, his warmth invading her, salving her grief.

'Am I forgiven?' asked Gruffydd Llwyd.

She was not listening. As she sat holding Madog, a blinding tunnel of sunshine shafted through the arrow-slit and engulfed her. Without warning, the slit widened before her. She saw the panorama of the valley. Of the world. Her inner blindness shattered and dispersed. Even at the height of her power it had never been like this. Kingdoms formed up to unroll before her, in surpassing beauty and poignant dread.

'Girl . . .' said the bard.

Trembling, she opened herself to the moment. There was no need to fear its dissolution; power rushed upon her, terrifying, almost insupportable. She felt as if she sat at the nucleus of a vast gale, being buffeted by voices of the unborn, seeing green lands yet undiscovered, the whole world a bauble for her spirit's examination. She thought she cried: 'Wait! Wait!' and the shattering vision slowed, conformed, and steadied to one small area. She smelled rain-washed heather, hidecloth and horses. She saw the pavilions of the English, and Davy Gam, emerging from a tent, scratching the sore socket beneath his eye-patch. There was the guard Fletcher, drunk; she smelled his reeking breath, knew he had been reprimanded lately. Then her heart shuddered as she saw the figure approaching him. Owen, golden in the sun, carrying his springald . . . Fletcher made a jest about it, and Owen turned away, cross and laughing; she saw his eyes, bright as amber honey. In ecstasy she hung upon his image but it was already changing, still Owen yet not Owen, his features ageing, his dress altering to the style of a time yet to be, his face fining, becoming sour, secretive . . .

passing quickly. Then Owen again, almost unrecognizable as a giant figure against a backcloth no longer of tents and hillside, but a gaudy chamber. Jewelled, he stood splay-legged, while a woman wept at his feet. Then he too was gone, to be replaced by the merest essence of Owen's features now refined in a woman whose magnificence proclaimed her suzerainty over empires. She stood by the sea, her long white hand extended to welcome in a fleet of carved fighting galleons heavy with gold. She wore a ransom of pearls, looped and cascading over her bodice and starry collar and woven into her hair, which was as red as Hywelis's own.

Now you see his greatness, said a voice in her head, and the shaft of sun folded itself and its visions away.

The bard was frightened. He searched her distended eyes.

'I thought you were dying!' he whispered. Then, incredulously: 'Is it . . . the sight?'

'Yes! And more! and more!'

'Tell the Lord.'

She set Madog on the chair and ran. I am redeemed; the words fled with her down the spiral, shouted triumph as she reached the hall. My lord, my well-loved father, let me serve you now! I can see all your fortune, even your enemies' movements, I can count their number, spy on their strategies, and all without stirring from your side! Father, my lord, here is the sight, the strength, renewed, doubled and redoubled time without number . . .

He was bending stiffly over the dying fire. Cafall had been carried to the dais, and his body was covered with a purple pall. She called the Lord's name, and he straightened, and instantly recognized what had passed within her, and his joy flamed up to mirror hers, as he stretched out his arms.

She took only two paces. What she saw, with the deep magic bearing her towards him, halted her as if by bowshot. For a moment she flung her hands over her eyes, vainly willing the truth to depart.

Smiling he came to meet her and she saw them. About the majesty of Owain Glyn Dŵr shone the corpse-candles, the stars of death, drawing him home at last.

Part Three

THE VICTOR

France, 1415

Our King went forth to Normandy,
With grace and might of chivalry,
There God for him wrought wondrously,
Wherefore England may call and cry –
Deo gratias . . .

Anon., c.a. 1415

The greatest fighting ship in England lay at anchor in Southampton Water. Woven in gold on her chief banner were three images of God and his Mother, flanked by the arms of St Edward, St George, and England. As she moved on the swell, a gilt crown glinted on her topcastle; her capstan bore a sceptre wrought with three fleurs-de-lys. At her deckhead stood a crowned gold leopard. She flew many forked banners and square pennoncelles embroidered with swans and antelopes, and her ensigns and standards were edged with feathers. Glowing about her scarlet waist were painted serpents and birds, and her bulwarks were tessellated and studded brightly with the quartered shields of the knights assembled on her deck. She was *La Trinité Royale*, the royal flagship, otherwise known as the *King's Chamber*.

Aboard, King Henry stood looking beyond the gaudy vessel's bulging belly. His fingers were curved about a dragon's head decorating a stanchion and they slid into its wooden mouth as if daring it to bite him. Slowly his gaze moved over the quay, then out along the narrow seapath where the last of the fleet came under oars to join the stunning flock of which *La Trinité* was the nucleus. Now fifteen hundred ships surrounded her. Their masts seemed to touch the clouds; sea and sky looked full of a massed intricate grandeur of sail at sight of which his heart rose in wondering glory. Even though he had planned for this moment for months, years, he was still moved. He clutched at the painted dragon's mouth, wary of his own emotion.

A storm petrel skimmed past his face, almost brushing the arrow-scar earned at Shrewsbury when he was sixteen. Those who were close to him said it had spoiled his looks, but secretly he cherished it as an honourable token of his first battle against the Welsh. His gaze moved from the incoming fleet, and he saw the flagship's master coming on deck from below: Stephen Thomas, the finest mariner in England. Only the best for this,

God's cause. The master went among the crew, giving orders, feeling a rope-stay, squinting at the broken froth of waves on the horizon. Henry watched silently, aware that others in their turn watched him, their king and leader.

He wore neither cap nor crown, and his brown hair was cropped close as a cannon-ball. Beneath a broad high brow and sharp nose, his cheeks and lips had a naturally florid, open-air look. His bright brown eyes were level, judicial, carrying deep within them only a spark of his unpredictable temper. He was lean, in his doublet of fine English wool, and had been so since an illness in his eighth year when physicians had poured bitter remedies into him and had bled him until he could hardly stand. Lost as to the nature of his malady, they had not asked whether his distress of body was linked with the spirit, or had wondered how deeply he had loved his mother, Mary de Bohun, married to Henry Boling-broke at twelve and dead at twenty-two after bearing six children.

He had recovered, but now he was wary of love, of any emotion. These things were not for kings, and king and heir he was born, tempestuous in the cradle, turning adolescently to vice, licentious as his grandfather John of Gaunt, whose passion for Katherine Swynford had spawned the powerful Beaufort family. He was thinking of Henry Beaufort, Bishop of Winchester, at the very moment when that prelate's bitterest enemy came, treading the salt-slick boards towards him. His younger brother, Humphrey, Duke of Gloucester, made no secret of hate or love or resentment.

Henry turned and stared out over the sea, glory nipping again at him, despite his vigilance. He thought of conquest. France. His undeniable heritage. The great Edward III, through his mother the She-Wolf of France, had laid a claim that he, Henry, would substantiate or die in the full of ambition. His full red lips parted to the sea air. From below, a galley-boy threw a pannikin of rubbish overboard and the scavenging gulls dived and screamed. The King's almost inaudible prayer mingled with the larine cries. O God, who hath sent us to the beginning of this August day, let us fall into no danger. Soon the tide would be full, and Stephen Thomas was watching every wave and cloud, with half an eye out for the sovereign's expected command. The royal ships vibrated gently round the *King's Chamber*, like leashed hounds. *La Trinité de la Tour* (the *Little Trinity*), the *Katherine* (named in honour of one of the sought-after prizes – a Valois princess), and the *Coq de la Toure*. Their bulwarks were lucent with gold leaf, their pavises, which shielded them against bowshot, were blue and green and carved with serpents, lions, falcons, all proof against the Evil Eye. Above, the painted antelopes and the reptiles and birds on the sails glowed, undulating as if restive after movement. A lookout clung to the yardarm like a spider. As far as Henry could see were the ships, and their very beauty seemed to make them omnipotent. Again he controlled his emotions. His brother of Gloucester, Earl of Pembroke, was almost at his side, and Humphrey was excitable enough without further infection. A hand slid over his own, pressing his fingers deeper into the dragon's wooden mouth. He heard a laugh.

'Sire, are you talking to yourself?'

'I was praying,' he said stiffly.

He withdrew his hand from that of the man who knew so much about him, of the old brawling days, the drunken nights when no woman, wife or virgin or slut, was safe from the royal brothers: himself and Humphrey, and John of Bedford, and Thomas of Clarence. The dead days of shame. His eyes darkened with his sincere intensity. *Domine, peccavi*. Lord, judge me not; not now.

Humphrey of Gloucester's sigh was drunk by the sea-wind. He knew his brother Harry better than Harry knew. He was content to follow him, be it in the streets of Coldharbour, rutting like a demented ram, or into the toils of this, God's cause. Humphrey, at twenty-five, was three years younger than his brother, young enough to regret the King's abrupt conversion and the end of play, but old enough to see that by following him there would be richer rewards than those of lifting a harlot's kirtle and drinking the nights into madness. And when this expedition was over he would, as always, go his own way. Harry might be given to God's cause but Humphrey believed firmly in temporal as well as eternal bliss. He had his library, his wardrobe crammed with vanity, his priceless artefacts. Poets acclaimed him as mentor and master. There were wealthy women with fine bodies who would be his, once he returned ennobled by his heroics in France. He leaned beside his brother, looking out to sea. Those momentarily naked eyes were full of deep guile and wilfulness, and even a secret monstrous strain of cruelty showed clear. In contrast, Harry looked innocent. His calm ruddy face often put Humphrey in mind of St Paul – the totally debauched utterly cleansed, and thus far holier than ordinarily good men.

The afternoon sun burned their bare heads. Mariners ran on naked feet about the decks, making ready for the signal to sail. Thomas, Duke of Clarence, was aboard the *Katherine*. The fourth royal brother, John, Duke of Bedford, had remained in London, acting as Lieutenant of England in the King's absence.

Harry turned abruptly and said: 'What are you thinking?'

'About St Paul.'

'Not, I hope, his voyage to Crete . . . that hazardous expedition.'

'He survived,' said Humphrey.

'I can never tell what you're thinking,' said the King, and studied the heavily handsome face.

'I was thinking, truth to tell, of the old days. Do you remember when we robbed those merchants in Chepe? And the woman . . .'

Harry said quietly: 'Those days only existed in another, bad life. We can only go through this new life with pure hearts. Have you made confession?'

'His Grace the Bishop of Winchester himself gave me absolution.' (And it took the best part of a day, Humphrey thought, remembering Beaufort's severe, ambitious face.)

'That's good. I am glad you saw my holy tutor. Would to God you two could love one another.'

'He's proud,' said Humphrey, flushing. 'Lord Bishop he may be, but he's a Beaufort, bastard stock. Of course – ' hastily, seeing his brother's expression – 'Lady Swynford was so beautiful, none could blame my grandsire Gaunt. Would I had known such a lady.' He spoke sincerely, fascinated by the legend of Swynford's body and wiles.

'The Beauforts are our cousins by blood,' said Harry. 'They deserve honour.'

And, thought Humphrey, how dearly they would love their rumps on England's throne! Had not King Richard, when he legitimized them, made the proviso that no Beaufort should ever lay claim to the crown we should have had risings from that family. He stared out to sea again.

'The tide is almost right.'

The last contingent of lords and principal commanders was climbing aboard: Sir Gilbert Umfraville, Sir John Cornwall; the King's cousin, the Duke of York, the Earl of Oxford, the veteran knight Sir John Greyndon, Sir Thomas Erpingham, a dozen others. Behind them came the armourer with a heavy pile of breastplates, helped by another man.

'Who's that, behind Allbright Mailmaker?' Harry squinted through sunlight. 'With the black eye-patch?'

'Davy Gam,' said Humphrey. 'Davydd ap Llewellyn ap Hywel. Glyn Dŵr's kinsman.'

'So it is. Glyn Dŵr died last year, didn't he?'

'So men say.' Humphrey laughed. 'They say he flew in the shape of a golden kestrel into the mountains. That the Devil came for him and was outsmarted. That his body lies incorruptible in his meadhall, with a sorceress crooning over it. They say . . .'

'I only asked if he were dead.' Harry touched the scar on his cheek. 'May he rest easy, wherever he is, the brave old fox!'

He did not wish to think of death. For a moment his eyes relinquished the bright harbour. His nostrils recalled his father's rotting body. He heard the spectral voice: 'Go with God, my son. Conquer. Then build the walls of Jerusalem against the Infidel.' It was then that he had felt the shame of his wasted youth and promise. He had eaten his father's sins that day; had felt buried under the weight of future atonement.

Another silent wave of prayer swept him. God, I am thy servant, not my father's. All that I accomplish shall be to thy glory. A cynical inner voice cut through: And to yours, Harry? When you bring France to England, when you harvest the rewards? You, with your crown in pawn for this foray? This is bad luck, to forecast victory. God! I have upheld thy

Church, I have hounded the Lollards. Even my loved old friend, Sir John Oldcastle, I imprisoned for heresy and sentenced to the burning death. Some hated me for it; they called me the Priests' Prince. They did not know my gladness in secret when Oldcastle escaped the Tower and fled to Wales. They did not know my heart when Badby the Evesham tailor was burned in chains. *They do not know how I am torn.*

He had stood so close to the blazing tun that the heat had scorched his own face, pleading with Badby to recant. The tailor's feet and ankles were already burned. 'Badby,' he had cried: 'I will pardon you!' At this the executioners had loosened the victim's chains and dragged him from the fire where he lay at Harry's feet.

'Say after me – the Bread is Christ's Body! Christ is incarnate in my confessor!'

And Badby, still conscious despite his roasted flesh, said clearly: 'The bread is bread. The priest is only a man.'

'I will give you threepence a day for life,' said Harry wildly, 'if you recant!'

Badby had managed a tortured smile.

'I cannot deny Wyclif's logic,' he whispered. 'In God's Name, how could Christ have eaten His own flesh at the Last Supper?'

In conscience it could not be let to pass. The flames had been doused, so there was the grotesquely painful business of kindling fresh faggots, of retrieving the hot chains to bind poor Badby anew. Grimly Harry had watched to the end, and later, sick at heart, had paid his own chaplains to sing Badby to redemption.

This I did for you, O God, and will do again to my best and dearest, should they offend thy Church. So let me be favoured with a safe passage, a holy victory, peace. Let me build the walls of Jerusalem and heal the Schism. One Pope at Avignon and one at Rome is heresy in itself. There must be only one Vicar of Christ after I have conquered France.

Humphrey does not understand the cause. John of Bedford is content to rule in London in my stead. Thomas of Clarence is out primarily for spoil. He invaded Maine, found Burgundy and Armagnac alike ready to *parler*, yet stripped the chapel

142

of Bruges and took the golden Cross containing the Nail . .
Sacrilege.

Harry, said the inner voice wearily. That was warrior's
bounty! Are you so saintly and greedless? He almost said aloud:
I am the weakest and most sinful of all. But I will brook no
sacrilege. And I can atone. The four-and-twenty bedesmen
singing continually at Windsor will protect my soul, doubly
soiled. Through my own excesses and through my father's
usurpation and his murder of Richard. Richard lies in magnificence at Westminster, and weighs on me like iron. Only, God,
give me victory, to be shared by dear friends.

A stab at his heart in the radiant afternoon among the lovely
painted ships. Dear friends are not here to share my moment.
Already I am betrayed.

In his Council chamber at Porchester, not long before this
embarkation, had knelt before him Edmund Mortimer, Earl
of March, whom King Richard had named as heir to the throne.
He was a weak cowardly man with neither wish nor chance to
claim his inheritance. His fear of Henry had proved less than
his fear of conspiracy discovered. He had come to reveal
an assassination plot and uprising. Stuttering with fright, he
had implicated Richard of Conisburgh of the House of York,
Earl of Cambridge, and Thomas Grey, and Henry, Lord
Scrope, three prominent members of the Council.

'Even the Lollards are involved,' March had said in a
glassy whisper. 'And the false mummet in Scotland, who so
resembles King Richard . . . they used me, Sire. They threatened
me . . .' He had gibbered, crawling on the floor.

He could not answer. His heart had pounded as if he had
been running in Windsor forest, outstripping a deer as he had
often done, then bringing it down bare-handed. And so he had
been running, through a forest of illusion and deceit, for
months, years. Scrope. Henry Scrope. How many nights had
he fallen asleep in the great bed at Coldharbour, in the warmth
of Scrope's arms?

March had gabbled on.

'The false mummet is Maudelyn, a chaplain. The rebels
call themselves King Richard's Nurslings, and openly flaunt
the White Hart.'

'Is Scrope the ringleader?' He was staring at some horses and saints on a wall-hanging. They were one vast shine of grief.

'He initiated everything. He's sworn to have you dead.'

He loved me. He remembered standing beside his mother's bier. She loved me, and left me. I was lonely; until Henry Scrope came to court, and held me close of nights, warm and laughing and loving. Many the time he comforted me, swam with me along the evil current of my dreams until their power was done and I slept in tranquillity. He could have killed me then. Better if he had.

'If you are lying, I'll hang you and burn your heart,' he had said quietly to the Earl of March.

'Would I lie?' March wept. 'Act now, for they are already well arrayed.'

He bade March rise, pardoned him, and summoned an armed party. The rebels were hunted down, though Maudelyn continued to hide behind the Scottish border. A bitter irony made Harry appoint March one of the principal peers to preside at the rebels' trial. Richard of Conisburgh and Grey were beheaded, but Scrope was hanged and his bowels burned before his eyes. This, too, Harry had watched to the end. Afterwards he had kept to his chamber alone for three days, emerging gaunt and distant and changed.

'The tide is right, Master Thomas is waiting.'

The small voice now gave him ghostly comfort. You were right, Harry. Perish your enemies; you acted like a king. And yet . . . would to God that Scrope stood beside me now, smiling, loving the look of the gilded vessels, his arm about my neck. Even Elmham, my chaplain, seems now to be part of the past, admiring me not for my piety but for my roguish lusts . . . I have only my brothers. My friends are gone.

He said, without thinking: 'Was it all lies? Henry Scrope hated the Lollards. He was most devout.' And Humphrey, overhearing, said uneasily: 'Harry, don't . . . *Carpe diem*.'

Yes. To live for the day . . . and then he saw, approaching, a young ascetic face, a good face, wise, attached to a long form in episcopal robes, and knew that there were friends left after all.

'His Grace my Lord Richard Courtenay, Bishop of Norwich,' announced an attendant clerk. The last of the ships arrived, falling to astern of the *King's Chamber* and striking her flag in honour of the sovereign.

'Your Grace is truly welcome aboard,' said Henry. The Bishop's pale young face smiled.

'Sire, I've brought the copies of your will.' Courtenay was one of the executors. Harry had forgotten none, not even his old nursemaid, Joan Waring, frail and senile. The Bishop's benign eyes studied and comforted him.

'You have fair omens, Sire,' he said. He pointed upwards. A flock of swans was circling the swaying masts. Moving closer, he said softly: 'It will be a good enterprise, Harry my son.' And as if he read his recent doubts: 'See. All your friends are here.'

He looked then, at a contingent of the men, not all of them familiar to him, but all sharing his cause and intent, from John Greyndon, knight, to Allbright Mailmaker. John Corbyn, Sergeant of the King's Tents and Pavilions. Thomas Morestede and William Bradwardyn, surgeons. John Waterton, esquire, Master of the King's Horse, and Robert Waterton, King's valet. Nicol Harewode, Clerk of the Stable, William Heryot, page and messenger of the King's Chamber. John Feriby, Clerk of the Wardrobe. Master Esmon Lacy, Dean of the King's Chapel. John Burnell and John Mildenhale, chaplains. Friars Alain Hert and John Brotherton; and the minstrels: John Cliff, Thomas Norys Tromper, Richard Pyper, Snaith Fidler 'and William Halliday. Many, many more. Davydd Gam's one bright eye caught his own in fearless, half-challenging amusement. The Welsh had come to him, and he was glad. Behind Gam he noticed an outstandingly handsome youth. Bright hair, strong shoulders, very straight back. Useful in a bowman.

Again he surveyed the fleet, knew of the hundreds of war horses and ponies tethered uneasily below, and to the last detail, the vast armaments carried: three iron guns twelve feet in length: the *London*, the *Messenger*, and, in tribute to the yet unseen princess, the *King's Daughter*, each capable of hurling five hundred pounds of shot. For two years, smiths at Bristol had been at work on these siege guns. There were also mangonels, arblasts and battering-rams, the most sophisticated devices of war that money could buy.

According to the Assize of Arms, each knight was allocated his full armour, helm, sword, knife and horse, and contracted to provide a force and muster it before the Exchequer, according to his wealth and ingenuity. Yet it was the bowmen who were beyond price, with their weapons of yew, hazel, ash or elm; the longbow and shortbow and crossbow, barbed, bodkin-tipped or forked, each discharge capable of covering three hundred yards and weakening the most heavily armoured cavalryman. Some arrows could pierce a four-inch wooden door.

There were pages, grooms, guides, mounted hobelars who could be used as scurriers and spies; smiths, armourers, painters and tentmakers, fletchers, carpenters, bowyers and masons. Wheelwrights, cordwainers, saddlers, quartermasters and farriers. Trumpeters, surgeons, chaplains. Hundreds of them above and below decks on the coloured ships. Officials of wardrobe and buttery, pantry, napery and spicery. Royal heralds: Leicester, Guienne, and Ireland King at Arms. Antelope Pursuivant and Chester Herald. Four master gunners, all experienced Dutchmen. These men and these armaments, together with the personal reputation he took aboard, blew away the King's doubt. This was his army, his friends. The swan flew rings above the craft, and Bishop Courtenay's eyes blessed him in silence. My reign began in snow, he thought, the worst blizzard for many years. It comes to the full in gold . . . he swayed a little on his feet, and Courtenay steadied him.

'Have you eaten lately?'

'Yes, I've eaten.'

'It is possible,' said the Bishop seriously, 'to mortify the flesh when there is no cause.'

Humphrey of Gloucester laughed.

'Your Grace, sometimes the King forgets to eat.'

This was not strictly true, but in the light of his new asceticism he had discovered that he could go sometimes for days without food or wine and often without sleep. He had thrown himself into the past months of preparation with a fanatical energy; few could match his pace.

'We must take wine before we sail,' Henry said to the Bishop. Humphrey called over his shoulder at the massed henchmen: 'Wine here!' It was ready in its flagon, on a silver salver with goblets, but there were so many waiting to do the King's will that their very number resulted in confusion and for an instant no one moved.

'Will none serve the King?' demanded Gloucester, and laughed, somewhat irritably.

Davy Gam was standing near to the salver. He whispered in Owen's ear: 'Chance, boy! Take it! It'll never come again!' and instantly Owen took the heavy silver into his hands, poured without fault three goblets of rich redness and bore steadily forward tray and flagons and wine without a drop spilled, and knelt at the King's feet. Harry looked down to see the sun ripen on the bent head. Somehow the clean light look of Owen cheered him even more than the sight of the ships or the swans.

'To victory,' he said.

Courtenay said, 'Amen,' and they drank.

For the first time in months Owen thought of Hywelis, and his future on her moonlit dreaming lips. Greatness, some day . . . vague. He would not wear out his welcome in this precious moment. Quietly he rose and backed away. Greatness? . . . the rest of her words had been forgotten. What he remembered best was his experience of her body, and even that was dimming, overlaid by similar escapades during the past months in England and dwarfed by the intoxication of the real adventure to come. He hoped no harm had befallen her, he wished her well, and presently forgot her.

'I see your stepmother comes to bid you *bon voyage*,' said the Bishop to Henry.

On the quay they could see the pinched white face of Queen Joanna of Navarre. She sat very still on a black horse; she was surrounded by priests come to pray for the fleet. Harry was surprised. There was no love lost between them and since his father's death she had been even more distant. She had always disapproved of him. He thought: to her, as well as to God, I will prove how I can amend. I will mantle England in glory . . .

'We will sail,' he said. Humphrey of Gloucester signalled

to the master. A bright thrill of clarions sounded. The flagship's mainsail was hoisted to half-mast, its ascent noted aboard each of the fifteen hundred ships, to the harbour mouth where the Earl of Dorset, as Admiral, prepared to lead out the convoy. The wind was right. The sails began to fill, and quickly the gap between the leading craft and her followers lengthened. A cheer arose from the people on the quay, drowning the chant of prayer from Queen Joanna's priests.

Suddenly aboard one of the ships, a Dutch vessel procured at great cost, an unguarded brazier tipped with the lurch of the deck. Fire poured on to the wooden boards. With incredible speed, pitch and paint and timber ignited. A sheet of flame whipped up the sails and, fanned by the wind, devoured tarry ropes, canvas and wood in seconds. Blazing, the topmast crashed across the deck of the vessel alongside. Men were running with their clothes on fire, jumping overboard; from below decks came the screams of terrified horses. The men aboard the *King's Chamber* watched in horror. Overhead the swans, distressed by the pitchy smoke, wheeled and flew out to sea.

Dry-tongued, Henry whispered: 'Jesu, sweet Jesu. It will spread.'

The Bishop's voice calmed him. 'No, my son. Look, they have it mastered already.'

Brave men stayed on the burning ships, throwing smouldering timbers overboard, dousing the blaze with a constant stream of water passed in buckets from hand to hand. Harry watched, silent, his eyes large with anxiety. In the flame he saw Badby's tormented face. The little voice within him said, Harry, you have roasted a man for his beliefs. And his mind answered unequivocally: Yes. And men could gladly burn me for my belief that this expedition will succeed. This knowledge is my rock. Badby, you were my sacrifice to God, whose cause this is.

The fire was quenched, almost as swiftly as it had begun. The swans returned, flying above the fleet as it set forth, on a bright wind, to France.

*

148

Owen stared at the town of Harfleur and thought it lovely and impregnable as a comely nun, with its two and a half miles of crenellated wall reflected in a deep moat. There were twenty-six towers along the wall, embellished with figures painted blue and gold; lions, dragons, snails, birds. Behind these, more towers crowned with tiny high turrets and golden spires curved like a nun's wimple falling softly into her neck. Harfleur specialized in weaving, dyeing and ship-building, and despite her fairy-tale appearance, was heavily fortified.

The fleet had anchored in the mouth of the Seine estuary off the *Chef de Caux*. 'Kidcocks', the army called it. Harfleur was the King's choice for the invasion. The French expected him to strike at Boulogne. Flemish troops kept guard from Nieuport to Sluys. And although Bordeaux was an English possession, it would have been folly to strike at the Seine valley or south-western France without a firm foothold in Normandy itself. From Harfleur he planned to force deep into the country's heart, to Paris herself. He had that day celebrated the Feast of the Assumption. The pavilions had been set up, latched with gleaming embroideries, and the priests had prayed for all the troops to hear; for England's victory, and for the prosperity of all Henry's subjects, English and French, for to him France and all within her territory were already his.

Sitting on the ground, Owen watched as the King left his tent to confer with emissaries from his brother the Duke of Clarence and the Earl of Suffolk. Clarence's detachment lay among farmlands north-east of Harfleur, and Suffolk's guarded the inland slopes. The siege guns and horses had been landed and the men had waited all day for their orders. They were already bored; some were sidling from camp towards the farms and vineyards, like truant children. Owen had no desire to follow them. He knew their intent: women, plunder, wine, and that they risked severe reprisal. The King had made himself plain regarding capital offences; killing or raping women, endangering the life of a woman with child, entering a church to plunder any hallowed vessel, ornament or book; any man who touched the Sacrament would be drawn and hanged. Yet still they crept away, towards the farmhouses and church spires. Little groups full of bravado on whom hot sun beat down, making them sweaty and lustful and crueller than at home.

A rank stench rose from the marsh upon which Harfleur was built. It mingled with the reek from the latrine pits and fly-infested midden where the animals were tethered. Bloated insects attacked Owen where he sat. His nerves were slightly overstrung from impatience. He had survived the three-day crossing and was ready for the fight. So far all he had killed (he slapped one blood-gorged insect) were these cursed stinging creatures. Already he had made himself unpopular with the men; a toady. The little scene aboard the *Trinité Royale* had not passed unnoticed. He had looked to Davy Gam, wondering how to explain to the others, but Gam had gone as an officer to help oversee Suffolk's detachment. So Owen sat waiting alone. He was thankful he would not have to put on full armour. The heat was terrible. His shirt clung to him and the foul smell of marsh gas worsened. He scratched and swore and heard a soft laugh behind him.

'Save your strength, friend, and let them bite. The waiting is only beginning.'

Legs came into view, then a black jerkin of boiled leather, a round face and sentimental dark eyes. The man sat down beside him, laying aside the longbow he carried and removing the arrows fletched with goosequills from his belt.

'I see you have a quiver for your darts,' he said without envy. 'One of the privileged.'

'It was issued with my bow.' The beloved springald had been superseded by order of the quartermaster. He did not like the tall bow half as well.

'I'm John Page,' said the man. 'Failed poet, amateur soldier.'

'Let a Welsh poet greet an English one,' said Owen.

'You make rhymes?'

'I try. But I sing them better.'

John Page smiled. His dark eyes glistened; they had the look of tears always near the brim.

'What's a poet doing as a soldier?' said Owen.

'I was impressed,' Page answered.

'I volunteered.'

'One of the few. Half these ships and more than half the men were pressed into this enterprise.'

Owen said: 'The men seem content enough.'

'There was a Frenchman, Froissart, not long dead. He said: Prowess is a lure few can resist. It is the mother and light of noble men. As the timber cannot have life without flame, so the man cannot come to honour or the world's glory without prowess. That's what they hope for, and why they seem content.'

'I know all about prowess,' said Owen softly. 'I am godson to Glyn Dŵr.' When Page confessed ignorance of the Lord, it was as if he had never heard of Ysbaddaden the giant. Owen was moved to murmur a very few words of 'Culhwch and Olwen', looking loftily ahead, as if communing with spirits.

'French I speak,' said Page. 'Little Welsh, though. What's it about?' and Owen told him.

'You should sing it to the King,' said Page. 'He'd enjoy the young hero and the battles and the boar-hunt. The beautiful maiden's another matter.' He laughed and lay back on the ground, brushing an ant from his face. 'It's no maiden he seeks, but a ravaged hag.' He sat up again. 'You don't follow? France is the woman he wants – and she's no longer lovely, with a madman on her shoulder and a child at her head and the dogs of Burgundy and Armagnac growling over her entrails. The Princess, Katherine, is her poor heart, which he must snatch for supremacy.'

'*She's* beautiful, at least?' said Owen, trying to salvage some romance.

John Page rubbed his round chin. 'I only spoke to one who ever saw her. She's been cloistered for years. But she visited Calais – my lord of Warwick said she was quiet and thin but not uncomely. She'll be about fourteen. But doubtless legend will give her the face of an angel. Legend's a hardy plant. You heard about the tennis balls . . .'

'Why, yes! The Dauphin offered them in insult for the King to play with – Harry said that he'd play a game of ball in France to make men weep.'

'All lies.' Page smiled. 'Had that been true, the King would

151

have flung himself on France a year ago, money or no money for troops and arms! But it's a good story, isn't it?' Then he said, musing: 'So you volunteered. I wager whoever recruited you never mentioned that the King might lose his holy war. That we might all end up in a ditch, outmatched five to one. The French are partial to throat-cutting,' he said merrily.

'It's a skill I'm willing to learn.'

'Just look at their defences!' said Page wonderingly, pointing. Harfleur's wall was pierced by the Rouen gate at the south-east, the Leure gate at the south-west and the Montivilliers gate in the north-east. Each was protected by portcullis and drawbridge and flanking towers, reflected in the moat. Every approach was barred by timbers and earthworks, and reinforced by freshly dug ditches deep in water. There was a barbican of ironbound tree-trunks nearly as high as the wall and broken by slits for the discharge of shot and burning oil. The garrison tower was prominently visible. Above it a scarlet standard, the oriflamme of France, hung in the humid air.

'They've a good commander, too. The Sire d'Estouteville. He sent back quite a sharp message when asked to surrender as an English subject. Now the Sire de Gaucourt's taken over, with at least three hundred more troops. See that moat! It will be the devil of a job to mine under the walls.'

'But we have good artillery,' said Owen. Little distant figures, carpenters and labourers, were building the gun emplacements. Wooden palisades had been erected to protect them as they worked. Already swarms of arrows swished and thudded home from behind the moated barbican. Men were digging the trenches along which additional guns were to be brought as near the town wall as possible. As Owen watched, a man unwarily straightening up in the trench was killed by a single shot. John Page was writing; he had a quill and a tiny inkhorn which he carried in his pouch. The sun had gone in but the humidity was worse. A drop of warm rain splashed down. One of the illicit raiding parties was returning, weaving wetly along the path through the marsh, driving a few calves and pigs, rolling a cask of wine and carrying baskets of apples and grapes. The leader was so drunk that he fell twice, his face in the swamp. He was dragging a woman along. Owen recognized him. It was John Fletcher, the sentry whom Hywelis had frightened over a year ago.

The woman was crying, swearing in French. She sank her teeth in Fletcher's wrist and he gave her a smack in the face that made her reel.

'Such chivalry!' said John Page.

'Hold your tongue, poet,' Fletcher said, staggering up to them. He began laughing uncontrollably. Hauling the woman, he lurched over to the winecask and wrenched out its bung. He flung himself on the ground, opening his jaws to the red stream, drinking until pushed away by others eager to take their turn. Then he seized a handful of little apples and green grapes, and crushed them into his face. He looked at Owen.

'You should have been with us, Welshman,' he said, belching. 'We had sport.'

'What do you intend for her, or need I ask?' said John Page, indicating the woman.

'I've brought her to be my con-concubine. All great men have 'em.' He belched again. 'Where's that shellfish?'

Like a warm tainted hand the foul air pressed down. Sweat streamed down Owen's back. He watched the men drag up a basket from which a powerful odour arose. Fletcher split open a handful of mussels, corroded with brine, and sucked at the little tongues within. He had gobbled a score before Page asked: 'Were those gathered in the marsh?'

'Ay, from the salt creeks.' Excitedly: 'There's thousands of 'em! We can live like lords!'

'They'll make you sick,' said Page.

Glassy-eyed from wine and the exertions of the raid, the others were sitting down, flapping at flies and munching the cockles and mussels. Fletcher had released the woman. She stood angrily, nervously watching him while he chewed on, stopping only for great draughts of the thin new wine. Presently these excesses had their effect; his head drooped and he stretched more languidly on the ground, his eyes closing.

'Well, it's your belly,' said Page, turning to look away towards the gun emplacements. One of Fletcher's friends was suddenly overcome, and leaned to vomit. The woman took a step towards Owen.

'Please,' she said. 'Please.'

He caught her hand and began to walk steadily with her to the edge of the marsh. She spoke to him in French and he answered her. She was small, gap-toothed, her hair wildly awry. She abused Fletcher in ornamental terms. He had fired her cottage, slain her cow and felled her grandfather.

'Devils!' she said vehemently. 'Already he raped my sister, then said she was too old and captured me instead. English devils!'

Owen pushed her towards the marsh path. Fletcher was snoring now and the others were throwing dice.

'Run, quickly.' But she pressed against his side, her expression changing.

'I will not stay for him.' She stroked his sweat-damp sleeve. 'He's a pig. But for you, then I would not mind.'

'Go,' he said. She stank of the marsh. And she was offended.

'Fool! Baby! Pigs and babies!' And spat.

He wiped his neck. He said: 'The King has issued orders about camp-followers. Any who come within three miles of camp are to have their left arm broken . . .'

'Swine!' she shrieked, and reiterated that the English were Satan's spawn and should beware the might of France, then ran sobbing across the marsh. Owen walked thoughtfully back to join John Page. Fletcher and his company lay in an untidy huddle, sure enough like pigs in a sty.

At that moment there was a wild trumpet-bray from the vicinity of the officers' tents. Almost immediately the first of the assembled guns spoke. There was a thunderbolt crash as a ball the size of a millstone hurtled to strike the barbican of Harfleur. The siege had begun.

Now he stood behind a curtain of wattle and iron, perforated with squints through which arrows could be discharged at the defenders of the beleaguered town. The French, with an elegant imprudence, were making little sallies out over the bridge from the barbican to loose a hail of shot and retreat, leaving English dead and, as often, falling slain themselves. The archers' task was to repel these assaults while the great guns did their work. Twenty men were needed to load and prime the *King's Daughter*, the *Messenger* and the *London* – ten to lift the ammunition alone, for the stones were five feet in diameter. Bending, running, heaving, men fainted in the now impossible heat, and were swiftly replaced. The guns had been brought near the walls of the town. Screens to protect the gunners were hinged and staked into the ground, lifted then lowered again as soon as the charge had been fired.

Owen drew the fletch back to his ear and loosed an arrow. He saw one of the Harfleur archers in the act of pulling a shortbow to his chest drop his weapon and, falling, clap a hand to his throat where Owen's barb now protruded. I killed him, he thought. How easy it is. A crossbow quarrel thudded through the planking on his left, impaling his neighbour to the screen like a writhing insect tortured by a child. The next moment John Page had come to replace him, inserting an arrow through the squint. His face was dirty with sweat; he smiled grimly.

'You've done a long stint,' he called.

'Sixteen hours today. Ten yesterday,' said Owen.

The siege guns seemed to have been roaring for ever. His back was on fire from the sun and the tension. His bow-arm felt as if it would never again be straight. His clothes were sodden and filthy, and the stinking marsh seemed to have worked down into his lungs. If he thought about it, it made him retch.

'How's your belly?' asked Page.

'Still calm and whole. *Diolch i Dduw.*'

Page aimed at a flicker of activity from the barbican. The French were coming out again on another lunatic foray that could sometimes prove spectacularly successful. Last time they had captured two apprentice gunners and a knight, dragging them back behind the town walls.

'Don't drink the wine,' said Page, like a litany. 'The shell-fish are poisonous. Leave the green fruit alone. I've just been round to the surgeons' tents. It's a filthy way to die. Worse than *that*, almost . . .'

A black veil of flies was settling on the corpse of the recently impaled archer.

'You have marshes in Wales, don't you?'

'Yes. But they're clean!'

The fretful polluted sun fringed Owen's tawny head and face with gold. The barrier shook as a volley of arrows landed just above his head. He and Page and the hundred or so other archers were loosing shot after shot as the French ran out, their assault covered from the walls by a profusion of gun-stones and arrows. They carried burning brands and small kegs of gunpowder which they lobbed at the protective screens and into the compound housing the provision wagons. There was a stutter of explosions; black smoke drifted along the line. Wagons and tents erupted; men running to douse the fires became targets for the French archers. The attackers ran back behind the barbican, leaping over bodies. Owen shot at the last fleeing figure but smoke from part of the blazing palisade spoiled his aim. The *King's Daughter* spoke shatteringly, her force throwing two of the gunners backwards into the trench. The vast ball whistled high over the defences of Harfleur and buried itself with a cataclysmic roar in the structure of the south-west gate. It collapsed, bringing down with it two of the golden towers with the painted swans and snails. A score of French were killed by their fall. Through the gap the town could be seen: more towers, dwellings, people running. A holy nun no longer, thought Owen. More like an antheap breached by a giant's foot. All down the line came weary cheering.

'What machines!' he said to Page in awe.

'Ay. But the *Messenger* at the other gate is out of commission. They're having to use the arblasts and mangonels. But it was a fair shot, I grant you.'

Owen wedged himself against the screen and felt for a fresh arrow. His neck muscles screamed with stress. Sweat dripped from his face. A bluebottle ventured on to his eyelid to drink, and he shivered. The stench of urine and ordure rose from the line where archers had relieved themselves during the long hours at the palisade. He tried to spit, and failed.

'Your flask's empty,' said Page, and passed a little leather bottle.

'Drink only sparingly. I don't even trust the water. But that

156

wine is death, like the fish and the fruit. I've never seen such sickness. Now, St Barbara, improve my aim!'

Evening was descending. The sky over the swamp was green and in the west like watery blood. Insects whined about the men's heads in a gluttonous cloud. A boy came to stand behind the line with a cask of tow-wrapped arrows, dipping them in pitch and fire and passing them to the archers, who discharged them, flaming, through the slit. Smoke scorched eyes, seared throats and stomachs. Harfleur had lighted missiles too; the dimming sky was crossed by parabolas of fire. In the flame-lit dusk the French were already shoring up the broken gate efficiently with bricks and mortar and sandbags. On top of the walls men lay with vats of sulphur and lime and hot fat. The river Lézarde which flowed through the town between the Leure and Montivilliers gates and was swelled by the tidal estuary had been fortified with chains and tree-trunks and iron stakes; the English fleet lay in constant danger, like the messengers sent by small craft to make contact with the captains beyond the marsh and the valley which had been flooded earlier by the French. While in camp the sickness grew; the awful bowel-rot that could bring death in a matter of hours. The only cheering rumour was that Harfleur was also plagued by this.

All night the great guns went on, as on every night, spewing out fiery millstones. The *Messenger* was repaired, and the *London* broke down. The heat changed to a clammy, noxious chill. Down the line men squatted groaning and passed blood. Complete exhaustion, filled with unreality, suddenly caught at Owen. He stared drunkenly at the whirling, arching fires. The palisade shook as flaming steel bit into it. A boy in charge of the pitch barrels rushed to fight the fire and was impaled as he worked. Owen's hand fumbled for a fresh arrow. His quiver was empty. He turned and spoke, insane with fatigue, to a burning bush nearby, then plunged face down through the smoke to the reeking earth, awakening to find himself in Hell.

All round where he lay were the sounds of men in torment, the whispering cries of the dying, the mumble of priests mingling with the occasional sharp rattle of death. The foetid air was like a heavy stone on his chest. On the torch-

157

lit tent walls the shadows of the doctors moving ceaselessly about their business were huge, grotesquely surging monsters. Beneath his hands the straw was slimed with blood; with trembling fingers he explored his own body, relieved to find it whole. But someone had lately died miserably here, leaving the legacy of his pain, a soaking corruption. The weary surgeons grumbled and cursed as they worked. Owen raised his spinning head and watched as they cut out arrow-heads and tried to succour a man with half his shoulder blown away by cannon-shot. They plugged gashes with powdered herbs and bound them with whatever linen was available. Yet such casualties were in the minority; death's real dominion bore a breath so foul it was almost unbearable. The wounded died cleanly compared with the hundreds taken by the dysentery; their end was horror and shame, their vitals dissolved in blood and filth.

Big John Fletcher was carried in, so pale as to be almost unrecognizable. He should by rights have died days ago; even now his breath stank of the unclean shellfish and the bad wine. But so far his strength had saved him, and its decline was dramatic. He was dying even as his friends lugged him into the sight of the overworked doctors. Crying for a priest, he lay in his own ordure, beginning to babble his confession almost before the chaplain had found a clean spot in which to kneel. Fletcher's rolling eyes found Owen; he paused in his catalogue of sins to cry despairingly: 'Your witchwoman warned me . . . she cursed me . . . Oh, Mary, mercy! I don't want to die!'

Owen thought: neither do I. Hywelis! And the answer came clear, a tiny forgotten voice: *you will be safe*, even while Fletcher died and Owen struggled to his knees, swaying. Hands gripped and drew him up, and, staring blearily into the one bright eye of Davy Gam, he heard his native tongue.

'*Diawl!* Boy, they said you were in here. Is it the belly-rot?'

Owen said stupidly: 'I don't know . . . would I be able to tell?' and Gam began to laugh. Mixed with the groans in the tent, it sounded like demons' laughter.

'*Duw!* Owen, you'd know, you'd know! Wounded then? No, I see you're not. What fool put you in here among the contagion? You're filthy, *bach*. Come to my pavilion.'

He supported Owen outside. Fainted, did you? no shame in that. Men were fainting every minute. There was not enough food, and too few to defend the gunners. It was quiet outside now, and the pre-dawn air smelled almost sweet after the surgeon's tent. Frogs sang from the marsh, and the birds were awakening. They walked up a little boggy rise towards the encampment. The officers' tents with their scalloped canopies looked like some weird mushroom growth coloured pale from the candlelight within. Near the glow Gam stopped and smiled at Owen's smoke-blackened face. Like a Moor you are, kinsman, a heathen.

'You're sure you've no flux, pain?'

'Only deathly tired.' Owen sighed deeply.

'We're both lucky. This pestilence spares none. The Duke of Clarence has taken to his bed. Morestede, the King's surgeon, is with him; it's grave.'

The King's brother ill. It was as if gods and saints were toppling. Unthinkable, to associate these with pain and stench and humiliation.

'Likewise,' said Davy, watching him, 'the Earls of March and Arundel. Did you think them immune, by birthright? Flesh, man! Flesh!'

The dawn was chill with the green death-smell from the marsh. Owen half-stumbled over a figure in the lee of a tent, a soldier collapsed in exhaustion or in the longest sleep of all.

'This is not how I dreamed of our enterprise,' he said with a tight throat.

'Nor any of us. If we could only get inland where the ground is pure. The King swore he would have Harfleur in eight days. Their resistance is magnificent. They are so clever. Nightly their spies slip through, God knows how . . . they've even reached the Dauphin at Vernon to apprise him of how matters go.'

'But their supplies must soon end,' said Owen. 'They can't last for ever.'

Watching the ground for further hazards he did not see that Gam had stopped and was down on one knee. Only when a slight shadow, flanked by two heavier guarding figures fell across him was he aware, and hurriedly knelt. Those feet he had studied aboard *La Trinité Royale*, when he had served the wine. Now warily he looked up. The King's face, its ruddiness tempered by dawnlight, looked drawn, the skin tight over the cheeks and the sharp nose. But the eyes were unwearied, the voice calm.

'How goes it, then?' he asked Davydd Gam.

'Sire, the same. I have just come from my lord of Suffolk's camp. His illness worsens. And the tower we breached yesterday has been shored up. Is your Grace in health?'

'Perfectly.' But Owen, lowering his eyes again, saw the tiniest betrayal of fatigue or uncertainty. The King's calf-muscles were swollen taut with fitness, an athlete's legs, yet they shuddered almost imperceptibly.

'We will smoke out these rats,' the King was saying. 'We'll have them on their knees, obeisant, with ropes round their gizzards just as the great Edward the Third did when he took Calais . . .'

Faintly from the pavilion where the Duke of Clarence lay sick filtered a plangent thread of tune. Like a hound scenting sport, the King's head turned.

'The Irish minstrel,' he said absently. 'He plays well.'

Words burst incontinently from Owen.

He said, excited, despite his tiredness: 'No, Sire. It's a Welsh harp. Good sycamore, strung more sturdily than the Irish, better proportioned. I play one at home.'

He bit his lip; once more he had broken protocol. Yet his glance flicked up once more to the King's face. It was unoffended.

'I, too,' said Henry's rather flat voice. 'I learned, between skirmishes, in Wales. I found it somewhat difficult. But how sweet a sound!' Then he gazed in belated recognition at Owen. 'My cup-bearer aboard ship! A minstrel too? As David soothed Saul, you shall play for me, once Harfleur is taken.'

'Jesu grant this soon,' said Gam.

Henry continued to survey Owen. He saw the crusted blood on his clothes.

'You're wounded. And hungry too, no doubt. The new victuals have come from Bordeaux. I would not have kept him

160

kneeling here,' he said to Gam, and Owen, ashamed of his filthy appearance, cried: 'No, Sire! I lay where a man had died . . .'

'Too many die,' said Henry shortly. He swung round as two men with lanterns hastened up behind him. A greybearded chaplain and a surgeon, his apron bloody black.

'Sire,' said the doctor. 'I must report the sickness. It's worse. Beyond control. Two thousand deathly ill, and fifteen hundred dead. It spreads faster than the black plague from which Christ preserve us.'

'Great God!' said Henry, almost to himself. 'Was it for this I pawned my lands, broke up my stepmother's jewels?'

'Sire,' said the chaplain. 'I must beg you come swiftly. His Grace the Bishop of Norwich asks for you. He is, I fear, *in extremis.*'

Music, ambition, regret, all fled Harry's mind. His dismay was apparent; his face grew old and stark.

'Courtenay sick? But he . . . he was so careful. He never touched the wine. My own butlers prepared his table . . .'

The good new bread and beef and salt, the fresh fish, brought from Bordeaux by wagons axle-deep in marsh, horses lashed over roads dirty with ambush. Yet Courtenay sick! Unbearable. Did God's cause demand other sacrifices, as dear as this? He drew sour air into his chest, and said:

'Why was I not earlier informed?'

'It took the Lord Bishop in a matter of hours.'

'But he was careful!' he repeated in disbelief. Abstemious, determined . . . my friend and ghostly comforter . . . *Discipline.* Be apart from emotion. Even this most terrible news must not undermine him. He loved the Bishop far better than his own brothers. And Courtenay's sickness served to epitomize the malady afflicting this enterprise. The abortive siege. The assured impertinence of Harfleur's garrison commander, the Sire d'Estouteville. A nightmare disillusion. Build the walls of Jerusalem, indeed! He could not even force the wicket gate of France! He thought: I shall never be able to return home if I fail. I shall go East, with the handful of sick men left to me, wandering the world till eternity, a lion no longer but a wounded jackal. Owen's face came into focus. These young men, so keen, as I was at Shrewsbury. Wasted now, as I was not. Are my fighting hopes so short lived? Am I visited with the sins of my father? Am I judged?

Yet he said calmly: 'Go, eat and rest before the day begins. There will be food and drink for you and all the wounded and weary. Be undismayed.'

The surgeon said urgently: 'Your Grace, the Bishop . . .' and Henry turned saying softly, yes, I come, walking away past the pavilions whose glow was dimmed against the growing dawn.

Owen got up. How strange he is, almost unconcerned, save for that trembling, that determination. And he acknowledged me, a nothing.

'He's confident,' he said to Davy Gam. 'And kind.'

Gam answered with derision. 'He conceals himself. He always does. He's full of doubts, but he'd tear out his heart rather than admit them. Kind . . . maybe, yes.' His voice softened. 'He noted your face, your words. He'll not forget you. He forgets nothing, no one.'

'I felt . . . he really cared for us.'

Gam rubbed the blindness beneath his eye-patch.

'He does, boy. And maybe in you he saw himself. Though he's no longer a youth. Yes, he cares. That's why we follow, and he knows it. We may follow him yet into Hell.'

It was accomplished. Harfleur had fallen. In his silk pavilion outside the walls, the King decided that Sir John Holland, saviour of the hour, should be created Earl of Huntingdon for his peerless service. It was appropriate that he should be given the title taken from his father by Henry's own father, Bolingbroke. Sir John had wrought miracles, although the laxness of the Dauphin at Vernon had played its part. Louis had virtually abandoned Harfleur which, with its diminished supplies, its sick and starving people, and its garrison's strength finally lowered, had weakened sufficiently for the final assault on the Leure gate to be successful. And now he prepared to receive the keys of the town. But his triumph was tempered by the wasted weeks, the thought of the burial pit filled with pointless death, and his heart was in private mourning.

Bitterness hardened his resolve that Harfleur should be made to pay for the grave or mortal sickness of March and Arundel and Suffolk and his brother of Clarence. Above all, for Courtenay. He sat very still, his embroidered gown spread out like stiff plumage, his eyes glinting with temper and grief. Harfleur should be humiliated duly. He did not stop to wonder whether this was what Courtenay would have wished, for that kindly wisdom was stilled for ever.

He had watched him die. Courtenay had been lucid, even eloquent throughout, and though his body was wrung out like a rag from the disease, he seemed remote and uncomplaining. Even the air within his tent remained sweet and decent. Harry had been watching while the Bishop dozed, a deathly sleep, the fine features marmoreal like an effigy's, the hands closed firmly about the crucifix on his breast. When he awoke, he smiled.

'It is your birthday, Harry.'

'It is?' He could hardly answer.

'And I have no gift. Save my love, my blessing.'

The King bowed his head. Courtenay murmured: 'I've been on such a long journey this day. A pilgrimage . . . I did not reach the shrine . . . so near . . .' He tried to sit, and Harry supported him.

'That's better,' Courtenay said, and Harry's heart lifted, but only for an instant.

The Bishop said: 'You must rest.' Then: 'But then, you never need to rest. Your strength is your shield, my son. Cherish it.'

Hoping in some way to imbue the Bishop with that envied strength, he placed his hand on the chill hand over the crucifix. Immediately he felt, through his own flesh, Courtenay's anguish. It lanced him, settling leech-like in his bowels. He knew all about contagion, but kept his hand steady on the Bishop's. Benedict Nichols, Bishop of Bangor, and Thomas Morestede, chief surgeon, stood silent behind him. Both had done all they could. He dismissed them and knelt at Courtenay's side. Into the sphere of this passing crept all other losses and deaths, long before Scrope's treachery to the death of his own young mother, Mary de Bohun. And now, this waste and robbery, all because Harfleur had defied him! In the bowels of Christ, he thought savagely, they were unworthy to be called *his* people!

He had offered them chivalry, honour, protection. In his preliminary letters to Charles of France, he had stressed that he only claimed what was his by right. He had had no scruples at styling himself King of England and France. He had ardently expressed his desire to avoid the slaughter of innocents. He had advised Charles to think of eternity, when both must answer to the Throne above. And the more concessions Charles had offered, the more his own dissatisfaction had grown. Not enough were the important principal towns and provinces, nor the 800,000 crowns, the dowry for the Princess, nor Katherine herself. He must have everything, or be seen to have failed. Then came the final spark that hit home. The emissary, the Archbishop of Bourges, had declared: 'Sir, the King of France is the true King, and with respect to those things to which you say you have a right, you have no lordship not even to the kingdom of England, which belongs to the true heirs of the late King Richard . . .'

Courtenay sighed. From the borders of that other kingdom his eyes watched, still caring, knowing Henry's doubt.

'Do not deny your cause.' He moved his fingers feebly beneath the King's hand.

'Is the cause good?' He would have said this to no living person, but Courtenay seemed no longer of the living.

'It is yours. Go and fight for it. If you betray it now, you betray yourself. Make war, then peace. But spare the innocent, my son.'

'I will spare Holy Church. None shall sully her. I will honour her and say: *in hoc signo vinces.*' Deep within, the shared pain moved. 'But will the cause be fulfilled?'

The Bishop stared up into the shadows of the tent, his free hand flat on his crucifix as if he shielded it.

'Will it? King Charles has come to Mantes himself, bringing the oriflamme of St Denis, to rally the people. He is saner than for years – strong enough to arm a great force . . . forgive me. I weary you.'

'No, no. Continue, my son.'

'I had hoped to persuade Jean sans Peur to my side, but it's said that Burgundy is ready to join Valois. The French will gladly enlist under such power.'

The Bishop's faint smile was macabre on his dying face.

'Harry . . . if you do not know these French you are unready to rule them. Their armies are not like your armies . . . their obedience is a flickering wanton light against your strong flame. They are afraid . . .'

He bent closer.

'Afraid?'

The Bishop's eyelids drooped. His voice was very weak.

'. . . more afraid of the tax-gatherers . . . than any invading army . . .'

Harry, staring at him, thought: Yes! and the structure of even their payment for their troops is not the stable convention that we know. Therefore the discipline will be poor . . . deserters numerous, morale variable . . . the French do not welcome a fight, otherwise why would Charles be so content, earlier, to *parler*? That Welsh boy, with the gold hair and the bright eyes and the dirty face . . . worth two of their elegant prancing knights. He saw the Bishop's eyes fall open again and was about to say: you have elated me! but saw that he was too late. Courtenay was over the border; he had reached the shrine. A little of its surpassing gold shone in his eyes. Harry closed it in with a tender downstroke of his hand. He was in a tumult of grief and enmity and fresh hope. In my singleness is security, he thought. My men seek no other leader, and there's the difference between England and France; when Armagnac captains refused to serve under a Burgundian, and when Jean sans Peur locked up his own son, Philip, rather than see him enlist in the ranks of Valois . . . confusion, faction! as potent weapons as the burning logs placed across the moat by Sir John Holland's men to fire the Leure gate or the gun-stones that had thereafter brought chaos into Harfleur as far as the church of St Martin. (God forgive me for St Martin!) From where he now sat he could see the ruined steeple and the still smoking bastion. Arundel and March might be deathly sick and Suffolk dead with two thousand others, and Clarence sent home to Southampton to die or recover. But the town was his. Hostages were taken. The cause was good. He prayed again, silent words which through their very familiarity were as integral and natural as the beating of his heart.

Beside him stood Humphrey of Gloucester, sumptuously robed and jewelled. Near him was Benedict Nichols, who had lately celebrated Mass in the smoking shell of St Martin, and by him the Earl of Dorset and Lord Fitzhugh, with the ancient Sir Thomas Erpingham, and John Holland, hero of the hour. On the King's right Sir Gilbert Umfraville held a pikestaff surmounted by the King's tilting helm and crown. Humphrey of Gloucester broke the waiting silence.

'How much longer, Sire?'

Henry said: 'Until my honour is satisfied and their penitence is complete.'

Their humiliation. He had ordained that the Sire de Gaucourt, the Sire de Bracquemont and twenty-four French hostages should proceed behind the Eucharist into the English pavilions, where they were to kneel before lesser knights. Each was wearing a felon's rope about his neck. Faces white or red, they looked like cattle going to market.

At last they knelt before him. The Sire de Gaucourt held the keys of the town upon a cushion. The rope chafed him and the sackcloth shirt he had been bidden to wear pricked his flesh. Henry stared over the hostages' heads while another half-hour passed and one of the penitents swooned. The tilting helm grew heavy on Sir Gilbert's pike. Old Erpingham's bladder swelled painfully. Finally Henry lowered his eyes. The Earl of Dorset brought the keys to him and he said:

'You have withheld my town from me for too long. Yet as you have given yourselves to my mercy, I shall not be merciless.'

He bade them rise. Agonized, they crawled upright.

'You shall sup with us.' And they bowed dispiritedly.

The French noblemen did justice to an elaborate meal, agitating bellies shrunken by the siege. They looked bewilderedly at Henry who harangued them from the dais, and wondered why he himself ate nothing. Harfleur, he declared, should

166

be an English town like Calais. The citizens would stay to rebuild, working in harness with emigrants from England who would settle by grants of demesne.

'Every man shall take the oath of allegiance save those wealthy enough to pay for their freedom, and these shall be sent captive to England until their ransom is raised. I release the Sire de Gaucourt and the Sire de Bracquemont and as many noble knights who are willing to be paroled, provided they bring ransom to Calais at an appointed time.'

Then, with slightly less arrogance: 'We need artisans to make Harfleur strong as the garrison town it is. But there will be no place for the infirm, the aged, or infants.'

One of the French knights dropped his goblet. Henry continued steadily, his voice drowning Courtenay's ghostly counsel (*spare the innocent!*): 'Women and children shall be given an escort as far as Lillebonne and five sous apiece for all. All men shall make a true declaration of their possessions. All moveables of value are forfeit. My brother of Gloucester shall be overseer, and false declaration will be punishable by hanging.'

Gloucester bowed in affirmation. The King rose. His head was spinning, while a griping ache that was nothing to do with hunger assailed him. He needed coolness, arched stone, and the sight of the Holy Rood.

The church of St Martin reeked of fire, but the altar was intact. Barefoot, Harry crossed the broken masonry in the chancel. A sharp piece of rubble sliced his foot and he went on, uncaring, trailing garnet drops. He fell prone before the altar. From a dark ruined corner a baby cried and its terrified mother stifled the sound with her breast.

The following morning the exodus began in a creeping file. The lame, the blind, the very young and very old, quitting the town gates beneath Henry's banner of St George. Women suckled infants in the early October mist. The slow line was quiet. In every hand was clutched the hot pittance of five sous, soon to be seized by robbers on the road.

Humphrey of Gloucester had been riding round the town, taking inventory and spoil. He had hanged no one, and was also disappointed at the lack of treasure and piqued by the moderation of the King's demands. Only a modest assortment of gold and silver plate had been taken aboard *La Trinité Royale*. In his pavilion he let an esquire divest him of his harness. The King was waiting for him.

'I could have acquired much more for you,' said Humphrey.

'I wish for no plunder. I am a builder, not a destroyer. All that is in Harfleur is mine.'

'What now?' Gloucester wiped sweat away. 'Faugh! Surrender hasn't made this place any less foul.'

'I plan a *chevauchée* into the heart of my kingdom.'

Gloucester whistled softly. 'With this depleted force? The *Holy Ghost* has just weighed anchor from Winchelsea. We should send home for reinforcements first.'

'There are none. You know that. All the men we brought are the flower of England's arm. Nine thousand, and over half are gone.' He rose, his face hollowed by fasting. 'We must leave at least a thousand to guard the garrison here. Yet we must go on.'

'To Paris? To pass Rouen with this little army? Harry,' he said quietly, 'God may be with this enterprise, but he doesn't suffer fools. There's a gathering force at Rouen under the Sire d'Albret . . . and Burgundy may still decide to throw its arm against you . . .'

Henry, his back turned, thought: How can I return to England having won one paltry town? There would be many ready to do more than jeer – those who mock my kingship, ready to see, in my ineffectuality, the curse of the usurper's son . . .

'But if we were to march to Calais,' Gloucester said thoughtfully, 'it would at least be a showing, that you are victor enough to traverse France northward, taking what you may in your path. It would underline your challenge to the Dauphin . . .'

'. . . still unanswered. I offered him personal combat – the prize being the succession to the throne upon Charles's demise. That youth must be either a coward or so debauched he lacks the strength to wield arms.'

'We could travel lightly. And fast! Slide beneath the noses of d'Albret and whoever Burgundy might care to send.

Speed!' He grew excited. 'Harry, you were always famed for it.'

'But there will be the Somme to cross.'

Humphrey thrust out his lip. 'Yes, Sire. It could be done. Yet it's a hazard.'

The King smiled suddenly. 'I always loved to cast the dice, my lord. Had you forgotten?'

Sir Gilbert Umfraville and Sir John Cornwall commanded the vanguard as the army set out for Calais on the hundred-and-twenty-mile march north heading towards Montivilliers. October mist steamed from the ground, lapping the horses' hooves to the pastern with white. Behind the van rode the King's party, Henry with Sir John Holland and Humphrey of Gloucester and other lords, the ancient knight Erpingham and Lord de Roos on either side. The Duke of York and the Earl of Oxford brought up the rear, and on both flanks of the whole cavalcade the footsoldiers, archers and light-horsemen ran or rode. The spirits of the men rose like the dispersing mist as hated Harfleur fell behind. Only essential supplies borne by mules and sumpter horses accompanied the train. There were provisions and armaments for eight days, but the great guns had been left behind at the garrison. Even the King's own baggage was of the minimum: his more important jewels and seals, the piece of the True Cross brought back from the Holy Land long ago by a Welsh crusader; harps and lutes and velvets, a few favourite hawks and hounds. The company rode in tight swift order with Henry as their nucleus, a gaunt-faced planet whose rays spread to encompass satellites on the perimeter: the Welsh, the Dutch, and the scantily clad Irish, short and black-eyed and fleet. Davydd Gam headed one of these flanks. Owen and John Page, who had been issued with tough little horses, rode close behind him.

That they marched at all was a minor triumph for Henry. The more experienced campaigners in his war council had been filled with trepidation. Sir Thomas Erpingham had reiterated Henry's own fear that although Burgundy might disdain to bear arms in the service of his royal cousin, the Duke was unpredictable and well likely to direct an offensive of his own against the invaders. At Rouen, the clever Sire d'Albret had a force which could move as swiftly as Henry once it knew what he was about. The argument continued past nightfall. Only when Arundel, although desperately ill, spoke up did the opposition quieten somewhat. He had been carried into the council pavilion and lay on a pallet. He raised his ghostly face to speak; Henry bent to listen, smelling the sweet rottenness of approaching death.

'Sire, your plan is good. At Calais you may rest and be reinforced,' (to which Henry said curtly: 'there *are* no reinforcements!') but Arundel went on, eyes clenched in a spasm of pain: 'Sire, I know the best place to ford the Somme . . . at the White Spot, *Blanche-Tâque*. It's nearest, and safest and was used by your great-grandfather on his way to Crécy . . .'

'He was better equipped than we are,' said old Erpingham.

Arundel disregarded this. 'Blanche-Tâque is five miles downstream from Abbeville. Twelve men can cross abreast.'

Further murmurs of dissent came from the advisers. Henry said steadily: 'My lord, I like your counsel. I'll send scurriers ahead to Calais, ordering the Lieutenant to keep Blanche-Tâque open and . . .'

'Beware Rouen,' said Arundel. Gasping, dew-faced with weakness: 'Squire, bring me my little map. Look, my liege.'

He spread the parchment between his shaking hands.

'Go by Fécamp, then Arques . . . Boves . . . but first send from Calais a party . . .'

'Yes!' Henry pounced his finger on the map. 'I'll have a detachment from Calais move south of the Somme to divert d'Albret away from our crossing.'

'That's it,' said Arundel, and let the parchment slide.

'This is great rashness, Sire,' said Lord de Roos.

The tent-flaps parted and two scurriers were bidden entry. Their tired faces were white in the torchlight, their clothes streaked with river-mud, and their news alarming. None less than the Marshal of France, Jean Boucicaut, was gathering a force on the opposite bank of the Seine estuary, at Honfleur. They had seen standards in the glow of many campfires, heard the sound of steel on anvil. Their number was hard to determine, but there were more than was comfortable.

Henry turned to his Council, saying: 'It seems we have no choice. Well, my lords? To Calais? or perish in this poison-pit?' No one spoke.

When he looked back at Arundel, the Earl was smiling.

'You have your way, Sire. Would to God I was riding with you, instead of going home to England.' (Then, with the quiet uncaring candour of the dying): 'I always loved you, Harry. My family were never King Richard's men. My lord, go with God. You are no usurper.'

Wisdom from the lips of death, once more! He looked at Arundel, stunned with gratitude. The cause is good, he thought. *The cause is good.*

Now they rode through the brightening autumn morning, and at Montivilliers, a few arrows hailed them from the walls. Archers drew their weapons. The command came at once. 'Hold! Do not answer; press on.' The vanguard began to move faster, the moist ground sucking at hooves and feet, the standards frisking. As the walls of Montivilliers fell behind, a greyish gleam to the east showed where the Lézarde narrowed to its end in a shallow lake. Page said to Owen: 'Two rivers to cross before the Somme – the Béthune and the Bresle. My grandsire fought at Crécy. Nursery tales. I know the whole campaign by heart.' He glanced towards the dwindling river. From its bank a little group of people, some of them half-naked, came hastening wearily. A woman, her eyes wild with hunger, reached Page's stirrup.

'Those poor devils out of Harfleur,' he said. 'The robbers took everything.'

Lamenting in broken English, the woman stretched out her hands, making irredeemable promises. Anything, for food for her child, her blind father. Page took his ration of hard salt pork from his pouch and tossed it to her, turning away before Owen saw more than a flash of his tears, which made him recall his own tears, when Glyn Dŵr had forbidden him this very campaign! That was hunger, too! he thought, and smote Page's knee affectionately as they left the ravaged little group behind.

October deepened, shrouded in mist-fine rain. By night

tents were raised for the nobles, the lesser ranks spread straw for themselves and the lowest wedged themselves into ditches and the branches of trees. The horses' legs were splashed hock-high with mud, the lords' armour shone with damp and the little, light-clad Irishmen were mired to the thigh. Yet, after Harfleur, it was clean mud, clean damp.

They were expected at Fécamp. A surprisingly well-prepared small army rushed out through the town gates and there was a skirmish. One of the English flanks detached itself and forced a little way into the town. Men fought hand-to-hand in the meadow under the walls and a salvo of arrows killed a dozen of Sir Gilbert Umfraville's men. Fairly swiftly the Fécamp assailants were beaten back or driven into the open country by mounted English firing after them, and the army moved briskly on, leaving a blaze and the high clamouring of a bell. Someone had fired the Abbey.

As the column of smoke behind became the size of a feather everything halted. A buzz of talk spread through the army and died. The ranks parted, revealing the King. Before him knelt one of the footsoldiers, and Humphrey of Gloucester stood near holding the soldier's leather pack and a gleaming silver vessel. A rope was placed about the man's neck, and he was led, thus haltered, through the ranks accompanied by a terse proclamation.

'This man has defiled Holy Church. He robbed the Abbey of the Pyx. The penalty is death.'

They hanged him from the branch of a young oak. The watchers were awed, not least by the knowledge that this man, now an example of holy wrath, had been openly complimented at Harfleur for his prowess by the King. Leaving him blue-faced and revolving gently in the damp air, they moved on. A few days brought them to the small stone town of Arques, where the Béthune flowed sluggishly beneath a narrow bridge and a *château-fort* stood high above the walls. The tramping medley of hoof and foot and wheel moved towards the bridge. The château's cannon opened fire, killing and wounding a dozen men at the mouth of the bridge. A screen of dust and shale rose, bisecting the company; horses reared and neighed, men shouted commands. Birds rose from the river, wheeling above the army and the smoke-wreathed nose of the cannon on the battlements and the scarlet oriflamme defiantly draped over the walls. At a command the vanguard turned and thundered back, away from the bridge. Someone called out: 'Do we retreat?' and the answer came back after a moment.

'The King will *parler*.'

A rider carrying the banner of St George left the vanguard and cantered towards the town gates. The cannon remained silent. After a while the castellan appeared, a portly figure flanked by two armed men, on the threshold of the main gate. The emissary addressed him from horseback; his banner flapped, brushing the horse's ears. The animal reared and the castellan took a step backwards. He listened, shook his head in evident discomfiture, and spread his hands, while his eyes strayed to the massed army waiting down the road. A wave of whispered reckless excitement spread back among the men, and then a little burst of cheering.

'The King has threatened to burn Arques to the ground.' said Davydd Gam delightedly. He strained to hear, and in a moment the word came back, sweeping with triumph. 'We may pass. *Duw!* That fat little Frenchman heard of our work at Harfleur!'

'Prowess,' said John Page softly. 'No better herald. I'm proud to be an Englishman.' And Davy shot him a cynical look.

As if the one burst of cannon-fire had sapped all his defiance, the castellan seemed at pains to show goodwill. In a few hours the army passed unmolested, taking with it twenty wagon-loads of fresh bread and wine, a welcome supplement to the dwindling rations. Eat, drink, and leave us in peace, said the castellan of Arques.

'*Now* we know how to conquer!' Humphrey of Gloucester strutted, huge-shadowed in the King's pavilion, which was dimly lit as by now the need to hoard candles had arisen. Henry sat listening, slightly irritated. His brother seemed full of energy, a wasteful undirected energy, and a cocksureness designed to tempt Providence.

'Just threaten!' he continued loudly. 'First Arques and now this godforsaken town, and another bridge safe behind us. By God! One has only to wave a lighted torch over their crops and they can't see our backs swiftly enough. At this pace, there'll be no need for battles!'

They were encamped across the Béthune outside the north walls of the town of Eu. The bridge had indeed surrendered to threats, but as Humphrey now chose to ignore, there had been a sharp skirmish during which more than fifty men on both sides had been lost. Henry could hear the thud of the gravediggers' spades. Not a pleasant sound, especially when allied to this lackwit boasting which, none the less, started in him a train of thought. Burning. Yes, men feared fire, that atavistic weapon of both godly and godless. Badby had feared it, but not enough to renege on his *credo*. Oldcastle must face it one day. And there were other, eternal flames . . . He frowned, hoping ardently that all went well in England, that the bedesmen continued to sing Richard's soul to Paradise; that John of Bedford's regency was steadfastly held. That Bishop Henry Beaufort was indulging in no controversies, and that Clarence was safely home and well again. He had been in great pain . . . And now Henry's busy mind failed to distract his body from its own little secret. Since Courtenay's death, there had been a little fretful pang deep in his belly signifying something not quite well within. So far, by drastic fasting, he had managed to keep it intermittently at bay. His skin was loose over his bones, his face cadaverous. Today the pain had sent him straining at the privy-stool several times. He had spoken of it to none. This was his private serpent, to be strangled by his will. Breathing deeply, feeling his lower ribs suck at the pang, he longed for Calais, for this struggle along the broken roads of upper Normandy to be at an end.

'. . . are you coming to table, Sire?'

He shook his head. 'You have my leave,' he said, seeing that his brother, bored by such an inattentive companion, was keen to depart, his mind on food, then books or women, his two passions. He had brought along part of his library and there were other rumours which Henry had not sought to confirm.

'Wait,' he said. 'I would like music before I pray and sleep.'

'I'll send your minstrels.'

'No, they are such a crowd. The Welshman, Davydd Gam's protégé. He said he could play and sing. I've time now to hear him!'

Owen was finishing his supper. He crammed the last of the horrible salt pork, dry as an old saddle, into his mouth and said indistinctly to Gloucester's esquire: 'Are you mocking me?'

'On your feet, lad,' said the man. 'God's Eyes! You're untidy. Haven't you a fresh doublet?'

'You can borrow mine,' said John Page wistfully. 'You're lucky, Owen. If the King likes you, he forgets nothing. Is the harp in key?'

'I hope so.' He tried the instrument, adjusted two strings by the little hooks that tuned it, then, satisfied, stood while Page and the esquire helped him to dress.

'I'm taller, broader than you. I shall burst your laces.'

'No matter. Come back and tell me what he said. I wish I could sing. Ask him if he likes poetry.'

The esquire took him through the dusk. Suddenly Owen felt sick. What songs? Would Welsh airs offend, remembering the long campaign against Glyn Dŵr? Would he request an unknown air, and be justly annoyed by ignorance? The sycamore harp slid between his wet palms. They were at the royal pavilion, past the guard, and Owen was within, kneeling before the gaunt man who sat in shadow.

Henry said in Welsh: 'Take the seat from the corner behind you. You cannot play standing up.'

He half-smiled at Owen's startled expression. The smile aged him, etching lines and sinews. The smile said: *I am Henry of Monmouth, Prince of Wales!*

'Show me the harp.'

He examined the instrument with minute care, turning it about so that the meagre light fell on its carvings. He studied its design, asking whose face, which bird or beast the ornaments on it represented. Suddenly confident, Owen answered him. For he remembered the long hours at Glyn Dŵr's feet, never failing to please. He was a prince, so why fear the man who

175

claimed the Lord's own title? Receiving back the harp, he looked into Henry's face. In the rusty flickering light a trace of the hollow half-smile remained. *If the King likes you . . .* Owen thought: I must make this come to pass. And I must not try too hard.

'How does the army suit you, Master Owen?'

(He knows my name.) 'Well, your Grace.' (Save that I'm always hungry, dirty, wet and bored to death with this trundling march north. Where are the battles we were promised?)

'What rank are you? Archer?'

'Horse-archer now, Sire.'

'A hobelar? Your horse is unarmoured?'

'Yes. Six pence a day, Sire.'

'You are rich, Owen.' The half-smile grew to genuine humour. 'I may ask for a loan.'

'All I have is yours, my liege.'

Henry laughed at the smooth earnest face. The laugh died instantly under a fiery stab in his bowels. He said, in a voice terse with pain: 'Play then, man.' Owen's mind raced like a rat. What song? Then a voice so clear that he almost jerked about to see who stood close, said to his mind: *He is sick. Soothe him.*

Glyn Dŵr at his most troubled had sought solace in his own composition, dedicated to the one Englishman he had loved. *Sweet Richard.* The victim of this troubled man's father. Politically a bad choice, perhaps, but a melody *par excellence.* So be it.

The minor cadences glided from his fingers and his lips carried with them the valley-breeze, the voice of the stream, a bright tune played on little flints, the ravine's mournful echo, the song of the whitethroat watching midnight lovers; the cry of Wales, of kings and lordlings, all powerful, all mortal, all equal. The last note fell like the eagle's dying wings. Feathered with love and artistry, the song lay spread for judgement. Owen looked up to see the King's head averted and moisture on his thin cheek.

After a time, Henry said: 'It was well done. I have a mind to send you to the minstrels. Snaith Fidler needs a prentice.'

The plaintive elegy stayed with him. He could see again Richard's face, knighting the young Harry on one of their Irish campaigns. Later Henry Bolingbroke had knighted his son a second time as if to eliminate the taint of the rival's hand. Now, hearing the sweet requiem, some of the torn loyalties were healed, some of the guilt assuaged. Then he saw that Owen was downcast.

'Sire . . . it is a great honour, but I would rather make war than merely trumpet for it.'

'So be it. Now, more music.'

Owen chose a psalm, and the King joined voice, tuneful, monkishly intoned within the hollow of his face.

'You are devout?' he asked when it was done.

'As the next man, Sire.' He answered very low.

Holy, disposed to war, and filled with the sounds I love. Young and shining too, his physical beauty undimmed even by these rugged days . . . he is my own youth, he is all beloved young men. He is Henry Scrope before his fall. An urge stirred. It would be so easy to take Owen, harp and all, into his arms, to bury care against the tanned smooth throat. He drew a harsh breath, and it was over. It was only tenderness, he told himself, and that's no sin; to want to bring Owen back to England whole and triumphant with all the others so eager to be chosen for these hazardous times. No sin in wishing to preserve beauty, health, or to abhor the image of beauty spoiled by the battle that must come before the winter. He decided he must find some position for Owen more defined than that of a mere horse-archer. If not in the minstrel troupe then in some capacity of value. It would need thought, and the time was not ripe. The climate among his own servants was for the most part known to him; they would consider Owen, not even an esquire, a rank upstart were he shown favour. The reverie went on. Through growing shadows Owen sat on, wondering. He had the uncomfortable feeling of watching at a corpse-side. His fingers trembled; the harp gave out a discordant twang.

'Yes, play again,' said the King distantly. Eyes, face, were dissolving in the gloom and all the last light seemed retained by Owen's fairness.

'I can scarcely see, Sire,' he said.

'Something more in Welsh; a saga, a story.'

'They are mortally long, your Grace. Hours they take. I can't do them honour, risking interruption.' He felt his face flush. Disobedience. Made bold by new nervousness, he said: 'And there is a lovely one that your Grace would enjoy when there is time. I can sing of Arthur's cousin who was without sin, chaste as flowers and noble as a singing mountain . . .'

The King moved slightly, his gown rasped in the near-darkness. He said: 'And what did this chaste knight?'

'He found the Great Boar. He confounded the fiercest giant in the world. He withstood all taunts . . .'

'He was taunted?' The voice was suddenly strong. 'His lineage and right were questioned?'

'Indeed, Sire!' There was nothing of the sort in the legend, but these things could and should be tailored for the listener, depending on the interpretative genius of the bard. Had the creators of many such stories been living, they would not have recognized their work.

'They were mad, who taunted him,' said Henry softly.

'Indeed, Sire.'

'And this knight – he had not always been chaste? He had revelled, and repented?'

Owen thought quickly. Rhetoric was familiar to him; he had often played instinctively on Glyn Dŵr's whims.

'He had been rash in youth. Thus he shone more brightly against the darkness of his past.' And bit his lip, and held his breath.

'It is well,' said the King deeply.

'And he conquered all,' Owen gabbled on, feeling suddenly weary. 'The princess, whose favour none other could attain; the giant – who was turned by the knight's prowess into a little child . . .'

'And the domain? The lands, the dower, the splendour? All were his by right, by force, by destiny?' The King was now sitting vibrant and straight.

'All, Sire,' said Owen. He let the harp slide down, where it rested against his knees.

Henry was silent again, while his spirit surged immoderately.

His emotional reflexes had been heightened by fasting to a degree of hallucination. He drowned in optimism. Tomorrow they would be pressing on to the ford at Blanche-Tâque, and soon would be in Calais with provisions to spare and the French outwitted. Believing what he wished to believe, he saw Owen as sent to him by fate this night, and through the now almost total darkness projected to him a wave of marvelling, unstable love.

'You've spoken well, *bach*,' he said in Welsh. 'Let us have light. Pour some wine.'

Owen lit a candle. From a side table he filled a goblet and, kneeling, served the King.

'For you also.'

He blushed. 'Wine is for knights, your Grace.'

'Also for poets and comforters. *Iechyd da!*'

Soberly they drank and Owen felt the flush of the good wine down to the soles of his feet. What in mercy's name have I done, other than say yes, and yes again? Behind him someone stood outside the tent, and coughed.

'My chaplain,' Henry said. 'I shall pray now, and sleep.' Then he added: 'Tomorrow you shall ride in the main body, near to us. And later we will find work for you in our Household.'

Greatness. The beginning? Owen picked up his harp and backed from the pavilion. He made his way very slowly past canvas and campfires, and in his own quarters found John Page drowsing over pen and parchment.

'You pleased him, then,' he said, without looking up. 'I believe that tomorrow he will break his fast.'

Owen, arranging his bedstraw more comfortably, raised an eyebrow.

'News travels fast in camp,' said Page, rolling up his poetry and settling himself for sleep.

The captured man looked like a small black-polled bird, his plumage mired where he had fallen in a bog trying to outrun his pursuers. Shrill and petulant, he spoke in an incomprehensible dialect as he was pushed forward to where the King and his advisers sat beneath a leafless tree.

'What tongue is that?' said Humphrey of Gloucester, frowning.

'He speaks the *langue d'oc*,' Henry said. 'Yet I wager it's an affectation.' To the sergeant in charge he said: 'Where was he found?'

'About six miles from the river, Sire, by our advance guard looking for the decoy contingent from Calais. He was quite alone.'

There was a further spate of wildly fluting syllables.

'He chatters like a jay,' said Gloucester in disgust.

The sergeant whipped out his misericord, a short killing-knife, and held it to the prisoner's throat.

'Speak French!' The chattering stopped. The dark eyes showed fear.

'Who are you, where have you come from and who is your commander?'

'I am of Bayonne, a servant of Marshal Boucicaut. I am to report back to him at Rouen when . . .' His lips closed up tight.

'When?' The blade moved; blood sprang, a small thick thread.

A terrified gabble: 'When your army is slaughtered at Blanche-Tâque . . . the river is full of sharp stakes and Marshal Boucicaut has six thousand men there.'

Henry leaned forward.

'You false-tongued, bragging Gascon! Boucicaut is a hundred miles south of here, at Honfleur.' He gestured violently. 'Take him. Behead him for his lies.'

The man's voice became a bird's screech of alarm.

'No, *grand seigneur*! It's the truth. Your army is doomed.'

There was silence. The sergeant put his knife away. Henry studied the Gascon for a moment. He said: 'Let us hear all of it, then. Take him away and feed him. Bring him to me in one hour.'

Later, information poured from the badly frightened man. To the hastily summoned war council it was apparent that swiftly though the *chevauchée* had moved, the French had moved faster. The legend of prowess at Harfleur which had eased their passage across two rivers, through Arques and Eu, had determined the French that such success should not be repeated. Most of the noble feuds in which Henry had rejoiced were suddenly, alarmingly mended.

'The Duke of Orléans has joined with a mighty force,' the Gascon said rapidly. 'Likewise the Dukes of Alençon and Bar, and the Dukes of Bourbon and Berry. They have discovered a great love and protectiveness for the realm of France.'

'And Burgundy?' Sir Gilbert Umfraville asked sharply.

'Of the Duke I cannot say. But many of his knights have joined of their own volition. The Duke of Brittany, who previously would have no dealings with the campaign, has brought twelve thousand men to the service of the crown. And the Comte de Richemont. And the Comte de Nevers. And the Duke of Brabant. All well equipped. Paris has offered six thousand men in arms. *Grand seigneur,*' he told Henry, 'you now ride against an army of thirty thousand men.'

'Bandits!' said Humphrey of Gloucester, vicious with shock. 'Pillagers, like birds of prey. Men who don't know a weapon's head from its nether end . . .'

'Thirty thousand men,' said the Gascon softly, 'who will drown your army in the Somme and in its own blood.'

Henry said: 'We are being watched from the northern bank?'

The black poll nodded. 'Marshal Boucicaut joined force with Constable d'Albret when he marched east from Honfleur. All the crossings round Abbeville are destroyed. You will be driven upstream, where they will kill you.'

'This is the truth?' Henry's voice was steady.

The Gascon wanted to say: as truly as all English are born with tails! but thought this too frivolous after his exposition of the English army's doom. He had taken the heart out of them, he thought. It was enough.

'By the sacred severed head of St Denis, it is the truth. When fate is fixed, there is no need for even a Gascon to lie. Will you now put me to the sword?'

Henry bowed slightly. 'Go unmolested. God does not march on the side of barbarism.' He turned to his councillors, who pressed about him, uneasy beside his strange calm.

The scouts whom he sent out verified that a large force was moving towards Péronne. Parties of d'Albret's and Boucicaut's men were glimpsed on the north bank well in advance of the English army. Meanwhile the tide swept into the Somme, filling the Blanche-Tâque ford, covering the deathly stakes and chains with which the river had been sown. The bridge at Abbeville was no more. And still the tight detachments of men with the flanking runners and outriders moved on through October's crackling gold, with a shiver of frost and winter that struck deep within belly and bone. Sir Gilbert Umfraville again commanded the van, although temporarily out of favour.

'We could, your Grace, return to Harfleur . . .'

He had been shocked at the anger in Henry's eyes.

'My lord, it is my intent to ride on Calais and reconnoitre there in safety. If you lack stomach for this *chevauchée*, there is a ship returning to England. The infirm will be on it. Join them as you please.'

Sir Gilbert had said no more.

Yet Calais fell further away as they veered south-east towards Pont Rémy and Hangest-sur-Somme in the search for a river crossing. As they passed north-west of Amiens, Calais became almost nebulous, a word, unattainable. And there was always the knowledge that their progress was watched and reported upon wherever the unseen army lay. The Picardy landscape was as deserted as the moon. Small farms from which all occupants had fled stood among stripped orchards and vineyards and empty granaries; slaughtering blocks were bloody from recently killed livestock, but the farmers had left nothing behind.

Owen rode as bidden in the King's detachment, among unfriendly strangers, and missing the company of John Page. He had had no more contact with Henry, but Davy Gam, galloping by with news of another broken bridge, halted, his one bright eye full of mocking approval, greeting him: '*Shwd mae!*' and: 'Favoured then, *bach*. Guard the King's Grace well.'

Owen dismounted to ease his little horse whose neck was now so thin it looked like a serpent's. Nearby a man was eating a fistful of hazelnuts. He caught Owen's eye and grimaced.

'The meat is finished,' he said bitterly, 'and so are we.'

Owen said: 'When we reach Calais . . .'

'Calais!' The man uttered a series of blasphemies and spat, then said, knowing and plaintive: 'You wouldn't have any wine, by chance? *They* have wine . . .' nodding enviously towards the Household knights.

Owen felt lonely and confused.

When they passed through the next deserted village the command came back to burn it, first warning any inhabitants who might have remained. In the thin frosty sunshine the army left this village and the next crumbling in a sea of flame. Dried dead leaves on the vines blazed under a black pall. Thus hoping to cover its passage, the army moved dispiritedly on. At night Owen went, against orders, down the drowsy lines of men to find John Page. He found him weeping, and sorry, gave him a blessing – '*Duw bo gyda chi*', and said, 'Don't lose hope, John.'

'I was thinking – ' Page wiped his nose on his sleeve – 'of the woman from Harfleur, the one I gave my meat to.'

'You can't have it back,' said Owen.

'I didn't mean that. I hadn't realized what a mean foe hunger really is. I pray,' he said, his voice trembling, 'that the Almighty will take pity on his unfortunates. All of them. That the glorious Virgin will mediate for us . . .'

Owen, sicker and sadder than ever, went back to his place.

Onward north-west of Amiens, through Crouy and Picquigny the army struggled, bellies groaning from the diet of nuts and berries, the horses faltering and lean on snatched sour grass. A constant flow of quiet swearing accompanied the march; a litany of despair. The men drank brackish water from the streams. Weariness, the overpowering lust to lie down and sleep for longer than the few hours allowed, assailed them. Yet none of their curses were aimed at the King, for they felt that he too was a victim of these fates, this eternal ambushed hopeless march. And at Boves, he silenced even their oaths for a while with a demonstration of his rage.

He came upon them drinking. A hoard of luxury had been

183

discovered, red wine in open casks left by fleeing villagers. Henry rode among the soldiers, striking out with a staff, his face pale with fury. Men lay droning happily on the ground, oblivious even of their sovereign. Others were filling their water-flasks from the barrels, trying to drink and hoard at the same time. Henry lashed a bending man across the shoulders and he rolled grinning on his back.

'All free! French wine!' he gurgled, and Henry would have struck him again, but Humphrey of Gloucester interposed.

'Harry . . . it would do no harm to let them fill their bottles for the march.' (He himself had already done so.)

'Bottles!' cried the King. The brown eyes in the thin face gleamed red. 'They've made bottles of their bellies! How can I take France with a bevy of sots!'

Humphrey recalled Harry singing in Coldharbour, more cupshotten than any of them. There's none, he thought, so virtuous as a reformed whore . . . but this is something deeper; as if he sought to take on him the sins of the world. So thinking, he gave orders to the sergeants, who smashed the casks; men wept like children.

Eight miles north-east of this minor tragedy they came to Corbie, and met sudden terror. A magnificent body of mounted French knights from Marshal Boucicaut's force attacked them at the bridge. There was a short hot skirmish, a flail of arrows from the English archers who, hastily assembled in battle order, saw for the first time the colour of their adversary. A force that glittered, the horses' powerful pounding legs a dappled gleam, their housings a flying rainbow. Over their armour, the knights' tabards were starred with the blue and gilt of the French lily. The cavalry poured forward, knocking half the archers flat. They bore the scarlet-tongued oriflamme of St Denis. Owen was one of those felled to the ground.

He lay while the wave swept over him, his face in the earth, his bow lying hard beneath him. Under the chaos, his thoughts moved like mice in a skein as pretty and mad as the French colours. I shall not die. I shall know greatness. Lie still, *bach*. A hoof hit his head glancingly. His mind was drenched in the blood of the oriflamme and darkened to peace.

Page said: 'Are you wakeful?'

'I think I'm dead.' He groaned, and sat up carefully.

'It's a scratch!' said Page. 'You're charmed, Owen.' A body with broken twisted limbs was being carried past.

'Their colours were beautiful,' said Owen. 'The colours of death are beautiful.'

Henry said to the few knights he had captured on the bridge:

'How are the French forces deployed? Where is d'Albret's army?'

He knew he would be given a fair answer. Under threat of death these prisoners, like the Gascon spy, always told everything. He now learned that his army was virtually trapped. The French on the north bank were moving across the route from Corbie to Péronne, cutting off the river. Only Nesle to the east was near enough; he might reach it first. He stared at the captives; their elegance was almost unruffled by the recent skirmish. Their gilded trefoils winked from their blue tabards. They could have been riding to a tourney. One face wore a complacent sneer which enraged him.

'Why do you laugh in our presence?' he demanded.

The Frenchman gave a little shrug.

'I was thinking of your poor archers. Such skill wasted by the speed of our horsemen. They scarcely had chance to draw a bow!'

Neither did they, Henry mused, his rage fading. With regret he thought of those fine weapons of polished elm, ash, hazel or best of all, yew. The arrows, fletched with duck or peacock feathers or parchment, should have brought down this gaudy cavalry . . .

'It was amusing,' said the French knight. 'While my adversary strove to reload from his quiver . . . *houpla!* my Bayard ran on and crushed him into the ground! To this art I trained the beast . . .'

Bayard. Strange that a horse's name should spark a memory so apposite to the moment that it seemed inspired. Henry sat quiet. The prisoners grew restive.

'My family will ransom me, English lord,' said one to Thomas Erpingham, who stood behind the King. 'We're rich.'

Henry said: 'Later,' and dismissed captives and escort. *Bayard*, he thought. At Nicopolis, where my father fought so long ago, the Sultan Bayard solved the problem of archers versus charging cavalry. *Les chevaux de frise!*

'The archers will grumble,' he said to Erpingham with a brilliant sudden smile.

'Sire?'

'When each man is ordered to bear, wherever he goes, a stout stake sharpened at both ends.'

'To fix in the earth like a fence before the charge?' Erpingham too was remembering.

'. . . thus giving each bowman time to load and reload . . . we'll see what amusement the French find in that!'

The war councillors admired the idea, but their faces remained tense. The Duke of York said: 'We are still shadowed by a mighty host!'

'We'll march to Nesle,' said Henry. 'The river is fordable there. At least it was last evening when the scouts came in.'

'Further east! *South*-east!' Edward of York said aghast. He thought with dull disquiet of the long looping dog-leg route deeper into France. They would not see Calais this side of Christmas. Perhaps he himself would never see Calais again.

'There's no other way,' Henry said. 'We must outmarch d'Albret.'

When the army moved off over the chalky terrain towards Chaulnes and Nesle, there was grumbling as he had forecast. The long staves were unwieldy. If used as an aid to walking, the sharp lower point caught in the ground and caused a stumble. Carried crosswise, eyes were endangered. So the army shouldered this extra burden and, grimly onmoving, looked like a plodding field of dragons' teeth.

Under threat of having their town burned, the people of Nesle were no less willing to capitulate than those at Arques and Eu. Henry's fretful temper grew when he saw the red strips of rag hung from the windows of cottage and farm. Again! the damned oriflamme, the symbol of stubbornness with which the French upheld their crown. He was unimpressed. These were *his* people. He sent soldiers into the homesteads to tear the emblem down, and there he billeted men who were still sick or wounded from past skirmishes, placing a guard in each dwelling to keep the invalids from secret murder. Constantly planning with his council, he knew little of what passed within these besieged houses. The army had learned discretion. The rapes, the softer liaisons, the drinking and looting were performed in stealth. For once such details escaped Henry's meticulous punitive mind, for he was preoccupied with acquiring the knowledge he craved.

He was roused from bed by a deputation anxious to see the last of the English army who, by its hidden excesses, had achieved perhaps more than their King could imagine. The whiteheaded town elders handed him words sweet as summer flowers.

'There are two fords north-west of here, English sires,' said the spokesman, leaning on an ashplant.

'How far?'

The old man shrugged. 'A day. Perhaps one and a half days. You will have to cross a swamp. There is a lower road to the ford at Béthencourt, another to Voyennes in the north. Both are unguarded.'

'When the kingdom is mine,' said Henry, 'I will see you have your reward.'

'Our reward is your departing!' said the ancient. 'Look for the causeway across the marsh.' Henry was already saying to his chief officers: 'Rouse and ready the men to move at dawn.'

So they went forward into shortening October, into mud and marsh and reeds. The pack-wagons took the Béthencourt road, the men-at-arms and archers made for Voyennes. Across the swampland the murky little Ingon river crawled to join the Somme. The causeway was a treacherous, crumbling, single-file plateau, and less than a mile from its end, the company was brought to a halt. The last stretch had been destroyed, leaving a vista of slime and deep pools fringed by coarse grass. It was too late to turn back or seek other crossings. Trees were felled and a row of nearby deserted cottages dismantled. Logs, doorframes, thatch, gates, and bundles of thicket were stacked to form a precarious road over which the company could reach the ford. Dawn yielded to day and then mid-day.

187

Henry stood at the head of the causeway, and as the frantic work upon it moved, so he moved, nearer the river, overseeing the repairs, giving orders, warnings. As each section grew he rode his horse on the wedged timbers, testing for safety.

A detachment of lightly armed bowmen had gone ahead across the swamp, springing from tussock to tussock towards the ford. They waded in waist-deep, fighting the little sharp currents and clambering up the further bank to form a bridge-head against any attack that might be threatening in the vicinity. Owen and John Page stood soaked and shivering with the others, but the little Irishmen, who wore nothing but a leather codpiece and discarded even that for the crossing, dried themselves by dancing about.

'You were nimble,' Page said to Owen. Page had slipped into the mud.

'There's a bog like that outside Glyndyfrdwy.' The old demesne and that night of his enlistment seemed far off, like something in another childish life, with no right of application in face of this reality.

'Look!' The causeway was completed. The first horse and wagon came, urged with cries, splashing down into the river. The horse's head was raised, its eyes rolled, the cartwheels drew a brown fan of ripples behind. A horseman followed, almost diving his mount into the water, and then another. The encouraging figure of the King could clearly be seen; he was waving the file on. It was nearly night; the army was wet, worked to exhaustion, but the Somme was gained. Mingled with the cackle of heron and the gurking of frogs, a little cheer arose, as if this fording had been a baptism of hope.

When they lay billeted around Athies and Monchy-Lagache, an hour from the river, the word Calais had form and meaning once more. At the end of this *chevauchée*, they would be able to renew themselves in home territory. Sleep came easy, even through sickness and privation, for the first time in weeks. None knew that in the King's pavilion, three French heralds knelt with solemn proclamation.

The unseen force was already very near, north at Péronne; all the great commanders, including Marshal Boucicaut and d'Albret, who had separately tracked the invasion from Rouen and now deployed their armies to sprawl across the only route to Calais. Likewise young Charles of Orléans, with his crack fighting force, and the old Duke of Berry, veteran of Poitiers; and the Duke of Bourbon. All the noble armies not already at Péronne were close enough to encircle and crush any forward movement. Only King Charles of France and the Dauphin Louis were absent. The Duke of Berry had persuaded them to stay behind. Though the puny half-dying English army posed no real threat, there were always mishaps not to be risked by the figurehead of France and his heir.

The courteous heralds' faces were in handsome diplomat mould. Their *côtes d'armes* swooned with colour. Behind them a page bore the oriflamme, windless on its staff like a skein of blood.

'Right puissant and mighty prince, great and noble is thy kingly power, as is reported among our lords.'

Civilly Henry inclined his head, while they told him they knew his intent to conquer the towns, castles and cities of the realm of France, and that for the sake of their country and their oaths, the lords were assembled to defend their rights.

'They inform thee by us that before thou comest to Calais they will meet thee to fight with thee and to be revenged of thy conduct.'

Henry caught the Duke of York's eye. Here on the high ground outside Péronne was a fine place for battle, with the advantage his. This he had already discussed with York, with Umfraville, Cornwall, Oxford, Camoys, Gloucester and Erpingham. He said quietly:

'Be all things according to the will of God. We shall take our way straight to Calais, and if our enemies try to disturb us it will not be without the utmost peril. We do not seek them out, neither shall we fear them. They shall not interrupt our journey without a great shedding of Christian blood.'

Their mission accomplished, the heralds bowed deeply, and Henry directed: 'Pay them for their courtesy.' A steward presented a bag of gold coins. As the tent-flaps closed, Humphrey of Gloucester blew out his cheeks.

'So! A battle, now?'

'We wait.' Henry rose. His eyes had a sheen of purpose. 'For a full day and night. If they make no move, we march on to Calais.'

Twelve hours later it began to rain heavily and continued when, at the second day's dawning, the army moved down into the valley towards Péronne. Loose shale and small branches broken off by the torrent streamed down the hill. Feet lost hold in the greasy mud. The rainfilled wind blew into eyes and tugged at sodden clothing. A frightened packhorse bolted with its burden and fell kicking into the little river Cologne. Under the walls of Péronne there was no sign of the enemy.

'They have moved back towards Bapaume.' Erpingham was astute and grim. 'Our position was too firm for them. They will attack our flanks, your Grace.'

Weirdly the great army yet unseen had vanished. Citizens fired a few shots from the walls of Péronne, soon retreating as Sir Gilbert Umfraville's party of horse raced in battle order towards the town. The army passed on to a crossroads. North-east, the fork led to Bapaume. Here the road had almost subsided and in the stew of mud, chilling to the heart, lay evidence of what faced the marchers.

An unimaginable host had passed this way. Tens upon tens of thousands of feet and hooves had churned the road. It was like a giant ploughed field as if all the horses in the world had trodden it and all fighting men ever born had set their mark upon it. Henry ordered a contingent of flank-guards to gallop off on the Bapaume road and the army went on towards Albert along the left fork. A heavy silence fell. Then, quietly at first and with growing exhortation, the chaplains in the King's party began to pray, while the rain poured, relentless as fear.

The scurrier, sent forward through the advance on the orders of Edward, Duke of York, spurred his horse and it sprang strongly upwards. The steep way, more mountain than hill, rose abruptly from the Ternoise valley at Blangy. Rain fogged its summit. The rider stood in his stirrups to relieve the strong surging back beneath him. The wet wind buffeted his face and tossed his hair. He was young and bold, and his mount picked for speed and strength. Yet as the rain choked his mouth and eyes he felt urgently alone. He could almost believe that there was nothing over the summit, and that once there he would step off the world.

They had marched fast, nearly forty miles in two days. Always westerly, doubly vigilant with the knowledge that to their right, beyond the flank-guards, the owners of those myriad prints kept course with them along the Bapaume road. Little stone villages and towns came and went; Albert, Forceville, Acheux. At Lecheux, the Comte de St Pol's château had leered from its crag with raised drawbridge and blank arrow-slits, token that the lord and his men had joined the war. For some hours before Blangy the way had been lost; they had missed the village where the night's billet had been planned. They had picked their tired way on to Frévent, sleeping briefly, then passing over the Ternoise bridge for a reconnaissance in the shadow of the hill.

The horse began to labour and the bold weary young man stroked its neck. We'll rest you soon, my boy. He planned to stand upon the ridge scanning the open country for some time, taking private ease, perhaps even closing his rain-sore eyes for a space. If he looked back he could see the little tents and insect figures of men and beasts. From his vantage point they were a small fussing knot. Those moving toys were riders passing from camp to camp, that tiny waving rag the King's standard. Very faintly he heard a trumpet call no louder than a midge's whine; the knot began to tighten as men rode in for council, and the volume of the company diminished further within the sprawling dish of the valley.

He reached the summit and looked out, wiping his eyes. Over the sheer drop before him the valley was clear as far as a small wood on the horizon, merging on the right with a dense forest, a million trees oddly luminous under the spearing rain. As he looked, the forest began to move. For a long moment his heart stopped. He closed his eyes, clenching them up tight. His pulse began again with a deathly galloping swiftness; he looked once more. His mind kept time with his pulse, gathering old pleasures for a last embrace: home, mother, father, his betrothed, a brown-eyed Kentish girl with plump breasts and a fine dowry; the archery contest won two years ago in sunshine, nights of gaming and cockfights, two sleek harriers, his saint's-day gift. These treasures rushed on him, relived in seconds, joys never to be repeated. For what filled his eyes from the ridge surely cancelled out all future.

The whole world glittered there, packed close yet spread out as far as man's eye could contain the sight. A rolling illimitable column, mighty as the hosts in the Bible, a legendary terror, a gargantuan forest dense as smoke. Lance upon lance, standard upon standard, an endless row of toothed weaponry, an incalculable number of death-devices: arblasts, mangonels, bombardes, veuglaires, crapaudins, ten times as deadly as the *King's Daughter* left behind at Harfleur.

Swearing softly, corpse-cold, he wheeled his mount and plunged downwards back towards the English encampment. The horse stumbled and slipped under his goading. Faintly he heard his own moaning voice. We knew they were many, O holy blessed Virgin! We knew they were many, but not this many! Mary, Mother of Our Lord, deliver us! And let me not vomit before his Grace of York . . . sustain me until I have told . . . that the whole world waits to fight with us!

The fine horses, great unwearied destriers, no kin to our pining starved mounts.

The matchless armed riders, well-fed, sprung full of health, a giant race beside our sick-bellied sadness.

The number!

He sped sobbing down towards the Duke's pavilion, one thought paramount.

I must find me a priest.

Humphrey of Gloucester kissed his French paramour with rough and final zest. She had been with him, carefully concealed, throughout the whole *chevauchée*. She was a blonde from Provence, thrice-widowed and sometime wealthy, whose passionate employment it was to follow armies. She did not care whose. She parted from the English lord with no regrets. She had passed a substantial degree of information to Boucicaut's agents during the weeks with Humphrey. Now work and play were done.

'I'll miss you, Madame,' he said. She smiled.

'I'll have Masses said for you when you are dead. Though doubtless you'll be ransomed. Did you know that you and your royal brother are worth a six at dice?'

'What?' Sharply he stepped from her.

'Ah, yes. Other nobles count a five, skilled men four, doctors and chaplains three and two, captains and sergeants one, but the poor archers, *hélas*! They're worth a blank! Are you not glad you weren't born an archer?'

Appalled, he said: 'They dice thus, for our persons?'

The lady was gathering up her jewels and, discreetly, some of Humphrey's into a bundle.

'To my countrymen, the English archer is lower than a worm. A clown, a fool. Adieu, my lord.'

'Wait until dusk,' he said uneasily.

On her way from the tent she walked suddenly into Owen, creeping with his guarded lantern down the line to chat with John Page. For an instant both he and she were badly frightened. She was wearing a cowled cloak; he thought she was a friar until he held up his light. Then she smiled and on tiptoe kissed him on the mouth, half mockingly, half because he was a beautiful young man soon to die. Her musky flowery perfume breathed over him. She walked rapidly away, pulling the cowl close. Stunned and delighted, Owen called softly after her – '*Hé, Madame!*' but she was already a friar again, a shadow, darkness, gone. The weirdest feeling came to him, as if the incident had happened before, perhaps in a dream, and was instantly dispelled by the next person he met – York's scurrier, coming from the chaplain, his face still glazed with shock. He challenged Owen, drawing a blade, and when reassured went off muttering. The words blew back through the rain-dark evening.

'Locusts,' Owen repeated to John Page. 'An innumerable horde like locusts, league on league, spreading across the Calais road, growing wider and deeper every moment. Are you listening?'

Page stuck his quill behind his ear.

'I was trying to set it down, what I've seen, and what I feel, and nothing comes. Now death seeks me, and fate holds me. Only prayer helps a little. And you, with your charmed life – have you made confession?'

'The priests are too busy.'

Suddenly Davydd Gam stood beside them, flanked by two sergeants. With an angry oath: '*Annwyl Crist!* Why are you from your place? I could have killed you for a spy!' And Owen rose quickly and Page hurriedly hid his writing and began to grease a bowstring.

'Yes. Ready your gear,' said Gam more kindly. 'We'll soon be moving upward on to the ridge.'

'To fight? *Now?*' said Owen.

Unexpectedly, oily terror churned his bowels.

'Chivalrous leaders do not carry war by night!' Davy smiled wryly. The throat-tightening panic grew in Owen. I am alone. Let me borrow your smile, your experience. Let me rub against your knowledge. This chance was all my desire. But I am alone, afraid, ashamed.

'I'll be riding close by you in the King's party.' Gam was watching him. 'But ask me not when or where we will fight. Only prepare yourself.'

His hand on Owen's shoulder, he said softly: 'What Glyn Dŵr would have given for this!'

'He hated the English . . .'

'Not all of them. He loved a fight. Remember him. Be worthy.'

Henry opened the treasure chest. Reverently he lifted out the crown. Even he had almost forgotten its beauty. Wrought of purest gold it was embellished with sapphires, rubies, and a hundred and twenty pearls the size of hazelnuts. The delicate fleurons of its circle lay snugly against the gold battle helm over which it would be worn. He regarded it for some moments while the lords crowded into his pavilion.

'Have all the men now seen the enemy?'

Sir Walter Hungerford, one of the chief advisers, nodded. His eyes were puffed and streaming from a heavy cold, the latest plague to sweep through camp.

For the past two hours the army had stood, dismounted, on the ridge, staring down to where the Tramecourt woods merged with that other fleshly forest in all its shattering immensity. Noise was muted. The loudest sounds were the nervous whickering of the horses and the unceasing murmur of the confessors as the soldiers knelt for absolution, and the wet wind moaned along the ridge. They had seen the massed monster below break and reform into thick columns which moved back into the densely wooded terrain behind the small village of Maisoncelles. Now these detachments lay across the country as far as could be seen, though it was difficult to know where enemy ended and trees began.

'Lord Jesu!' Hungerford's voice was choked with cold and emotion. 'Sire, the Gascon didn't lie. We are outmatched four to one. Would to God we had ten thousand more bowmen!'

There was something almost rapt about the cadaverous smile that touched the red-brown eyes as Henry said:

'By Heaven's grace on whom I have relied for my victory I would not, if I could, increase our number by one. For those whom I have are the people of God!'

He rose from his seat, lean and vibrant, looking older than his twenty-eight years.

'Do you not believe that the Almighty with these, his humble few, is able to conquer the haughty opposition that waits so proudly out there?'

He held up the crown close to his eyes, so that the jewels ran into rainbow prisms and the pearls glowed like running tears. 'Tonight, we move down into the valley, south of the trees. I feel that Almighty God planted those trees for a purpose. He has us all in his protection. When the men are encamped again, I shall go and tell them so.'

George Benet, master cordwainer, worked under canvas while the rain drummed above. With a long curved needle he drove into Cordovan morocco leather, fashioning the last eyelet through which gold laces would pass, and trimming the edge with minute stitches. He worked close to a tiny light shielded from the midnight world outside by his crouching apprentice. Finally he laid down the supple shoes fashioned for a man's slim light feet, and sighed deeply. The apprentice gave a sudden bellowing sneeze.

'Quiet, you knave. Do you want to lose your right ear?'

Absolute silence had been ordered through this night, on pain of ear-lopping for inferior persons and loss of horse and armour for any knight. At sundown the tense, excitable army had been shouting around the village, looking for billets and bedding, the armourers racketing with hammer and file, even the animals infected with noisy anxiety.

'His Grace wants the French to think we've run away. Keep your carcass over that light!' He stroked the soles of the little shoes. 'Fine work, although I say it . . .' Next moment he was hastily on his feet, managing to kick the youth into a kneeling position at the same time. The King's face materialized, ghostly between the weak glint of shaded lanterns. He was in half-armour, and smiling.

'How goes it, Master Benet?'

'You do me great honour, Sire.'

Henry said to the apprentice, 'Get up, child. Are you ready for the morrow?'

The youth, who had never before been so close to the sovereign, nodded dumbly. While Benet marvelled: out of all this host of servants he remembered my name! Henry's eyes were benign, with a look so calm it was almost of fulfilment.

'Are you busy?'

'There's much mending to do after the march, your Grace. But these – ' he pushed the new shoes forward shyly – 'are holy work.'

Henry studied them in the gloom, touching them with tender curiosity.

'Beautiful,' he said.

'Tomorrow – today now,' murmured Benet, 'is our patron's day, the Guild will be performing in London. These shoes would have been worn by the man who plays Our Lord. But I have made them anyway in honour of the saint.' With hanging head: 'I would deem it greater honour if your Grace would accept them as a gift of love.'

In the dimness, sudden tears burned Henry's eyes. I have marched them, worked them to death and near death, and still they speak of love. He said steadily: 'We are pleased and we will cherish them. But you will live to make me many more pairs of shoes. You know that God is with us and will never desert us?'

Benet bowed his head. Withdrawing into the blackness and the rain, the King said: 'My calendar is out of sorts after this march. What day is it? Which saint has you in his care?'

Benet smiled proudly. 'We have two, my liege, both shoemakers. Today is Saint Crispin and Crispinian.'

Through the soaking dark and the quiet lines he moved on. His foot brushed against a threadbare soldier, lying curled against a fire of dead ashes, his bare feet in a pool of rain. He never stirred, his exhausted face was bland as the dead. Scores of similar shapes littered Henry's progress. Their longbows were stacked close at hand; they lay with arms clasped about sheaves of arrows and the sharp stake each had carried for eight days was planted nearby in the ground. Further on a man knelt upright in the mud, whispering urgently to a priest. Henry passed them stealthily, his head averted. What sin could that man have, to look so sorrowful? Could he bear a burden as great as mine? My children. My people of God. He trod carefully so as not to disturb the sleepers as he went.

Towards the end of the line a smith quietly sharpened daggers and a dozen bowmen were notching their arrows and waxing their strings with goose-grease. He stopped and spoke to them.

'I shall not forget your prowess at Harfleur, your tenacity and courage during these last weeks. Now the Almighty has you in his hand. Today, tomorrow, and for ever.'

They shivered in their ragged loose shirts, wondering how soon they might see the Almighty face to face. Yet, at the serene rapt smile that bade them goodnight, much of their fear abated.

In Gloucester's pavilion the Duke was wakeful, uneasy. He

motioned a page for wine for Henry but the King declined, dismissing pages and guard. Humphrey drained a goblet.

'You drink overmuch,' said the King.

'I heard something earlier that set me drinking,' said his brother. 'The French have painted a cart in which they plan to parade you captive through the streets of Paris! After they've finished the throat-cutting!'

Henry said mildly: 'Tomorrow they will be the captives. Have you no faith?'

'I'm full of faith,' said Humphrey, and poured more wine.

'I spoke to Erpingham. He's a good and great commander, so sagacious. We are agreed that combat must be joined as soon after dawn as possible. I cannot waste the men another day. They are debilitated already. A few more hours will finish them. My last challenge to be allowed to pass unhindered to Calais has been refused. So, by God, there *will* be throat-cutting on Crispin's Day, and ours will be the blades!'

Humphrey knelt to kiss his brother's hand. 'My life and sword are yours,' he said. He sighed. 'By my faith, I know not why, Harry, but I am comforted.'

Henry left him and walked on, flanked by his escort. Two figures approached, and did him homage.

'Davydd ap Llewellyn ap Hywel here, Sire. We were seeking your Grace. My scurrier brings news from within the French camp.'

'They're merry, Sire,' said the scout. 'But that you can hear for yourself.' Across the half-mile of country, tossed on the rainy wind, came shouts, laughter, the barking of dogs, and music, a flageolet's weird high wail and the heartbeat throb of a tabor. Roaring campfires glowed on the skyline.

'I hid in the Tramecourt woods, then penetrated their lines. It was quite easy. Then I caught a boy.' Grimly: 'I persuaded him to sing to me.'

'Tell me.'

'They are magnificently arrayed. Some knights are so proud that they are spending the night in the saddle rather than foul their harness in the mud. There's at least ninety pounds of steel on their backs. They look like giants, not men.'

'Ninety pounds!' said Henry thoughtfully.

'Ay, Sire. And I heard of their plan for the archers. They are to be killed or sold in bunches of twenty as slaves. All left living are to have three fingers of their right hand severed so that they may nevermore draw a bow.'

'Now tell me of the commanders.'

'Boucicaut, d'Albret. The Dukes of Orléans, Alençon and Bar, Bourbon and Berry. The Counts of Eu and Richemont, Sir Ferry de Lorraine, the Sire de Heilly, Guillaume Martel, Ganiot de Bournonville. Others, a chivalry too numerous to name.'

'What of Burgundy?'

'The story goes that Jean sans Peur wished to attend a christening feast and may not be here for days. His young brother, Anthony, Duke of Brabant is still awaited, but his son, Philip, has been forbidden the affray.'

'Go on.'

'Something else, Sire. There is much rivalry and disorder. A general feeling of rebellion. Even the card-players form factions and curse one another in the name of whoever is their master.'

Discipline! Indiscipline! He thought: again their weakness. That vast disparate army! And what commander could do what I have done, enforce this blessed stillness, these muted lights and fires, this constant watch and ward?

'Are they well fed and well provisioned?'

'Yes, Sire. And they know that we starve.'

Henry gave a grim chuckle. 'So! We'll deepen our silence. Let them think we have pined and withered where we lie. You have done more than well and you shall be rewarded. Remember now that God is with us. Never, never doubt.'

Davy Gam said in soft wonderment: '*Duw annwyl!* Your Grace is an inspiration . . .' He knelt and took the hem of Henry's sodden cloak to his lips.

He was moved again, but gave no sign.

'It will soon be dawn. I shall complete my progress and then put on my *côte d'armes.*'

He went on to where the horses were quartered, most of them lying down with the grooms snuggled beside them for warmth. In the gloom a great white stallion shone like a ghost. It turned to him knowingly, dropping its nose into his hand.

'Fear nothing,' he told the stable-boys, the baggage-boys and farriers. 'All will be well.'

Almost at the end of his progress he came on Owen, standing rigid in the lee of a tent, his hand curled tightly about his longbow. Owen had forgotten that once he had been told he would always be safe. There was room for nothing but this crippling fear. He hardly noticed when the King came forward to speak to him.

'You're afraid,' Henry said softly.

'*Duw a'n cymorth!*' Owen whispered.

'Amen.' The King's voice was grave. 'And He *will* help us indeed. *Cymerwch nerth oddiwrth Dduw a byddwch ddewr!*' And turned to include his own escort, repeating: 'Have courage; take strength from God!'

He thought as he walked away: Almighty, spare him. My good talisman, with his little sycamore harp!

With dawn, the rain ceased suddenly as if satisfied with a havoc of wet clothes and sneezes. For three hours both armies had been drawn up at the appointed place on Artois plain, the English in a field of young corn, the French flanked by the woodland less than a mile to the north. As they waited the day brightened and some small birds alighted to peck among the furrows deepened by the horses' feet.

Henry sat on a little grey pony and stared across the field. Behind him a page held the snow-white destrier, groomed to a glassy sheen, its housings blue and gold, golden tassels hanging from its bridle. A little way off was Edward, Duke of York, commanding the adjoining vanguard to the right, while on the left a keen-eyed knight, Lord Camoys, watched with them. His horse was restive, his nerves taut as wet hemp. Henry had chosen Camoys to lead the left attack with soldiers brought up from the rear. Thus three main bodies formed the vanguard. The men stood four deep behind the commanders, quilled with an assortment of killing-tools: lances, clubs, spiked maces and axes. Small deadly knives were thrust through their belts and some carried a sharp double-edged sword. Interspersed with these three bodies were the archers, drawn up in wedge-shaped groups each like a half-diamond, the base line steady, the sides of the apex trimmed to a hair. On either wing of the company more archers formed flanks curving inwards, ready to encircle a charging enemy. The tall bows bristled beside their heads, their waists were crammed with arrows and beside each man the stout sharp stake was planted firm.

Lord Camoys's horse reared and he fought its restlessness with a soothing oath. He had not expected the honour of commanding the left advance. During the night he and others had ridden to reconnoitre the field of battle, reporting it as fairly favourable to Henry.

'I had thought your Grace's brother would be in my place,' he said, still struggling with his plunging mount.

Henry said, never taking his eyes from the distant French line: 'My lord of Gloucester will do well in the rearguard. Once it begins he will come forward and reinforce us.'

He continued to stare, incredulity growing in him. Not at the vastness of the French force which this morning looked greater than yesterday, but at the position in which they were drawn up. To their left the Tramecourt woods sprawled densely; even closer to their right another thick wood on a little hill girdled some farm dwellings and a derelict-looking castle.

'Sweet Jesu, mercy!' he said under his breath. 'God *did* plant those trees to a purpose!'

Camoys looked hard where the King looked.

'Can they not realize?' said Henry softly. 'They are so many!'

'They're proud,' said Camoys.

'The first deadly sin. See how the cannon on their flanks is hindered, almost masked by woodland!'

'And the mangonels and arblasts . . . they should be placed well clear . . .'

'And look how the knights are bunched together in the front line!'

They were so close that it seemed a solid wall of silver-grey confronted the observers, intermittently blazoned with colours of shameless loveliness: purple, jade, bright mustard gold, rich cerise, sapphire, and azure and leaf green. Central to this bouquet of beauty and steel the oriflamme tossed, a scarlet vein glistening as its bearer moved flauntingly about. The standards of so many lords and dukes seemed to outnumber the common soldiery by ten to one. The first two lines of dismounted pikemen stood six deep, while small companies of archers stood at intervals between them. Behind the foot-soldiers were the cavalry on mounts unarmoured save for gay silk housings.

'Can you ascertain who commands each party? Describe the standards if you will,' Henry said, as the French colours billowed clearer in a light wind.

'To their right vanguard: Bourbon. Then d'Albret, Bouci-caut . . .' Camoys strained to see. 'Now, here's another standard . . . jostling to join the first battalion – the Duke of Orléans, I think, and on the end, my lord of Eu. Rearward . . . Vendôme commands their left . . . many more, Lammartin, or it could be St Pol . . . and Marle, or Fauquemberghes . . . many more. Too many.' He shook his head, half blinded from interpreting the colours at a distance, and when he looked at the King the whites of his eyes were bloodily veined.

Henry's gaze wandered away to the left. 'What is that village and castle, westward?'

'They call it Agincourt, your Grace.'

Henry looked again at the French army. 'What vainglory!' Then, with a chilling laugh: 'And see how the woods hem it in!'

He turned to gaze at his own lords and captains heading the neat taut wedges of footsoldiers and bowmen. A sense of completion that was almost joy rose in him at sight of their good battle order, their quiet controlled stance, the undisputing loyalty which seemed to shine from them. Sir Gilbert Umfra-ville, Sir John Cornwall, Edward of York, Sir John Greyndon, Suffolk, inheritor of his dead father's earldom since Harfleur, Dorset and Oxford, Humphrey of Gloucester, now looking fresh and unworried. Sir Walter Hungerford and priceless Erpingham. Sir John Holland. Davydd ap Llewellyn ap Hywel.

But no Clarence, no Arundel, no dear Courtenay. And no loving traitors, either. Again he surveyed his army. Not only the captains but those who had marched or ridden starving jades over two hundred and sixty miles at his bidding. Waiting, tattered, bareheaded, shoeless, the leather having rotted like that of their gloves. Some wore no breeches at all, their bare buttocks were red and rain-chapped as the wind lifted their shirts. These and the Irish contingent gave the party an occasional nude savagery not unpleasing in the circumstances. The sergeants and captains had chain hauberks and the less dilapidated of the archers still had black jackets lined with mail. It was a beggar's army, until one looked at the faces. Under the streaked mud there was no fear, only an unbearable impatience. And with this bold hankering came nobility.

Integrated with the rest were the Household craftsmen, those who oiled the wheels of this rough life. Like Allbright Mailmaker with his serving armourers, John Covyn, Sergeant of the royal tents and pavilions and his attendant yeomen. The surgeons, doctors and leeches. John Waterton, Master of Horse, and Gerard de la Strade who had groomed to its present glory the white beast waiting behind the King. Guy Midelton and John Milton, who guided Henry through the lines by night on his progress of comfort. Richard Berre and his saddlers. Carpenters and labourers. John Feriby, Clerk of the Wardrobe. George Benet, master cordwainer. Almoners: Thomas Bridde and Estephin Payn. John de Bordin, Doctor in Laws, with his clerk and archers. And rolling to join the waiting ranks were the baggage carts from Maisoncelles with the pack-mules and men too sick to fight. In attendance were the Household priests: Dean Esmon Lacy with his chaplains, friars and the young weary priests for whom the long night had been heavy with the grief of penitent men.

The minstrels: John Cliffe, Tom Norys Tromper, Panel and Peut Tromper, Richard Pyper, and his brothers Meysham and Broune, Snaith Fidler, Thomas Hardiberd, with trumpets, fifes, shawms and drums. Henry had listened to their sweetness in times of waiting. Now they would scream of glory or death, beside the banners of the three royal heralds, Leicester,

Guienne and Ireland, and the great standard of Antelope Pursuivant.

Vested for the Mass, behind a great gold cross, the Dean approached, leading chaplains carrying the Pyx and Eucharist. Singing-boys began a chant, their voices icy on the thin breeze. Cloud-filtered sunlight touched the Cross, the gold mitre, the chasubles. Henry dismounted and took off his mantle. He was revealed in magnificence. He wore full armour, its silver burnished to blue. Over it lay his *côte d'armes*, bright with the leopards and fleurs-de-lys of England and France. The priests began to pray loudly, as he had instructed. About their feet, one small bird still pecked fearlessly in the furrows.

'Remember us, O Lord! Our enemies are gathered together and boast in their might. Scatter their strength and disperse them, that they may know that there is none other that fighteth for us, but only Thou, O God.'

'Amen.' The word resounded deep in thousands of throats. In that moment every man was sinless, without will or desire other than to be led, lying between the great pale hands of fate. The Mass wound its sonorous coil about the King. He received the Sacrament; in his lifted face the full red lips shone like a wound. Then he rose and his body-servants crowned him with helm and diadem. The jewels gave grace to the morning, glittering blue and carmine and pearl. There was a little gasp from the men. Mounted on the white horse, his sword was placed in his hand. In the ranks there was silence, while his words came forth in a roar.

'Hear me, all of ye! I am come into France to recover my lawful inheritance. In this quarrel ye may surely and freely fight. Remember! that ye were born in England's great realm where your fathers and wives and children now dwell, and there ye must strive to return with great glory and fame. As the Kings of England before me have gained many noble victories over the French, so must each man do his utmost to preserve his honour and that of the crown of England!

'Archers! Noble archers! Hear me!' The bright brown eyes snapped and came alight with wilful red. 'Have ye heard what this vainglorious host plan for your shame?'

As he told them they looked down involuntarily at their right hands, at the fingers already tried and sentenced to mutilation. Murmuring arose. It grew, a running storm of outrage, and, as the taunt was passed on, burgeoned into a sound like the snarl of a winter wolf.

He waited, then continued even louder:

'This haughty company speak also of selling back my great lords and earls to England. And I choose death! rather than charge England with the payment of my ransom! But first, I choose victory. I will hold those who boast and threaten themselves to ransom! I charge ye all to do the same!'

The wolves were wild now, the clamour growing; men in the rearguard who could not hear had the King's words passed back and a new reverberation of wrathful excitement was flung back and forth on the fringes of the army. Owen, trembling but now completely unafraid, sat his horse near to Davydd Gam. A hobelar lurched his mount in between them, saying with a mouth made toothless by the bad diet yet full of rapture: 'Ransom, eh? I'll get me a fine French lord, and see myself right for life!'

New heart came into the men, a bursting ambition. They forgot their pathetic gear, their cold bare feet and heads. The naked Irishmen cursed in their own weird tongue, while the whole army strained to see the arrogant mystery which menaced them and whose downfall they now ardently desired.

'Give no quarter!' the King was yelling. 'Slay as if they were the Infidel! Our cause is that of God!'

Across the boggy field, the French continued to stand, with banner upon banner nudging one another so closely that at times they became locked together in warring colours. It was a legion of steel. The myriad counts and dukes were living carapaces, encased from head to foot in bolted metal. Their great helmets bore chain aventails riveted at the base, imprisoning the wearer's neck. Steel plate cast about legs met steel boots at the ankle. Hands in gloves of boiled leather were further weighted by mailed gauntlets. Shining elbow-joints met thick rings of chain mail and merged into steel rivets at the shoulder. Within this metal might, the sweat streamed down. Yet the knights looked jealously at one another, nudging their horses forward, so that each individual's pride could be viewed to the full, and old grudges cooled by being first in line. The front rank undulated like a steelbound serpent. The first battalion broke and fragmented, reforming untidily as tempers surged. The archers, trying to maintain their battle order, found themselves forced into chaos by the thrusting nobles, and the flanking gunners were driven outwards nearer to the trees. With each jostle, the horses plunged fetlock-deep into the mud.

His exhortation finished, Henry waited while half an hour dragged by. Behind him his army lay quiet again though still vibrant; before him the distant play of coloured movement continued, indecisive.

He called for Sir Thomas Erpingham.

'Why do they wait?'

Erpingham said: 'Maybe they remember Quintus Fabius Maximus . . .'

'To harass us to defeat without a battle?'

'Ay. That the mere sight of their glory will drive us to run!'

'By the God of Heaven, we will run!' said Henry. 'Now! Towards them! Will you ready the bowmen, my lord?'

Twenty years seemed to drop from Erpingham. He turned and rode to the archers. At his sergeants' commands the wedges tightened still further. Each elbow formed an angle as the first arrow was notched. Sir Thomas smiled encouragingly as he went among the men. Then he threw his marshal's baton high and cried: '*Nestroque!*' the word of approval and intent. The King and his lords dismounted; the horses were led back through the ranks. In the forefront the royal standard was raised. The light wind caught and flexed it firm. The entire army dipped and knelt, each man signing the sodden ground with the cross and taking a handful of mud to his lips: 'As I, O God, came of dust, let this be thy sacrament, and should I fall, let me return to Him who made me . . .'

'Banners advance! In the name of Jesus, Mary, St George!'

The trumpets sounded in blood-freezing indisputable assent. The call shivered the flesh of even the men in the sick-tents, who raised their heads to curse or pray. Then, moving at a light march over the field, the advance in its three tight divisions went forward, seeming to diminish in size the nearer it came to the monstrous wall of steel ahead.

The small bird abandoned its furrow and took to the air. For a while it flew above the advance, singing, irrelevant, benign.

As the gap between the two armies narrowed to within bowshot range it could be seen that the front line of the enemy had dismounted and stood, solidly mailed, weapons in hand, shining feet dulled at last in the liquid mud. The faces beneath the great helmets became defined. Ruddy and white, clean-shaven or lushly moustached, aloof or expressionless. Behind the leaders the deep rows of footsoldiers clustered untidily, each groping for a place. Horsemen were riding round from the rear to reinforce the wings where the cream of the horseflesh waited; tall fine-blooded destriers like those who had flattened Henry's archers at Corbie. Hampered by the pushing of the nobles, the bowmen in between were still trying to maintain battle order. They carried iron crossbows with intricate gaffles and winders; there was not a longbow to be seen. The English advanced to within three hundred yards, and Charles d'Albret issued the battle-cry.

'*Montjoie! St Denis!*'

The scarlet oriflamme beat the air. The steel wall moved forward, the silver serpent ready to become a lunging fish. Across the gap Erpingham cried a command and a trumpet sounded staccato like a hunting horn. In dense, light-running waves, the archers swept forward with their sharpened stakes, planting them deep at an angle in the ground, like wicked extra warriors pointing towards the enemy. The *chevaux de frise* were formed, standing firm from the incurving flanks to the centre where the bowmen, now back in their places, were deployed between the King and his lords, with space to draw the fletch back to the cheek and feel the sixty pounds' weight of the hauled string.

Owen stood sideways, aligned with his fellows, his right arm crooked in the hold, the fingers of his left hand firmly about the wood. He bent his left knee and dug the other heel deep in the slime. The bow felt sweet, smooth as the harp. Through half-closed eyes he measured the silver monster. It blurred and heaved with teeth, claws. He whispered: 'The *Twrch Trwyth*!' The Giant Boar: he knew his enemy at last.

Further up the line John Page steadied the notch on the hemp and gasped under the prolonged hold. Lines of un-written verse, never to be remembered, scurried through him. His weeping was done for the moment and his eyes were as hard as any.

Humphrey of Gloucester gripped his lance, gazed at the sumptuous banners and guessed at the jewels. He longed to rush forward, seize the oriflamme standard from Guillaume Martel and beat about him until the noblemen fell apart like dolls, rained jewels and gold and ransoms . . . Harry! I should be leading this affray!

Davydd ap Llewellyn ap Hywel murmured from a bloody mind: Grand they are. Have at them. Eh, Lord of Sycharth, my old one? Under this brave mad prince I do battle, but in my heart it's for the honour of Wales. D'you hear, Glyn Dŵr?

Lord Camoys settled his bascinet more firmly on his head and cleared his eyes with a gloved hand. He saw his home, the park beyond the moat in Oxfordshire, where the fallow deer grazed. That pasture had never been tilled, it was thick with thyme and mint and marjoram, feeding the sweetest venison in England. He thought, with love: may my son cherish that meadow. May it bloom aromatic for a thousand years. Let me see my heritage, Stonor, again: let my son be braver than I feel today . . .

Suffolk found difficulty in breathing. For courage he had drunk a lot of wine last night. Bad wine had killed his father at Harfleur. His blood pounded, his face grew hot with dread.

Edward of York tried to count the weapons opposite him. Some of the French knights had broken their lances off short for more fighting space, yet still mailed shoulder brushed mailed shoulder. He noticed a spot of rust on his own sword. Armourers grow slovenly, he thought.

Erpingham watched his archers with pride. They would stay poised until they broke under the tension. Old battles filled him. Crécy, Poitiers; what had the French learned from them? What else beside the Fabian tactics from that great commander Bertrand Duguesclin? Have they control over their men as I have over mine? And he knew the answer, and smiled.

In the sky over the woods, the King saw St George. He saw him plainly. His head was bare, his sword raised. The bloody cross on his white surcoat was mirrored by cloud and repeated below on the breasts of the men-at-arms. It was enough. He raised his arm to Erpingham. The trumpets screamed again. The sky became black with surging English arrows.

It was as if night had blown up on a tumult of rushing wind, or a million migrating birds flying at top speed, filling air and shadowing earth, their noise almost drowning the yells in the weird darkness – *Montjoie! For Harry! For Jesus! A Denis!* From the French wings came a stutter of cannon-fire and a score of stone balls split the English flanks and a few men fell, but the razor-tipped arrows were finding their mark. They were aimed at faces or where the mail was weakest, at the join of neck and shoulder, elbow or knee. Some of the French took the barbs on their helmets, but many were directly hit, in eye or brow or gullet. Sire Ferry de Lorraine, who had pushed forward to fight near Charles of Orléans, took an arrow in the forehead. Its impact penetrated the steel behind his skull by inches and he fell backwards, a big man made giant by the weight of his mail. He crashed down upon two knights behind him and bore them down with him into the mud. Entombed by the steel shells they wore, they could not rise, but lay crushed, lashing their weighted limbs feebly. In the sight of this and similar calamities the French began their advance in earnest. A further rain of arrows hurtled from the English longbows. The French crossbowmen, cramped in line and hindered by the mechanics of their weapons, tried to reply; they fumbled with crankins and winders, cursing their adversaries' speed and skill.

The French cavalry moved forward at a lumbering gallop, a great ruthless force erupting from the wings and gathering speed. The horses' hides, the blinding colours and gold embellishments sparkled, themselves a battle cry. Grimly

209

the archers continued firing, with the precise threefold drill of Notch! Stretch! Loose! their muscles waxing and waning beneath their scarecrow garments. And the sky was black again with sharp-tipped rain, while the mounted host thundered down, intent on crushing once and for all these despised ones. They were unworthy to do battle with the chivalry of France, yet their gadfly shafts had a sting.

They had nearly reached their goal when the leaders saw the *chevaux de frise*, which at a distance had blended with the surrounding clay. The knight commander, trying desperately to haul in his spurred excited horse, turned in the saddle to scream a warning. At that instant an arrow thudded into his temple and he fell forward while his horse died under him, spitted through the heart by twelve inches of wood. The others thundered up close behind, the riders tearing vainly on the bridles as impetus carried the charge on to the stakes and the horses began to scream, terrible, womanly cries. They plunged with breasts and bellies impaled, spouting jets of arterial blood over the English archers, bolting in agony with the stakes still in them, running in all directions, disembowelled. Nearly all the riders were thrown heavily. One knight crashed at Owen's feet. Cast like a giant insect, immobilized by countless pounds of armour, he stared into Owen's glazed and naked face. All around writhed a chaos of shrieking beasts and groaning men. One great stallion, dragging its rider by the stirrup, ran through the wedge of archers and fell in a welter of blood near the King and his Household. Clawing at the mud and his own harness, the chevalier at Owen's feet tried desperately to rise. Someone thrust an axe into Owen's hand and yelled unintelligibly. He struck down hard across the French knight's gasping throat. The great steel shape heaved and stilled.

All around, the archers had cast down their bows and were snatching up other weapons, some dropped by the French, swords, daggers, maces, and with these they laid about them, smashing faces, stabbing between rivets at neck and armpit, raising clubs dripping with blood and brains to beat down on the glorious force that had been rendered defenceless by its own armour. Some were dead already, crushed by their mounts or by the weight of those who had fallen on top of them. Others writhed haplessly on the ground, to be killed or dragged away by groups of bowmen to the sergeant in charge of ransoms. For there was gold here as well as blood, although the cream of the nobility still waited beyond the mêlée. Erpingham strode up and down the line restoring order, his surcoat bloodstained, his mouth tight. He quelled any premature rejoicing, and again the trumpets sounded.

Now approaching, the rolling columns of footsoldiers marshalled under the banner of d'Albret seemed wider and greater than ever. Although their forward march was fragmented by wounded men, refugees from the first charge who staggered back among them, and maddened horses crashing in and out of their lines, they came on at a steady rush. Back in their formation, the English bowmen loosed a fresh salvo of great accuracy which checked the enemy approach, although even as these began to fall a fresh force could be seen in the distance and behind this a further row of horsemen standing to arms where the woods began. Yet the trees grew where the French advance progressed, driving the ranks closer together, blocking them in, whereas Henry's army occupied a wide field. The detachments of archers were free to run, deploying themselves to an outward advantage, moving swiftly, halting to fire at the sides of the approaching columns, catching the weaknesses in the armour, and again, the French who fell brought down their companions by sheer proximity so that they lay piled in helpless drifts of steel.

Yet wave after wave came on, and Henry went forth in gladness to meet them. On either side he heard the humming song of the arrows. Psalms ran in his head. Ice-cold, flanked by his Household, he strode forward, the flamecrossed surcoat of St George still etched on his mind and his banners. Endeavour blazed about him as the jewelled crown circled his helm in shimmering approval. Ice-cold he was, yet he burned to prove himself in skill and prowess, this day, tomorrow, for ever. The knights about him, taut with dedication, drew nearer to their charge, feeling the bounding rhythms of his zeal. He went towards the shining close-packed death like a lover to his bride. The hoarse shouts of *Montjoie!* were music. He was jewelled, lean, starved almost to ecstasy, and, like the knights who ran beside him, ready for death or honour yet at the same time able to judge how the royally hatched front line of the new advance, heavy with weapons, was already being forced into a conglomerate horde. The archers continued to fire an irrepressible storm at its flanks and the trees crowded inwards. The ducal host, doubly encompassed, nudged and bolstered one another and the sounds of mail plunging upon mail were heard over the battle-cries. There was a subtle desperation in those cries. Henry heard it and communicated it with a wild look, a terse comment, to the running men who tried to shield him.

Bourbon, d'Albret, Boucicaut, and Eu. These were the shapely bright standards charging through the mud, and with them Charles d'Orléans (he recognized the peacock feathers and broom), and then a tide of steel smashed down, many, too many for anyone's good. Under the powerful impact, the English line swayed and fell back. The shock ran through three detachments from Lord Camoys to the Duke of York, but the main collision was sustained by the King's party. Henry, clearly marked by his gold helm and crown, howled a challenge; he raised his sword and laid about him, while his Household whirled their axes protectively, cleaving hands from wrists, embedding blades in faces, moving like dancers to avoid the rushing unwieldy onslaught. The noise was like a thousand blacksmiths at work as the lightly clad Englishmen struck at the writhing sea of armour all about them. The cries of *Montjoie!* diminished, and the English line surged forward again, pressing the steel giants still harassed by the bowmen and crushed in upon one another by the trees. Their cannon were silent; their crossbowmen, pushed sideways, had ceased trying to load their antique weapons. By now the knights themselves were so crushed and hindered that they could find neither space nor strength to lift their arms. The charge had become like the butting of a hornless bull.

Impotently they thrashed about, began to stumble and fall. The entire line, off balance, panicked as it tried to parry the blows hammering from all sides. Under an assault from Lord Camoys's party twenty fell, some not even wounded but swiftly suffocating beneath piled armed bodies. The assault looked like a house of cards, brushed by a wanton hand. Cheering rose from the archers, who, maddened by prowess, left their places again to join the affray. Owen, his jacket stiff with blood, went to work with an axe and a broken lance. Davy Gam, his one eye like a fiend's, smashed three French knights to the ground with a broadsword as if he were lopping daffodils in Tanat Vale. Everywhere the mud was reddening in runnels and lakes where mailed feet slithered; the archers' bare legs were scarlet and the naked Irishmen, yammering their war-lust, looked as if they had rolled in a slaughterhouse. Soon deep piles of French corpses towered higher than a man's head. The bowmen leaped to scale these pyramids, to strike downwards, then swoop like buzzards to cut the throats of those who lay groaning. Strewn among the carnage were hundreds of weapons and pieces of armour. The mighty advance, ruined by its own splendour, was no more, and across the clearing field, a horde of French were in retreat.

Suddenly a brave further flock swept down, blundering through the mailed mounds, seeking with grunts and oaths to strike at the nimble bowmen who were smashing about with halberds and spiked maces. A party of knights, led by Brunelet de Masinguëhen and Ganiot de Bournonville made for the King. De Masinguëhen's sword, its hilt flashing with gems, arched through Henry's bodyguard, killing one of the House-hold knights and landing obliquely on the King's helm, denting the gold and slicing off one of the fleurons on the crown. His head ringing, Henry growled in fury and lashed out. Two knights went down, and the bodyguard redoubled their strokes, fighting shoulder to shoulder with the King, killing and maiming until the danger was past. Henry's slight figure seemed to be in all places at once, battling with a speed and surety weirdly inspired; a sliver of a man richly possessed by elementals.

It was becoming difficult to move about the field as fresh heaps of slain gathered. The archers were looting, tearing off gauntlets to snatch jewels from fingers, taking the fingers themselves in grim reprisal for the enemy's earlier threat. Prisoners were being led away to be ransomed. Among the prizes were Marshal Boucicaut, speechless with disbelieving horror, the Duke of Bourbon, the Counts of Richemont, Eu and Vendôme. Taken personally by Henry's escort was Charles, Duke of Orléans. Unhelmed, he knelt, his young face glacial as a sleepwalker's.

'*Alors! mon cousin!*' said Henry, and smiled terribly.

'I yield,' whispered the Duke.

At that moment a clamour arose at the King's left side. A fresh force had arrived, led by the Duke of Alençon, who had galloped off to apprehend the deserters and now rode fast with them through the pockets of combat towards Humphrey of Gloucester, who was joyfully beating the brains from the escort of the Count of Fauquemberghes. One of Alençon's knights thrust low with a dagger. It slid under the plates of Humphrey's cuirass and into his belly, and he was down. Instantly Henry grasped the situation. He whirled and sprang, gathering men as he went, between the little groups of combatants. His escort ran with him and others followed the call of his trumpeters and his own hoarse cry: '*M'aidez!*' Among these were Davy Gam and Owen. They plunged into the mêlée surrounding Humphrey's prone figure and closed with the men about to administer the *coup de grâce*. Owen's axe half-severed a man's arm at the shoulder. Davy was laughing as he struck and stabbed, drawing the attack away from Humphrey, who groaned as he was carried out of danger. Owen heard Davy cursing in Welsh, laughing again, pounding with a mace at a man who came with raised blade at the King, hacking at another's face until it exploded in a fountain of blood. They fought one on either side of the King, shielding him to the tune of Davy's fiendish laughter which was suddenly cut off short. From behind a Frenchman had drawn his knife halfway across Davy's throat, plunging it deep into the great vein at the angle of his jaw.

Humphrey's assailants had been routed, and the Duke of Alençon, instigator of the fight and wounded, came limping towards Henry, sword in hand.

'I yield . . .' he began, and Henry stretched out his hand in assent. One of the Household, blind with zeal and seeing only the drawn sword, leaped between them, axe spinning. Alençon's head bounced like a bauble on the ground.

Owen knelt by Davy Gam. He drew his head on to his shoulder, and pressed his hands over the awful wound, but the blood gushed through his fingers and soaked him, running down his arm on to his chest. Davy's one darkening eye searched outwards. Owen bent near his lips and watched them say: 'Good fight, *bach. Duw annwyl!* . . . my prince . . .'

A shadow fell across them; Owen looked up at the King's haggard bloodflecked face.

'He saved my noble brother. Is the surgeon coming? The priest?' Then he heard the bloodfilled whisper.

'How goes the battle?'

'I think the day is ours. Through God and those like you. I salute your valour, Davydd ap Llewellyn ap Hywel.'

With his sword he touched the dying man on either shoulder.

'In the Name of the Father, Son and Holy Ghost, I create thee a knight.' His voice was overlaid by the murmuring of the priest who knelt at Davy's head.

'Today . . . we were all your slaves,' Davy whispered joyously, and died.

The final assaults occurred at noon after a lull in which hundreds of kites and big black crows, fighting raucously among themselves, came down to feast upon the dead. They rose in a dark storm before the sudden late arrival of the Duke of Brabant.

He came hastily to face the unbelievable carnage he now saw for the first time. Directly contravening the orders of Jean sans Peur, and bringing a few Burgundian knights, he joined the battle with all the followers he could muster from the third line of mounted men who watched uncertainly beyond the trees. He saw some knights of Charles of Orléans in retreat as he hastened upon the field, and cried to them to join him. The leaders stared at him without recognition. Brabant's haste had caused him to forget his *côte d'armes.* So he cried: '*Je suis Brabant! M'aidez!*'

'*Nous sommes Armagnacs,*' the cold hard answer came back. 'We do not fight for Burgundy.'

Brabant, appalled but unsurprised, cast round for something to wear over his armour. He seized a trumpet from one of his heralds. The colours of its banner were similar to his own. He slashed a hole in the cloth and struggled into the makeshift tabard, then bravely led a charge forward, straight into a mêlée dominated by Henry. Within minutes he was unhorsed, his person given over to a grinning footsoldier, and most of his men dying in their blood.

The looting continued. All over the field the English had given up the fight, and, drunk with incredulous rapture, were sitting at ease on the prone steelcased forms of their prisoners. Smoke drifted from the villages of Tramecourt and Agincourt, where the houses harbouring fugitives had been set on fire under the command of Sir John Cornwall. From one dwelling a figure, wounded in the leg, erupted, rolling almost beneath Sir John's feet.

'Sire Gilbert de Lannoy,' he gasped. 'I am yours. My ransom is set at twelve thousand crowns.'

There was a great warhorse tethered nearby. Jewels winked from its bridle.

'Twelve thousand, and the horse.'

The chevalier nodded gratefully. '*Oui*. Save me, for the love of God!' Cornwall's esquires helped the wounded knight away.

Meanwhile, having witnessed the Duke of Brabant's brave charge and been inspired by it, Marle and Fauquemberghes, their forces much depleted, were riding round recruiting those who had dropped from the fight. It was not easy. Just as Burgundians would not do battle under Armagnac, those who had lost their commanders refused to serve under any other banner. Gascons, Bretons and Poitevins threw down their arms. In all the company finally gathered numbered scarcely six hundred but with these the two Dukes, inflamed and vengeful, spurred forward. The English army was surprised, just as it had been earlier when the baggage wagons, abandoned by sentries mindful only of looting, had been plundered by some French villagers. A jewel chest was gone and some of Humphrey's precious library, and an ornamental sword. News of this dereliction of duty was brought to Henry just as the fresh attack from Marle and Fauquemberghes began. He sent for Erpingham, safe steady Erpingham, peppered all over with blood but unscathed. Henry himself looked a hundred years old; his face was like a bleached bone.

'This will not do!' he said wildly. 'The men are growing negligent. Their minds are full of ransoms, not fighting.'

'Your Grace promised them ransoms.'

Henry glanced towards the skirmishes: Edward of York was battling strongly against Charles d'Albret whom all had thought slain. Further left Lord Camoys closed in a bout with the Duke of Marle. But elsewhere there was indolence; men ringed their hostages and gloated like yokels at a country fair.

'Now I must disappoint them,' he said. He gave a command to the sergeant. Groans of fury followed.

'Kill the prisoners!' Henry said, short-breathed. 'I promised ransoms; I also promised throat-cutting. But spare the nobility!'

The Duke of Brabant, wealthy, royal yet unrecognizable in his strange garment, stared into his captor's eyes. 'Worthless,' the man grumbled, and struck down with his blade. Just before he died the Duke cried once more, '*Je suis Brabant!*'

Edward of York stabbed upward, killing his opponent. Pressed closely left and right by the men of Fauquemberghes and Marle and the heavy retaliation of the English, he slipped in the mud and crashed backwards. Marle and Fauquemberghes were dead. I am unharmed, he thought – but what passes? He struggled as three hundred pounds of armed man fell on top of him. He pawed at it, saw the anguished face at which he had stared over a distance in the first moment of confrontation in the field. It was Charles d'Albret; his arms flailing like a steel windmill, gripping York involuntarily about the throat as his own life ebbed. Another terrible weight fell on them both. York, unwounded yet dying, found his face crushed against that of the French commander. Like monstrous lovers they convulsed. The final gap was mended. The battle was over.

And the carrion crows returned, replacing the benign

brown birds who had witnessed the beginning. Large and death-dark, their descendants would come back to feed upon these bloody fields after just five hundred years.

Home, then. Calais, then home. The men, numb with incredulous joy, ceased grumbling over the loss of their prisoners. Rations of wine and ale and food in plenty were issued and the tall tales began, waxing through the days and nights, to be repeated in England for generations. The stories had no need of embellishment. The reality was fabulous.

Some eight thousand French were dead. Among the English the casualties, not all of them mortal, numbered scarcely one hundred.

The steel serpent had been dismembered into countless noble segments. Dead were d'Albret, Châtillon of Dampierre, the Admiral of France, Rambures, commander of the artillery, Guichard Dauphin, grand hospitaller to King Charles, Brabant, Bar, Alençon, Nevers, Marle, Lorraine, Blamont, Granpré, de Roucy, Fauquemberghes, Bourdon, with other chevaliers of honour too numerous to recount. In the light of this matchless triumph the men forgave Henry even when ordered to dispose of much of the acquired loot, which would have needed extra pack-trains to carry it to Calais and would have sunk the ships bearing the army home. Part of the plunder was stowed in a vast barn on the edge of Tramecourt where thousands of French corpses already lay. Pitch and fire were applied to the structure. The ensuing blaze seemed to scorch the sky. The stench was terrible. The English dead were also disposed of by fire, save for the slain lords and officers: York, Suffolk, Sir Richard Kyghley, Sir Davydd ap Llewellyn ap Hywel. Their flesh had been boiled from the bones ready for shipment to England where they would be buried.

The orange glow flowed against the walls of Henry's pavilion where he sat on the evening of the third day. Montjoie Herald had conceded the victory. And now a wave of dreadful melancholy, so sudden and inappropriate that it made him shiver, dropped upon Henry. Holy God! he thought, hearing the laughter and song from outside, jubilation runs like a hare through my army, and no wonder. But can they not realize, as I do, that this is only a beginning? The French, after their catastrophic defeat, will soon be renewed, gorged with the lust for vengeance. Doubly savage, I must return next spring and face them again. I feel so weary. Now I must fight this crippling *accidie* and question Charles of Orléans, who sits opposite me, shocked silly, and my royal subject.

'What was your latest news from Paris?'

'Would to God I were there,' replied the Duke.

Henry thought: you will not see Paris for a long time. There will be no ransom for you until I have conquered France anew.

'You gave birth to a butchery,' said Charles. 'To slaughter the prisoners was shameful, criminal.'

Henry was past thought, past judgement, part of a heredity of victors. He said: 'Did not your countrymen do likewise, at Nicopolis?' Charles was silent.

'What of the King of France?'

'He is in grave madness again,' he said sadly. 'And it's rumoured that the Dauphin Louis is dying.'

'How so?' Ten years younger than I, thought Henry. Debauchery has carried him off.

'There's talk of poison at the hands of my father's murderer . . . the Burgundy assassin, Jean sans Peur.' Tears came to his eyes.

Henry said evenly: 'How are you sure? Could it not be your own faction, Armagnac?'

He knew enough of Armagnac and the powerful Count Bernard whose daughter, Bonne, Charles had married, to accord him respect, for the new leader of the Orléanist party was more potent than the murdered Duke Louis had been; while Charles was thinking regretlessly of Bonne, whose pinched shrewish face he might not see again for years. Suddenly he longed for Isabelle, his beloved 'Madame'. But Isabelle was dead.

'Come, cousin,' said Henry not ungently. 'There's no merit in holding back. Who will gain supremacy now?'

'Armagnac.' Charles wiped his eyes on silk. 'We will wrest the Constable's baton from the King, in face of Jean sans

Peur's ambition. Armagnac will end the factions, the constant brawls and murders . . .'

'Can you be sure?' Henry leaned forward, the muted fires gleaming in his eyes.

'No,' said Charles helplessly. 'But I can hope!'

Henry sat back, satisfied. Let France remain in a state of chaos. And let me gain Burgundy against the fierce Armagnac! Feeling a little less despondent, he said:

'What more? The Princess Katherine? How and where is she?'

'She's well, and with her mother in Paris, the last I knew.'

'How does she look?' said Henry curiously.

Oddly, Charles's clearest picture of Katherine was as on that dreadful day at Blois. Time had ceased for her there in his memory.

'She is still much a child, even at fourteen.' Then: 'Sire, I'm weary.' Henry rose, motioning the guard to escort the Duke to bed.

Later he went outside across the rosy flame-lit field, black with scavenging birds, to visit the surgeon's tent where Humphrey lay in some pain, but able to grin at his brother.

'Is he mending?'

'Ay, your Grace,' said the surgeon. 'There's some proud flesh, but I think it will be well.'

'All's well, eh, Harry?' said Humphrey of Gloucester. 'All is very well!'

I must pray. I must sleep. Henry left the tent abruptly, feeling a strange dementia. All round, the men were singing a *Deo Gratias*. He stared at the raging red pyre that bubbled and stank, and saw clearly the tortured resolute face of Badby. Great God! He clenched his fists and looked up at the blood-shot sky. Great God, I did that for Thee! And this I did at Agincourt in Thy Name. God, I am no ingrate. But what has been achieved? Many dead, a few ransoms, the long campaign just beginning. You gave me the day. Now give me peace of mind.

Music, the healer. As David soothed Saul . . . He turned to his escort and said:

'Bring me the harpist, the bowman, the Welshman.'

Tomorrow, he decided, I will hold the celebratory Mass. But tonight I must have reassurance, the mystical concessions of old legend, whose significance I do not fully understand myself. I, who should not need strength seek it now, now that the battle is over and the men rejoice. My stepmother's jewels, my lands, are still in pawn and the stench of my father's usurpation once more in my nostrils. And yet – as he entered the pavilion with the hellish light wavering on its walls – the first step is taken, the first veil drawn upon self-doubt . . .

Owen, fresh as a lark and slightly drunk, entered with his harp and a light step. As before, Henry motioned him to sit.

'Shall I play holy things, Sire?'

Henry's thin hand covered his eyes, he spoke without lifting his head.

'There was something you once told me of . . . a ballad, concerning some fair young knight . . .'

'Culhwch,' Owen said eagerly.

'That is the one, then.'

'Oh, your Grace,' Owen burst out intemperately, 'was it not all a miracle, a mighty victory?'

'Sing of Culhwch.'

Ruefully, Owen said: 'It should, by rights, take hours in the telling.'

'Then tell of the essence.' He searched among labyrinths of wanting, the magic, the only words. 'He confounded the fiercest giant . . .'

'. . . in the world. He had been rash in youth. Thus he shone more brightly against the darkness of his past. And he conquered – the princess, and the giant who was turned into a little child in face of his prowess, and the mighty Boar . . .'

'And the domain?'

'All lands, all dower, all splendour. His by right.'

Silence. Then Henry looked up, smiling frailly.

'I saw you fighting, Owen ap Meredyth ap Tydier. I shall reward you now.'

Duw annwyl! He will knight me as he did poor Davy. Owen's shining hopes flew crazily. Then the King said:

'I shall create you an esquire of the Wardrobe. You will

be under the jurisdiction of Master John Feriby from now on, in my Household.'

'It is an honour, Sire,' Owen said jerkily. The King's eyes looked past him, to where the corpse-pyre made a pattern on the canvas of the tent.

'Now, sing,' said King Henry.

The first note dropped, silver on the silver of the voice. For a brief moment player and listener shared an identical thought. *Is this the greatness of which I dreamed?*

Part Four

THE TREATY
France and England, 1420–22

Il est ecrit,
Pur voir et eil,
Per mariage pure
C'est guerre ne dure.

(From Katherine's Coronation feast, 1421).

She still had a cough, relic of the old fever, and now there was no Dame Alphonse to bring her the sweetbriar necklet, for Alphonse was dead and Poissy a place of the past. The cough was more an indication of nervousness than ill-health, intermittent and sometimes an embarrassment. And in her mother's household there were plenty to care for her, a plethora of abigails and béguines, like benign sheepdogs round a rather independent little lamb, for Katherine of Valois was learning how to care for herself.

A woman now, nurtured as the bait she was, treated by Isabeau with an eerie indulgence, she had developed a secret self, a mental sanctum, detached, full of private conclusions and often passionate thoughts. Her will was strong, although not as strong as she would have wished. She was fairly biddable. She had survived, through a concealed, wary determination. She was tall, her face serene, her bearing steady. Her colour was ivory with a musk-rose flush on the cheekbones. Her great dark eyes were thoughtful, often distant, her lips wide and sleek, and her smile still sometimes transformed her, so that the eyes bloomed mysterious as black satin. It was almost a wanton smile. It challenged, teased. None could see Katherine smile without acknowledging her curious glamour, neither could they guess that the smile was often only a propitiation, a defence that sheltered her spirit.

She was smiling now at some witticism of her mother's. They sat together in the bower at Troyes under a stained-glass oriel, its light glinting on their finery. Katherine's dark hair hung below her waist and shone with filaments of gold and green and red under the sunlit glass. About her head she wore a filet of gold and pearls. A tight crimson gown, faced from neck to hem with ermine, constrained her long body. Small sapphires punctuated the collar. A loose mantle of cloth of gold was draped about her shoulders. Beneath all this, her rigid flesh prickled with sweat. The sun was fierce for May, and they were waiting, still waiting, as they had waited in other bowers, other manors, through stress and hope, since Agincourt.

Isabeau watched her daughter, and tried another jest. If only the girl would laugh more! all might yet be saved. When sullen, she could look almost plain. The portrait sent recently to Henry of England had a false smile plastered upon it, and she was doubtful of its efficacy. Worry dragged at her, as she sat in her sumptuous blue sarcenet and sipped Burgundy. She shifted her spreading hips upon the window-seat and tapped her feet. She was heavy with ambition as well as anxiety, and, like Katherine, she thought often of the dead. Dauphin Louis for one, her fierce, bibulous little son, gone to his grave before his twentieth year, rotted by debauchery and full of spleen at the incredible catastrophe sustained by France in 1415. Such was Isabeau's reputation that men said she, the mother, had administered poison. She smiled wryly. At least it could be said that she did not mourn Louis. He had become truculent, an embarrassment, furious at her negotiations with the English King because they rocked his own dreams of supremacy, hating her association with Jean sans Peur of Burgundy, the enemy turned lover. She had plotted and schemed at Tours and Troyes with Jean sans Peur, encouraging him to keep the bloody feud between Burgundy and Armagnac running, so that Parisian Armagnacs were murdered in their beds and factions festered like a sore. How easy it had been for the invader to return from England and resume his conqueror's trail through France!

The whole of Normandy was now virtually Henry's. Many towns had been captured by him and his captains: his brothers Clarence and Gloucester; Umfraville, March, Salisbury and Warwick and Exeter. Touques was his, and Auvillars, Caen (besieged cruelly by Clarence and Warwick); Creully and Villars Bocage in the west of Caen, the castle of Alençon; Falaise (the birthplace of Henry's own mother), Bayeux, Cherbourg, Louviers and Pont de L'Arche, eight miles from Rouen. Then Rouen itself, which had undergone a siege from which even Isabeau's rock-hard sensibilities recoiled, though she cared nothing for the common people and had not wept for years. What was the English poet's name? Paynter? No, Page,

John Page. His ballads were read in both England and France. Untutored, a common soldier, he had written from his eyewitness heart.

> And also their bread was near hard gone,
> And flesh, save horseflesh, had they none;
> They ate also both dogs and cats,
> And also both mice and rats . . .

The French soldiers had turned the citizens of Rouen out to starve into the drenching town-ditch, ruthlessly forfeiting French lives for their own survival. Beyond the moat the English force refused to let them pass, and there they had lain, the dead and the living.

> And then they ate both roots and rind,
> And dew of the grass that they might find,
> All love and kindness was gone aside,
> When each from the other their meat might hide.

Babies had been born in the moat, while nearby corpses lay unburied. Babies who were hauled on pulleys up to the battlements to be baptized, then lowered again to their deaths in the pit. Skeletal girls had struggled as far as the enemy lines to sell their bodies for a crust. There had been women suckling dead infants, and babies hanging on the breasts of their dead mothers.

> At every gate they were put out,
> Many a hundred in a rout . . .
> And all they cried at once then,
> 'Have mercy on us, ye Englishmen.'

Isabeau drank wine, and tried to think with detachment about the present situation. Her own son, the third and present Dauphin, Charles, and his enmity for Jean sans Peur had been at the root of that carnage, albeit indirectly. Just as she herself was to blame, for the factions seeking to destroy one another, even as the English King had desired. Henry had played one off against the other while babies were born and died in that ditch of Purgatory, flooded by rain and the tears of illimitable suffering. So it was, she thought. Life! Fate! I must not grow soft or pliant in my age. Her eyes turned severely on Katherine. Smile, woman! Smile, salvation!

She had stayed in her fortified manors, fringed by the howling strife, cultivating Katherine like a magic herb and up-holding Jean sans Peur. Burgundy, the crafty old warrior, had come to her like a miracle at the time when she needed him most. Despite his murder of Louis of Orléans, she had welcomed him gratefully; they were in complete accord. Shrewd and cool, he was a man to match her own strength at last. She knew and approved of the knowledge that he was hand in glove with the invader, holding back his troops from the defence of the realm and rejoicing to see Armagnac's forces harassed, beleaguered, betrayed. When Bernard, Count of Armagnac, was murdered in a Paris street-brawl to lie naked and mocked by the Burgundians for three days, she and Jean sans Peur had celebrated with a revel lasting twice as long. King Charles was not present on that occasion. He had a turret-wing to himself at Troyes, and stayed there most of the time, unstable, muttering of old sins and regrets, useless as a broken cannon. A scrapheap of a man.

The second Dauphin, Jean, who had been as tiresomely obstructive of her private schemes as his brother Louis had been, was also dead. Young Jean had been dedicated to the Armagnacs, to the Dukes of Brittany and Berry, and, like Louis, had feared for his own succession at the hands of his mother and Burgundy, and when Henry of England ruled France through marriage to its Princess. Jean sans Peur was blamed for the Dauphin Jean's death; people spoke of poison. None would ever know the truth. It was of no account. The prime consideration was to treat with Henry of England, for he had proved stronger and cleverer than any, and was an ally devoutly to be wooed.

By St Denis! she thought. How many dead! Even Jean sans Peur now, and men had judged him immortal. Struck down at a meeting with the new Dauphin, Charles, on the bridge of Montereau. Before this event, further towns had fallen to the English: Lavilleterte and Bouconvillers, Gisors, Meulan, Montjoie and St Germain, Château-Gaillard. News of Burgundy's death had come back to Isabeau in garbled versions. He and the Dauphin had met in a small barricaded square east of the river on the periphery of the bridge. Jean sans Peur had disliked the venue but had finally acquiesced, saying that something must be risked in the cause of peace.

Although Burgundy, to the rage of the Dauphin Charles, had long been intriguing with Henry, giving and receiving promises, they had quarrelled after the terrible siege and fall of Rouen, and Jean sans Peur had dismissed as null all the tentative negotiations that had gone before. So he had agreed to meet the Dauphin for exploratory talks. He was annoyed with Henry, and toyed for once with the idea of the factions healed and a united front presented to the conqueror. Learning of this proposal, Henry, who had been keeping truce, launched an offensive on Pontoise, and then reached the gates of Paris, from which Isabeau and Jean sans Peur were forced to run by night.

It had been early September (less than a year ago, she mused) that Burgundy, accompanied by seven hundred armed men, arrived at the Montereau bridge and entered the enclosure with a small entourage. One of the Dauphin's chief officers, Tanneguy du Chatel, greeted him there. Jean embraced him, praising his fidelity, then knelt to the Dauphin who was leaning, fully armed, upon a wooden frontier set up on the bridge. What then ensued had never been clear. A few insults of no real weight had been uttered by the Dauphin to the Duke. Jean sans Peur, rising to his feet, found his sword caught up in his velvet mantle. In order to untangle it, he took the sword by the hilt. There were shouts of outrage from the Dauphin's party – he draws a weapon before our lord! – and Tanneguy du Chatel whirled his axe across the Duke's throat. Then all the Dauphin's men fell on him, stabbing and gouging him to death, while the heir of France, still leaning on the barrier, watched without a sign or a word.

It was so sudden that the seven hundred fighting men drawn up outside remained uninvolved. Perhaps, she thought, they saw only a distant scuffle. Perhaps they were traitors – who could tell? The Dauphin Charles was later helped by his friends into the castle at Montereau. Was he appalled by the savage finality of it all? Although he was Armagnac through and through and that day two murders had been avenged; Louis of Orléans, and Count Bernard. He was only sixteen years old, and perhaps confused by inexperience . . .

Whatever the truth, Jean sans Peur was dead. Of all Isabeau's paramours he had been the most useful, the most likeable. There would be none to match him, with his ruthless wit. His long heavy face returned to her sometimes in stabs of regret. And now there was only Henry of England, the symbol of survival, the prime concept by which she and Katherine stood alone to gain. For in her heart Isabeau knew the Dauphin to be merely the tool of strong conspirators, and his father was continually quaking-mad.

'Sit straight!' she said suddenly, although Katherine was sitting as if she had a rod against her spine. 'The gown looks well. Would to God you had more jewels. I could hang those marauders with my own hands.'

Henry, after his first meeting with Katherine almost a year ago, had sent her a gift of gems worth one hundred thousand crowns. (Unfortunately they had been stolen in transit by robbers, Frenchmen for all that, on the road to Troyes.) He must therefore have admired her. Did he carry her face in his thoughts, like a troubadour? Unlikely, from what Isabeau knew of Henry. Was the portrait an uninspired reminder, with its manufactured smile? None could persuade Katherine to smile, the week of the painting. She had murmured that she was mourning the anniversary of a death. Whose? when there were so many dead, and who knew who was loved or hated?

Katherine now listened to the sporadic conversation of her mother as to the rumblings of a far-off battle, dangerous but too distant to be of account. They were waiting; they would eternally be waiting, for news of a second chance to meet Henry of England, for a messenger to slide through the studded oak door and possibly be harangued by Isabeau for not bringing the desired words. Katherine was accustomed to waiting. Her mind was trained to drift from poignant memory to curious recollection – from a little white dog now dead to the willow tree at Poissy – to Belle, whose remembrance no longer hurt, being welded to her own spirit. Constant within that private dominion, a silent counsellor whose essence was truer than a memory and more potent than a ghost.

Nearby stood a harp, its woodwork carved with roses and acorns. At her mother's bidding she had become adept upon it. Henry loved the harp. That was one of the subjects that had arisen in their brief conversation. And near the harp was a caged nightingale, an insignificant brown bird who would go for weeks without singing and then burst into a desperate abandon of melody. Silently Katherine rehearsed a *chanson* newly learned, thinking without understanding of the love it celebrated.

> *J'ay prins amours a ma devise,*
> *Pour conquérir joyeuseté,*
> *Heureux seray en cet esté*
> *Se puis venir a mon emprinse.*

Such a happy, courtly song! And how hot it was in this room, in these clothes! The gown was pinned to her back by sweat. Scattered at random in her mind were courts and castles and dowries and stolen jewels and strange lands and somewhere love. She dreamed of open fields; meadows, and brisk trembling air, and mountains. And love? Why, Henry of England was her love. She had been rehearsed in this thought, yet her long glossy lips curved a little cynically and the black eyes came on fire with humour.

He and she had met at last nearly a year ago near the bridge at Pontoise. A high day in Katherine's lifeless almanac. The first and possibly the last meeting. Perhaps she would die before they met again. Of longing for Henry? The smile turned to a chuckle. Isabeau looked up approvingly and the nightingale cocked its captive head, closed its pin-sized eyes and prepared itself for another recital, perhaps in about two months' time.

It had been almost as hot as now, with May slipping into June, and she had been even more royally robed, as she sat in the barge with her mother, her trembling, glassy-eyed father, and Jean sans Peur, who had kept his hand on her shoulder as they approached the Île Belle in the Seine near where the rendezvous had been arranged. Noxious odours rose from the river and she was glad of the Duke's proximity; his clothes were rich with Venetian perfumes. He murmured encouragement, his voice vibrant against her unbound hair: 'When the King sees you, *ma belle*, he'll forget all about his Aragon princess!'

She had scarcely been aware that Henry was contemplating an Aragonese liaison, nor that he was trying to bring all Europe to his side by arranging marriages for his brothers Bedford and Gloucester, wooing the German and Hainault courts. In between making diplomatic representations to Genoa, Flanders and the Archbishops of Treves and Mayence in aid of his proposed war against the Infidel. Treaties and abortive treaties, unfulfilled pledges and cancelled meetings came thick and fast without her knowledge. She was, however, aware that Rouen, its population vastly decimated by the siege, was being held to ransom for 300,000 crowns, and that Henry was building a palace among its ruins.

'Smile, *doucette!*' the Duke of Burgundy whispered, and she obeyed, glancing back at her parents. Isabeau, fanned with peacock feathers by a page, was watching her as usual. The King of France closely surveyed his own hands and fingernails, his lips trembling. The barge, hung with cloth of gold, moved steadily on towards the meadow outside the west gate of Meulan, north of the river. Beribboned pavilions had been set up, and palisades ringed three enclosures; one for the French, one for the English, and one, holding the largest pavilion, a neutral meeting-place dressed with the lilies and leopards of the two countries. Deep trenches had been dug to mark the territorial boundaries and for further defence, lines of stakes planted along their edge. Henry was bringing English bowmen. A small city had arisen in the Meulan field. Noblemen of both countries had erected smaller tents of rivalling magnificence, coloured and tasselled with gold and set in neat patterns, like little jewelled streets.

There were as many of these tents on Henry's side of the palisade as his most recently captured towns: Montivilliers, Lillebonne, Fécamp, Etrepagny, Tancarville, Dieppe, Gournay, Neufchâtel en Bray. La Roche Guyon (thought to be invincible but whose foundations had been undermined by Warwick); Eu (for the second time), Honfleur, and Ivry, taken by Humphrey of Gloucester.

The oaths of chivalry had been sworn, the terms offered. Katherine could hardly believe that she was the focus of their extravagance. Her dowry was named by Henry at 800,000 crowns. To this Isabeau objected, saying that 600,000 crowns was still owing as the sum taken to England by Isabelle for Richard. In response, Henry reminded them of the ransom for King John, captured by the Black Prince, and never fully reimbursed. Jean sans Peur mentioned Katherine's jewellery, assets which would accompany her. The answer was brisk: these jewels could not match even one bauble of Henry's, for example the 'Great Harry', a crown pawned for his Agincourt campaign. He also demanded his own kingdom in France, including all the conquests of Edward III and his own gains in Normandy. Touraine, Anjou, Maine, Brittany, Flanders, Ponthieu and Montreuil were but a few of the claims he sought. Above all he must be regent and son-in-law to King Charles, and upon the sovereign's demise, supreme ruler.

This sovereign, upon whom all such decisions should have fallen, swayed to his feet as the craft was moored and trumpeters played a fanfare. His face was milky-pale, his eyes withdrawn. He knew neither where nor what he was. Gently Jean sans Peur pressed him down into his red silk chair.

'Stay! Rest, *grand seigneur*!' he said, as if to a well-bred hound. And to Katherine: 'You also, Madame.' He stepped from the barge and joined Isabeau in a litter where boys dressed as angels were playing pipes and shawms and women fussed to arrange the Queen's gold robes. Katherine waited for a further two days at the castle of Meulan, with her father, until she was escorted by the Count of St Pol into the great pavilion. She wore the most costly of her new dresses, green velvet panelled with intricate silver brocade, so heavy and hot she could scarcely walk, and adding to its weight a vast downfall of ermine attached to a high-arched coronet. When her women had placed the coronet on her head they had caught some of her fine hairs round a jewelled floret; this pained her. She was pale and her dark eyes immense.

It was dim in the pavilion after the brightness outside. A stake was planted in the middle of the cloth of gold carpet, a halfway mark between the nations, and there she knelt with her mother and Burgundy. She saw the shapes of noblemen, the transient brilliance of jewels in the gloom, a movement of dark robes and bright heraldry, and peering up, sought to tally the old description given by Dame Alphonse.

'His head was bare, his cheek florid. He has a scar on his face. Aged about three-and-twenty. He looks clever.'

Three men stepped forward, making deep obeisance, all tallish as they rose, but this must be Henry in the centre. He came to take her hands and lift her for a brief embrace. His full lips pursed to kiss her. Yes, he was florid, but patchily, over the weathered cheekbones. Steady eyes in a thin restless face. An old scar. But two-and-thirty now, to her eighteen. Clever, yes. A stubborn cleverness in face and body. His hands were strong, his mouth slightly moist. She thought, with an insight that amazed even herself: he is unwell. Devoured by something – what?

'*La Belle Katherine.*' A good, mature, mellow voice. 'The portrait lied.' He spoke good French too, nearly as perfect as the Earl of Warwick, whose long, welcoming address had lately finished.

She had known the painting was not good. She lifted her face and smiled her brilliant seductive smile.

'He showed you to be fair. But you are lovely. *Comme une ange.*'

Then Henry presented his brothers. Thomas, Duke of Clarence, capturer of castles. He looked war-weary. His breath none too sweet, he kissed her, as did Humphrey of Gloucester. This one was different. She looked up, startled, into his eyes. Then away, quickly, back into that secret inner sanctum where dwelt Belle and her ghostly advisers. They were whispering, an instant chaos of warning. *Beware him! Beware!* then the moment snapped and she found herself murmuring the rehearsed greeting, though now avoiding the eyes in which she had seen an unmistakable evil.

That, in retrospect, was her clearest impression of the meeting. The rest, recalled in the stifling room at Troyes, was vague, not unpleasant. Henry had seated her at his right hand in the gorgeous pavilion, had studied her carefully but with courtesy and a severe clerkish charm. She had felt that no detail of her went unobserved – not the way she drank or took her food, and when she asked for water with her wine, she fancied a spark of approval gleamed in his eyes. Choristers sang a motet during the feast, and this was when they talked of music. The harp, said Henry, was his favourite instrument, and as if in illustration of his discourse, behind a screen a musician pulled down a pellucid fountain of bright notes, his light tenor voice winding a skein about their conversation. A strange voice; she heard it sometimes even now, on the edge of dreams.

'That,' explained Henry, 'is the Welsh harp you hear. A difficult skill to master. The tuning . . .' The music attracted her, overlaying Henry's descriptions of technique – she feigned attention, nodding demurely. He had promised her a harp and here it now stood, beside the sulky nightingale.

Above his head a banner, held by two attendants and embroidered in blue and gold thread, had read: UNE SANS PLUS. She had forgotten then that he was dabbling with Aragon. Naïvely she had thought his attention, his desires, were hers. She had trusted the *raison*.

The negotiations had failed through the fault of Jean sans Peur, now for ever silent. He had been afraid of those in his own party who resented Henry's terms, and dared not risk losing partisans to the Dauphin and Armagnac. So the tents at Pontoise were dismantled, the French royal family resumed their river journey and Henry, when he returned a month later expecting a final settlement, found an empty field. That was when he had sent the jewels. And after that he began a further campaign, throwing a force from Nantes against Pontoise itself, the stronghold of the Burgundians. Now Pontoise was fallen, the trenches overgrown with grass, the scars where the bright pavilions had stood healed by a year.

She could well have married him. He was pleasant enough, she could not imagine him wine-flushed and raging like her mother, or gibbering insanely like her father. He had an appealing stability. Meanwhile, there was this limbo of un-knowing. She would sit for ever, cooked by clothes, in the bower at Troyes, a virgin in her nineteenth year. Her sisters, perhaps even Marie the nun, must have seen more of life. Dear lovely Belle had had love and death for bedfellows. Briefly she thought of Charles of Orléans, held for five years since Agincourt. Still Henry's captive, still writing his sad songs in the Tower of London.

And then a messenger scratched urgently upon the door, and the nightingale, without warning, began to sing.

A paperchase of seabirds, flying downriver, followed the cavalcade as it approached the spires and turrets of Troyes. Flanked by horsemen and followed by hundreds of foot-soldiers, Henry rode beside Philip, the new Duke of Burgundy. They rode so close that the sleek quarters of their mounts jostled together. Philip leaned slightly towards the English king as if in physical token of his complete amity. The young Duke wore a large black hat, the folds of its chaperon trailing over one shoulder. Over a black woollen tunic, a mantle of the same stuff enveloped him down to his spurs. The only relief in this gloom came from a gold crucifix and an enamelled collar across his chest from which hung his emblem, a small gold ram. His face was as hollow and serious as Henry's. Beneath deli-cate brows his black Valois eyes were tragic. He had mourned his father, Jean sans Peur, for a year. The murder had utterly dislocated his life and his intentions. Neither warrior nor strategist himself, he had found himself waking nightly, weeping, crying *Death to Armagnac!* Death in particular to the Dauphin Charles, death, or ruin. Innocent of how to achieve this, pious and gentle and nicknamed 'The Good', he had turned in desperation to the English king, armed with treaties and concessions. In Henry's strength he saw a weapon for his vengeance. And like most Frenchmen, the fate and eventual suzerainty over his own country took second place to his personal desires. When they had met at Christmas for the preliminaries of the vast Treaty which now travelled with them, he had practically promised Henry the earth.

'If you will fight against the Dauphin, my father's assassin – ' his voice almost strangled with longing – 'Cousin, my own fair cousin Katherine shall be yours. You shall have all that you desire.'

Henry had not been surprised. Carefully conscious that he was now not only the conqueror but also the prime arbiter in this internecine strife, he had weighed the Treaty in terms

236

of its acceptance by those towns he had so far left unbesieged. Paris was not one such, for he had it virtually surrounded, but when he passed by from Rouen to Troyes he saw the walls crowded with a throng obviously delighted by the prospect of a peaceful settlement. Seven masters from the University of Paris had helped to draw up the Treaty. Seven French envoys had addressed the Parlement's chamber of representatives, whose reaction had been unequivocal assent. Paris itself, though near starvation, sent four cartloads of wine to Henry, a gesture of friendship. These he received sombrely gracious, accepting them as his due.

Wine was the conversation now as they rode. Against Philip's mourning dress, Henry's scarlet gown, worn over full armour, had a bloody gaiety. Before him a page bore his tilting helm from which, instead of a *panache*, a fox's brush moved glossily in the wind. This quirk of fashion set him apart, as a man savage and vulpine in combat rather than one enamoured of silk fripperies.

'Some of the Loire yield I found much to my taste,' Henry said. 'There's one with a flinty pleasing palate of which I took a little.'

'The area is rich in minerals. Did your armies appreciate the wine?'

'I forbade them to drink unless each cup was mixed with three parts water. I do not brook intemperance.'

Philip glanced behind at the lined barbarous faces of young men grown old in service, who had triumphed in the clashing maw of Agincourt and returned for further conquests. He looked at Henry with even greater respect for his discipline of such men.

'I am ever grateful to you, my liege,' he said, 'for the letter you sent in sympathy of my father's death.'

'Queen Isabeau wrote me in equal cordiality,' said Henry. He thought how blatantly she too had shown readiness to come to terms. Now he could dare to be generous. The death of Jean sans Peur could be the final solution to the vacillations and feuds which continued even while France fell at Henry's command. His own letter to Philip had been warm yet stern. There could be no reneging on promises or oaths as Jean sans

Peur had done. Meanwhile Philip's grieving mother fanned the flame, writing in complaint to the Pope, harassing the University of Paris, whose patron Jean sans Peur had been, to rise in arms against the Dauphin. And the campaign of vengeance had already begun; Philip and Henry's combined forces had launched a successful attack on Tremblay, an Armagnac *château-fort*, their armies fighting well together, with only a little friendly rivalry. And now, although this expedition to Troyes was one of diplomacy, it had been thought prudent to arm the men in case of a Dauphinist ambush on the road.

'Queen Isabeau will be glad to see you,' said Philip.

'So will *our dear father*, the King.' The ghost of a smile brushed Henry's thin cheek.

'Ah. The King,' Philip said less happily. Then: 'I trust you found the Princess pleasing. She is a good maid, most devout and modest.'

'That is what I thought.'

The heralds on the walls of Troyes raised their trumpets. Banners rippled, azure and scarlet and gold. Henry spoke honestly; he had been impressed with Katherine and by a letter she had sent him, doubtless written under dictation but sweetly and simply penned. He could not recall her face, save that it was nothing like the portrait which he had scarcely had chance to study. He wished she had written in English, little knowing that she had wanted to but had feared errors; Henry's own letters were exemplary, with all the prepositions spelled right.

The dignitaries of Troyes came out to do them homage. Prominent among the vested prelates was the old Archbishop of Sens. Pale-faced, he looked at Henry with unmistakable supplication. As they rode on towards their royal lodging in the Hôtel de Ville, Philip said:

'The Archbishop is greatly troubled. The Armagnacs have turned him out of his diocese,' and Henry answered firmly: 'If he's the one who will join me to the Princess Katherine, he shall see an end to trouble!' His eyes flicked over the crowd of nobles travelling with them through the cobbled streets. In a chariot drawn by two pale horses sat a lady, leaning outwards with a kind of desperate confined energy. Exceptionally blonde, glittering braids fell to her waist from beneath a towering crescent of white veiling. Young and rosy, her small mouth was twisted with discontent. Henry knew her: Jacqueline, Princess of Hainault, widow of the second Dauphin, Jean of Touraine, and niece of Jean sans Peur. Now another husband, the new Duke of Brabant, rode before her on a prancer, and her eyes, set upon him, matched the distaste on her lips.

'All's not well between my cousins Dame Jacqueline and Brabant,' Philip said softly.

Young Brabant bowed to Henry without enmity. He was rather an ugly young man. He gripped his restless horse with skinny legs, while his wife's beautiful eyes bored like basilisks into his unknowing back.

I had hoped, thought Henry, to marry Dame Jake to my brother of Bedford. A useful link with Burgundy, and more, she is heiress to Hainault, Zeeland and Holland. Then, suddenly aware, he watched acutely where the lady's eyes went next, although at the same time managing to ride on and bow and converse. Humphrey of Gloucester had spurred up to ride beside Jacqueline's litter, and her eyes were no longer bored or cross. When Humphrey, resplendent in sapphire silk, doffed his hat to her, her eyelids dropped as though scalded. So, thought Henry. He has the good looks – he can make ladies fall in love . . . he might have done better than I with Katherine but he could not have bested me in the field. He filed away the knowledge of Jacqueline's coy longing, and rode on.

The citizens, sensible that the forthcoming treaty might mean an end to looting, ransoms and ruin, had prepared a welcome. Burgundian poets and chroniclers from all the noble households edged the streets. A frenzied spate of minstrelsy flowed from wagons, courtyards and balconies. The song changed from street to street, the tail of one tune merging into another key and then another. A song would be left behind in minutes, drowned by the hollow tabor of hooves, to be replaced discordantly by the next, diffused, dying then emerging changed in the next square or swallowed by trumpets.

He was reminded of his triumphal entry into London five years ago with his war-weary armies. There had been singing boys and girls, blessings and the roar of the *Deo Gratias* anthem. While he, still sick from the melancholy that follows great triumph as it sometimes follows love, had endured it all like one dead. All he could think of, under the waving banners and the showered coins and flowers, was that his conquest was left unfinished, and that, in further holy settlement he must find and burn Oldcastle, the Lollard. And this he had done . . .

In London little birds, their feathers painted gold, had been freed to flutter about him, settling on his shoulders as he rode over London Bridge. They fell on him like small soft missiles, choked and dying from the paint. On the Bridge two almost pagan giant figures held the keys of the City and an immense laurel wreath of silver and gold. Inside a brocade pavilion was a twenty-feet-high effigy of St George, his helmet covered with more laurel and studded with pearls. Men and boys with laurel in their hair had sung and, as now, the singing had risen and faded and become diffuse, garbled, competitive, its beauty overwhelmed by zeal. One tune in unison would have been enough. But that singing, like this singing, was like the tune of life itself, the clashes and uncertainties, the pains and joys, the facets of the spirit ever at war, ever seeking the one true music.

On Cornhill, old men dressed as the prophets had sung, bowing down: *Cantate Domino canticum novum, Alleluia!* Well, they should sing a new song again, he thought, dismounting with Philip at the Hôtel de Ville. Upon his next return home he would glory in it all, this time he would not fast through all the banquets that had been prepared for him. The way was open, and achievement within his hand.

Owen ap Meredyth ap Tydier rode among the train, a rightful and experienced member of the King's Household. He did not sing; his talent was too precious for street-bawling. He had been present at the robing of the King for this journey, had helped Henry with his long scarlet boots, and he had given the tilting helm a rub, although it already had a glassy sheen. He had touched the fox's brush, soft as a girl's hair, and full of strange crisp lights.

And touching it, seeing it now bouncing in the wind, he thought of Madog. With Madog came Hywelis. He had

240

thought of neither for over five years. But the feel of the brush was the feel of Madog, and it woke in him a long memory like an unfashionable caress, one that he quickly put aside.

Charles of France did not rise from his dais as Henry strode through the crowded hall towards him. He watched the red-mantled figure vaguely. Somewhere in him was the notion that the gaunt man who came with such purpose was important. The idea swam about in his consciousness, then evaporated, becoming part of the inconsequential greyness that hid memory and anticipation alike. The figure came on. Not dangerous, so long as it did not touch him, for he was precious today, his limbs and eyes and hands made of finest spun crystal, the whole enclosed in a brittle egg of glass . . . Two women knelt on either side of him. The tall stoutish one, well-nosed and flushed, was smiling. The younger one was very still but her vibrations made him uneasy; she could crack his delicate shell. Her heavy gold robe too looked sharp, it was stiff enough to stand in points about her as she knelt. He shifted an inch away. The man was at his feet now, on one knee, and behind him another dressed in black did likewise, and there were so many people . . . Charles gazed down the packed hall blindly. Drool ran down his chin.

Henry looked at his Princess. For a fleeting second he saw the image of her father in her and was filled with doubt. Then he assessed the two pairs of dark eyes and the shielding look common to them both, and was reassured. In Charles it hid true madness; in Katherine, only innocence and a discreet detachment. Then Queen Isabeau's hands, wine-hot and with the grip of a man, reached out to him. He bent to kiss her on both cheeks and she rose, nearly pulling him off balance with the weight of clothes and flesh.

'Welcome, great sovereign lord.'

'My dear mother,' said Henry. 'Greetings.'

'Our dear son,' Isabeau said.

Katherine stumbled slightly on her robe as she got up and Henry caught her. Her soft breast met the steel cuirass under his mantle as they stood and he kissed her formally. Her cheeks were peach-soft; she smelled of honey and lilies. She was long and lissom and strong, with wide slender shoulders and a vibrancy apparent even to his politic abstracted mind. He felt the unique potential flouncing within her. Beneath the dresses and overdresses and the heated *ennui*, beneath all the stressful longings was – Katherine. And Henry, the anxious victor, racked by old guilts and conquests, was suddenly lightened, filled with hope. This was better than that first meeting. She was new, promising, far more than a figurehead of the Treaty that would, God willing, be signed tomorrow. She was the virgin of legend, chained to the rock of circumstance, and he the hero who would unfetter her. She was the white maiden that Owen ap Tydier had sung to him about. He thought: I'll have him sing this day, to charm that poor tortured soul, her father, whom devils have by the heart . . . it would be an act of grace. He kissed the Princess again, spontaneously, and a little sigh of pleasure rose from the courtiers.

'My dear Katherine,' he said in English. 'My dear wife.'

His face was red. She smiled gently, her dark eyes, like those of an Eastern woman, grew moist and rich. Her small white teeth glistened. Through the coloured windows the sun strengthened, painting with blue and green and gold all those who stood lost beneath its power.

Inside the Cathedral Church of St Peter all was dim and sombre, and cool despite the multitude gathered to watch the signing of the Treaty. Massive pillars fanned upwards into vaulting, delicate traceries starred with saints and monsters. In every aisle there were tombs, stone witnesses to the rustle of robes, the prayers, the silences, and then the sounds of feet approaching the High Altar. Philip escorted Isabeau and Katherine, while Henry led the way to the place of signing. At the rear of the procession came the knight whom Henry had chosen for Katherine's especial protection after the betrothal – Sire Louis de Robsart. He was under orders not to let the Princess out of his sight. Henry, inherently wary, was still prepared for treachery; an abduction of Katherine was a contingency he had not overlooked.

The carved tombs sat in shadow, then blazed with chips of colour as the sun came through the windows overhead.

The Treaty, carried along its great length by six clerks directed by the Archbishop of Sens, was read and signed by Henry and Philip, and the great seals of France and England appended. Philip acted as the King's deputy, as Charles had withdrawn to his apartments, and, listening to the new Welsh minstrel, was refusing to stir. The Treaty was rolled again while the sun passed behind cloud and the tombs sank into fuller gloom even at the moment's consummation.

Jean sans Peur's murder was the hole through which I entered France, thought Henry, moved. I am lord and regent of France and England. Philip and the other nobles were swearing their eternal devotion to the terms of the Treaty.

I am King of France, when Charles dies. When will the Dauphin, at his hunting lodge at Bourges, learn of these matters? It matters not, for he, like Katherine's sisters, are disinherited, and I am on the track of his spoor. And whatever I shall capture from him shall revert to France, my new heritage.

There were clauses concerning the lords whose Normandy estates had fallen to Henry; he promised to recompense them with the lands which he should take from the Dauphin.

He was to be styled, by King Charles: 'Our very dear son Henry King of England and heir of France.' Charles in mercy was to be left to maunder out his days in whichever palace he chose to dwell, kindly tended by Frenchmen of his choice.

The two kingdoms, although united, were to be separate, neither enforcing its laws upon the other.

Charles, Henry and Philip were bound to keep faith, never to make separate treaties with the Armagnac party. And Katherine, whose finger he now crowned with the great betrothal ring which had been worn by Mary, his mother, was to receive 40,000 crowns a year as Queen of England. The dowry had been satisfactorily agreed.

I, Henry, promise I shall not call myself King of France while the King of France shall live. The country shall be governed by a French council with me, Henry, at its head. The Treaty must be ratified by a personal meeting with King Charles. Well, that meeting had come about, like a meeting with a child or an animal . . . I hope, thought Henry, that Owen ap Tydier sings well for that poor creature this day.

Oh, holy God! How the great Edward III would have rejoiced! Great dead ones, have I not redeemed myself?

Katherine's hand in his was sweet, pearly as a wild orchid. It was a capable, long hand, built to make music or mould about the head of a swaddled child. My wife, my bride. He bent to her, although she was almost as tall as he, and felt the last tension sliding from his bones. She raised her face, and for the third time returned his kiss. He became glad and pliant. The stern tombs folded themselves in deeper shadow.

'Home?' said Humphrey of Gloucester. He stared at his brother. 'To England? *Now?*'

Unlaced, he had been lounging, eating fruit from a gold dish in his apartments at the Hôtel de Ville, and had only hastily put himself to rights before Henry strode in after a cursory announcement from a frightened page.

'I shall miss your wedding feast.'

'You think too much of revelry.' Henry paced to the window. Above the moated palace garden house-martins played, diving and sweeping, expending, he thought, needless energy in sport. He controlled some of his anger and walked back to where Humphrey stood, belching from too many ripe peaches.

'You are to be my regent in England, replacing our brother of Bedford. It's time that John was relieved. And I need him here for the new campaign with Philip. Clarence has more than enough to do. The garrison will benefit from a fresh commander.'

'But, my lord, why now?'

'You know why.' And Humphrey looked away, guilty as an orchard-raiding schoolboy.

'I could hardly believe it,' Henry said, 'had my servants not told me – what you did and said to the lady. Were you drunk?'

Humphrey was crimson with resentment and humiliation. Harry, your new grandeur makes you a tyrant. You string up my desires as unthinkingly as you hanged those who rifled the Church. Yes, you've achieved all, but by God! luck played its part. I could have done just as well.

He burst out: 'You are to marry in three days' time, and get heirs for yourself, while I and my brother of Bedford remain bachelor. Your Grace, I crave permission to marry.'

Almost pityingly Henry looked at him.

'Sweet Christ! How do you intend to marry someone else's wife?'

'Harry, all's not well with that marriage. Jacqueline is truly unhappy with Brabant.'

'Who ever equated happiness with marriage? In God's name, how could you risk offending Brabant? and his cousin of Burgundy . . . Humphrey – ' he sat down – 'what *did* you promise her? I mistrust servants' tattle.'

'Only that some day I would take her to England – ' his eyelids fluttered mischievously – 'to live with me under the greatest ruler since Alexander.'

The ruler blew an exasperated breath.

'You are mad. What works in you that you should jeopardize all we have gained?'

'Her marriage,' said Humphrey, 'may not last for ever.'

'Pah! Brabant is young and strong. God willing, he will live long and help me take the remainder of France from the Armagnacs.'

'There is divorce,' said Humphrey carefully.

'So you would alienate his Holiness too! By the Mass! Was the wound you took on Artois plain in your head, not your belly? Have you forgotten my holy quest? To build Jerusalem . . .'

Gloucester allowed him to expound on this for some time. Then he repeated meekly: 'I must marry. John of Bedford must marry.'

'Have you a bride for him, too?' Henry said coldly.

'That I have. Philip's sister Anne. A useful coupling. *She's* not married. She's young and rich and doubtless fruitful.'

'Ay!' Rage diverted, as was Humphrey's intent, Henry stared thoughtfully ahead. He said:

'Before we march on Montereau – where Philip wishes to

settle the debt of his father's murder – I'll propose the match. I doubt he will gainsay me.' He smiled suddenly, the quarrel dead in his mind and, he imagined, in Humphrey's.

'I must prepare for my wedding.'

Humphrey thought: I am glad to be taking ship for England, after all. For *he* will be the nucleus of attention, and Dame Jacqueline well guarded by her husband. Also it's time I set my eye on what machinations presently occupy that conniving Bishop, that upstart Beaufort, back at home . . . yet before I go I must establish my claim.

When Henry had left he came abruptly to his feet. Swiftly he passed through long marble hallways and came to the door of Katherine's solar. A page opened. Ladies were sitting at their tapestry, one played a lute and another caressed a small red squirrel on a chain. Pray God the harridan isn't there! He was relieved after a glance. Isabeau, the all-seeing martinet, the reformed courtesan and constant schemer, was absent on God knew what mission.

He was admitted, and Louis de Robsart, portly and suffering in the heat, gave him greeting. Jacqueline sat near Henry's bride. His mind burned, seeing about the Hainault woman a glittering sea of prosperity and influence. Her bright braids were pure gold, her lips hard rubies. Principalities framed her in his imagination. But she was also lovely, and it was not in his nature to woo a crone, as some did, deformed or with one eye looking eastward. She was desirable and have her he would, husband or no husband.

'I have a wedding gift for the Princess,' he told de Robsart. He saw Jacqueline's body stiffen at his words. 'A little jewel – possibly unworthy. It would aid me if one of her ladies might give her opinion before her Highness sees my poor offering. I hear that Dame Jake has superb taste. If she could view the bauble?'

Louis de Robsart was anxious only for his royal charge. Whatever her handmaidens did was outside his province. Jacqueline got up hurriedly, spilling her tapestry silks in a bright river. The little squirrel began to play with them like a cat.

Humphrey hastened down the stairs, Jacqueline almost treading on his heels. She wore a gown of cream sendal laced to the throat with a crosswork of gold. Her horned headdress was nearly as wide as the staircase, and was swathed in pale blue veiling. Outside the palace the sun was bright on a lawn edged with orange lilies and on the lake and moat. At the far end of the garden a sentry sweated out his duty. Otherwise they were invisible, save for one tiny window in the turret room they had just left. Clear of the outer door, Humphrey threw himself on his knees.

'There is no jewel,' he said hoarsely. 'I have already submitted my wedding gifts.'

'For a moment I was jealous,' she said artlessly.

'You thought I came worshipping Katherine? She is only a dear sister-to-be.' He reached for her hands, taking them to his heart. 'There is a jewel *here*, though . . . sharp, it pains me beyond life. Lady, I am in Hell.' He raised his face and stared obliquely at the sun until his eyes watered and ran.

'See how I weep! All my days are a mockery. Farewell is a word for a wicked tongue. I bleed and burn and die. Sweet Jacqueline, never did man love before, never will he love again. Let love be slain, let lovers kiss no more. Let fortune itself be ill-fated, for parting us thus!'

Her face drained white. 'Parting? Us?'

'Yes.' More tears fell. 'It's my punishment for daring to worship you. My beauty, my goddess. Pray for me when I am gone back to England. I shall not live long away from your presence. I can say no more.'

He bowed his head. There was a pebble under his left knee, and he wriggled in real pain. Chaucer slid conveniently into his mind. He murmured:

> '*The grete joye that was betwix hem two*
> *Whan they be met, ther may no tunge telle,*
> *Ther is no more, but unto bed they go,*
> *And thus in joye and blisse I lete hem dwelle;*
> *This worthy Mars, that is of knighthod welle,*
> *The flour of fairness lappeth in his armes,*
> *And Venus kisseth Mars, the god of armes . . .*'

'How fortunate he was!' he said softly, 'but this poor

247

unworthy Mars is bound for England, cheated of bliss . . .'

She was blushing. He thought: I've gone too far. The verse is daring for one used to the dispassionate couplets of the Hainault poets. But she said: 'My lord. Am I sinful?'

He got up. The pebble had lodged in his kneecap through his hose, and he longed to jump about and swear. He said tenderly: 'You, Venus? Why, sin fled in shame at the sight of your birth. Sinful?'

'To love,' she whispered, 'and to hate . . . Brabant. I wish he had died in battle, like his kinsman.'

Trying to remember whether Brabant was old enough to have been in the battle, Humphrey said: 'Lady. You are a saint.'

'But I love you!' she cried suddenly and so loud he was startled. Then she began to bawl as lustily as a child. Her pink mouth turned down, her small pink nose began to run as if her eyes alone could not cope with the cascade. Great hiccuping sobs escaped her. Gratified and astonished, he thought: they will hear us across the river. Harry will be after me again. I must stem this row. He seized her in his arms. He had never found chance to kiss her, but now he tasted the salt on her cheeks and the inside of her eager mouth, while she, tears finished, writhed in tiny meaningless protest. He became tumultuously aroused, and ripped at the little gold laces of her bodice, baring her breasts to be kissed. He drew away once, demanding: 'Do you still love me?' and she sighed, yes, yes, as he pushed her into the alcove where the turret jutted from the building. He was ready to claim in that moment all the lands, castles and splendours that were hers, not to mention her wonderfully unresisting body.

The sentry turned and began to walk towards them. Humphrey stepped back, breathing heavily.

'I am coming with you to England,' she said, quickly knotting her broken laces.

'No!' he said, with anguish. 'The King forbids it. I dare not go against him.'

She was starting to cry again and he said angrily: 'Would you have your kinsmen follow me and slay me in combat?'

'No, my lord! But what are we to do?' She flung her arms

248

about him, tipping her great headdress sideways.

'Persuade King Henry,' she begged. 'He loves you . . . I cannot live without my dear lord: I will take poison.'

'The King loves me. But he loves policies and conquest more. He is Burgundy's man and you are their chattel, instead of my dear wife.'

Sobbing, she said: 'Then I shall speak to him!'

'No, better than that, sweeting.' Inspiration had come to him. 'Speak to Katherine. Harry is, I believe, passing pleased with her; she may have influence. Test her soft heart; plead. Aren't you her favoured gentlewoman?'

She nodded, smiling again.

'You shall be with me in England. When Katherine's ship comes into Dover, I will be on the quay. And we shall be married, and damn the Pope's displeasure! I shall love my Venus' (with little kisses). 'Be of good heart.'

They stood embraced, he silently self-congratulating. Dame Jake should handle all negotiations, while he remained in London. The sentry had walked back to the end of the garden. Humphrey renewed his caresses. Temporary bliss warmed her fretful heart. Love flowed in her like warm honey. While in him, avarice and lust joined in a demon dance.

Katherine, in the turret window where she had moved for better light to thread her needle, stared down at them. That was love, then. She would learn more of it herself in three days' time. Now it was like a scene in an illuminated romance, and equally unreal. Yet she watched with deep pleasured interest, and her blood grew curious.

'Don't stop,' said Thomas Harvey, entering the room at Troyes where Owen was practising. 'I like to watch you dance. How are you so light on your feet?'

'I don't know.' Owen wiped the dew from his brow and sat down. Thomas Harvey, the King's Servitor, came further into the room, accompanied by Robert Waterton, the royal valet. These were the two most affable men in the Household. Owen liked them. Others in the main were so unfriendly that often he preferred his own company. He was a man between

249

two camps, craftsman at music and Esquire of the Wardrobe but accepted by neither. He was once and for ever a Welsh upstart brought in on the King's whim. Snaith Fidler, Pyper and Tromper talked darkly about Guild laws, old precedents, seeking ways to discredit this unqualified usurper who sang and played better than any of them. The quiet, favoured, solitary one. Now he had learned to dance. He had picked up the skill rather than being taught by the royal troupe of entertainers. It challenged; it needed great physical stamina. He had begun to improvise. In secret he was fashioning an illustrative medley to accompany the ballad of Culhwch and Olwen. It involved the portrayal in swift succession of the giant, the knight, the shell-hooved horse, the fighting-Boar, the flowing-gaited Princess. He was very unsatisfied with his attempts. As in his life, he had come so far and no further.

He dwelt in a busy hive, rewarded with scant praise. Apart from his minstrelsy, he was responsible to John Feriby, Clerk of the Wardrobe, together with Tom Tunbrigge and Robert Spore, Yeomen of the Household, William Topnell, Master Tailor. He helped to oversee the laundering and ironing of the royal linen, the preservation and repair of the silks, cloth of gold and Dasmascus, the sendal and fine Holland shirts, the cloth of Rennes. The hundred pairs of hide boots and Spanish leather shoes, the turban-shaped chaperons which Henry, hating their Infidel connotations, seldom wore, and the beautiful mantles with their starry emblems. When in London he went with others into Chepeside for murrey and wool, for tawny satins and for coffers of ermine and swansdown and fox. The armour was not his responsibility, nor the crowns, the heavy collars and carcanets, the precious rings, But he knew the King's taste, and he had discovered an instinct for fashion, colour, in both men and women – what flattered, what concealed, what enhanced. So he learned, and drew on growing expertise, and sang, and danced his secret dances, pounding out their intricacies until his feet bled and the sweat ran in rivers as heavy as at the Harfleur palisade. A strange existence. Although most of the men were hostile, there were, he had discovered, unlooked-for, most delightful compensations.

Thomas Harvey was gazing out of the window. There was

meadowland and trees as far as the moat and walls of Troyes. Wandering, coiffed head turning in unmistakable search, was a small slim figure.

'I can see Blanchette,' he said.

'Oh, *Duw*!' said Owen.

'She's looking for you. And she was there yesterday and the day before.' Waterton joined him at the window.

'You weary of them very quickly,' he said. 'She's crying. Oh, she's weeping, Owen!'

Owen got up. 'I've work to do,' he said.

Duw! How they wept. Always it ended like this, inevitable from the moment they sought him out, so pretty and graceful with their rounded bodies and their honeyed accents and their delicious difficulties in pronouncing his name. It was fatal to smile at them or speak to them other than distantly or formally. When the first smile, the first word had been exchanged, they made themselves irresistible, with their long-lidded downturned glances, their little folded hands, their pampered feet. French girls, English girls, Flemish girls. He could remember only half of their names. He was initially amazed how quickly they came to him. It was not something of which he was particularly proud. Not all were light or wanton, but he knew without doubt that after only the shortest time he would be in their beds, or they in his, or shining and naked as a peeled almond in the meadow-grass or wherever his search for pleasure bore them. They brought him rapturous well-being, and consolation in black days when Snaith Fidler was particularly rancorous from the belly-gripes that had plagued him ever since Harfleur. They brought him the burning salt of consummation, then dropped him to the little death. He enjoyed and relished them charmingly, giving them no promises, and then swiftly forgot them in work, or singing which was joy, not work. And then they cried. *Duw annwyl!* how they wept. Marie, Blanchette, Alys, Odile . . . their tears alienated him by the thought that what had begun so prettily should end in bitter tantrums.

'She's gone now,' said Waterton, coming away from the window. 'Someone will make you weep one day, Owen Tydier.'

Owen said: 'I doubt.'

'I see your eye is better,' said Harvey, grinning not unkindly.

Ghislaine's brother had sought him out. Owen's eye had been closed for days by the enraged fist. He had knocked two of the brother's teeth out and then had seen the knife drawn on him. Thanks to Ghislaine, he was still alive; she had hurled herself screaming between them to protect not brother but seducer. Ghislaine was now a nun, somewhere near Chinon. No, he was not proud. Neither was he ashamed. It happened. It was so.

'I must go,' he said. 'It's nearly sundown.'

The Guild members were furious when Henry had appointed Owen to make music for the mad King. Only by the knowledge that they too might play afterwards had they tolerated the idea. Owen had been happy to oblige. He saw little of Henry at close quarters yet always they met in what, save for the chasm of blood and birthright, could have been friendship.

'Do not play loudly,' Henry had told him. 'The slightest noise affrights him. He's very ill these days.'

So, at sunrise and sundown, daily at Troyes, Owen sat before the small glacial figure, feeling the corns on his finger-tips harden as interminably he played harp or lute and sang. While on the dais, Charles rocked and trembled and sometimes smiled, and Owen's mind, detached, pursued the latest steps for his dance . . . there was a place where they were unjust, ill-matched to the beauty of the first sight of the giant's daughter:

> *'And her eyes! their look*
> *Was lovelier than the thrice-mewed hawk*
> *And her breast was softer than the sun,*
> *Where she trod, four white clover flowers*
> *Grew beneath her feet.*
> *All were longing-filled and she was called . . .'*

Olwen. A special dance for her, lithe, fragile, yet bounteous with power, for Olwen can change the world.

The softest ripple glided from the strings, dewdrops on a spiderweb of sound.

'*Pastourelle en un vergier,*
Ouy complaindre et gémir,
Disant 'las! en quel dangier
Me fait amours maintenir . . .'

King Charles's lolling head struggled upright; he croaked out, breaking the song:

'That's pretty, Jacques.'

'Your Grace is mercifully most kind.'

Why '*Jacques*'? Owen always wondered. Some dim memory, perhaps, some dead minstrel. Anyway he had trained himself to respond. He looked with pity at the forlorn figure on the dais. Charles's eyes constantly dilated, then retreated as if from some awful foe. A King! thought Owen, and remembering Glyn Dŵr, princely even in age and bitterness, and Harry, immoveably majestic, a little contempt joined the pity. Ease my soul, Jacques. Sing the *Magnificat primi toni.*

Owen sighed. But Snaith Fidler and the others were listening behind the screen, so he struck the first chord and then the doleful inverted second, and began the chant. On the back of his neck he felt a draught from the opening door; it blew through the turgid chamber and with it came the scent of lilies and honey and rosewater. He heard the hushed movement of silk gowns and the rough drag of a brocade train across the tiles. As Charles's attention had wandered, he halved his chords and sang more softly still.

Out of the tail of his eye he saw the ladies approaching. He recognized Jacqueline of Hainault and Queen Isabeau. The nun he did not know, nor the princess who walked beside her. Christine de Pisan, the Italian poetess came with them, wearing a white habit. The foremost figure, seen previously only at a far distance, was unmistakably identifiable by the splendour of her robes. King Harry's betrothed.

The fine strong profile came level with him, and the body held rigidly against the stress of the train. Playing mechanically, he studied her. She was dreadfully weary. There was a film of sweat on her long throat. Very recently she had rearranged her coronet, pushing it back; an angry red weal showed on her forehead. Her thick dark hair fell slightly tangled, below her hips. She halted before the dais. He could have touched the great carved jewel on her left hand. He deplored the colours chosen for her gown; that murky green and harsh gold trim sapped what little colour she had and threw up heavy reflections. He approved of the red in the train; it brought up the lights in her hair . . . Suddenly, insanely, he was reminded of Hywelis, who had loved him and let him go.

The perfume was Katherine's. It circled him as she knelt slowly before the King. Queen Isabeau's voice, loud and nasal, drowned the harp's plaint.

'Dear lord and husband! Here is your daughter, come to bid you adieu! Give her a blessing for tomorrow's wedding-day!'

Charles smiled wistfully. 'I have no children. I have always longed for children. Who are you, maiden? How gay you look! But be careful – stand away from me . . .'

Gay was hardly the word. Owen played some wrong notes. Her left hand where it had touched the tiles had bestowed a damp oval mark. The perfume changed subtly. It was like the feral smell of Madog, chained and moon-howling, yet far from unpleasant.

'Kiss your father!' cried Queen Isabeau.

Owen could see fresh sweat gather in the Princess's palm. His heart began to beat thickly, in almost painful strokes, as after too much wine or love-making. Her fear became a powerful elemental and whirled him with her into it. He stopped playing. She mounted the dais and embraced the King. He squirmed from her. She persisted, deliberately kissing him on the lips. When she descended from him he was maggot-white and staring.

'I warned you, lady,' he whispered, 'none should touch me. Go away, before you do me mortal hurt.'

'Oh, my father!' said Katherine in a terrible voice, and bowed her head. Jacqueline of Hainault burst into sobs, the nun began to tell her beads, Isabeau gave a loud cluck of impatience, and Christine de Pisan unfeelingly took out her writing-tablets and began to scratch a memoir of the moment. Owen thought desperately: Princess, don't weep! He found himself trembling. This was real grief, not the petulant tears of infatuated women; real fear, primal and rooted in an old deep agony . . . her face was sliding into defeat. Smile, Princess! His mind impertinently urged her, and, racked by wild sympathy, the urge infected his harpist's fingers and he did a terrible thing.

There was a nursery rhyme that Megan at Glyndyfrdwy used to sing while baking, and the knaves would join chorus. Even Gruffydd Llwyd would wag his beard to it. Glyn Dŵr had sung it to his grandchildren. It was called *Dinogad's Petticoat*. Dinogad's father went hunting for marten's fur to gown his little girl . . .

> *'Whistle, whistle and whistle again!*
> *Then we'll sing-o, a lusty strain,*
> *To his dogs so swift he'd whistle and sing –*
> *Gaff, Gaff, catch him then, bring!'*

His voice cracked on the last note. The loud merry echo hung above him like a sword. Every pair of eyes swivelled to his face. He smiled, giving a little shrug that said: Demons possessed me! and met all the eyes like a fool. Some were outraged; the King was rocking about with his hands over his ears. But Christine de Pisan was looking at Owen with professional interest, and Katherine was smiling.

Why, she's like a child! He smiled back. The damage was done. No more serenading the royal madman, and Harry doubtless displeased. Their smiles tangled together in a bright shaft of sunlight, although it may have been relief lighting up the glum chamber with an excess of illusion. Then she turned away, still smiling, and left with her womenfolk, while physicians took over the room with their astrolabes and herbals and blood-irons, crowding about the dais. Owen picked up his harp and departed. The lusty tune's ghost lapped him round.

That smile! I would have her dressed in rose, or saffron, or pale amber, or in dark gleaming silk to complement her skin and eyes. I would like to make her laugh. Gaff, Gaff, catch him then, bring!

Belle, my sister! this is no betrayal. She raised her hand in asseveration before Henri de Choisy, Archbishop of Sens.

Sparklets streamed from the great betrothal ring. The shadows in the Cathedral of St Jean lifted and ran like water under the prying sun. That bright sun had shone during all these predestined days and now, like a benign relation, waited to see that all was accomplished. Crystal voices meshed and hung upon the final anthem. Henry's hand shook slightly as her own rested in it.

He is as anxious as I that all should go with dignity, befitting this joining of nations. We are all nervous. The Archbishop's voice is unsteady as he pronounces the blessing. His eyes are still suppliant, he is ashamed to sue for favours to a foreign invader. I do not share the shame. Belle's little loving voice is stilled for the moment. She called Henry terrible names and his father was a creature vile beyond belief. Yet all is past and gone. I am Henry's wife. I have no experience of the world or of men. Yet this is my man, my husband. He has ravished my realm, but he has bowed to me. And I must, at last, consider myself. Belle, whom I love, whose old grudges I was asked to share; Belle, whose portrait's colours are darkened by time, may have been a little blinded by hatred. For in his way, I think this is a gentle man.

Even the coronet felt easier on her brow, it was a new beautiful diadem with high arched florets. She raised her eyes, for the first time in her life surveying the assembled nobility as more than an equal. To where her mother stood she sent the captive scorn of years. I am free of you, terrible Isabeau, even though bound by memory, for I still remember that night when I lay at the gate of death and you played cards. You cannot hold or touch me now. I have an army at my side. Oblivious, the Queen-Mother stood smiling, next to Philip of Burgundy in his doleful black.

As it was Trinity Sunday there was an interminable anthem during which Katherine and Henry stood, then knelt, and stood, and were anointed, kissed and blessed, until the ceremony was finally over and it was time for the wedding feast. The sun had dipped and a swallow, which had caused a distraction by its swooping irreverent acrobatics, flew to roost in the mouth of a stone lion. Katherine thought light-headedly: Once I was ragged, frail and dying. Now I am Queen of England. The swallow has found her a nest where she may lay her young, and tell them that she once saw *me*!

The pantner came with his long towel draped about his neck, bearing on his outstretched left arm the seven loaves of eating bread and the four trencher loaves, and carrying the vast salt-cellar for the royal table. He set down the two knives with their haft outwards before the carver, and took out his own knives with which he shaped the plates from the round trencher loaves, squaring and smoothing the edges. Kneeling, he received the slice of bread from the assay loaf, and the ewerer came forward with two basins, straining water through fine linen and testing it as fit for the washing of royal hands. Plainsong grace filled the hall.

Katherine and Henry ate from the same dish. Food had never tasted so good to her. At one moment, seeing how little he ate, she stopped and looked at him obliquely. He said: 'The banquet is to your taste?'

'Ah yes, my lord. I was very hungry.'

She glanced round the assembly and saw that Humphrey of Gloucester was absent. Unreasonable, to feel such relief. She drank ale. The hot weather had turned most of the wine to vinegar. Shyly she raised her goblet to Henry, and he returned her courtesy with a smile so preoccupied it dampened her spirits for a moment. Then she thought: I am fanciful, I make much of little. And why should I fear Gloucester, who has done me no wrong? I see Jacqueline there with red eyes for love of him. My fear was misdirected on the part of that inner counsellor of mine. The dish before her was refilled with the fourth part of the first course, a Crustade Lombard. Eagerly she bit into the crisp pastry, tasting the succulent fruit and beef marrow within.

'You eat heartily, Katherine.'

The ale had gone to her head, just a little. She said: 'Does that displease your Grace?'

He frowned. 'No, no, certainly not. You are so slender, Katherine.'

She looked quickly away, and saw the swelling curves of Anne of Burgundy, brought here for her betrothal with John

257

of Bedford to be negotiated. She said foolishly: 'It grieves me that my lord finds me uncomely.'

Almost before the words were out, he said: 'Dear Katherine, you misjudge me. If you only knew how pleasing I find you!'

She smiled again. He put his hand on hers, saying softly: 'Why, even the angels . . .'

'Your Grace,' Louis de Robsart was kneeling at the dais. 'Word has reached us that the Duke of Bedford is in Paris.'

Henry's hand left hers at once. She felt the lack of it, and for comfort, took more pie. It had lost its savour. She slipped it beneath the damask cloth where a hound's furry jaws snapped it up. She started on a hot bread roll stuffed with cinnamon and Corinth raisins.

'And what is the situation in Paris now?' Henry asked.

'Paris is yours, Sire. Even now they drive the last of the Armagnacs from the streets. The river is silted up with Dauphinist corpses. The City's anxious to receive you and the Queen.'

'Ah!' Henry's brown eyes gleamed. 'Then we'll go there with all speed. Katherine! Welcome awaits us in Paris.'

She fluttered her fingers in the perfumed water by her plate, and dried them on the surnape. She edged the clean hand towards Henry's, and he held it again.

'When do we go to England? I long to see England.'

'And England longs for you, Madame.'

'I've seen nothing. You have seen so much, so many cities, counties, peoples.'

This amused him. 'My dear! I've seen blood and mud and sickness. One battlefield's the same as any other, one dead man like the next. At Harfleur, my friends died a dog's death.'

A great dish of raw fruit in syrup came with the next course, a subtlety of spun sugar. There were early golden plums, grapes and green figs. The tartness pleased her palate. She offered a washed fig to Henry. 'They're delicious.' He was about to decline but saw her disappointment. He ate the fig.

'I will serve you, my lord.' She busied herself snipping grapes, splitting open the yellow plums and placing them in his hand. He indulged her, and she, able to eat no more for the moment, took pleasure in watching him.

'Tell me about the last campaign,' she said.

'It was successful.' He was surprised that she should want to hear. 'But I did not think Rouen could withstand us for so long.'

He looked sharply at her; she had lost colour.

'Too much food?' he asked, ready to motion to a page for napkins. 'You feel sick?'

'I didn't want to hear about Rouen,' she said faintly. 'I heard what was done with the babies.'

He was silent for a few moments. Then he said: 'Put it from your mind. You will have babies of your own, God willing. So think no more, Katherine, of sieges and leaguers. They are not your concern.'

'And there is peace in England, where I may go with you. Soon?'

'As soon as possible. But I have campaigns to finish and the crucial part is yet to come. And then – my life's ambition, my work for God – to drive back the Infidel . . .'

Pain, unexpected as a night assassin, speared his bowels. I should not have taken the fruit. Down, damned pain, cursed legacy of Harfleur! I thought I had you outmatched long ago. Die, intruder of my wedding-day! He closed his eyes and broke into a pallid sweat. Katherine was afraid. She glanced towards her mother, who lolled, cup in hand, against the shoulder of Philip of Burgundy, to his obvious embarrassment. Was her protector already brought low? She said softly, 'Harry . . .' in uncertain accents, stressing the last syllable. He drew a deep breath and opened his eyes. The sight of her anxious face stirred him sweetly even in pain.

'Be easy, Madame,' he said. 'All's well, dear wife.'

Thomas, Duke of Clarence leaned across.

'I've arranged jousting as part of the festival. I trust this will please the Queen's Grace.'

Henry shook his head. 'No time, Thomas,' he said, each word an unguessed-at effort. 'There'll be jousting in earnest. At Montereau, at Sens.'

At Sens lies my debt to the Archbishop. Thus he thought as later, Henri de Choisy, stammering-pale, came with a score of priests and noblemen to bless the bed where Henry and

Katherine lay naked, the stiff brocade drawn to their chins, their bodies straightly moulded as if in effigy. Her long dark hair lay outside the coverlet like some rich reposing beast. Her breathing was swift and soft; he heard it through the long ritual prayers. The sacred wine and soup was brought and they sipped from it, token gestures, Henry fearing sickness and Katherine already sated. '*Benedicat Deus corpora vestra et animas vestras.*' Incense swirled and lodged in the bed-hangings. Three times the holy water fell, dampening the bed like rain while they lay stiffly together. He called *me* slender! Katherine thought, feeling the sharp hip-bone against her under the mounded clothes. I must make him eat, cherish him. He is all I have.

Musicians were playing softly outside the antechamber. There was the harp-note again and the voice with the wild, barely controlled merriment that had cheered her in a dark moment, now coiling about a psalm. Jacques, her father's comforter . . .

'You have given me my bride, *Monseigneur Archevesque*,' said Henry as de Choisy snuffed candles and prepared to withdraw. 'Soon I will restore yours – the diocese of Sens – the Church!'

Darkness covered the chamber. The faint music ceased. After a while she said: 'Is all well, Henry?'

As he did not move or speak she felt for his hand. He caught hold of her quite roughly, grazing her face on his cheekbone, holding her close, still silent.

'Is all well?' Hers was the loneliest, the last voice alive in the world. 'Harry?'

Then he said: 'All's very well, dear Katherine.' She lay waiting, knowing yet not knowing what to expect. She had heard vaguely of discomforts and ecstasies, neither of which occurred now. His extreme thinness worried her. She liked his kisses and returned them ardently, all the time thinking: *Freedom*. I am a Queen. Unassailable. The thoughts so redeemed her that there was no room for disappointment. She drifted into a light doze, and after some time heard him say:

'When I have done, there will be no Infidel left to conquer!'

And she, who had been following her own half-dream, said: 'To think you might have married my sister!' But Belle should not hang sorrowing above this marriage-bed. She said candidly: 'She had no good word for you . . . because of Richard. She was wrong, Harry.'

Sainte Vierge! he *is* ill. From head to foot he was filmed with sweat. An intermittent rigor shook him. She leaned on her elbow, wishing for a light. She touched her lips to his eyes and tasted salt.

'It was not my fault,' he said, his words dragged out. 'Don't speak of Richard or my father, or of Courtenay who died for me, or Oldcastle and Badby whom I put to the flame. If you love me, Katherine, do not speak of the past. All my life I've fought with ghosts. Give me your hand . . . such a strong hand. If there is any mercy owing to me, be my comforter.'

'With all my heart,' she said steadily, 'I give you my love, Harry. We will do well together.'

The pain had him again, it was so fierce she could almost feel it in her own nerves. Carefully she drew his head on to her breast, and with her soft toes began to rub his horny, freezing feet. He lay, teeth clenched, willing the pain away. In the pitch darkness red flashes danced, each flash a pain. I cannot be ill. With Montereau and Sens and Paris ahead I have no time to be ill. The porcupine emblem of the Armagnacs danced redly on the black, quilled with agony. Katherine whispered: 'Your physicians . . .' and he said as violently as the pain permitted: 'No! For God's love, it's nothing. Don't take your arm away, it helps me.'

She was coughing, a little dry cough, and he thought: poor Katherine! what a travesty of a wedding-night! What demon sent this plague just now? It shall be close between us. She will not tell; God willing, I may trust her. One word to the Armagnacs of this weakness and I am lost . . . or Philip . . . he should not know, he might think it a diplomatic illness and lose faith . . .

'Pain is good for the soul,' he said, as it ebbed a little and he lay cautiously still. 'I shall fast tomorrow. Then, sweet wife, I'll do more justice to your beauty . . .'

'Sleep, Harry,' she said. Her arm was numb, but she held him closer. The cough had parched her throat. There was wine on the night-table but nothing would move her from his comfort. This was not the loving she had witnessed between Jacqueline and Gloucester, but suddenly she was glad, proud to hold with tenderness rather than be held in such a storm. Jacqueline was mad with love . . . her two husbands had both been very young. Humphrey, like Henry, aged by comparison . . . fascinating . . . Jacqueline had undressed her tonight, whispering, don't forget! Madame, ask if I may go with you to England . . . sleep was forming a circle about her. Within it, Jacqueline's face shimmered and pleaded, she pushed it away, there was no time. Later, she'd ask him . . . the face returned and she stroked the soft hair reassuringly.

In his fevered sleep, Henry felt the caress. It drew him down and away to a place he had not visited for years. The great warrior was a child again, in the arms of Mary de Bohun, his dead mother.

Two days later, in a litter drawn by eight white horses, one of Henry's wedding gifts, she accompanied him and his army to Sens. The horses were not perfectly matched, and, paradoxically, this enhanced their perfection. One was dappled like a pearl, one white as a snowbird, one had a freckling of black on its quarters and one was whiter than whiteness, with pale blue eyes where the others' were dark, sad and generous between long lashes. Between an armed escort, the horses bore her *charrette* smoothly along. She looked out on the pale moving river of their grace, and adored them.

She had prayed that he would not leave her behind. Last night she had lain alone while he, somewhere unknown, conferred with his ministers. Then word had come for her to make ready. She understood his preoccupation with affairs. Yet she obeyed with joy, glad to be travelling through fair weather past terraces of vines, only sorry he was not nearer. She had come this way before, in a false life, a nightmare now powerless to alarm. Ahead she could see his standards, the blue and gold of France and England quarterly, with France Ancient borne by a pursuivant as a mark of respect to King Charles, who, drugged with music and poppy-juice, rode in a closed litter far behind. Isabeau too was travelling in an equipage far less glorious than her daughter's. Her suggestion: that Charles should come to Sens. Henry had agreed. There was always the danger that the Dauphin might attempt his father's abduction. The French royal household was on the move.

Some of the ladies had never been far from the court. They treated this expedition as a holiday. The presence of so many strong men had gone to their heads. Giggling mingled with the hoarse shouts of the commanders and the soldiers' oaths. Pages ran alongside with packs of small Italian greyhounds, and falconers bore peregrines and hawks on ribboned rods. Katherine knew without doubt that this would annoy Henry. His own party, jogging urgently ahead of the long cavalcade, seemed segregated from frivolity by a wall of steel-clad men. She knew that this enterprise was important to him. The Archbishop of Sens, with his priestly attendants, rode near him, where she longed to be. Instead, she had for company Jacqueline, weeping or laughing, beside herself with excitement and private frustrations.

'There goes the Pig!' she cried, as young Brabant galloped by.

'You shouldn't speak so of your husband.'

'Oh, Kéti!' She was almost the only person now who used the old pet-name. It touched Katherine, and Jacqueline knew it. 'When true love comes, all other men are pigs. Besides, Brabant's father killed my father, the great and good William of Holland . . .'

'It's past,' said Katherine. (*Do not speak of the past. Be my comforter.*)

'Does the English king please you?' Jacqueline asked impertinently. 'He looked very pale this morning. Is he well?'

A warning little cloud settled on Katherine's features. Incapable of leaving the subject, Jacqueline said: 'Is he a strong man?'

Katherine knew exactly what was meant. She said: 'The strongest, the best. *And* I do not care that he fights against my brother. *And* if Madame of Hainault does not stop this insupportable probing she will not come with me to England!'

263

A troupe of minstrels on horseback cantered past the eight white horses, startling them. Clarions sounded; the men sang a little war-song, riding. Jacqueline leaned from the litter.

'Look, Kéti! *There's* a handsome!'

'I thought you said all other men were pigs.' But Katherine looked where Jacqueline looked, saw bright curling hair, bright eyes, blue flecked with gold, the gold seeking supremacy, catching the sunlight almost like blind eyes. Snatched song, warring with the trumpets. Gaff, Gaff, catch him then, bring!

'Yes,' she said, and leaned back on her cushion, suddenly weary and wanting Henry, wondering if his pain had returned, sending up a little prayer for his easement. Ahead, his standards blew, winking at her reassuringly. He was wearing his crown about the battle-helm. Jacqueline knows nothing about love. There are no bursting stars, no angels singing. Only a sick tormented man finding solace in the arms of one who herself was the familiar of sickness and torment. *Harree . . .* she whispered, turning her face away from her companion. He has his pet-names too. For many years we shall do well together.

The bridge at Sens had been destroyed by the Dauphin's party still in possession and several outlying dwellings burned; they smoked among blackened cornfields. The porcupine standard of the Armagnacs hung from the town walls. From the safe distance of her pavilion, ringed with armed men under de Robsart's command, Katherine watched the little figures begin the siege, saw the cannon belching drifts of smoke as tiny and innocuous as snuffed candles. She guessed that her brother the Dauphin Charles was not there. He preferred to wage war remotely and had likely remained in his Bourges château. Patiently she waited and on the third day Henry came to her lodging where they shared a meal. She thought: he looks better, *grace à Dieu!* His colour was bright. He kissed her. She thought he had even put on a little flesh.

'Does it go well?' she asked, so softly that he had to bend close. The pavilion was filling with men, all the great generals and commanders.

'Better than expected. Madame – have you all you need?'

She looked straight into his eyes. I need constant news of

your safety. I need you here to enhance my peace. She dropped her glance and missed his tender look that said: *I know*.

'The siege will soon be over.' He turned from her to Sir John Cornwall who was saying, 'Sire, there is an emissary outside our lines. I think he wishes to *parler*.'

'The one with the torn banners and the dirty face? Bid him visit a barber and change his clothes before he comes to our presence. There are great ladies here.'

This time she caught his look of affection. He murmured: 'I am so pleased with you, my Katherine. Be patient.'

'Do you ever think of me?' she whispered, and bit her lip.

'No.' But he smiled, the smile cancelled the hurt. 'That way, battles are lost. I must live only upon the moment . . .' Then stopped, thinking: what eyes she has! They fill her whole face with darkness and light, a mystery. She is still my mystery. Sudden anguished panic made him take de Robsart aside to say: 'With your blood, guard her. Double her escort!' He thought: what would become of her if I were slain?

Sens fell within the week through attrition, which was the way he liked it best. There were few casualties, and he was pleased with the way Philip had handled the deployment of his forces, despite a certain impetuousness that sometimes marred his judgement. Paler than ever, still wearing his black, Philip had been in favour of storming the walls of Sens, even when the citizens were ready to surrender the keys. He wept when they entered the gates. So did the Archbishop, passing once more into his cathedral.

'God will reward you, *grand seigneur*,' he said. 'Blessings on you and your bride.'

'And upon you and yours.' Henry thought: I have kept my word. Holy Church blesses me! A wave of thanksgiving invaded him. Henri de Choisy was bearing from the cathedral the holy relics, a piece of the True Cross, a bone from St Denis's foot, for him to kiss. Looking about him he saw King Charles, mute, being borne on a litter which for all he knew might be set on the road to Hell. He said to the Archbishop: 'I pray you, take them first to our dear father. It is his privilege.'

Then Henry saw the eight white horses. Their drivers had whipped them up on Katherine's orders. They came like

265

a stream of living pearls, their belled trappings echoing his own joy. It was not only the taking of Sens that gladdened and released him; it was her. She was leaning forward, her coiled dark hair escaping from the elaborate headdress, her eyes seeking him over the heads of the excited soldiery and courtiers. He went quickly forward, seizing the leading horses' bridles and bearing them strongly backwards to a halt. She alighted and ran to him.

'Is it over?'

'For the moment.' He kissed her, and wanted to go on kissing her, but modesty in face of the crowd inhibited him. He had sent servants ahead to make ready the best lodging in Sens. For the first time in years, his desires were channelled into something other than the gains of war . . .

'Now, will you think of me?' She was smiling, radiant. He caught her up and lifted her into the *charrette*.

'Of you,' he said. 'Of you, Madame, and nothing else.' To the coachman: 'Stand down! I will drive the horses!'

The pearly river moved forward, deep into the captured town of the Armagnacs.

The honeyed time was over, and she was diminished, as by the loss of a limb. She had been raised to a height, and the abyss to which she had now been lowered was deeper than in the black times of old uncertainty. She thought of the babies at the siege of Rouen, winched up from the moat for the kiss of God, then cast back down the swifter to meet Him. For Henry had taken her, loved her, and was gone.

North he had departed, with his army, following the Yonne to Montereau. The sun had gone too, leaving a chill rain like the tears she could not shed. Louis de Robsart had broken the news that Henry thought it best that she remain in Sens. The reason he gave was that the campaign was becoming too dangerous, but she knew better. The laughing ladies, the hawks and playthings, misplaced revelries, had posed a threat to discipline. If only he had told her himself during the nights when he had bound her to himself until she was bemused by contentment! There had been no Archbishop to dew the bed with solemnity, no malaise to sap Henry's power. It had been her turn to lie safely in his arms, listening to his drowsy voice lapping her in sweetness. The pledge never to talk of the past was honoured, but neither would he discuss the future. Only now did she realize that on campaign he lived from day to hazardous day. There was also the bitter knowledge that, away from her, he put her from his mind.

When she had heard of his impending departure, all that had passed between them seemed for a moment oddly soiled and shameful. For she had discovered in herself a wellspring of abandonment almost too powerful to contain. Shared with him, it was beauty and goodness; here in the abyss, she was reminded only of her mother, of the succession of paramours taken for policy or lust, all of whom had met terrible ends. God preserve me, she thought, from such an inheritance! Yet she had recognized her own carnality. It couched within her, an animal, a coiled, purring need. Her shame was such that she could not voice it even to her chaplain. Terrible regrets and embarrassments assailed her. How wildly she had laughed when Harry had said, breathless with delight:

'Forgive me, Katherine! I've lived like a monk of late, and now . . .'

'My monk! Now the monk sheds his habit . . . Harry, Harry!' She had met his passion like a soldier in close mortal combat. She had made him very happy, and in herself had lit a fire to burn for ever.

When they said farewell in the courtyard at Sens, she hardly knew him. He was a steel man in a host of steel men, his face closed, his mouth set. Harry of the night was gone, locked away by another implacable being. Shining brigandines covered his frail flesh. Then there was only the spark of hooves on the cobbles, the banners diminishing to little coloured blurs, and her own tearing loss.

'Madame has been weeping,' said Jacqueline. She sat at Katherine's feet, teasing a kitten with a bobbin on a thread.

'I have not,' said Katherine. I leave all the weeping to you. Long ago I learned that tears solve nothing. My eyes are red from sleeplessness in that great empty bed. She looked down at her own hands. They were trembling and for a moment seemed to have a strange transparency.

'The flowers of *agrimoine* are good for the eyes. Shall I distil some for you?'

'You sound like an old nun who once cared for me.'

'Me! A nun!' Jacqueline laughed shrilly. Katherine thought bitterly: you are part of my trouble. Had you and the others tempered their glee I should be riding with my lord, quiet and stern and soldierly as he would wish. Had he wanted it I would have put on armour!

'Kéti, don't look at me like that! Don't be so sad!'

'Husbands are often away. I didn't realize it.'

'Yes, they are, thank God! Madame, you *will* take me with you to England! Please . . .'

'You only want to be with Gloucester.' Katherine frowned. Let Jacqueline wait. No need to tell her yet that Harry was almost brought round to the idea – it had taken all her persuasions. 'As for divorce,' she said, 'you will be excommunicated.'

'Faugh!' cried Jacqueline, and as others would protest for generations: 'What does the Pope know of love?'

Minstrels were playing continuously outside the chamber. Someone was singing, an air so rapturous and melancholy that it hurt the heart. Katherine pulled her tapestry screen towards her and stabbed her needle deep. She started carefully to embroider an acanthus leaf.

'Send them away,' she told Jacqueline. 'I wish for quietness.'

'It was the handsome one,' Jacqueline said brightly, returning.

'There are no handsome men,' replied Katherine, and bit off a thread.

'Father, my noble father!' The cry echoed round the dusty little church as Philip knelt by the recently opened coffin. A spider had woven veils across the fleshless face of Jean sans Peur, and rats had been at his eyes, dislodging the two silver pennies. The parish priest of Montereau had made some attempt at embalming the Duke after his assassins had left him on the bridge, but most of the body was rotted like its

268

cheap shroud; it was hard to distinguish between cloth and flesh.

Infected by Philip's grief, Henry swallowed tears. He said: 'May Almighty God have mercy on his soul. We must send for salt and myrrh to mend the damage done to him.'

Philip's face blazed red and white. 'This is damage that cannot be mended, my lord. As for God! Let Him witness that I will not leave a soul alive in Montereau!'

Henry bit his lip. This ill-judged emotionalism was a facet of Philip that he feared. He had already been disturbed by the overheated manner in which Montereau had been taken. Screaming Philip's challenge, flailing the banners with the gold-fleeced ram, the Burgundians had stormed the town like madmen. For one terrible moment it seemed that the barely controlled ranks would break when they came on to the bridge, hurled up their siege-ladders and then themselves over the walls. He looked down at his own mailed shoes, rusted with blood to the ankles. Through the church walls he could hear the screams as Dauphinists were chased, clubbed and stabbed to death in the streets.

'Where do you wish him taken?' he asked, deliberately calm.

Philip rose, wiping his eyes. 'The Charterhouse at Dijon. With other heroes of his line.'

'My brother of Clarence will attend to it. You and I have work to do. Not in haste or rage, my lord, but with expediency. We have the town. Now we must capture the castle.'

Philip said: 'The castle! the garrison hides within the castle, with their families. We'll raze it to the ground.' But he seemed suddenly exhausted, his voice was feeble.

'Why decimate the populace?' Henry asked. 'Rather, have them work for us to build Montereau anew.' He found himself once more in command. Already he had set up a bridge across the Seine linking the force on the right bank of the Yonne where his cannon were trained on the castle. While Philip had been mourning his father's corpse for the past two hours, Henry had captured eleven hostages, who now knelt beside the moat, begging the garrison's captain, Guillaume de Chaumont, to surrender, or see them hanged.

Summoning his escort, he went outside. The walls of the little church were splashed with red flowers, long-stemmed where the blood ran down. A drizzle of rain was pinkening the red on the flagstones. Glinting silver caught his eye in a doorway; a holy vessel. Earlier, men must have been fighting in the church. As he looked, an English footsoldier ran past, stooped and caught up the silver plate, thrusting it into his belt and running on.

'Take him,' Henry said softly to the guard.

Shortly the man confessed. He had stolen the salver, leaving it to be later retrieved, and he had murdered the priest protecting it. Henry knew his grimy face; one of his most courageous soldiers, due for promotion to armiger, who had been in the front line at every battle and siege. For a second he found himself poised on the edge of mercy. Then he ordered:

'Build the gallows close to the castle walls. He shall hang with our enemies.'

Priests were with the hostages, hearing confession. Guillaume de Chaumont stood armed upon the walls, bellowing that he would never surrender the garrison; below, the raging Burgundians and the quietly ranked English listened.

'In God's mercy, let us see our loved ones before we die!' cried the hostages, and women with babies, young boys and greybeard fathers came to look over the battlements. Dreadful lamenting drifted down across the moat.

'Command him one more time,' Henry said tightly to the captives' spokesman. Again de Chaumont wagged his head and roared defiance. On either side of him, stood huge bearded men wearing fleeced tunics over their harness.

'Are those the Scots?' asked Philip of Burgundy.

'Yes,' Henry said grimly. 'There are hundreds in there. That barbarous race with whom my father tussled and whose king we've held in London Tower for these past fourteen years. I might have known the Scots would ally themselves to Armagnac!'

There was one woman, leaning dangerously over the crenellations of the wall, her hands outstretched imploringly to where her husband knelt, a rope about his neck. Her long

270

dark hair streamed, her black eyes were full of tragic light. Henry looked away swiftly.

'By St Mary Virgin! Have done!' He signalled to the executioners. The weeping stopped abruptly. Death was played out in absolute silence. Then a raven, perching on the highest turret, emitted a hoarse bark and others began to circle, landing heavily. Henry looked up again. The woman had gone. In the town the fighting had recommenced. Thomas of Clarence came to stand by him, and they stared at the twelve lolling heads.

'And now they'll surrender,' said Clarence. 'Mark me.'

'I know,' Henry said. 'Were I inside that castle, I'd cut de Chaumont in pieces. The stubborn fool.'

'There's a message. Bedford will be with us in a day. He's bringing Scottish James from London at your orders. God willing, he may persuade his subjects to desert their cause. Also a reinforcement's on its way. Fifteen hundred. Mostly bowmen. And Count Lewis of the Rhine is coming, with seven hundred men. Your last letter convinced him, Harry . . .'

He could not get the woman, the dark eyes and hair, from his mind. *I live only upon the moment*; he had said it himself. I do not think of you . . . battles are lost that way. He knew now that he had lied to himself; bewildered, he felt the subtle change, and sought vainly to expunge it. He said: 'Is the messenger still here?' and Clarence pointed to a man standing on the river bank beside a foamy horse.

No time to write a long letter; the castle would fall before night came. What message then? He knew that she was well, de Robsart's courier reported almost daily . . . but it was not enough.

'I wish to send greetings to my Queen,' he began stiffly, 'to inform her of my fair health and successful feat of arms in this place . . .'

The clerk kneeling before him scratched away, then waited. God's mercy! Henry thought. Madness, truth. Like the wines of old of which I drank too deep. I need her.

'Say that when we have built her a house . . .'

'A house,' muttered the clerk, writing busily.

'In Melun,' said Henry, and saw Philip's eyes kindle with

a near-mad joy, for Melun held the Dauphin's chief castle, where he might well be in person.

'. . . where she may live with us in great joy and comfort –' haltingly, and hearing his voice harsh with disguised longing – 'then we will send for her.'

The November fog smoked lithely about the walls of the new stone mansion. In their haste for completion the glaziers had skimped their labour on the windows and into the chamber where Owen was working on his dance crept grey puffs of mist. Acrid gunpowder mingled with it. He could hear the distant rumble of the bombardes and the sharper explosions from the small cannon, the crapaudins and veuglaires, all blasting their way into the fourth month of the siege of Melun.

The dance was nearly right, except for the ending. Its creation eluded him, for its essence was man and woman in one, yielding yet virile; almost impossible to form its pattern without the music. He had to listen in his mind. Poised, he turned to look back at the four white clovers, bequeathed by Olwen's mystic feet. It was coming . . . it was almost perfect . . . now, now . . . A tremendous explosion came from the siege lines. The ill-fitting windows rattled. Owen lost his balance, almost fell. He swore, all the old Welsh words; he kicked a leather bucket across the room, forgetting it was lined with steel and he wore soft shoes. Thomas Harvey, laughing at him in the doorway, clapped his hands to his ears.

'I wish I could curse like that! Even in English. What ails you now?'

'My work,' Owen said crossly.

He walked across the room, flexing his bruised toes. Someone had left a little Book of Hours open on a bench. A saint was being boiled alive in a vast cauldron, under which knaves stoked the fire. Smirking over prayerful hands, he seemed almost to be enjoying the experience. Saints, it appeared, had all things made easy.

'You love your music, your dancing!' said Harvey, surprised. 'As for the Wardrobe duties, pay no heed to Master Feriby.

He was always a crossgrained wretch.'

Owen glared down at the simmering saint. 'Once,' he said bitterly, 'I was a soldier, and I stood for weeks behind a palisade like those out there. I fought near the King and his brother – I was part of the *galanastra* – the slaughter – on Artois plain. The great knight Gam, whom Christ assoil, died in my arms. Now I'm a prancing tamed ape, a mender of holes in velvet, a singing salver of consciences. *Y diafol!* They've turned me into a lady!'

Harvey said: 'You've made yourself too useful, soothing Mad Charles.'

'Maybe. Would to God I was out there fighting. Tell me the news.'

'Today the King beheaded de Chaumont – not Guillaume, but Bertrand, his cousin.'

'*That* de Chaumont! He was one of our best captains at Agincourt, he fought under the King's standard.'

'He was found guilty of corrupting the Melun garrison. The Armagnacs bribed him to let some prisoners escape. The King said he would have given 50,000 nobles rather than hear of such treason. Clarence and Burgundy pleaded . . . but Harry said had it been his own brothers he would have done the same.'

Owen nodded, unsurprised. 'What more?'

'In Melun itself, it's Harfleur all over again. The belly-rot is raging. They're starving; the town ditch is full of corpses. Stop complaining! You're snug in the royal house with enough food, and your other comforts!' He winked. 'I admire your present choice, I must admit.'

Owen's latest mistress, acquired in Sens, was the silver-blonde Jeanne, sixteen years old and known as Jeanne la Picarde. On several occasions he had had her among the piled furs and velvets, in the room where the winter wardrobe was stored. Harvey had one day opened the door. I do not always behave gently, he thought, and, for excuse: among the English I am not deemed a gentleman. At home, I have consanguinity with princes.

He was very fond of Jeanne. She never wept; she had the wit not to pursue him, and an appealing graciousness. He had

273

not spoken to her of love, it was against his principles, and he hated the false courtly speeches that were in fashion, yet it would not have been difficult to do so. That is, until a few weeks ago. He couldn't remember exactly when the feeling began, not of boredom with her, but more of failed attainment, something lost. A hunger like an unrecognized disease, quite outside his diagnosis. He knew it to be no fault of hers; this made it doubly mysterious.

Harvey was still talking. 'Everyone thinks the end of the siege is near, but there have been some unhappy moments. Apart from the Dauphin's raiding parties – he, by the way, still lies about twenty miles from the action – some of the Burgundian troops have been deserting to his standard. And King James has had little influence with his Scotsmen, who stay with Armagnac. It appears that there were Scotsmen on the bridge where they killed John the Fearless, so *they'll* be for the rope, if Philip has any say in the matter!'

'Are they still fighting in the mines?'

'Most of the warfare goes on underground.' Harvey chuckled. 'Yesterday the Gascon, Arnaud of Barbazan, went down below, trumpets sounding, bells ringing. And who did he meet there in the dark? King Harry himself! They struck at one another for minutes until the Gascon realized and withdrew, saying the honour was too much for him! They're chopping the axe handles off short to fight down there better. I hate to see a good axe mutilated.'

'Are the town walls breached?'

'Daily, but they fill them up again overnight. It *must* end soon. It *must*.'

'Listen,' said Owen.

They were silent. The fog seemed to be clearing, a thin ray of sunshine silvered Owen's fair head. The drifts of mist through the ill-fitting windows smelled purer; the gunsmoke odour was dispersing.

'The firing has stopped.' They looked at one another. They waited for long moments. A sparrow cheeped irritably outside the window.

'They're resting. Gathering reinforcements.'

'Wait!' Harvey sharply raised his hand. Then he flung the

window wide letting in gusts of sunlit damp. Very far away, cheering arose.

'It's ended!' Harvey's face shone. He slapped Owen on the back, and then performed a hopping dance all round the room. Owen thought: I should be glad too, but what's it to me? Something is eating me, other than being armourless and housebound, which annuls all my small pleasures, takes the shine from my wit and my responses. Another town taken, another woman bedded, another listener satisfied, another dance created. All insignificant landmarks down my lonely road. Once, I was promised greatness or some such arrant nonsense. I am nearly twenty-two. And, with excessive melancholy: I should have died in the field like Davy, and become immortal.

'God be praised,' said Harvey, unexpectedly wiping away tears. 'Four months in this cursed place has made a dotard of me.'

A page's head, with popping eyes, came round the door.

'Melun is taken!' he cried, then added: 'And Master Tydier is summoned to the French king's apartments.'

I'll take the lute today, Owen thought. And, he decided, I shall give him a *bergerette* by Gilles Binchois, that brilliant young Burgundian musician whom I envy so, for he is also a soldier. Mad Charles will have to endure it. I am overrun with psalms.

'Have a care,' said Thomas Harvey, sitting down breathless from his dance on the Book of Hours. 'Remember the eyes!'

Lately, Henry had commanded that none should look a royal person in the face. Even the Marshal of France, Sire de l'Isle Adam, had been reprimanded. When he had remarked that it was the French custom not to address anyone, whatever his estate, with a downcast countenance, Henry had replied coldly: *'It is not ours!'*

Harvey mused: 'There's only one person I can identify without looking at or hearing. The Queen's Grace.'

'The perfume,' said Owen. One of the lute-strings looked worn; he frowned. He hoped it would not snap today and frighten Charles. 'Her perfume.'

'Yes. I knew the day she took up residence here . . . it's very seductive. Harry must like it, he visits her whenever he can . . .'

'Yes.' Owen took a sudden dislike to the look of the lute, it was a bad design, an ugly shape. He felt an insane desire to break it across his knee.

'. . . otherwise she keeps close within her bower, with that glorious Hainault woman,' said Harvey.

Owen left him and went along to the wing inhabited by King Charles. The passage window was open and Isabeau's voice, raised in anger at a tiring-woman, floated from the opposite tower through the thinning fog. Further down the passage were the apartments of Harry and his Queen. Jacqueline of Hainault passed him and gave him a provocative look which he registered efficiently from beneath lowered lashes. He was admitted to the French king's presence. He watched his own feet move over the parti-coloured tiles until Charles's slippers came into view. He was startled by the merry greeting.

'Welcome, troubadour! Welcome, Jacques! Wash your mouth out with wine before you sing. Look up, man, don't be nervous!'

Here was a predicament, but, Harry being absent, he obeyed. He was astonished at the change he saw. Charles's eyes were sparkling, he had a goblet in his perfectly steady hand, and his ravaged face was almost handsome.

'God's greeting, *grand seigneur*,' Owen murmured.

'Gramercy. See, the sun is returning. This weather has given me *la grippe*, but I feel better today. You may play as lustily as you please.'

Just what I intended, thought Owen. He gratefully drained the cup of wine offered by a page, and sat down with his lute. Then Charles said: 'A moment!' The door opened. Owen slid his eyes round, cautiously waiting to see whether it was safe to raise them. There was no need. Lilies and roses and honey, and more, a musky, almost peppery odour, distilled in one warm woman's flesh. The Queen was moving swiftly to the dais, she was somewhat *deshabillée*, her dark hair in a thick plait over one shoulder; her gown was pink wool, her mantle

276

lemon silk. She was attended by two handmaidens. A lamp might have been lit from her, she had a sheen, a rapturous glow, a blithe contentment that engulfed him as she passed by.

She ran up lightly on to the dais. Charles rose to embrace her, fearless, willing, changed; no more tears, no shrinking away.

'Katherine, my dear child, my little one. What passes?'

'Melun has surrendered at last. The King's Grace will be here within the hour, and then we're going to Paris!'

'Paris!' cried Charles. 'Sacred city! Shall I be with you, daughter?'

'Of course, of course. The whole court. Harry's coming. It's wonderful. He's safe, unharmed.'

She turned on the dais as if to welcome all into her bliss. Owen raised his head fully and looked at her. Had it meant hanging he would still have done it. In the time she had been at Melun he had scarcely seen her. Now he saw her changed. No longer childlike, but flowered in beauty, graceful as an undine. He looked at her eyes, her mouth, her body. He saw the signs of love in her, as in a mirror. A terrible joy and grief laid hands on him; a knowledge so fierce that the room darkened in his sight.

And then he knew the nature of his vague disease, and why Jeanne la Picarde had ceased to please him.

Together they circled Paris eastward to enter by the royal gate under the headless stone figure of St Denis. It was Advent Sunday. Crowned, Henry and Katherine went first, on matching horses, followed by the Burgundians and King Charles, no longer in his closed litter but mounted, with Isabeau a few paces behind. Bishops and Archbishops waited in a sunburst of rich vestments, bearing the relics of the Passion pledged by St Baldwin to the Sainte-Chapelle. The reliquary, borne under a silk canopy, was dulled by the November damp. The day was cold, unpleasant; the bellying wall of the old town, the Enceinte Philip-Augustus, was cloyed with moisture. Katherine folded her hands within her sleeves; a knight led her horse. The relics were offered for Henry to kiss. Once again he asked they should be taken first to Charles. While the priests moved in procession between the stamping, tired horses, he spoke softly to Katherine.

'The journey has wearied you. We shall soon be lodged.'

'No, I'm well,' she answered, and as he turned away again, she searched the narrow, clever, close-cropped profile and, dismayed, knew that he himself was far from well. He had that look, an ageing fleshlessness about him, the pallor showing through the war-weathered complexion, the too-straight posture employed to combat what could be a slight pain or a crippling agony. Could nothing ever be perfect? She had eagerly anticipated Paris and returning cherished, protected, to exorcize all frightful memories. Determination blossomed: I will nurse and heal him. I will have recourse to the old remedies of Dame Alphonse. Given with love and prayer, these can prove effective. I will be his doctor, the only one he can trust to keep a close mouth. He is sick, yet thinks only of my welfare! And yet – and yet this same man will hang his dearest friend for treachery. Would he, I wonder, ever show me that ruthlessness? I think, I trust, it would need to be a mortal sin . . . She laid a hand on his sleeve, and he turned to smile at her, a smile severe with pain.

The blessing over, the procession moved through the precincts of St Eustache, by Les Halles towards St Honoré, and everywhere there was a pageant. A dozen St Denises knelt before the block, to rise triumphant. Everywhere choristers gilded strophes of praise, and even the nuns of the Célestins had come out to bow. On the corners the conduits belched wine. Men and women were falling drunk, and Katherine felt ashamed of the city. And with the drunken desperate gaiety, came a whispering: *there goes the foreigner.* See how Charles takes second place? Our King is Henry? No King of ours! The pageantry, music, prayers, were all a sham. There was a rash of outrage under the smooth skin of welcome. And in the next street loomed the cause, tangible, horrible. Three dead infants lay on a dungheap, not a morsel on the pathetic wasted bones. Then, through the gaunt eyes of the revellers, Katherine saw how the long siege had weakened Paris. The civil strife within had bred starvation as surely as in Rouen. Some who guzzled at the festive conduits were like living skeletons. Like pictures in her old breviary – three pretty women hawking and dancing, and on the facing page the same three stripped of flesh, entrails visible. The vast and incontrovertible lesson of mortality.

She shivered, wrapping about her the mantle of Icelandic wolfskin Henry had given her, trying to ignore the whispers which, now recognized, grew more insistent. She wanted to cry aloud: your hunger is not my husband's fault! The accursed warring dynasty of Valois is to blame! Acknowledge the saviour who brings you peace! I blame my brother Charles, and that wicked wretch riding behind with her fixed lascivious smile. I blame Burgundy and Armagnac. France is Henry's now. France and England are one, and I am their mother.

'Harry.' She spoke quietly, averting her eyes and mind from the ugliness and hostility, though watching him, she knew he felt it too. 'Are we to lie at the Louvre?'

'You and I. Your father has expressed his wish to go to the Hôtel de St Paul.'

'He was very unhappy there, long ago. Perhaps he wishes to face his demons.'

He twisted on his horse to study her. 'To face his demons . . . a good phrase, Katherine. Anyway, that is what he wants.'

'And my mother?'

'She wishes to come to the Louvre.' He saw her eyes cloud, and said: 'I can command her, you know.'

'I think,' said Katherine quietly, 'all women should be with their husbands. Also . . .'

'Also, she should not be given the chance to steal more jewels,' said Henry, and laughed aloud. She had seldom heard him laugh before. It went oddly with his stern, fateful ageless-ness. But she laughed too, even though they were passing by the end of a bread queue stretching all the way from Les Halles, and that a grey harridan was shaking her fist at them and crying in outrage: 'Eight deniers for a stick of bread!'

'Queen Isabeau shall lie at the Hôtel de St Paul,' he said, and Katherine kissed him with her eyes.

While the people chewed roots and haggled with the ex-tortionate food merchants, the dignitaries of Paris had hung cloth of gold for the royal party. Near the palace a crowd waited, forgetting their hunger to gape. The cheering began as Katherine appeared. As she rode her horse along the costly carpet laid to the gate of the Louvre, wild compliments singed her ears, praising her beauty, her bearing, her new majesty. Charles and Isabeau were greeted with equal enthusiasm. Very occasionally someone cried diplomatically: 'God guard King Henry!' She longed to take his hand and hold it high, give him a rightful share of the affection lavished on her. For, seeing his unsmiling face, his rigid pose, the people ceased even their lukewarm praise and turned from him, muttering. What a vain hope that Paris could ever love him! They acknowledge him as conqueror and arbiter, but they will never love him. I shall love him, in place of Paris and the world. And Poperin pears are said to be good for his complaint. I shall have some placed before him at supper.

But there were no pears to be had, and anyway that evening he ate nothing. She had little speech with him; he was intent throughout the feast on what John of Bedford had to say. They leaned close, talking very seriously, though in the noisy packed hall she could catch hardly a word. Also she had a new companion at her left hand, and a surprising one. King James I of Scotland, seemingly unblemished by his years of captivity, was a plumpish, pleasant young man in his mid-twenties, and he talked, in good French, as frantically as if he had just discovered speech.

'*Ma reine*,' he said, eating fast and looking about him bemused. 'This is a privilege. I did not think I would be honoured to join the feast today.'

She let him talk. Fourteen years was a long time to be imprisoned. She asked him about the Tower of London, where Charles of Orléans had first been taken.

'One has all one needs. I was on my way to be schooled in France when King Henry Bolingbroke's army took my ship off Flamborough Head. In the Tower I continued my education. I have my poetry. Chaucer! my dear master, my inspiration!' He watched in childlike pleasure as an entertainer in the body of the hall swallowed fire and danced on his hands.

'I would give my life to be truly free again,' he said sadly.

'But then you would be bound by death,' said Katherine. 'Cannot your countrymen ransom you?'

'They're bent only on fighting. They scarcely recognize me. Madame . . .' Instinctively she knew that a request was imminent. It must be common knowledge that with Henry, she had some persuasive powers. To wit, Jacqueline's desires, which he had not refused. Indeed, he had admitted that since signing the Treaty of Canterbury with Sigismund of Bohemia he had the Holy Roman Empire on his side. As for Pope Martin, now supreme, the Great Schism having been healed by England, dispensations had been granted and could be again, to annul Jacqueline's marriage to Brabant . . . She looked at Henry now, tenderly, at his grave gaunt cheek inclined towards Bedford, then she turned back to James.

'What is it you wish of me?'

'If the King's Grace would only let me stay at large . . .'

'You would need to affiance yourself wholly to his cause, and fight under his standard.'

'This I'd do.' Then, more softly: 'There's something else . . . Madame, I am a poet come face to face with a living poem. I saw her walking in the gardens below the Maiden's Tower. Her name – ' his voice shook – 'is Joan Beaufort, niece of your great Bishop. Madame – ' he pushed his trencher of food away – 'if you know anything of love . . . Before, I was almost content. But now . . .'

I know of love, thought Katherine. She said: 'You wish to marry her?' That's a match which might not displease Henry, for Joan is his relative, albeit by bastard blood. Such an alliance with the troublesome Scots could be useful. See how politic I am becoming! She smiled delightfully at the thought, and James, watching her, desired the married state more than ever. Music, sweet and plangent, curled about the hall from the minstrel troupe. Katherine, her glance unseeingly brushing Owen's bright bent head, said: 'Be easy, my lord. I will help you, to my power.'

Henry was rising from the dais, the company following suit. John of Bedford still kept close to him, talking tersely, spreading his hands. In looks they were not unalike. He had the same brown eyes and cropped hair, but his face was fleshy in comparison with Henry's. She had seen his full lips smile kindly, but at present they were tight with some ruthless disquiet. On Henry's arm she left the chamber between bowing French and English, and, with her women, went to her chamber to wait for him. She did not mean to sleep, but she was weary from the long day.

She was awakened about midnight. He stood fully clothed by her bed, with a taper in his hand. Its wavering light explored the bones and hollows of his face. She sat up. From the antechamber came the sound of peaceful snoring. He had come so quietly that none had awakened.

'Harry, you should rest,' she whispered.

He set down the light and sat upon the bed. He began almost absently to stroke her bare shoulder and the swathes of rich dark hair.

'I have been praying,' he said. 'I know now the true nature of my malady. John told me this evening. I have been bewitched.'

'Bewitched!' A sudden chill gripped her brow and spread to her throat. She began to cough. His long fingers moved to the source of the cough, and soothed it into silence.

'My stepmother, Joanna of Navarre. She's always hated me. She has laid a curse on me back in England, to waste my bowels in agony and weaken my power. Being the widow of old Duke John, she still feels allegiance towards Brittany and resents the truce I made with them . . . her Spanish blood is versed in sorcery. I never knew her intent was as fierce as this. She grudged me the jewels and money I had from her for my campaigns. But I left her endowed with enough for her comfort. By the Mass! I've never warred with a woman before!'

'They're much as men,' murmured Katherine. He gave her a cynical look, but went on stroking her, and talking.

'She had accomplices: Randolf, her Franciscan confessor, and two members of her household skilled in demonology. The truth came out before my brother left England. She has compassed and imagined my death in the most horrible manner that can be devised.'

He spoke almost with excited triumph.

'I'm glad that I know,' he said. 'I have warned God and Our Blessed Lady. They have always fought for me. I have an army in that other world.'

'How goes the ailment now?' whispered Katherine.

'Much easier.' He looked at her ardently. 'Katherine, do you still long for England?'

More and more, she told him. If only to see him receive the worship he deserved.

'Then we'll be there, shortly after Christmas. Will that please you? The people will fall down at sight of you. You will be crowned in Westminster.'

She said: 'It is Harry the people will cry for, not Katherine. She will be busy with her prayers, for your safe coming and going, your eternal protection.' She knelt up on the bed, her long hair mantled them both. She held him close. 'None shall harm you, while I live.'

'My Katherine,' he said, deeply moved. He put her from him so he could look at her. 'This I must tell you. When I first came to France in blood and justice, you were the prize I sought, the proof of my endeavours. You understand.'

She smiled. 'Harry, I know, I understand.'

'But never – ' and he smoothed back her hair and began slowly to kiss each long gleaming eye – 'never did I dream that I would love you so.'

The welcome began from the moment they were carried ashore at Dover on the stout backs of the Barons of the Cinque Ports, of which Henry was Warden. It excelled any Katherine had known and was almost terrifying in its extravagance. It was Candlemas Day and the sea was fresh and lively, with great waves running across the tide as if to claw at the sheer cliffs, whose white chalk was ribbed with lichen like a precious mosaic. An enormous English lord had plucked her from the longboat as if she were a kitten. She clung to the piled furs about his neck, sorrowing for the ruin of his velvet skirts in the salt water, though this seemed to bother him not at all. As he carried her he cried praises, snatched from his lips by the roar of the sea. A thousand people were on the beach and a multitude blackened the cliff-top. Square banners and pennoncelles blew wildly, golden croziers and embroidered canopies borne above the clergy caught the February light all along the edge of the waves. Trumpets scored the air with frantic, acid braying and seabirds screamed. A choir broke into the *Deo Gratias*, and was drowned by a massed cheer so violent with excitement that it jolted Katherine's heart. A few yards away Henry rode the neck of a vast baron as he might a horse, stretching his arms high in greeting as they neared the shore. Behind, the Duke of Bedford, the Earls of March and Warwick, James of Scotland and the other lords were being rowed ashore. In the anchored fleet were hundreds more of Henry's great captains and counsellors, waiting their turn together with the Household and the ladies, among them Jacqueline, half mad with joy. Katherine wondered about her eight white horses. When last seen they were being winched aboard a raft; she hoped they would be handled gently.

She had believed the English to be a strange, savage, mercenary race, and cold. She wondered how many other lies she had believed. *Sainte Vierge!* there was nothing cold about their King! In her retrospective rapture she half-throttled the baron, he did not seem to mind and went on roaring her praises. To think I once imagined I was born unlucky! I am the most fortunate, blessed lady in Christendom! Henry was ashore; men were falling on their faces before him in the wet sand. He was holding out his arms still, as if to embrace them all. My dear companion, she thought, my joy-maker. Oh, Belle, how truly wrong you were!

For several hours her feet never touched English soil. She was carried everywhere in the arms of great knights who almost fought one another for the privilege, and in chariots each one more sumptuous than its predecessor. She heard oaths of fealty in accents which her command of English sometimes found unintelligible. Swept by the tumult of generosity, she saw tears and laughter in the streets and crowds gathered so thickly in the flat fields of Kent that she feared England would tip into the sea. At Canterbury she wept a little from the beauty of the singing and the jewelled miracle of St Thomas's shrine. She was parted at Canterbury from Henry, who, with an escort riding fast horses, galloped ahead to ensure that in London everything was ready for her coming. At every halt he made he sent back greetings and tributes; soon a wagonload of gifts followed her train.

Gradually the striped fields and Kentish orchards gave way to the slopes of the North Down and the sprawling forests of Eltham. The Archbishop of Canterbury, Henry Chichele, rode with her, accompanied by his priests and the precious relics that were to add lustre to her coronation. Henry had spoken affectionately of Chichele, who had been his confessor in earlier times, and she found his presence reassuring. As they travelled he rehearsed her in procedure for the forthcoming ceremony. Her own chaplain, Johan Boyars, chosen by Henry, was with them and she found him sympathetic too. It would be a long and arduous occasion, they said. Yet she was already a queen, divine, immune, strong. Also in the company was Henry Beaufort, Bishop of Winchester, thirty-six years old and so proud and princely that at first she mistook him for an unknown brother of the King. His face was strong; his hooked nose was flanked by grey eyes as judicial and unblinking as an owl's. But he addressed her with greater deference than any, and put himself about immeasurably for her slightest whim.

Katherine marvelled at the palace of Eltham, its round blunt towers so different from the pinnacled turrets and delicate spires of the French châteaux. The garden had lily-lakes and swans and climbing roses and there Henry rejoined the main party. With him came Humphrey of Gloucester. He greeted her effusively, throwing himself upon his knees with much panache, calling her *'Madame la reine'* and *'ma chère sœur'*. Rising, he asked permission to salute her as a brother. From the tail of her eye she saw Beaufort's expression. The owl had changed to an eagle; his face was grey with fury. She felt the unmistakable hatred that sparked between him and Gloucester. Then Humphrey kissed her on the mouth, she felt the lightning probe of his tongue between her lips; her face flamed. But he was already kneeling again, a meek unpleasant little smile vanishing in his downward look. She longed to wipe her mouth, but Henry was beside her, urging her into the great hall where more gifts were arriving. Her flesh still crawled from the kiss. But there was Jacqueline, on the brink of tears because Humphrey had not yet greeted her! *C'est mystérieux*, she thought.

'See them bow down!' said Henry, as they rode into London from Blackheath plain where the mayor and aldermen and citizens had assembled wearing white cloaks and red caps, and flanked by their Guild banners. Henry rode close to her, proudly protective, as the roaring acclaim of the city swirled about them. Great statues of St George and the Virgin had been built and towered, holding out the keys of the City. The narrow streets had been made narrower by elaborate wooden castles filled with knights. Below, boys and girls shimmered in silver and gold paint, men pranced in jewelled mummery. Falcons, tigers and elephants, angels, prophets, martyrs and virgins; children wearing green leaves danced about the procession like a living forest. A gold lion with a dozen men inside its skin capered by Katherine's horse and rolled its eyes, and she laughed in joy, riding under a canopy of evergreen and tapestries strung across the street, darkening the sky. Someone freed a shower of white doves. Bells battered her ears. When she reached the Tower of London to be prepared for her coronation, she was dizzy and trembling. She had felt the love of the English people – a love for their king which rebounded on her in generous measure. A sense of destiny and tremendous rightness took hold of her, supporting her throughout the long ceremony which passed without a flaw.

The ensuing feast lasted all day. As it was Lent no meat was served, but a variety of fish. Stewed eels, fish jelly coloured with columbine flowers, a cream of almond soup thick with bream, sole, chub and barbel. All delicious, all so salt that deep draughts of wine were needed for accompaniment. The wines of Champagne and Gascony and the Loire; Burgundy wine and the light red wines of Gloucestershire; the mead of Kent and Sussex. There was carp, turbot and tench in cream, perch with gudgeon sauce. Roast porpoise and crab in its shell. Fresh sturgeon, dressed with whelks.

She sat upon the King's bench in Westminster Hall. A thousand people occupied the benches on either side of the great chamber. Music played. The table damask was dressed with early violets and coils of greenery. Snowdrops had been mixed with the floor-rushes. Whatever her feelings about Humphrey, he had organized the feast to perfection. Yet there was one dish she knew Henry had ordered especially, remembering how she had enjoyed it on their wedding-day. The Crustade Lombard, with fish and fruit in pastry. It stood nearly a foot high before her place, decorated with hawthorn leaves and berries, the pastry sculpted with the arms of Henry and Katherine and the SS collar of Lancaster. Another subtlety showed a pelican on her nest with St Katherine and her wheel. A scroll, held in the saint's hand, read:

C'est signe et du roy
Parer tenez joy,
Et tout sa gent
Elle met sa content.

as if to emphasize the joy and contentment she had indeed given him. There was also a pastry image of St Barnabas with robes of spun sugar and a legend reading:

It is written,
It may be seen for sure,
In marriage pure,
No strifes endure.

Behind Barnabas was a marchpane tiger with a mirror in its paws and a knight fully armed, holding a tiger cub. The tiger's face was that of her brother the Dauphin, and the knight was unmistakably Henry. By legend the sight of a mirror tamed a wild beast. In a savage way the image pleased her; it was the final closing of the door on an old, bad life.

Henry was filled with tenderness and relief that she was safely crowned. Now I must keep her in secure contentment, he thought. She sat, radiant in her white gown, relishing the banquet. The greatest in England waited on her: Lord Audley, the Duchess of York, the Countess of Huntingdon, Margaret, Duchess of Clarence, and the Countess of Kent, who sat at Katherine's feet, ready with the finger bowls. The Earl of March held the priceless gold sceptre Henry had given her for her coronation. Sir Richard Neville poured her wine and Sir James Stuart served her food. Lord Clifford acted as pantner, with the loaves balanced on his arm. Lord Grey of Ruthyn held the pile of surnapes. At her right hand sat the Archbishop of Canterbury, Chichele, and next to him, Bishop Henry Beaufort. On her left, King James of Scotland. He was at liberty, through Katherine's intercession. Henry thought: I could not resist her plea, and she was right: I will make him a good soldier when I return to France. He shall marry Joan Beaufort, and God send them happy as we are!

And, standing respectfully before the Queen throughout the banquet, was Humphrey of Gloucester. Henry was not pleased with Gloucester. The reports of his conduct in England had been far from encouraging. The constant enmity between him and Beaufort was no longer to be taken lightly as Humphrey's mere grudge against high-risen bastard blood. It was a festering hate that might one day break out and do grave harm. Henry thought: I wish I had left him in France, after all. Rather let him expend his energies controlling my territories there than stirring up this aggravation in England. But my good brother, Clarence, had to be given his chance. Clarence was so disappointed when he was shipped home sick from Harfleur. He missed all the glory. So let him remain in France as my regent. I have promised Philip and King Charles I shall return by midsummer. Let Clarence hold my gains till then.

As for Queen Joanna, she is safely immured in the manor of Rotherhithe, and her fellow necromancers in the Tower. And God is on my side. There is the proof, that delicate, dark-eyed, loving face talking so charmingly to King James. God is with me. God will protect us both for ever. Amen.

Katherine, attuned to his thoughts, leaned to look at him. Praise be, he is well, he is happy. Tonight we shall lie together in this friendly palace of Westminster. Peace and the joys of the night shall be with us. Her glance strayed along the table-decorations, the glazed and gilded fish, the sweets and flowers. Nearly every item bore the *raison* that stretched, repeated, in a silken banner raised the length of the board. Worked in gold and sugar and green leaves, it printed itself upon her heart. UNE SANS PLUS! Henry's *raison*, and therefore hers. *One alone.*

*

288

Dress warmly, she was told. The North of England is a wilderness, swept by barbaric winds, where spring comes late. Henry had gone on ahead to greet his people, jesting that in the northern territories it was rumoured he had died in France! She fancied his smile was a little strained and found his wit incomprehensible. Although at Windsor, where he had left her to prepare at leisure for the journey, he confided the threefold purpose of his progress north. First, he needed to address the corporation of as many towns as possible, telling them of his gains abroad and his need of further funds to return and consolidate these triumphs and establish the condominium with Burgundy. His finances were straitened. Most of the battle-ransoms had been exhausted. There were fresh armies to finance for what he hoped would be the final return to France. And then would come his life's true work: the crusade against the Infidel, the fateful, inevitable journey East. Philip of Burgundy would be with him in Jerusalem. He had sworn it upon the most sacred relics, in Melun. The debt would be repaid.

Secondly, in the north there were rumours of fresh Lollard heresies. Leicester, for example; this was the womb of Wyclif's teachings; he had been rector of Lutterworth for some years. And even the burning of Oldcastle had rebounded unsettlingly upon the True Faith. Folk had gathered about his stake in ungodly fervour to rub his ashes into their eyes.

Lastly, Katherine was to be shown to the people. The proof! the prize! By now it was a tender jest between them. They would kneel together before the Easter candles, kindled to lighten the northerners' dark souls led astray by the voice of heathen. And before he departed, he had shown her some other candles. A hundred candles burning before the tomb of King Richard in Westminster Abbey. In the side aisles, monks tongued a constant liturgy, echoed by the arching stones and undulating like the shadows cast about the King and Queen as they stood where Richard had been interred anew by his murderer's son.

'The candles must never be allowed to go out.' Henry wept, fresh tears from an old well, and she knew better than to offer comfort, for this was part of the forbidden, undying past. Yet she thought of Belle, and sighed at the complex mysteries of it all.

'Richard!' he murmured. 'I'll light another candle for you in Jerusalem!'

She was in fair spirits when he left for the North. They would not be parted for long, and she was surrounded by servants and retainers and a hierarchy of nobles. John of Bedford was increasingly kind to her. Humphrey of Gloucester she contrived almost to ignore. Bishop Beaufort was there to attend to her spiritual needs. Her ladies: her cousin Anne of Burgundy, Bedford's betrothed; Margaret, Duchess of Clarence; Philippa, Duchess of York. Jacqueline, so full of gratitude that, to please Katherine, she managed to refrain from speaking too much of her beloved Humphrey. A host of servants of wardrobe and bedchamber. Dames Belknap, Troutbeck and Coucy, who cherished her tirelessly, at bed and bath. A strange little tiring-woman named Guillemot, who from the first had looked at her with childlike adoration. Katherine learned that their wages were paid, like Jacqueline's maintenance at court and Dr Boyars's salary, out of the estates of the disgraced Queen Joanna. She knew this to be Henry's punishment, and pitied those who crossed him.

She learned more of Henry as the chariot, drawn by the eight white horses, bore her north. With her travelled Margaret of Clarence, who at one time had been married to John, the brother of Bishop Henry Beaufort. She seemed to love to dwell in the past. Old feuds were dredged up for Katherine's bewildered ear. How the Bishop, years ago, had cheated her of her late husband's estate. How Thomas of Clarence and Henry fell out over it. Also there was some strange story of Beaufort hiring an assassin to hide in Henry's chamber. How subsequently Arundel was made Chancellor in place of Beaufort. And Thomas of Clarence had worsened things by persuading his father to dismiss Henry from the Privy Council and appoint him, Thomas, instead.

'Thomas was always impetuous,' she said. 'All the brothers squabbled when they were young. Once my husband was sent to France on a campaign that should have been Henry's. Your noble lord was bitterly upset.'

'Yet he bears no grudge.' Katherine thought: he was determined to let Clarence have his chance in France this time.

'Yes, impetuous,' said Margaret, looking worried. 'He resented his absence from the Agincourt affair. God grant he will not try to make conquests alone. He boasted before he left that he could have won that battle without the English bowmen!'

She began to tell her rosary. The entourage rumbled over the flat fields of Leicestershire and the town, a welcoming party at its gate, came into view. Katherine saw Henry's standard. Old dead feuds fled her mind, as if Margaret had never embarked on the telling of them. Her carriage halted, and maids congregated to dress her hair, Master Feriby's minions came running to drape her in fresh, scented furs. A man with thick golden hair knelt to clothe her feet in sweet soft leather. Then Henry's horse bore him boundingly towards her and Leicester seemed the comeliest town in Christendom, Lollards or no Lollards.

Owen, uncaring in the deathly sickness of his love, raised his eyes to watch the royal embrace. *I have touched her feet.* I could have kissed them, and have had my lips cut off. No punishment. There's no heart in me ever to kiss again.

I must somehow get over this. It is only because she is unattainable, because I can't have her. It is nothing of the kind. I love her. *Am byth.* For ever.

Pontefract, rising starkly from the frigid moor, seemed even more forbidding than Nottingham's gloomy rock, where they had travelled soon after Easter. Their welcome continued, but more discreetly. People shouted less in the north. Near-foreigners themselves, continually harassed by Scottish raiding parties, they regarded anything foreign with some suspicion. Yet she smiled, bowed, did all that Henry advised, and warmth, more genuine for its initial reticence, eventually surrounded her. She prayed at countless holy shrines, gave and received gifts, listened to the recital of Henry's conquests on every city street and village green. She lay one night at the Augustinian priory of Nostell, then made her way to Pontefract, Henry continuing northwards. Immured in this fortress was someone she wished to see. It crossed her mind that it would be easy to secrete funds and information to this important captive: her own cousin and brother-in-law Charles of Orléans. It was in her power to betray Henry to Armagnac. And by his trust, she knew that he paid her the greatest compliment of her life.

As he embraced her farewell, there was an extra dimension in his concern, shared as yet by a secret few. Then he lectured her physicians, to see that she was warm and watched and rested, and rode away with backward looks, lovingly mystified as at the site of a miracle.

She was escorted up a stone spiral, passing by round pillars strictly functional and lacking in ornamentation. She entered a well-furnished room that took her back instantly to the tragic castle at Blois. Everywhere there were the devices of Orléans, the peacock feathers and broom on the hangings, the pineapple and the porcupine, spiked, nervous, arrogant. A great fire burned in the hearth. Charles sat in the window. He had put on weight. She would not have recognized him as the keen youth who once wooed Belle with such tenacity. His secretary, Antoine l'Astisan, looked much as on that ride to Blois years ago; time had merely turned him grey. Charles rose, bent his knee, then embraced her. He did not seem overjoyed to see her, unlike l'Astisan, who shed tears at sight of her. Plagued by memory, he thought: *Grâce à Dieu*, she is happy at last! Would that my master could be also . . .

'Well, Kéti,' said Orléans. 'By St Denis, you are fine.' He stroked the sleeve of her rose velvet gown.

She hardly knew what to say. She asked if he were content at Pontefract.

'Well enough. Windsor bored me, and the Tower is fiendishly hot in summer. The north suits my mood. This place is full of ghosts to howl with me in my dolour. I have my faithful Antoine, my servants, my chaplain. What should I lack?' His laugh was like a dog's shrill aggression. He was changed.

Don't ask me to intercede for you, she thought, wondering if he had heard of her success over James of Scotland's liberty. You are different. You would be only too ready to lead

Armagnac once more against my lord. She looked about at the flamboyant peacocks and the quilled stormy emblems.

He said: 'Have you made a tour of this place? Shall I summon my guard and have them show it to you? There is a room at the base of this tower where Henry Bolingbroke had Richard done to death. What irony that both husbands of Madame should end their lives in this fortress!'

'Your life is not ended, Charles.'

'It might as well be. Marshal Boucicaut and the Duke of Bourbon are also here. We never meet. Boucicaut is half-mad, and the Duke unwell.'

'Do you still write poetry?' Katherine said uncomfortably. His face was glazed with melancholy. She thought of James of Scotland – captivity seemed to breed verse.

'Yes. Mostly of Madame. I wish I were with her in Paradise.' He sat down heavily at the table and Katherine joined him. 'Night and day my thoughts never stray from her. And you, your Grace?' he said, with an edge of malice. 'Where is your great lord? Why is he not here with you?'

'He has gone on, to pray at York, and to St John at Beverley.' She pronounced it *Bevair-lee*, and Charles's malice stretched into a smile.

'You are quite the Englishwoman. And yet the conqueror leaves you here alone. Doubtless he visits his paramours in the North.' This was so ridiculous that Katherine burst out laughing. Even if Harry had the inclination, he certainly had no time.

'No, Charles. I do not ride with him. *Je suis enceinte, tu sais.*'

'Ah,' he said gloomily. 'A child. Madame died from a child. My daughter, widowed herself now. Death blew his stinking breath upon my princess. My love killed her.'

'I shall not die from a child,' said Katherine.

'A child can kill,' he said. 'I loved Madame. Now she lies in the Célestins, lapped in quicksilver and fine linen, but still mine!'

He began to weep. L'Astisan filled a cup with spiced ale and set it before him. With a sweep of his hand Charles knocked it away. It spilled over some sheets of manuscript on the table. The coloured inks ran and shreds of gold leaf floated on top of the liquid. L'Astisan looked despairingly at Katherine.

'Shall I leave you?' But Charles caught her hand and held it. They sat silent.

'Do you remember how we met in the Sainte-Chapelle?' His head was bowed over the ruined illuminations. 'She was always my love and I was hers.'

'She loved King Richard,' Katherine said. She did not intend to hurt him. It was the truth.

'It was a child's love,' he said. 'She was maiden when she came to me. Richard loved only Anne of Bohemia.'

'I wonder . . .' said Katherine softly.

'She will be mine in Heaven!' He rose violently and went to the window, looking out on the wild sweep of moorland. 'What do you care? These old passions do not touch you. You have betrayed your own country!' She looked at his bowed shoulders, portly as those of an old man, and said, in angerless pity:

'What did my own country bring me but fear and strife? As for love, and Paradise, I have thought on these things, and if it's true there will be no taking or giving in marriage, neither will there be ownership! Charles . . .'

'Then who shall have whom in Heaven?' he asked sadly.

'We shall all be one love, having expiated our sins.' She went and laid her hand on his shoulder. 'Charles, remember her words – I have never forgotten them. Love is the only candle in this dark old world.'

He did not reply.

'Think of eternity!' Katherine said. 'In the merciful bowels of Christ, think of eternity!'

'Not your words,' he said, soft and savage. 'The conqueror's words to your father. You are his mammet, Kéti.'

'I am his dear companion,' she said.

Still looking through the window, he said: 'I was glad to learn that your brother murdered Jean sans Peur. He who struck down my father in the dark of Paris!'

'Your father! My uncle!' cried Katherine. 'Charles, let's not quarrel. The past is gone. When I return to Paris I'll have Masses said at Belle's tomb in the Célestins for you.'

He turned, his face radiant under the tear-tracks.

'You promise?' To l'Astisan: 'Give her Grace money, much money. And a great choir to sing for her? Kéti, make it soon!'

'As soon as my baby is born and I can go to France,' she said. 'I promise. Now show me your poems before I leave you.'

One was so lovely it brought tears despite her new tranquillity.

> *The torch is set of piteous sighs*
> *Which was with sorrow set aflame,*
> *The tomb is made also the same –*
> *Of careful cry depicted all with tears,*
> *This which is richly writ about,*
> *That here, lo! lieth without doubt,*
> *The whole treasure of wordly bliss . . .*

She kissed him, and gave him her blessing. Then, thoughtfully, she descended to her own apartments. What a heritage of love was in that poem! If Belle were not dead, one could envy her . . . She found herself longing for Henry's presence, after the near-frenzy of Orléans. Little sounds from the lodgings of others blew down the cold halls of Pontefract: Jacqueline laughing, someone scolding a servant, someone singing. Sounds that touched her ears and were cut off like dreams at daybreak by stone pillars or a labyrinth of galleries. The scolding and the laughter faded but the singing followed in her mind. She retraced her steps to its source. That same gay, wild, tenor-bell of a voice, but with all its gaiety gone, replaced by an anguish like that of Orléans's poems. Through an open door she looked where the singer sat with a lute across his knees. He sang on, moving her to think: never did I know that Jacques could sing like that! He did not see her. His eyes stared ahead. Whatever sunlight there was in the grey chamber had rushed to gather about his head, in the gold hair curling at his temples and brow and touching the tanned face and the blue, blind-looking eyes with gold.

The chatelaine at her waist swung as she halted and its keys made a sound. He was on his knees as if poleaxed. She said: 'You have a pleasing voice, Jacques. One day you shall sing for me.'

Grief, rage, and longing filled him. *Annwyl Crist!* I knew I was nothing, but not that I was invisible! I have sung for you night after night, morning after morning, at your door and the great ceremonies that crown your life! I have brushed your gowns and guarded your furs, I have practised in pursuit of your pleasure until my throat was raw and my fingers half-crippled. I have thought of nothing but you. I can't remember a time when I did not think of you. Once you sent me away because my melodies made you sad, but you do not know that all my songs come from a dead heart. That because of you I am no longer a man! When I tried to lie with Jeanne again it was a frightening failure. When I tried to pretend that she was you, it was an unspeakable sacrilege. For my dream is you, and I would sleep for ever. Last night I had a dream, Cathryn (for that's your name, your only name, in my tongue, the best tongue, the language of the gods) – that you and I stood together on a mountain and you rested your face, chilled by the Welsh wind, upon my heart, and you were mine, and *Duw annwyl!* I wish I were dead.

He looked up fearlessly into her eyes. Part of the essence of his look broke through her innocence. *Sainte Vierge!* she thought. *Comme il est féroce!* She turned away, saying: 'I've disturbed your good music, I am sorry. Continue, Jacques,' and left, a little disturbed herself. He looked as if he hated me.

From her apartments she had a view of the bailey and the main gate of the castle; outside tall trees were struggling into leaf. She felt a slight queasiness, and touched her belly wonderingly, it was so slender and tight, hard to imagine a tiny manikin stood there, with Henry's eyes and close-cropped hair. She caressed the place where its heart might be. She smiled in ignorant bliss. A movement on the hill-brow behind the trees caught her eye. Riders, coming fast. King's men! He could not have returned so soon. What pleasure if he had! She waited, hands still clasped on her belly. The coloured banners floated down the hill in the wake of the galloping horses. They were tired, they wavered and strained for home as the gate was raised. John of Bedford was out in the bailey talking to the dismounting men. Henry was not with them.

Bedford came to her in a few minutes. His face was quite grey. Something has happened to Henry. I cannot support it.

I can. I must. I am his wife, a queen.

John of Bedford said: 'The news is very grave, *ma reine*. The King is on his way from York. We are all to go south immediately.'

He looked so devastated that she had to ask: 'For God's love, my lord, what's happened? Is the King well?'

'He is well. But our brother of Clarence has been killed in France. The Dauphin was triumphant at a great battle near Baugé. And now all that Harry conquered stands in jeopardy.'

Letters. Letters. He dictated more than two score letters to a frantic scribble of clerks; instructions to all his captains who still held the French possessions so dearly gained. She sat quietly, listening to his rapid words which illustrated his diplomacy and grasp, his memory for detail, his skilled discrimination and judgement of approach. A soft letter to a pliant, easily-flattered castellan. A letter which threatened death to one who understood severity. But always the same message. Keep my conquests safe. Guard them with every arm you possess, with every strategy within your power. A team of fast couriers, every hour upon the hour, departed to take ship at Dover or Southampton. If he could have thrown his heart across the Channel he would have done it. After hours of vital deliberation and instruction he turned to Humphrey of Gloucester, to Bedford, and to Katherine. She knew that this meant France for him again, sooner than had been anticipated, and that she would be parted from him for some time. The coming child meant too much to him to risk her health on the journey. And parts of Upper Anjou, deemed his securest possession, were, if rumour ran correctly, once more awash with blood.

When the last courier had gone, he dismissed his counsellors and went with her to privacy. She took his face in her hands. He kissed her.

'My dear companion,' she said.

'The knight I mourn most is Sir Gilbert Umfraville.' He looked wan and sad. 'There was a knight, Katherine! He fought so mightily on Artois plain, the archers loved him.

That fool brother of mine, God rest his soul, thought he could dispense with the archers at Baugé! The Armagnacs cut my best fighting force to shreds, captured my noble Sir John Holland and Somerset, killed Umfraville . . .' He sat down heavily, staring grimly ahead.

'Clarence was envious of your prowess,' she said softly.

'Yes, jealous. As, I fear, is Gloucester. Bedford is the most loyal of all my brothers. Katherine. When I'm in France, stay close by John of Bedford. He will look after you.'

She said: 'I think Humphrey . . .' and bit back the words. Ridiculous to say *I think he'd do me harm*, even to Harry. He looked at her keenly, his tired eyes narrowing.

'What of him? Has he displeased you? He shall hear from me . . .'

'No, no,' she said hastily. 'He upsets only Bishop Beaufort. He will be more settled when he's married.'

'That's more or less arranged,' Henry said impatiently. 'And praise God, Philip seems unperturbed. Perhaps Brabant is glad to be rid of the Hainault wench after all. And she will bring money into England from her estates. God knows I need money in face of this new catastrophe.'

'And his Holiness?'

'His Holiness Pope Martin owes me a favour,' Henry said grimly. 'He will agree to the annulment. Although he has ceased to love me, it seems. He remarked after Baugé that the Scots are the antidote to the English! appearing pleased. There were many Scottish lords fighting under Armagnac – Archibald of Wigtown, Stewart, Earl of Buchan, and *they* had archers! Clarence's cavalry were stunned by the hail of fire. He rode across the bridge wearing a gold crown, as I once did. He died, as I did not. Had it not been for Salisbury's countercharge into Maine, I should have lost more lands. As it is I have lost much, and must ride to regain it.'

She had summoned servants with food and wine for Henry and now dismissed them, kneeling beside his chair to serve him herself. He protested. 'No, Katherine. You are my queen, not my servitor.'

'I am your dear love,' she said, with a fluttering dark secret look. She set a brace of little birds roasted in honey before him.

'Can you eat? Has the pain returned?' She had not dared ask before.

'No, I feel strong, despite everything. And you?' His gaze swept her ardently, tired though he was. 'When will my son be born?' He gnawed hungrily at the little fowl.

'They say towards Christmastime. We'll rejoice over him together.'

'If I am back by then,' he said flatly. Her heart dipped, she turned her face away. Eight months! He rinsed his fingers and dried them on the surnape. He turned her cheek to his.

'Be of good heart. Bear and baptize my son in the faith of the Holy Spirit. Name him after me. Let him come into this wicked world strong and just and loving God. Don't be downcast, my Katherine.'

She rested her head on his chest. The gold collar of SS was cool and hard to her face. She felt the vital impatient beat of his heart, like an augury of the swift journey that was imminent. She clung to him, gathering the safety of Now against the emptiness ahead.

As it happened, the departure was delayed for another five weeks while they rode south through April into May, seeing spring take hold of the countryside in a flutter of blossom and green leaves. The couriers continued to stream to all points of the realm collecting the promised funds for the campaign. The money came in from lords too old to fight or infant lords bound by family loyalty; from all Englishmen who, stirred by Henry's past exploits, now shared his present anxiety. Ships were fitted out, new cannon cast, weapons forged. Nine hundred knights and three thousand bowmen prepared again for war. In early May Katherine was back at Windsor, and Henry in the Painted Chamber at Westminster where Parliament was in session. The Speaker, Thomas Chaucer, spoke eloquently of the King, and the Treaty of Troyes was ratified. Debates were accelerated under the growing tension and Henry, sparing neither himself nor his ministers, worked for days at a stretch. He signed treaties long in abeyance, ordered fleets to stand off the Scottish ports to safeguard against further defection to Armagnac, and posted border guards to that end. He dealt with lesser matters: the Commons requested that England should be given the monopoly of wool exports to Burgundy, prohibiting competition from Scotland and Spain. The Lollard problem was discussed; he set up further commissions of enquiry. Bishop Langley commended him publicly for attributing his past conquests to God and not man, and, watching Henry doing the work of ten, the Chancellor wondered indeed with what secret power God had endowed the King.

And then it was June, and the ships ready to sail. The roses bloomed in the pleasaunce at Windsor. The scent of summer jasmine and honeysuckle swept through the window of Katherine's bower. Two new harps Henry had recently purchased for them stood, as yet unplayed, in a corner. A linnet in a cage chirped dolefully for the world outside.

He came alone and stood before her, his mind full of a thousand matters overlaid by the impotence of all farewells. He thought she looked pale, attenuated, but she stood graceful and straight, her hands folded over the tiny curve at her waist. She in turn was relieved by his bright colour, his vigour. It would have been unbearable had he been ill at the start of this enterprise.

'I am for Dover now, Madame,' he said, as if formality could lessen pain.

'God speed,' she said faintly. 'God be with you.'

He stood as if frozen, then took her into an embrace that made her gasp for breath. She fancied for an instant that the child writhed in protest, but the child was too young to move, he was a good child and would not abhor his father's touch, and he was to be dedicated to God. She had sworn it . . .

She kissed his neck as he held her. He had been barbered more severely than usual and there was a white line between the weathered skin and the short hair. She kissed the scar on his face. He thrust his hand in her long hair and groaned. Over his shoulder she saw gilded strings, gold-painted wood.

'We never used the harps,' she said with a sobbing laugh.

'If you need new strings,' he said, as wildly, 'John Bore in London is the vendor. Send Owen Tydier, he knows the kind.'

'I know of no Owen Tydier,' she said weeping.

'You call him Jacques . . . your father called him so. A Welshman.' He kissed her eyes. 'My dear wife, it's time.'

'Do not think of me,' she drew back, composed, inwardly shivering.

'No,' he said.

'But write to me.'

'Whenever possible.'

'And in God's mercy return soon. Or send for me.'

'I give my word.'

She knew then she must cease clinging with outworn phrases and let him go. She foresaw the sad hard summer, the endless conversations with the unborn child. She watched from the window until the army gathered below had rolled gleaming away through the gate. On impulse she opened the linnet's cage. The small bird stood uncertainly on one leg, then dived with a swift flick of wings into the living air outside. She thought: he shall sing my dear companion on his way.

'He has your eyes,' said Jacqueline of Hainault, hanging dotingly over the cradle.

'He favours my father,' said Katherine. The baby, bound from neck to toes in a case of starched ribbing, gazed up opaquely. He had a sad, ancient look, as vulnerable as one of the monkeys in the menagerie at Windsor. On the milky pearl of his neck a chafe glowed red. Katherine slid her finger beneath the swaddling. Once again the laundress had used too much arrowroot. Jacqueline should dismiss her. Poor baby. *Mon pauvre petit prince.* The great eyes swam about like dark fish between the pale bald lids. The resemblance to Valois was truly unearthly, like Charles on the verge of a nerve-storm. *Bébé,* she said softly, and the eyes crept back towards her, seeming to look at her with sober trust.

'He was so good at the christening,' Jacqueline said for the hundredth time. 'The lovely prince.'

A great crucifix swung from Jacqueline's breast. The tiny Henry's eyes found a target and fixed on it. Jacqueline whispered: 'Look! already he embraces the image of Our Lord!'

Humphrey of Gloucester touched Katherine's arm reverently.

'He will be as devout as his parents, *ma chère sœur*.' Near the crib hung his own christening gift, a solid gold wand inlaid with sapphires.

'He will be happy,' Katherine answered. She turned to smile at Gloucester, thinking: how we have all changed! Since Henry's departure, she had had occasion to revise her opinion of Humphrey of Gloucester. He had become a paragon. None could have been more tender, thoughtful, or respectful. During the summer, and the winter of her lying-in, he had addressed himself to her welfare exclusively, and gradually her glacial feelings towards him had thawed. Had he been Henry he could not have ministered to her more efficiently. It was Humphrey who had found the best wetnurse in England, Humphrey who, whenever she felt dispirited, had sent Jacqueline to cheer her or come himself. Totally reformed, he had not uttered a murmur when Bishop Beaufort and John of Bedford were appointed the prince's sponsors at the christening. In her presence, at least, he had shown civility to the Bishop, lest their enmity should cause her pain. Best of all, he had brought her the news of Henry, snatching the rolls from the couriers almost before the regent, Bedford, had had time to see them. For that alone, she thought, I shall ever be in his debt.

We have all changed. Even Jacqueline, who looks almost matronly. At first there was a little jealousy from her, but I explained. Humphrey takes his duties seriously. It is well that he does. For John of Bedford, to whom Harry bade me cling close, is always too busy. Immured in Council, writing more letters than Harry did, desperately worried about the outcome in France and itching to be there. Well that I did not depend on him for my comfort during these months! During the summer when I became great and sick and weary, an autumn during which I thought I should burst like a pod, a winter of fulfilled joy.

She looked again at the pale, old-eyed baby. St Nicholas's child! What better day on which to be born. His future is assured; the saint of youth shall succour him. If only his father could see him. I am nearly a year older since our leavetaking. Is this a new spring, or did time stop then? Are not those the same bright nestlings outside my window, the same puff of honeysuckle striving towards the light against the stones of Windsor? There are things that have not changed. New greenness on old towers. But in me, *hélas*! the same ache and waste and wanting. That love-need, that terrible, carnal need.

'Don't be sad, *ma reine*,' said Humphrey. 'See how the prince thrives. Is he warm enough?' He touched the baby Henry's brow with a ringed finger. There was a raging fire in the hearth and all the windows were tightly closed. It had been a dreadful winter, but, according to reports, nothing like so fierce as in France.

She had not heard from Harry since the christening. He had written, bidding her hear a Mass to the Trinity for the baby. Since then she had heard many Masses. There had been only three loving letters altogether since his departure. From their content she had the feeling that there should have been more, but Humphrey said they had been lost on the journey. Ships had foundered, couriers had been waylaid. She had to be content. If Humphrey said it, then it was so.

He took her arm and moved with her from the cradle where Dame Alice Boteler the nurse, and Anne of Burgundy and the Duchess of Clarence congregated. He said softly: 'I have news of Harry.'

'Why didn't you tell me before?'

'I only learned myself today. Bedford has instructions from him – he has the rolls in Council now. I must go there shortly.'

'Is Harry well?'

'Yes. But the army has suffered much, at Meaux. They sat all winter outside the gates. Men died of hunger, and the bloody flux . . .'

'You're sure he's well?' Her face was white.

'*Ma sœur*, have I ever lied?'

Not that I know, her little inner counsellor said, and she dismissed it as unworthy. Our feud was in my uncertain wits. It never really existed.

He said: 'The Armagnacs tried to push towards Paris, but Salisbury fought them back at Chartres. Philip of Burgundy has been indisposed – I wonder if this was a diplomatic illness? He didn't fight with Harry against Jacques d'Harcourt in Picardy. The Dauphin declared he would fight in person near Beaugency and left his new wife at Bourges . . .'

'Marie d'Anjou?'

'Yes. Sweet and docile by all accounts. Anyway, your brother didn't show himself after all. Harry captured the lands surrounding Orléans. He lost a lot of men, but he continued, to the Yonne; Villeneuve surrendered. Then he reached the Marne, and Meaux. A hive of bandits like the Bastard of Vaurus and Pierron de Luppé in command. The enemy never slept. Even with Philip back to aid him, and Exeter and Salisbury, Harry suffered an ordeal. Men dropped like frozen birds . . . the sickness . . .'

'He was victorious.' The descriptions distressed her immeasurably. 'And he is safe.'

'Yes. Meaux capitulated after a siege of seven months. And Harry hanged the Bastard of Vaurus from his own tree, where he used to strangle women and innocents for sport!'

Katherine looked at the cradle, wishing the infant was old enough to hear of his father's prowess.

'He's undone part of Clarence's mischief. He rules the recaptured lands peaceably. He's willing to treat with the Dauphin. Your father, alas!' he said delicately, 'is once more in no condition to partake in rejoicing or grief. He's mad again, Katherine.'

So. She was sad, but more anxious about Harry. 'Will my lord be coming home?'

'There are more campaigns. He has asked for reinforcements, that is why Bedford is now in Council. Next month, a new army will cross the sea.' And then, very softly: 'Why should you not go with it?'

The ache of ten months spread illimitably within her.

'I will not join him uninvited.'

'Write to him,' said Humphrey. 'You could be with him next month, in Paris!'

They looked at one another like conspirators, he nodding encouragement, she thoughtful, troubled.

'Bedford would care for the baby . . .' Humphrey shook his

head. 'No, Bedford is summoned to France to lead the new contingent.'

'Then the prince would have to come with me.'

Humphrey took her hand, squeezing it. His rings made her wince. 'Katherine. That little soul is heir to two great kingdoms! Would you risk a dynasty? Rough spring tides, ambushes in France . . . Think again.'

Paris, next month. Paris, and Henry. She looked down at her own hands. They seemed so frail, one could almost see the bones within. The ache of months seemed to shatter her.

'What if he should refuse?'

'He refuses you nothing. Remember Jacqueline and me! Remember James of Scotland, Joan Beaufort!'

'But the prince,' she said.

'I will care for the prince,' said Humphrey of Gloucester.

She stood, swayed, agonized. Paris, and Harry. The end to all doubt and hunger. The ache already dulling under anticipation.

'Leave the prince with me. Go and find joy in France with your dear lord. I'll send for your clerk. The messenger leaves within the hour. Go, Katherine.'

Something in his voice decided her irrevocably, and at last she understood a little of Jacqueline's long bewitchment.

'Write!' he said urgently. 'Write to him, now!'

Dispensing with the clerk, she wrote in her own hand, the most loving letter possible. Six weeks later she was with Henry, near Paris, in the forest castle of Vincennes.

He stood at the window as night gave way to the early dawn of late July. A faint silvery blush crept over the sky to the east. The monks from the nearby abbey had sung matins some time ago, their voices like bells beneath the sea. From the tower of Vincennes watchmen had called the hour, but how late it was Henry had no idea. Pain rowelled and racked him. All his will had to be directed to the struggle within. Everything else was incidental, and the beautiful breaking dawn a chimera.

Behind him in the shadowed bed, Katherine slept deeply. He heard her slow measured breathing mingling with the wind stirring in the forest that grew densely to the castle walls. He tried to breathe with her rhythm and that of the hushing trees. He pulled the ermine robe tighter about his thin body and endured as he had never endured in his life. A bird, awakening, gave one shrill intricate call, like a minstrel trying out his instrument. The pain within heard it and leaped into fresh life. He bit his lips and waited, clenched, until it abated and resumed its steady, dragging ache.

Very carefully he turned his head. By the waning nightlight on the side table her sleeping face was like a pale pearl against her dark hair. Her mouth was open; she slept like a child. The touching comparison brought tears to his eyes while the pain, having bred an ineffable sense of waste and sadness, loosed its hold as it always did before returning, doubly envenomed. Bitterly, he congratulated himself on having kept from her how bad the pain really was. Or had he? She had landed at Harfleur two months earlier; they had been reunited at the Louvre in Paris. Then at the Hôtel de Nesle they had attended a pageant: *The Mystery of the Life of St George*. At the moment when the saint closed in combat with the Turkish knight, the pain struck intelligently at Henry's vitals. The hall was semi-dark but she had seen his face turn greenish with agony. And she had said quietly: 'Humphrey lied.' 'It's nothing,' he had told her. 'Humphrey didn't know that I was slightly indisposed at Meaux, like Philip. I am glad Humphrey is behaving himself better,' and somehow was able to turn his attention again to the play.

He had been desperately ill at Meaux. It was as if the seven years of intermittent pain had fed upon itself and like a hydra grown new heads since that first spasm at Harfleur. Lying in the freezing, snow-drenched pavilion, he had realized that the pain was an adversary no longer to be quelled by will, or prayer, or even fasting. Greedily, the pain gave off shoots which struck down his men in the snowfilled ditches, where they expired bleeding from the bowels, crying on the Virgin and their families. He had bled too, a terrifying, weakening flux, for hours no longer a king, scarcely a man, but a shivering, undignified mass of punished flesh. When the news came that he had a son born on December 6th, he had been so light-headed with agony that it meant nothing. Only afterwards, in a blessed interim of recovery, could he rejoice.

He was now convinced that this was a punishment for his sins. Not for burning of Badby and Oldcastle – that was God's work. But maybe for the babies at Rouen and the hanging of hostages, and the licentiousness of youth, and perhaps still for the sins of Henry Bolingbroke, their essence remembered in the burning candles at Richard's tombside. And above all, for his failure to reach, as yet, the walls of Jerusalem in the True Faith. Could my heart and spirit have gone there, independent of this wretched flesh, the Infidel would have been driven back years ago. I have failed. This pain is my just requital.

It was not witchcraft after all. Why should Joanna of Navarre, whom I ordered to be released from Rotherhithe months ago, have machinated against my army as well as me? The most powerful sorceress could not have wrought malice on such a scale. The thought of Meaux, the hunger, ice and snow and mud, chased a shiver over him and one of the hydra-heads lifted inside him. Better to think of other things. My little prince, seven months old. Katherine described him well. I'm glad he favours her in face, instead of this haggard old warrior who looks so much older than his thirty-five years. Before the year is out I'll hold him and see his face light up as he looks on Holy Cross and the Passion of Our Saviour.

Katherine, dreaming, gave a little moan. She licked her lips in sleep, a strangely sensual little gesture. I would like to lie with her, he thought, but even her soft touch is like flame on my skin. She understands; she demands nothing save to be with me, and she suffered that rough crossing not long after bearing the child. She is more beautiful since the child, not so slender; her flesh shines like a lamplit Madonna. She turned, still asleep, and threw out a long pale arm across the bed. The pain raised its head again. He sought fresh fancies in which to hide from it.

A fine castle, this Vincennes. Louis the Tenth died here, and, nearly one hundred years ago the last Capetian King, Charles the Fourth, who was succeeded by his regent, Philip of Valois. And with Philip began the great war, the line of rightful conquests begun by Edward III, whose work I strive to finish.

Not my work, but yours, Edward. Not my fault, Richard, but yours, my father. Not my way, O God, but Thine. UNE SANS PLUS! It was written everywhere, on the bedhangings, the scrolls of armaments hanging from the walls, woven in silk, carved in steel. One cause. One faith. One wife. One son. The pain came eagerly to join the rhythm of his thoughts, invading the whisper of the breeze-hung forest, the woman's quiet breaths, the small sleepy chatter of the birds. He leaned forward the better to meet it, while it washed and flamed about him, up to the top of the towers renovated and decorated with saints and monsters by Charles the Fifth of France, and down again to his own crucified loins.

Outside the door, the castle was stirring with little sounds of steel on stone, and muted voices. Already his army of reinforcements was readying itself for the day. He recognized one voice; John Swanwyth, the doctor whom he had summoned from London. It had had to be done, whether or not the Armagnacs got wind of his condition. Swanwyth was reputed to be the cleverest surgeon in England. Ostensibly he was there to look after Katherine. He thought: she's not easily deceived. And God forfend she should have to drink the vile potions which the good doctor brews for me! Tincture of Dioscorides, bitter as the black sloes from which it was derived, and supposed to alleviate hæmorrhage. The crocus, the Sun-sign saffron ruled by Leo for colic and spasm. A very dangerous remedy, said Swanwyth, if taken to excess. And draughts of the juice of cinnamon bark with enough grains of Paris to make Chaucer's murdered child, in the *Tales*, sing a whole litany. And the last I could swear was poison. He told me it was an extreme remedy to combat evil of the fundament. I think there was a powdered emerald in it. At any rate it lit green fire in me.

The dawn light grew stronger, sprinkling the trees outside with gold. Someone scratched at the door. He gathered his strength and moved to open it a crack. His valet, Robert Waterton, stood there, eyes lowered. He was one trusted to be privy to the King's secret agony. He knew of the night's torment; he could smell the pain. Henry came out.

'Robert,' he said softly. 'Look at me.'

'Oh, sweet Jesus Christ,' said Robert, seeing the King's face. It was far worse than he had dreamed.

'Be soft,' Henry said. 'Don't rouse the Queen. Is the courier here?'

'Sire, he's ridden from Cosne. He's behind me.' In the shadows of the antechamber a figure rose from its knees. Waterton held up a light for Henry to break the seal embossed with the gold ram and read the news from Philip of Burgundy. It was what he expected. The Dauphin was besieging Cosne near the borders of Philip's Duchy and reinforcements were called for. The King's presence was urgently desired.

'Are the men ready?' He felt too tired to summon the sergeants who waited along the hallway, and asked the valet.

'All ready, Sire. His Grace of Bedford is prepared to march. Will you break your fast?'

'Bring my armour.' He turned back into the bedchamber. It was four days' ride to Cosne, and five with a fully equipped contingent. The pain was asleep as if stunned by its victim's audacity. And so was Katherine, her moist lips still slightly parted. He bent over them, then froze. Better this way. She would worry, and put up arguments. She would remind him of conquests already made, that Normandy and most of Picardy were his, also the Île de France and Northern Champagne, Maine, and the Orléannais. She would beg him to let Philip and Bedford deal with this present skirmish alone. But he had never reneged on the compact with Philip, and this was no time to start. There had been a recent Dauphinist plot to capture Paris . . . This war! he thought, in sudden despair. It will go on for ever. Surely it is sent by the Devil to keep me from Jerusalem . . . In his mind there sprang the image of Jerusalem, its sloping red-tiled roofs and little arched streets, ringing with holy bells, a new city of perfect faith rising from the snarling desert of the heathen. Gilbert de Lannoy, Philip's Chamberlain, had been sent to reconnoitre, to Alexandria and Constantinople, and yesterday word had arrived at Vincennes to say that the reports were favourable, the way open . . . Katherine sighed in her sleep. She was so lovely, so pliant and gracious and good. Sleep on, my sweet Katherine. My dear companion. With great stealth he moved from the chamber. By now the birds were in full harmony outside. A robin pecked at the sill, singing sweetly of the death of kings, in the great castle of Vincennes.

The seabird stood on the prow of the boat, its implacable topaz eye pitiless and oblique as that of an Egyptian prince. It rode in comfort down the Seine, having embarked, glutted with fish, at Corbeil. Corbeil was less than a day's march from the castle in the forest, but it was where the pain had conquered at last.

John of Bedford had been riding fast at the head of the troops when the King's outrider galloped up with the news. Bedford turned and rode down the mile-long line of marching men to where the royal standard and the Cross of St George drooped from their staves. He found Henry lying in a litter, his head on Waterton's chest, the valet's arms about him. They had taken off his helm and unbuckled his cuirass. He said clearly: 'John. I can go no further,' and closed his eyes. He was so still that Bedford thought him dead. With disbelieving horror he climbed into the litter beside him. He was relieved to hear the faint breaths.

'Rest, Harry,' he said. 'We'll set up camp here. Your doctors will ease you.' He made a frantic gesture to the henchmen who sped off to summon Swanwyth and his fellow physicians.

'Are you in pain?' he said softly. When the strongest in the world gives up, what hope for the rest of us?

'Not so much. But something breaks and wastes in me. I am so weary.' He opened his eyes. He said, gasping: 'You must go on. Appoint Salisbury and Exeter the captains as usual. Do not fear the Dauphin . . . he'll run away, as is his custom. See . . . that King Charles is safe. I heard he was mortally ill.'

Waterton shifted to hold him more comfortably. 'Thank you, good Robert,' he said, and lost consciousness. Bedford looked at the valet's wild, grief-torn face. 'Take him back to Bois de Vincennes,' he said quickly. 'Tell him I will come as soon as I can. But go by river. It will be easier for him.'

Descending from the litter, he remounted and spurred back along the line. In the fields on either side of the army peasants straightened their backs to curse softly. It was the start of the wine harvest and already the passing of errant hooves and wheels showed a trail of havoc among the laden vines. There was a little thunder about; the sky was a heavy lemon-grey.

And now Waterton lifted the King into the boat moored ready between the fishermen's nets. The greedy voices of the seabirds were deafening; they swooped and hung in the hope of plunder. Robert was amazed at the frailty of the man he carried and laid on cushions in the boat's stern. Henry's eyes were still closed; his breathing was shallow. Waterton saw pearls of blood staining the arm of his jacket, and was awed by the fact that royal blood bore the same garnet gloss as that of common men . . . The oars were dipped, the boat moved midstream and down the Seine, which reflected the yellowish sky. It was then that the bird had alighted to stand on the prow, sideways, like an archer.

Down to Charenton they rowed on the quiet river. On either bank a forest of great oaks doubled its dead-still image in the water. The birds had stopped singing, and the plash of oars was the only sound. The King's standard had been hoisted but hung inert, folding itself away like a memory. Henry opened his eyes. The pain awoke too, but this time like a fond acquaintance preparing to depart, with one last urgent grip. In the boat's bows sat three priests in black. Trying to focus on them he imagined them as three female figures, and the old story of King Arthur drifted upon him. But what was a Welsh king doing in France? Then he thought with what seemed logic: I am Henry of Monmouth and Prince of Wales. Therefore I am Arthur. Arthur and his three mourning Queens, rowing down to Avalon.

'Charenton,' someone said. He struggled to sit up, and succeeded. 'I will ride,' he said. 'I will not be carried to Vincennes like a woman!'

Arthur and his three Queens! The glamour of the analogy lit a last small flame of impossible determination. For Arthur was immortal, and there was work to be done. Vaguely he heard the doctors, servants, confessors pleading with him, then found himself swaying upright on the river bank, where his horse stood before him, white as winter mist and as unreal, a descendant of the great stallion he had ridden at Agincourt. It wore a gold-embossed saddle with a high cantle for him to lean against. He was lifted and sat astride, two knights riding close on either side, supporting him. Ten paces forward, and the pain returned, furiously affronted, so that he ground his teeth and moaned. Twenty paces, and the saddle was wet with his blood. So he was taken down, insensible, and placed in a litter, and so brought back to Vincennes, to the curtained chamber, and the whispering host, and the lighted candles all about him. The days and nights coalesced into a little eternity of prayer and waiting, while the forest outside passed on the message from tree to tree, of greatness humbled, and the leaves rattled in terror and the bark groaned under the threat of storm-winds and the knowledge that kings must die and that they were less than kings and should also fear the axe.

From time to time the shadows that crowded nearer about the bed took him away to the utmost ends of a great universe, and reluctantly returned him at longer and longer intervals, when he dimly heard small sounds; the prayers and psalms for his recovery, and hour on hour, a woman's little fretful coughing. He rocked and drifted on the shadows, longing to go wherever they willed him, yet clinging despite their power, striving to reach the other side of the ranks and rows of gleaming French chivalry massed so tightly that their armour rubbed together; to break through the wall of starry banners and be free to ride the empty plain and reach the city. He knew it lay beyond. It called him, with its sloping little red roofs and holy bells and the shrine that had long been fashioned in his heart.

'Mars is square to Saturn in Virgo, his Grace's birthsign,' said Swanwyth. 'Greatly unfavourable for all enteric disorders.'

Suddenly the shadows were gone about their other business. Voices and sounds were clear, tiresomely insistent. That time he had been so near he could almost see the gates of the city, smell the incense from the shrine. But here was Bedford, bending close, unshaven, Warwick and Exeter, peering sadly beneath the bed-canopy which was gilded overall with UNE SANS PLUS. Bedford was telling him that the skirmish was over, that the campaign had gone just as he had forecast, and, incredibly, that his illness had lasted three weeks.

'Rest, Harry,' he said. 'You'll soon be well.'

Everything was so lucid. He began to talk, while Bedford beckoned the clerks to set down all that the King said. Important and unimportant things, and matters of tender pain.

'I ask pardon of all I have wronged. I give thanks to all who have fought for me so bravely, who have done my will without question, who have given all or part of their lives to my service. Would that I could have repaid them better.'

'There will be time,' said Bedford, but Henry shook his head. The wonderful clarity must not be interrupted.

'I wish you, my lord John of Bedford, to command Normandy until my son is of age to rule. You are to be regent of France unless Philip objects and wants the title for himself. England must never quarrel with Burgundy; our strength lies there. And Charles of Orléans must be kept prisoner until the war with Armagnac is over and all France is subject to the Treaty.'

'And in England?'

'My brother of Gloucester shall be Lord Protector over the prince . . . you, my lord of Warwick, and my lord of Hungerford, shall support him in this. But John . . .' His voice grew stronger. 'You are to be the final arbiter in England over the safety, destiny and upbringing of my son. It is my decree that Humphrey of Gloucester's power be limited so far as seems just and reasonable.'

And then he said, quite simply and softly:

'I commit to your care the Queen's Grace. Comfort her. Comfort my dear companion, my Katherine.' Lastly, sounding much weaker: 'Now send for my executors – I must show you my will.'

'Ah, your Grace!' said Exeter sadly. Henry looked at the doctors, and Swanwyth replied in a whisper: 'Sire, except for the favour of God, we judge you cannot survive two hours more,' and Bedford murmured: 'We have sent for the Queen. She is sleeping, but . . .'

'She has watched and prayed for hours, days,' said Warwick, tears in his eyes. Henry smiled faintly. Let her sleep a little longer. Sleep on, sweet Katherine. The shadows return, I see them growing in the corners, coming to touch the gilded UNE SANS PLUS . . . friendly, soft. I will ride with them for a while. It was midnight and the monks in the nearby abbey began to sing matins. Wreathed by the sepia shadows came Bishop Courtenay's face, still rapt as on the moment of his passing in the pavilion at Harfleur, and full of love, speaking without sound of the Four Last Things, and of other, unexpected matters – the nothingness to come, the black velvet æons of waiting and then somewhere at the eternal outer limits of the universe – the reckoning. And with that word came a swirl of painfilled images – the mountained bodies on Artois plain, the crushed flowers of France, the drooping heads of the hanged hostages. Sounds, too; over the plainsong of the monks, a woman weeping, her voice that of the eternal widow robbed by war. Courtenay's face was still close, his lips still moving, now speaking of guilt, the guilt of kings and warriors. This made him cry aloud, striving to rise and frightening away the shadows so that they rushed into the corners of the room.

'You lie!' he cried. 'My portion *is* with the Lord Jesus!'

Now the confessor came, and the breviary and the glinting cross and holy vessels were the only foci of stern comfort before his eyes, and he spoke with humility of all the years of doubt, all the actions judged to be well-judged and right; nothing hasty or in anger but none the less actions dealing death to others, and midway he broke off and desired all the chaplains to recite the Seven Penitential Psalms, which contained the verse: '*Benigne fac ex benevolentia tua Sioni, aedifica muros Hierusalem . . .*' and at this reminder of the greatest crime, his sin by default, he broke in again saying:

'Good Lord, Thou knowest that mine intent has been and yet is if I might live, to re-edify the walls of Jerusalem . . .' thinking even now: could I only be spared one more year!

His hand was clasped about the crucifix. Outside, the watchman called the hour; it was the last day of August, 1422. Beyond the bed stood the woman. Dark and pale, aged about twenty-one . . . his mother, Mary de Bohun. Death had stolen none of her douce beauty and sweetness. She was coughing, a little dry cough, trying to stifle it with a slim shaking hand. His mother had no cough, childbirth had killed her. There was

314

only one who coughed like that, when sad or afraid.

'Oh, my dear companion,' he whispered. She stepped forward a pace, then was still, so that the priests could continue and administer the Blessed Sacrament and the Extreme Unction. Afterwards he again interrupted the prayers and chanting with a long lucid whispered speech which seemed so important, although it was compounded of old emotions known by all close to him.

'It was not ambitious lust for dominion nor for empty glory . . . nor for any other cause that drew me to the wars . . . but only that by suing for my right I might at once gain peace . . . and my own rights . . .'

Courtenay's ghostly countenance again crept forward to mingle with the weary living faces. It smiled and nodded, and said distinctly: *I am your advocate . . .*

'. . . I was fully instructed by men of the holiest life . . . that I ought and could . . . with this intention begin the wars . . . prosecute them, and justly finish them . . .'

But it is unfinished! A spasm not of pain but of disembodiment took hold of him as the last of his life began to ebb away. He held steadily to the Cross.

'. . . without danger to my soul,' he whispered.

Servants were opening the windows ready for his soul's departing. Everything was dim yet shimmering. The kneeling figures about the bed were a chiaroscuro, unformed save for their essence, but that essence was strong, full of tender consolation. The chaplain's *Ego te absolvo* settled within him like balm. The pain was gone, it had never existed. The shadows were sweeping forward again, taller, majestic, like a trailing black velvet robe held engulfingly high. His grip on the crucifix slackened, for all he tried faithfully to hold it. He looked up to where the *raison* of UNE SANS PLUS swam together into a gilded bar, to where the pale face with the dark jewel-like eyes leaned down.

Queen Katherine laid her hand over his and over the crucifix. And with her touch a momentous thing occurred. He no longer saw faces or shadows, or the dimming manifestations of love and sorrow. He saw the city, builded anew.

It was not as he had dreamed. There were no little rose-red

tiles, nor sloping dwellings, and no narrow arched streets. There was only a vast citadel, white as a perfect rose, whiter and more scintillating than the softest bleached sand, rising in immensity like a gleaming tree in flower. He moved forward to embrace it and its brightness blinded him, so that he closed his eyes.

Part Five

THE DREAM
England, *1424*

O thoughtful herte, plonged in dystresse,
With slomber of slouthe this longe winter's night –
Out of the slepe of mortal hevinesse
Awake anon! and loke upon the light
Of thilke star . . .

John Lydgate, 1370–1450

Rain, blown into fine patterns by an east wind, whirled about Windsor. It drenched the oaks in the meadow and darkened the hides of the grazing fallow deer. August? more like November! the wet-faced guard, ranged on the high walkways between the towers, remarked to one another. Below, soaked to his silk tunic, Humphrey of Gloucester rode in from Westminster at a gallop with a handful of servants and a vile temper. His mount's sides bled from his rage. Weighted by his sodden cloak, he dismounted and threw his reins to a groom, who thought: my lord Duke, you're a swine! Several nights of poulticing needed here, and good mounts not easy to find these days. Money was tight, if one's betters were to be believed. He led the shivering horse away and Humphrey went rapidly across the green and entered the castle. He had apartments at Windsor, as in nearly every manor, and there more servants waited with dry clothes and a bath. Stripped, hairless and broad, slightly paunchy from too much wine, he submitted to these valets, cursing them continually for water too hot, soap too abrasive, herbals too pungent. At last he flung himself from their frightened hands and towelled himself as if to rub the skin from his body. And I wish, he thought, grinding his teeth, that this flesh were Beaufort's and I flayed him thus with knives.

He had stormed from the Council meeting, although knowing this to be unwise. There would be wry laughter, ponderous Latin quips from Chichele, capped smirkingly by Henry Beaufort, that bastard Bishop who, since Harry's death, seemed even more boastful of his flawed kinship with the royal House. Beaufort! the product of old Gaunt's lust, even now preparing himself to be enthroned as a great prince of the Church, a Cardinal. Beaufort! who, from that first Parliament two months after Harry's death had with the utmost efficiency set out to block Humphrey's power. He must have schemed for this, for years, all the time I was away nearly getting myself killed in France. How had it been so easy for him to obtain the support of lords and commons, gain triumph at that Parliament two years ago? The sole glories of which I dreamed as Protector of the Realm and the infant King, all are made null! He has hamstrung me! He flung the towel away and thrust his arms into a velvet robe. Me! Regent! Blood-uncle to the King!

'Get out,' he said, and thankfully the valets fled, gathering up the paraphernalia of the bath, which was a travelling tub in glazed leather festooned with gold tassels. Humphrey pulled a bench close to the roaring fire and continued to torment himself with memories of injustice. That opening of Parliament had fallen on a crisp November day. He had been dressed like a popinjay, befitting his new status, ready to sway kingdoms; riding close to the widowed Queen who sat veiled and ghostly in her carriage, the infant in her lap. Doubly bereaved (news had lately reached her of the death of her father in France), she had been mute and rigid, the child also waxen-stiff, both pairs of dark eyes withdrawn, shadowed. Two little dolls! to guard and guide and subjugate! Strength surged in him as he had ascended King's Bench. He was glad that Bedford had remained in France, leaving the field clear. He had prepared his memorandum to submit to the lords stating that he had been granted *tutelam et defensionem principales* of the infant King as per the codicil in the royal will. And then the opposition began, shattering him. They objected to his premise that if he were to administer the estates of a minor and as those estates constituted the realm itself, he, Humphrey, was no less than sovereign ruler. They objected strongly to his interpretation of the wording. True, he was designated custodian and regent. Yet (and for the first time in his life he feared apoplexy) he was to open, conduct and dissolve Parliament *de assensu concilii*. All his decisions were to be subject to the consent of his peers. His status was fatally prejudiced. And Beaufort was behind it! One had only to look at him, hear the bland speeches obviously well-prepared for this contingency, see the nodding heads, the faces that said: we can make or break. We can keep Parliament in session for twelve months or dissolve it within a week if we wish. And you, my lord of Gloucester, Earl of Pembroke, are as much a figurehead as that pale infant yawning on the dais.

He stared into the fire, his eyes watering, recalling the sermon preached by Archbishop Chichele, so pointed in its allegory that some of the lords had laughed aloud. The story of Jethro and Moses, Jethro (Chichele) advising Moses (Humphrey) to delegate his authority in governing, to take counsel from the wise men about him, not to weary himself with overwork (over-ambition). Even after two years the sermon still smarted. Beaufort and Chichele had concocted it together. Hamstrung! by clever priests and lawyers, with their talk of Romanist interpretation and their objections to the word *tutela*, which meant that Humphrey, had he had his way, would have been answerable in all things only to the sovereign, a baby!

Katherine of course had not been mentioned *in tutela*. She had sat there, veiled and inert, apart from the barbed explosive atmosphere and his own humiliation. Afterwards he had tried to speak to her: like trying to converse with Lazarus before the miracle. Well, she should speak with him today. That was why he had come to Windsor, raging from the Council meeting. Harry once said: 'The death of Jean sans Peur was the gateway by which I entered France.' Such a small thing really, leading to such triumphs. Time he turned his attention to small things, like that quiet widow in the further turret. His mind lashed back to Beaufort, whom the Council had this day considered for a large monetary grant in furtherance of his ecclesiastical duties. This day! when, according to the Exchequer, the economy was so straitened by the cost of keeping in luxury French prisoners still awaiting ransom, not to mention the garrisons' wages at Calais, Scotland, the Marches. Some of the lords' salaries were months in arrears. Humphrey himself had been so far fortunate in having 8,000 marks from the receivers of the Duchy of Lancaster. But it was not enough.

Thomas Chaucer, the one-time Speaker, was a cousin of the Beauforts, a common wine merchant. His presence and the new articles he had brought forward today were the final thrust that had sent Humphrey foaming from the Chamber. Obviously aimed at the Protector's power, these articles requested that all offices and benefices not directly excepted should be filled solely on the Council's assent, that all favours, wardships and marriages should be theirs to distribute; that no individual should have correspondence with foreign countries without the approval of a quorum of six. And this was a terrible blow. Hainault! He bit his index finger until it bled. Another plan aborted! The rich pickings of his long courtship taken out of his hands. Jacqueline virtually dowerless, now that Philip of Burgundy, somewhat belatedly, had shown outrage at what he claimed was the kidnapping of his kinsman Brabant's bride.

Everything seemed changed since Harry's death. Philip, God knew, had once been complaisant enough. His gratitude seemed outworn. Humphrey thought: everyone now shows his true colours. And here am I, saddled with clinging, cloying Jacqueline of whom I am heartily weary, and whose inheritance appears further away than ever. Even the Hainaulters refuse to co-operate. He had challenged Philip to mortal combat over Jacqueline's estates. The procedure would have been perfectly honourable, chivalric. He stared at the crumbling fire. And who had prevented it? None other than that silent widow in Windsor's Upper Ward. Katherine, who as Queen-Dowager should have known better than to interfere, should know her place like Queen Joanna, now a recluse at King's Langley. He had not dreamed Katherine capable of such initiative. When he had asked her about it, his temper curdling under his smile, she had raised those great black eyes saying gently: 'Harry would not have wished it. He said we were to cleave always to Burgundy. I was there.' She must have been influenced to write that diplomatic letter, by Bedford on one of his brief visits to England, or by . . . he chewed his raw finger again . . . Beaufort.

The fire was dying. Rain on the windows darkened the room. He yelled angrily for his servants. Immediately there was a tapping on the door; his flesh prickled. He knew that tapping. Outside stood the only person alive who could frighten as well as enchant him.

She was so slender and darkclad and sinuous that for a moment he fancied she entered while the oak was still fast, like the elementals who come through keyholes to steal the wits from a sleeper. Beneath a skull-cap trimmed with rabbit fur her small face was smiling, showing pretty little teeth. She curtseyed formally, bowing her head. Scooped low at the nape, her dress revealed the luminous pallor of her perfect back. Under her arm she carried a pile of jewel-bound manuscripts.

He rose and greeted her. 'Lady Eleanor Cobham.'

'My lord,' said her cool voice. 'I have only come to return your books. The Queen-Dowager and your lady wife have finished with them.'

She straightened, seeming to waver and grow to an extravagant height, and he thought of a black kitten, bonelessly stretching up a wall. Yet she was far from tall, and minutely slim.

'You're sad today,' she said. 'The Council angered you. Yet they are but men . . .'

'Toadies, traitors,' he said thickly, 'but grossly empowered.'

'Men,' said Eleanor Cobham, silk-soft. 'Mortal, fallible. They lack your kingly blood.'

He stepped forward to take her in his arms. She kept the pile of books outstretched between them. Her eyes, the same colour as the rabbit-fur, dilated.

'Eleanor,' he said, in genuine pleading for one moment of her strange joy. At all other times he could only watch her, armed with comb or lute or words of consolation, in attendance on the petulant Jacqueline. In the Queen's apartments or her mistress's bower she never looked at him, almost insolently denying his existence. It was driving him frantic.

'Perhaps your Grace should examine the titles,' she said, 'in case any are missing. Alas! your lady and the Queen-Dowager have scant interest in books these days. Both are so *triste* . . .' And the fur-grey eyes darkened further in what could have been satisfaction or sympathy or merely the patterns of the reflected rain. His fingers brushed hers as he took the manuscripts. Never in his life could he remember a woman who had stirred him so. He had, just once, possessed her cool body, in joy, in uncharacteristic gratitude, yet she still seemed untouched by him. Cursing Jacqueline, the Council, and the way the world used him, he began to wish she had not come, bringing this new torment. Sighing, he glanced at the books.

Several were the late King's property and had found their way into Humphrey's own library during the chaos of the early funereal days. Chaucer's *Troilus* was stamped with the arms of the Prince of Wales, and should by rights be with the infant Henry. There was Hoccleve – *De Regimine Principum* – a vast tome, and Lydgate – *The Life of Our Lady*. Well, both these scholars were his protégés; he was entitled to enjoy them. But hiding beneath *The Cuckoo and the Nightingale* was a slim black book which, aghast, he nearly dropped.

'Sweet Christ, Eleanor! Has *this* been in the Queen's apartments?'

She took the book from him.

'A mistake,' she said simply. 'None has seen it, save you and I. I promised its safe return, and here it is.'

He sat down slowly. His face felt very cold.

'For safety it should be burned, I've often thought so,' he whispered. 'As you and I could burn for touching it even in ignorance.'

'I tried the Egyptian spell,' she said, so calmly that his skin crept. 'I bled three mice to death and named them Beaufort.' (And one other, which I named Jacqueline, she thought.)

'You risked that? For me?'

'For you. Only a beginning. In time, I'll get you kingdoms, fair kingdoms by foul means. No fouler means than kingdoms often fall to,' she added.

It came to him forcibly that she was a blood relative of Sir John Oldcastle who had burned for heresy of a different colour, Lollardy, which compared to this seemed an innocent pastime. 'You must lend me the others, the demonology books,' she was saying. She knew his every possession, every cranny of his mind, his prickly, tortuous secrets. 'These – ' tapping the black book – 'are elementary matters. I taught Joanna of Navarre all she wished to know . . .'

'But she was discovered,' he said uncertainly.

'She was very careless. My lord, you can be a great wizard.' The amorous, small-toothed smile came again. 'And I will be your familiar, your black Eleanor, your Nell-cat!'

He rose up and embraced her then, spilling the precious illuminations to the floor. Even in his arms she seemed illusory, a supple shadow, a puff of scented smoke, a tingling ghost-mist. He thought of Jacqueline, grown plump and indolent and whining, he thought of the torments of the Council meeting, and clutched at Eleanor Cobham as at salvation, with Hell-fire a reasonable tithe for the riches of the world. She drew away too soon, leaving him hapless, hungry. The grey eyes unflickeringly probed him, old eyes in a young face, eyes that had known everything from the remotest times, had opened on the world fast in their knowledge. Humphrey, loving his first great love, was robbed of the courtliness, the rehearsed excitations of poetry previously his tools. Anyway he would never again quote Chaucer to a woman. He was against all the Chaucer family, since the Council meeting.

He watched her shining nape as she knelt to retrieve the manuscripts. Straightening a crumpled leaf, she said: 'Will you be at Windsor long?' and he remembered the purpose of his visit.

'As long as it takes to discover what, if anything, is exercising the Queen-Dowager's mind,' he said grimly.

'She's had a letter – ' Eleanor rose – 'from Bedford at Rouen.'

'Congratulating her no doubt on her skill in averting the duel,' he said.

'And she has written two. But I was unable to discover their contents.'

'She writes too many letters.' Humphrey sucked in his lip.

'One to James of Scotland. I think she plans to visit him at Hertford; she lent him her manor there.'

Humphrey made a disgusted noise. 'There's yet another foothold for the Beaufort brood! I would have prevented that marriage, but Harry approved it. So Joan Beaufort joins the climbing ranks. She'll have a kingdom, now that James is restored.'

'I dreamed last night,' said Eleanor, 'of Beaufort, lying on his bed. A spider, as big as a hound, hung above him. It lowered itself and forced into his mouth. He was screaming . . .' Then she said, dispassionately: 'Beaufort is very deferential to the Queen-Dowager.'

The room had grown very cold. Humphrey said: 'She's a

thorn in my flesh, that widow of Harry's. Who are her clerks? Are they corruptible?'

'Perhaps. Louis de Robsart guards her affairs, but I will discover all, to my power. And, my dear lord, remember. You still have wardship over the prince!'

She was at the door, smiling, an odd young smile in contrast to her old eyes. You and I will be married, she thought. It is predestined, and the day not so far off.

'Yes,' Humphrey was cheered at last. 'I still have the prince!'

Within the Upper Ward, traditional lodging of royalty, reached by angled stairways and galleries from tower to tower, the Queen-Dowager, not quite twenty-three years old, kept close within herself. Now and then she coughed her brittle cough. Jacqueline hung close, talking incessantly, unheard, unanswered. Katherine's maids, Belknap, Troutbeck and Coucy, waited for commands that never came. And, standing with her back against the wall, little Guillemot, the bedchamber maid, watched her adored mistress with great sadness. The two harps, bought by Henry, stood still unplayed, their strings furred with dust. This was one of the bad days, the women thought. A bad month; naturally, the anniversary. It had been the same last August. Her Grace was born under Scorpio, thought Troutbeck. Such are prey to great passions, joy and sorrow cuts them deeper than most. There was a wine stain on the Queen's grey gown. She drinks rather a lot, thought Troutbeck, but she's out of her black at least. In the beginning she wanted to wear white, saying it was the custom of mourning Queens in France.

UNE SANS PLUS! What tragic irony the *raison* held now. It had been limned in radiance on the gorgeous funeral canopy as the long procession wound from Vincennes to Abbeville, Hesdin, Montreuil, Boulogne and Calais, then overseas to where the weepers waited, inconsolable, at Dover. UNE SANS PLUS! Yes, she was the one alone, in this secret private place that she had drawn about herself against shock and fear that would otherwise have engulfed her. Wine helped: some days she could pretend that Harry was only on campaign.

They had boiled the flesh from the King's bones and placed them in the casket, first moulding a complete death-mask of head and face and body, and fixing this effigy on top of the canopied bier. The mask was crowned with an imperial diadem of gold and rubies, and clothed in the purple, trimmed with ermines. The right hand held a sceptre and the left an orb. Louis de Robsart, the Duke of Exeter, and March had overseen the tributes and smoothed the passage home. Masses were sung at every town through which they passed. She had not wept until Dover, not even at the abbey of St Ostian where the monks sang so sweetly that everyone was in tears. It was on England's shore that the pain flung itself over her. Then she had been glad of James, dear James, giving comfort where there was no comfort, repaying whatever kindness she may have shown him. James of Scotland, ceaselessly at her side. Unlike Bedford, who, although bidden to look after her, had been forced to remain in France.

And then she was in a foreign country, an embarrassment to the crowds who had cheered her once. Perhaps this was why James took her suffering upon him, having once been as displaced as she. He was not far from her now, a mere two days' ride, but she wished he were here at Windsor. He might even know what to advise about the little King. And at the thought of the baby Henry a tremor broke through her detachment, and her mind raced. None would harm him at Kennington Palace, where he now lay; he was the King. But he was so small! She had seen Dame Alice Boteler slap him once. In answer to Katherine's protest the woman had primly quoted the Privy Council's edict, written as from the infant himself:

'We request Dame Alice from time to time reasonably to chastise us, as the case may require, without being held accountable or molested for the same at any future time. The well beloved Dame Alice is to teach us courtesy and nurture and many things convenient for our royal person to learn.'

She had not seen him for two months. The Protector had impressed upon her that the teaching of courtesy and nurture could only be effective away from all frivolous influence. Like training a dog, he had explained; the fewer the masters the swifter the obedience. Well, she had seen the way Humphrey trained his dogs; the analogy sickened her. Eight weeks since she had seen her son, and twice as long before that, when she had taken him to an opening of Parliament. Then it had been a day almost of happiness.

They were to pass the Saturday night at Staines before going on to Westminster the following day. Somehow the question of their lodging had been overlooked, their host indisposed, she had forgotten which. They had come finally to a common tavern, whose name she had also forgotten. She remembered a roaring fire, mulled ale in which slices of pippin floated, a delicious duckling roasted with chestnuts. A distinct lack of ceremony! The tap-wench, round as a cask with three teeth missing in her merry pink face, had been called Betty – Bet. Bet had snatched the King of England from his nurse's arms and settled him on the soft rollicking terrain of her lap. Jigging him, singing him an inexhaustible stream of ditties, spooning broth into his unprotesting mouth. Sending her own children to fetch their crude toys for his pleasure. His eyes had rolled with amazement, he had begun to chuckle and then to laugh. None had ever heard him laugh like that before or since. When he had begun to drowse before the great fire, Bet had covered his hands and feet with kisses; the whole scene had scandalized nurses and physicians and warmed Katherine's heart.

The following morning when they were due to leave for Westminster, Henry had other ideas. Whether it was the duckling broth, so exotic after his wetnurse's milk, or Bet's riotous lap, or the little wooden horse of which he would not let go, no one could say. However, when lifted into the chariot he began to scream, and went black in the face. See! the attendants said, awed: how holy he is! he refuses to travel on the Lord's Day! So he was lifted down and restored to the arms of Bet, for several further hours of lovely play . . .

And would to God I had left him there, Katherine thought. There was love there, kindness. Sweet St Nicholas, protect my little prince. Dear Harry! if you have time, look down from beyond the stars and keep him safe.

Distressed, she forced her mind to other things. When had the silversmiths called on her? Half a year ago? Time was tangled, inconsequential. But the work was finished, Harry now had a fitting memorial in St Edward's Chapel, beneath the H-shaped chantry in fine Caen stone. She had designed the memorial herself; a life-size effigy in oak plated with silver-gilt, the head in its jousting helm made of solid silver, his sword and armour and his achievements fittingly displayed. The arms of France and England. France and England he would have been truly, had he but outlived her father by another two months! Would poor mad Charles be sane again in Heaven? while Isabeau pursued her ageless career of debauchery and the Dauphin, the 'King of Bourges', claimed a larger kingdom and sought annulment of the Treaty of Troyes. She had written to her brother, congratulating him on the birth of his son, Louis. She had been moved by a desperate family feeling, a longing for future peace. It was useless; both the Dauphin and Bedford were adamant – the campaigns would continue. The wastefulness appalled her – the fighting, killing, the crushed crawling ants of armies. All so vainglorious compared to the power of those few words to her after the entry into Paris: 'You were the prize I sought . . . but never did I dream that I would love you so . . .'

Harry had come to her bed that night, the night of those words . . . so tender, filling her, completing her. She shivered. She drank some wine from the cup that stood beside her chair. She thought again of the prince, her baby, under Duke Humphrey's tutelage. This strange weather would not suit him; he easily took cold. Her unease became agony. He was paler than ever last time she saw him, in his white velvet doublet, standing on thin black-hosed legs, addressing her formally as '*Ma Reine*'. He has very long lashes, a bony un-childlike face . . . they cannot harm or neglect him. He is the King. Nicholas, Nicholas, with your crook and your little lamb, leave all your other charges and guard my son! Be mother and father to him. His mother is void, a shell of barren wanhope. His father has gone before his time into that other world. Harry, you took my safety and my peace. Your face is hard to remember. The lack of you remains, the dreadful lack, so ominous. I fear the future. So much an end to everything. How could you leave me so alone?

But where there's an end there must be a beginning. Life is an unending circle.

The strange little secret voice was so confident that, startled, she looked about her. The women still stood there, silent. Jacqueline was stabbing her tapestry, quiet at last. The two harps were like elegant watchers with their dusty gilded shanks. Eleanor Cobham had just slipped back into the room. Katherine rose, and Guillemot hurried to serve her, but Eleanor was there first.

'Dear Madame – you look chilled. May I pour you more wine, send for your furs?'

Katherine felt a pressure on her shoulder, looked to see Jacqueline, glaring, bright with rouge over a sickly pallor.

'I will attend her Grace,' she said. 'Kéti, may we walk together in the pleasaunce? This inactivity makes me ill.'

Katherine felt jealousy, venom, pass between Jacqueline and Eleanor. She could not be troubled to assess its cause.

'It's too cold,' she said.

'His Grace the Duke of Gloucester begs audience,' said Louis de Robsart in the doorway.

Humphrey entered in yellow cloth of gold, on a gust of bonhomie. Danger and brightness came with him. Jacqueline grew paler and more starkly rouged: Eleanor Cobham withdrew into a shadow created by herself.

'*Ma chère sœur!*' said Humphrey. 'How fair you are today!' He kissed Katherine's hand.

And there's today's first lie, she thought. Whenever I trouble to look in the mirror I see a face so withdrawn it is almost featureless. It did not worry her, unlike Jacqueline, who, beset by a storm of troubles, still sought comeliness with lead pastes and the juice of crushed insects. In vain: her husband's eyes encompassed all the women, and he smiled more sweetly at little Guillemot than at his wife. It was a sharp smile, and finally lodged in Katherine.

'But your Grace seems sad,' and his eyes took in the winestain on her gown. 'Permit me . . . why does your Grace not wear more jewels? It troubles me that you should sit so lifeless, when all know how you can shine!'

How formal he was! Gone the soft touch, the concern that

had eased her when Harry was in France. Oh, many-coated Humphrey! with the answer known so well!

'Most of my jewels I pawned,' she said steadily, 'to pay for my husband's memorial.'

The dower to which she was entitled as the King's widow had to stretch a long way. There were palaces which she scarcely saw to maintain, and a mystery of servants. One small manor, she often thought, would have been enough.

'I passed your stable,' said Humphrey. 'Do you no longer have the eight white horses?'

She studied her own frail fingernails minutely. The pearly team had been more to her than any jewels. Watching them go, brave and gay and rippling like the top of a wave, had been like a second farewell to Harry. Humphrey knew this. *Sainte Vierge!* he was so cruel. How could she ever have been otherwise deluded?

'My lord,' she said. 'How is my son, the King's Grace?'

Humphrey cried in delight: 'Madame! So holy! he astounds his tutors. Yesterday he lisped a psalm, I forget which – '

'Yes,' she said, looking up, 'but is he well?'

'Just a little cold he had. His Grace has forty servants to wait on him and the best doctors in England.'

'I wish to see him,' said Katherine. '*La grippe* is dangerous in the young.' The sharp smile seemed to bruise her eyes.

'It was only a little cold,' Humphrey said gently. 'He is again at his lessons.'

'I wish to see him.' She was twisting and turning the ring on her finger. 'I wish to come with you to Kennington Palace.'

'I shall be honoured. But his Grace is not at Kennington. He's at King's Langley for now.'

She said sharply: 'With Queen Joanna?' Joanna, who once had Harry bewitched. Ah, no.

'Joanna is being removed to Havering. I thought it fitting that his Grace had a change of scene.'

She thought wildly: they are at liberty to bear my little son to the further ends of this strange country! I am powerless. It's my own childhood over again. Isabeau . . . Tonnerre, the storm, the sickness . . . coughing seized her, sweat sprang out on her face. Eleanor Cobham knelt beside her, offering a warm and bitter brew, one of the herbal concoctions for which she was famed. Humphrey said: 'Your Grace is weary. She should take to her bed . . . Queen Joanna spends most of her time in bed. Bed is beneficial to ladies . . .' and without warning, Jacqueline burst into a sobbing roar, and fled from the room.

'I will have the King's physician visit you,' said Humphrey, when there was quiet again. 'With that chest-cough, it would be unwise for you to come near the sovereign. We'll have you well again . . .' He went on and on. Katherine, exhausted, thought: I can't fight him, he is a chimera, he attacks from below, behind, before . . . St Nicholas. Protect my son.

Humphrey was looking at the gilded harps. 'These are beautiful. If your Grace is temporarily embarrassed for funds, I will pay a good price.'

She said hoarsely: 'They're not for sale.'

Not the harps, upon which she and Harry were to have made music into their old age. Gloucester stroked a dusty arpeggio from one with the back of his fingers. Instantly two strings broke in a cloud of resinous gold.

'The weather,' he said knowledgeably. 'The gut expands in sunshine and sudden cold shrinks it beyond endurance.'

Beyond endurance, she thought. Ah yes. The kisses, the joy. Gone for ever.

'Especially if they lie unused,' said Humphrey. Then: 'Have you heard lately from our brother of Bedford? There is rumour that he is coming home.'

She stared at the broken harp. The gold filament curled outwards like the stamen of a flower; a watery shaft of sunlight made it shine. It breaks. But it does not bend. And it can be mended. She even remembered the harpmaker's name. John Bore. Henry had told her. Get Owen Tydier to see to it – you call him Jacques – he is a Welshman. Humphrey was waiting for her answer. Yes. They break, but they do not bend. And they can be mended.

'My lord Duke. I do not listen to rumour.'

When he had gone, she sat, reflectively sipping her wine. The women resumed their waiting stance. Then Jacqueline burst into the chamber again, her maquillage grotesquely streaked from weeping. 'Kéti, Kéti, I must speak to you. Get rid of these wenches.' She was down on her knees.

'Now, Jacqueline,' said Katherine patiently. 'We're alone. Dry your eyes, don't clutch me so.' What a weeper she is. But this is something serious.

'He talks of leaving me,' said Jacqueline in a horrified whisper. Tears splashed to join the wine-stain on Katherine's skirt. 'Just now. In the antechamber. He spoke . . . of annulling our marriage . . . says the Pope never agreed . . . I am still . . . Brabant! Burgundy!' She buried her head in Katherine's lap.

'He . . . intends to disobey the Council . . . go to Hainault . . . demand my dowry . . . if my lands . . . not forthcoming . . .'

'I can't hear you,' said Katherine.

Jacqueline raised her ruined face.

'. . . he is tired of me. There are other women. I love him.' Her eyes were demented. 'From the first time he embraced me . . . *I am consumed*. Oh, Katherine, how can you know? You're a Queen.'

And of all the foolishness you've ever uttered, Jacqueline, there is the crown. Are Queens so sacrosanct, or am I so wickedly unnatural? If you only knew my thoughts, the riptide of my blood, my crying, constant need! My agonizing urges which constitute the main part of Harry's loss. I need his body. In the dark night I know myself alone, unfinished, cheated. My wanting is unashamed even in face of regal death – it cries for consolation. The fact that he is dead does not rob it of an iota of its power. The shameless animal still couches within me, stronger now. I am only twenty-two years old. I am chaste. Not for lack of opportunity; certain lords have looked at me and I knew them eager to offer me consolation. Yet I found them distasteful. I am chaste. I am not like my mother. I can, if only barely, control this dreadful need. Yes, Jacqueline. I know.

'He is so changed,' Jacqueline was whimpering, and Katherine answered after a time. 'No. He was always like this. Unscrupulous, cruel, scheming. We saw a counterfeit Humphrey when we loved him or were his friend. I feared him once, then trusted him. I fear him now.'

'But I love him! What shall I do?' Jacqueline rose, haggard, defeated. 'You were always able to arrange things – you spoke

335

in favour of our marriage . . . tell me what to do.'

'He'll go to Hainault,' said Katherine. The sun was making diamonds on the rain-wet window. 'The Council will be furious but he will have his way. So go with him. Do not let him from your sight. Cleave close . . .'

As I should have done. I could have had many months more with Harry, child or no child, had I but gone with him to France. Perhaps with love and care I could have stayed that killing sickness. And this last thought was so unbearable that she began to cough again, waving Jacqueline away, needing solitude, while the last of the rain dried under sunshine that crept to touch, at last, the wounded, yearning harp.

The monk rose from his knees and looked down at the man lying insensible on the straw pallet. He wadded up a blood-and pus-soaked bandage and gave a final pat to the new dressing covering the dreadful gash on the man's thigh. The linen looked very white against the tawny flesh. Such a strong man, the monk thought; he looked at the nakedness, dispassionately seeing the beautiful length of thigh muscle covered with fine gold hairs, the strength of the manhood revealed, the hard slim belly. But such a sick man! the wound did not seem to be improving, there were black streaks visible to the groin. The monk sighed for more skill. He relied on the daisy and the dangerous aconite, poulticed with prayers; the gash was still flushed and oozing. He covered his patient with a grimy blanket. He touched the brow to judge the fever. A good face, too, handsome features like those carved by a clever mason. Perhaps too handsome, and the mouth! even in pain that showed now, with consciousness returning – it was an angel-devil's mouth. Or a devil-angel's mouth. Young virgins, thought the monk, should beware that mouth. But he may have to lose that leg. The monk sighed again, and moved away. In the corner of the cell his patient's belongings were stacked, his sword and knife, his money-belt, his cloak, still hard and stained with sea-water. A soldier. A foreign soldier, judging by his tongue in delirium. It was three weeks since he had been dumped senseless at the porter's lodge by a cart coming from the harbour. Obviously someone had been too busy or too callous to play the Samaritan any further. One blessing; he had not been robbed.

He was almost at the door when the man spoke, wildly.

'*Annwyl Crist! Dyna drosedd aflan!*'

The monk hurried back.

'Damned Lombards!' said Owen clearly. 'What a filthy trick! They've taken all the Duke's silver plate!'

His eyes were open and seen properly by the monk for the first time. Fever-brilliant blue eyes, with gold flecks swarming in the fever.

'My son. Are you mending?'

'The baggage!' said Owen. 'Stop them!'

He tried to sit up, the pain from his leg flattened him instantly. The monk's dark shape wavered and was replaced by images bred in the fiery heat of the wound. The battle-ground at Verneuil swam far away and he was back on the ship, lying wedged in the forecastle between two tuns of wine, his teeth chattering with fever as the high seas roared over his raw leg, salt mixed with blood, the whipcrack flutter of canvas and groan of timbers drowning his own agonized cries. A woolship coming back home from Calais with a cargo of wounded men and wine, her hold and part of her deck crammed with the yield of Bordeaux and Burgundy . . . The monk's face crept back into his sight.

'Dover,' said Owen.

'Not Dover, my son.' The monk was mixing poppy-juice in a little vial. 'Southampton.'

Out of the dream's turmoil came the shouts of captain and crew as a September storm ripped the sea apart and hurled the *Petite Marie* round the southern tip of England, spewing her up into Southampton Water . . .

. . . he knelt on the deck and offered wine to Harry the King. Swans flew overhead, good omens like elongated pearls. Davy Gam chuckled in approval . . .

'But that's nine years ago!' he said in amazement.

'Drink.' Bitter and syrupy, the juice went down. He slept again, a little cooler, and the cell door opened and someone entered without sound. Lissom, long-handed, sweet-hearted, she lay beside him, so light that not a blade of straw was displaced. She spoke to him in the soft tongue of the beasts and the wind and the flowers. Across his cheek lay her hair with the look of fire and the scent of water and he knew she had washed it in the spring that leaps from the breast of Eglwyseg Mountain. The pain made him moan.

'Hywelis,' he said. 'Help me.'

'*Cariad*,' she answered. 'My love.'

She slid down and pressed her lips and her keen bright fox-face against the dreadful foul oozing wound and she was there, neither dream nor memory but real, flesh and scent and bone. He could even see the blood beating gently in her pale blue-veined wrists, they were holding out a posset of beaten eggs and milk.

'Try to eat a little, my son,' said the monk.

'The woman. The woman. Where is she?'

'No women here, my son.' A soldier. Mind always on women or war. The monk carefully unwrapped the wound and appraised it. The redness had paled considerably, the edges of the gash looked moist, the black streaks were receding. He raised his gaunt, cloister-white face and smiled.

'St Francis heard me. I was afraid the leg would have to come off, and I've not the skill.'

'*Diolch i Dduw!*' Owen sat up against the monk's arm. He ate a little of the posset, felt strength returning. She was here, he told the monk. A friend, whom I haven't seen for years.

'Then, my son,' (with bent head) 'it must have been her spirit, sent from the grave to assuage you.'

'No.' The wound was itching, its heat had gone. 'She's not dead.' He wondered, without much concern, whether he would ever dance again. 'I'd have known if she were dead.' (So I would. How, I do not know. But I would.)

'Spirits,' said the monk very softly, 'can sometimes apport themselves of the living.' He removed the empty bowl, applied fresh bandages. 'Sleep now. Sleep again.'

Owen wanted to say how good, how kind, but time spiralled and caught him in blackness, with the fever pouring away in a good sweat, and no visions or visitations this time. Only

338

a dream of his own making. The dream of anguish and longing that he both dreaded and craved. It could have been two years or twenty years, the dream was the same. For ever loved, for ever lost, the dream hung like a homing lantern never to be reached by the lonely traveller across the endless moor.

He called the dream by name: Cathryn, Cathryn . . . and it came, obedient to hurt his heart. Weeping at your father's madness. Laughing and shining at Gaff, Gaff, catch him then, bring! Lilies and roses, honey and musk. The thick dark braid over one shoulder. In love! at Melun! sorry and glad I was that you were in love. Your feet, your lovely feet, clothed by me in soft hide, I could have kissed them and been punished for it. And you have a pleasing voice, Jacques, you shall sing me a song one day . . . in love, in love, I can't remember a time when I did not think of you, or want you, or dream of you beside me upon some shining mountain, your face chilled by the Welsh wind, and mine, mine . . .

. . . and the worst part, the most barren, bitterest part, the part that made me stay behind in France, knowing it useless to follow you further. The last sight of you, in mourning for Harry. Your face, when the King's bones and the fabricated corpse were lifted aboard the bier. I knew then that even the dream had gone from me. You were utterly remote, where once you were merely unattainable. Lost in your loss, you were a star on the further side of heaven. That is why I stayed in France these two years, keeping what little essence I had left of you close within my heart. These last two years have been the most unhappy in my life . . .

He began to weep, and woke with tears streaming, and a voice cutting through the unbearable pain of the dream, a voice from the past. He wiped his face and lay, trying to place the voice.

'In here, is he? When I heard there was a soldier lying sick, I had to come. Is he bad?'

The voice and steps approached the bed. Owen saw a round face, dark sentimental eyes, and for a moment his mind smelled pitch-smoke and heard the roar of armaments against the Harfleur palisade. John Page. No longer in black leather jerkin but elegant with a fine worsted tunic and deerskin thigh-boots. He carried a leather satchel.

'Dark in here!' said Page. 'And stinking!' The monk threw open the one dirty little window and departed. Page whistled.

'Saint Mary Virgin! Welshman!' He held out his strong well-kept hand. 'I thought you were dead!'

'Likewise,' said Owen with a feeble grin. He took the hand. Page looked at the straw bursting through the pallet, the grimy coverlet. 'What a wretched state you're in! What a hellish hole!'

'The monks have been very good to me.' Clinging to Page's hand, he groaned upright.

'You're still with the wars?' Page asked. 'I thought you'd have left active service when Harry died.' He bowed his head in a little gesture of memoriam.

'I left *active* service long before he died,' Owen said. 'Not everyone came home with the corpse. I attached myself to the Duke of Bedford, in the Wardrobe service.' Talking made him sweat more. Page wiped his brow with a square of fine linen. 'Near the Loire . . . there was a big battle on the Verneuil-Danville road. We were guarding Bedford's baggage. A party of Lombards ambushed us.' He showed Page his leg. 'The blade must have been poisoned. Someone carried me aboard ship and put me down here . . .'

'I heard that Bedford was coming home.'

'Impossible. The wars are hotter than ever . . . Dauphin proclaimed King of France . . . he has a great force, Scots and Italian mercenaries . . . Bedford and Salisbury are both hard pressed. Could I have some water?'

Again, Page's little flask, after all these years. 'Don't drink the wine,' he said, laughing. 'Remember?'

'I don't even trust the water!' Affection sprang with the memory. 'How fine you are, John. Still a poet?'

'I'm in the service of Bishop Beaufort! I'm one of his emissaries to the Customs here. He holds the commission on Southampton and its subsidiaries. He enjoys all profits, and should this port be closed, he's to have the Port of London. Already he's received eleven thousand pounds in revenue. He's been financing your French campaign. Did you know that Harry, God rest him, borrowed over twenty thousand from the Bishop, with most of the Crown jewels as security?' He laughed. 'Humphrey of Gloucester's chewing his doublet with rage – says Beaufort seeks to defraud the Crown of its treasure. The feud's no longer a jest. And the little King sits in the middle – a little bone! with Gloucester, Beaufort and Bedford (though I'm not calling *him* a dog, you understand) snarling over wardship of him. Beaufort will soon be Cardinal Archbishop and then Humphrey will blow up – like that cannon we once saw, remember? Gloucester's solid rage. He and my master think of little else but money. Yet I've no complaints – I've a post with a pension and the Bishop treats me fair.' He laid his hand on Owen's bandaged leg. 'It feels very wet. What's the monk been treating it with? No matter. I've access to the best doctors in the port. We'll soon have you walking.'

'I was a dancer,' said Owen. 'First a soldier, then a dancer.'

'Well, you'll jig again,' said Page kindly. 'Have you any plans?'

'I thought I'd go back to Wales,' he said. 'Home.'

Page said: 'I forgot to tell you. I heard your name some weeks back, when I was at Windsor. They wanted some harps mended, or some such.'

'Who are "they"?'

'Queen Katherine. She was asking for you . . .'

Warmth. The cell filling with light. The leg gloriously painful under the pounding of the blood. Page's face shimmered, his lips talked on, unheard. Why? Why didn't I know, in every part of me, wherever I was, that she had spoken my name? *Duw annwyl!* the miracle. The dream. He could smell the lilies and roses and honey and the subtle musk of her body. A surge of feeling gripped his heart, and something else, so magnificent in its reassurance and power that he gasped. He had felt it very seldom for two years. Only in dreams that ended in sickening barren loss. Now it was back, warm and transfixing and beautiful. Swiftly he pulled the covers over his loins before Page could see.

'Are you listening?' said Page. 'I said some compatriots of yours are at court. They asked for you too. John ap Meredyth and Howell ap Llewellyn.'

'Kinsmen,' said Owen faintly. 'Of Glyn Dŵr and me. From

Gwydir. John. John. I must get up. I must get well. Bring me your surgeons. I have money, I can pay. And stay by me. I must go to London.'

In the shell of a room that was part of the crumbling fabric of ruined Glyndyfrdwy, Hywelis lay cold and stiff on the floor. Anyone seeing her would think her dead, but there was none to see. After a long while she stirred. She got up in agony. Her red hair was damp with the sweat of her long journey; she bound it with a thong. She fell twice, crossing the room, and crawled raggedly to her feet. A day and a night had passed. She was a little frightened; this time her spirit had been reluctant to return.

She went through to another ruined chamber where the new generation lay mewling in its high-sided basket of rushes. She picked out the largest of the male cubs and held it up. Madog's grandson. This was the one; he had the badger-blaze. The line was pure. The rest could go back to the vixen. She might reject them, they would die. They were expendable. She rocked the cub in her arms, crooning to it through the terrible festering sore on her mouth.

And then it seemed that nothing could go wrong, that both the wound and the weakness had just been awaiting banishment like naughty courtiers at a royal word. The doctor brought by Page was a skilled Levantine Jew. He poked and prodded at the residue of proud flesh in the wound, while Owen clenched his teeth on Page's leather satchel, making a permanent imprint, and Page watched, his own eyes watering with sympathy. Still a poet, Owen thought; still soft of heart. Wonderful, blessed John! He had not mentioned her name again, and Owen did not dare, yet his mind was still filled with light. The doctor wadded the wound with crushed cinnamon bark. Soon there was little to see, other than a wide rosy channel filling with new tissue. Soon, he was on his feet.

Page, out of charity but also anxious to show off his new status, behaved like a prince. Owen needed a horse, and a horse was at the door. Owen needed a cart, and one was borrowed from the Customs office. Owen needed information as to the harps. Page had it. One William Menston had taken them down to Bore's in Fleet for repair. For a moment his heart dipped, as he thought the chance had been lost. Yet the same Menston had not troubled to reclaim them. All well; thanks to all-knowing John Page. Page, Owen thought, has been sent to me. By God, or perhaps by Drwynwen, to whom he had once or twice prayed. The love-goddess of Anglesey.

He ordered new clothes, and a barber. He found he could not shave himself. But you're better! said Page, and Owen could hardly say: it's too soon. My hands still shake from the knowledge that within a short time I may be in the same room with her. He wanted to laugh, and cry. He felt slightly mad. Yet one determined thought rose from the tumult: I shall look at her. Whatever the current edicts and courtesies. I shall look at her. And she will look at me. *I say it will be so.*

You'll find your place still open at court, Page said. All your old friends are there. Robert Waterton (though he's somewhat changed, he can't seem to stop mourning Harry's death) – Tom Harvey. They're short of staff in the Wardrobe. Several were pensioned off; Gervais died. There'll be no difficulty. It was almost as if Page knew. He could not know, Owen thought.

No, nothing could go wrong, from the perfect fit of the blue doublet and hose, the good elegant fall of the tawny cloak, to the fact that even after paying the Jew he still had a good portion of his French wages intact. There were honest people left in the world. He was in love with the world. There was an intermittent stiffness in his thigh. When you reach London, Page told him, have yourself massaged in the old Roman manner. (Grinning.) There's a new place in Southwark. A friend said that a real Nubian girl, black as warsmoke, gave him new life – and he was sixty! What would you say, John, if I told you that no woman has touched me, and I have touched no woman, for over two years? though I am only twenty-five or so . . . you would not believe me.

No woman has touched me, but one has rooted in me like a flowering tree. The dream entwines about me, possessing my heart, my veins, my vitals. That's why my hands still shake as I bid Page an affectionate farewell and crack the whip over the head of this good noble horse, who takes me again into the service of joy.

And then Fleet; driving past the prison and the shops hung with guild banners and the close-hugged dwellings, their lintels carved with angels and flowers and fruit. The prison, where folk lie rotting, all love lost; the houses, where folk dwell never having known love, at least not like this . . . urging the wagon through the press of citizens, while the scribes worked diligently in their doorways and traders cried their wares. Moving on, oblivious of the rubbish lacing the cobbles, the fish-guts and slops and parchment shavings; seeing nothing that was not fair. A golden haze caught permanently within his eye. The carved angels looked serenely on him with *her* face. Their wooden draperies were *her* soft garments that once again he might tend and store and cherish. And in his mind, the lily and rose and honey of her blotted out the smell of the spilled ale in the taverns, the clerk's pungent ink, the heavy dankness of the river. London's reek was purified. The dream was near.

Then to John Bore's, a place often visited before, dark, yet glittering with instruments old and new. Long-stemmed clarions stacked like wide-mouthed lilies in the corner, fifes and whistles and shawms in velvet-lined cases; the curving double-reeded cromorne, the psaltery, the three-stringed viële with its bow shaped almost identically to an archer's weapon. Battle-drums and round-bellied little tabors. Harps of all kinds; the small metal-stringed ones and the larger gut-strung ornamental harps; he saw immediately the royal pair, two slim gold birds with backspread wings.

John Bore greeted him with pleasure, begged for the news of France (his son being there and no letter for a year), and showed disapproval at William Menston's tardiness in collecting the Queen-Dowager's property.

'I was about to deliver them myself. They're expensive pieces. A liability. They cost nearly nine livres sterling and that was in 'twenty-one . . . Will you pay, or am I to send the reckoning?'

'I'll pay,' Owen said.

They carried the harps into the street and laid them on the straw bed prepared for them in the cart. Very tender, said Bore approvingly. But then you always did treat an instrument like a woman. Have you still the little Welsh harp? I've a new Italian one, lovely work . . . but you're in a hurry. Come again, Master Tydier. Good musicians are always welcome in my house.

The sun was beginning to dip when he reached Windsor. Soon, now. The dream was nearer. He could hardly breathe. The gate-ward recognized him after a moment, and demanded news, which in courtesy had to be given; the whole tale, the battles, ambushes, looting and knifework.

'I wish I were back in the fighting,' he said. He peered into the cart. 'What have you there, Master Owen? Angels' skeletons?'

Owen told him.

'Well. Enterprising of you. You'll need a couple of boys to help you to the Upper Ward with those things. Sire Louis de Robsart will take charge of them.'

He turned to bellow at a couple of pages dicing in the courtyard behind.

Owen said very carefully: 'I thought I might return them to her Grace in person, and explain . . .'

The guard laughed. No reason for him to laugh, Owen thought.

'Her Grace is no longer here. And don't ask me her whereabouts. The last we heard was that she had gone to find her son, and the Devil knows where he is today! King he may be, God save him, but ruled, is our young ruler, by the caprices of the Council! Here, come in the gatehouse a moment. That leg must pain you, you're ghostly.' The pages came dawdling up. He smacked one across the ear. 'You took your time.'

'Leave the harps with me,' Owen said, sitting down on an arrowchest. His blood was so sluggish he thought his heart might stop. It would be very easy for it to stop. 'They are my sole responsibility.'

Then said no more, seeing that nothing now could go right.

*

'Dear Katherine,' said James of Scotland, 'is there nothing on my table to tempt you?'

'Please eat, Katherine!' said Joan Beaufort, the new bride, flushed and pretty and concerned. 'You used to eat so heartily – you astonished us all!'

She smiled fraily at them both. She had been at Hertford Castle for three days, and this was the final banquet, for James and Joan were leaving for Scotland in the morning. The cooks, surpassing themselves, had taken away her appetite. Their mountainous concoctions reminded her of other feasts, when Harry, fasting to appease his pain, had watched her gorging. Like an indulgent father. Now she pushed away the '*Douce Âme*' – a capon in honied milk, hyssop and pine-nuts coloured with saffron. The carver approached and bared the contents of another great dish with a flourish.

'A cockatrice!' said James. Mythology lay before them. Half a swan and half a piglet had been sewn together, roasted and glazed. Great bowls of salad came to the table, garlic, onions, mint, rosemary, rue, leeks. Goblets were filled with heavy Calabrian wine. James raised his cup.

'To your Grace's health and happiness,' he said.

He drank. Joan drank. After a moment Katherine drank. She swallowed the whole cupful in one draught. The times she had watched Queen Isabeau do that! A little comfort began to spread through her.

'Alas, your happiness,' James said softly. 'But how can I wish you other than happiness.' He took Joan's hand and kissed it. 'We owe you everything, Katherine.'

'*De rien,*' she said. Her cup was refilled. 'May your joy last longer than mine, James.' She drank.

Tumblers were in the hall, leaping through fire-hoops. Joan touched her arm.

'But you saw him, Madame . . . that was something after all.'

'For a day!' said Katherine bitterly. 'They'd moved him from King's Langley to Eltham. I wasted time finding him. He was in a room full of people, he seemed scarcely to know me. *Sainte Vierge!*' She shivered. 'Dame Boteler . . . I hate that woman. Then Humphrey came and I coughed and he sent me to lie down and fetched his physician, that *maudit* Swanwyth, whom I swear helped to kill Harry with his nostrums . . .'

'Katherine,' said James under the yelps of the acrobats, 'don't take Gloucester's medicines.'

She drank. Her mouth twisted in a smile. 'Sweet James. What would it profit him to poison me?'

James's hand lay on Joan's thigh under the table. Katherine looked away quickly. Her goblet was refilled by an admiring servitor; her trencher was loaded with rabbit in syrup.

'Has he ever made an attempt to pay court to you, Katherine?' said James.

'It would be against consanguinity,' said Joan. She leaned her head lovingly for an instant on James's shoulder.

'Yes . . . but if he were in your favour – he would gain power. He would do anything to outmatch the Bishop!'

James looked tenderly at his wife. 'I must always uphold the Bishop.'

And so must I, thought Katherine. My enemy's enemy must be my friend? 'Though I love you anyway, *mes chèrs amis*,' she said aloud. The feast is splendid, though there is no Crustade Lombard, no Harry. The sympathy is warming. And tomorrow I shall lose them, too!

'Scotland is so far away,' she said. She drank. Did Isabeau drink to kill the pain, or salute the taste? A team of bagpipers had entered the hall. Another dish arrived on the table. Roast goose with garlic stuffing, in a lake of galingale, sage, parsley and wine, where grapes, cubed pears and quinces made little islands.

'It's *Sauce "Madame"*, Katherine,' cried Joan over the bagpipes' yowling. 'Invented by King Richard for your late beloved sister. Please eat,' she begged.

Katherine bowed to the carver, who cut her a slice and ladled sauce over it. So I will eat to the dead. And drink. Mother, I could drink side by side with you now. There is a kiss mark on Joan's neck, where James has forgotten himself. Last night, or the night before. Mother, I am more like you than I feared. This feeling, this envious lust in me, must be inherited debauchery. Yet I am chaste. Oh, my dear friends, I am chaste. Don't touch, don't kiss before my eyes! She wanted to put her forehead down on the table and groan.

'Some figs, Katherine,' Joan said. 'They're good for the blood. How pale you are, *doucette*!'

Figs had made Harry ill, on their wedding-night. I want another wedding-night. I am chaste. Oh, God.

The bagpipers had left and now a man beat a drum while a monkey juggled with two oranges. James liked his entertainments noisy, after years in the prison-house.

'I wish I could hear sad songs,' said Katherine unsteadily. 'Shall I ever marry again?'

Joan's face was smoothly reassuring.

'But naturally, Madame . . . The Council will doubtless propose a match . . .'

'The Devil have the Council,' said Katherine quietly. Her eyes, enormous in her drawn white face, moved over the hall. Fat lords, thin lords, drunken lords. Lords so old they looked like effigies, with saurian faces, withered shanks. Young lords appraising one another's jewellery. Half-witted earls, dukes notorious for their lechery. The wine soured her mouth.

'I know one who would think himself in Paradise to marry you,' said Joan. 'Edmund, my brother.'

'But sadly,' said Katherine with her twisted smile, 'he is a prisoner in France. Harry tried to ransom him but the bargain failed. I'd love you for a sister, Joan.'

'I am King Harry's first cousin,' said Joan proudly, 'albeit through the bar sinister.'

'You are truly royal, Joan,' said Katherine thickly. The hall was spinning gently. 'In France we count our friends by their deeds, not their lineage.' (*Bet at the tavern, the kindness, the baby's laughter.*) 'Here, there are degrees of greatness . . . each man better than the man beneath.' Her hands shook; she spilled wine. 'What a weight for the fundamental man to bear!'

'But, Madame, it must be so.' Joan was puzzled. 'Or there would be uprisings, revolutions . . .'

'Every man is equal in the sight of God.' Katherine pushed her untasted food away. She swayed a little where she sat.

'No, Katherine,' said James, overhearing, 'there must be master and man. There must be leaders.' He had his arm round

Joan's little shoulders, he smiled at her, a secret smile. The hall stopped spinning; it was fuzzed with tears. A group of minstrels had replaced the monkey and were playing a jaunty, complicated *pastourelle*. The treble singer was a little off-key. There was a new course before her, coffin-shaped pastries filled with pork and fruit. I long for sadness. A sad song, a song of lovers lost.

'Must you go to Scotland?' she said suddenly. 'Can't you stay? I'll give you Hertford Castle . . .'

They looked at her kindly.

'It's a fine castle,' Katherine said wildly. 'It was built on ancient foundations to protect London from the Danes.'

'But, Madame,' said James tenderly, 'my own kingdom awaits me!'

Silent, she looked away. The minstrels had finished. Someone called for the jester. At the end of the hall a door opened. Very faintly came a voice raised in protest. The arras swayed as if blows were being struck behind it and a rumbling noise ensued. Elderly guests who had succumbed to the feast woke abruptly, feeling for their purses. A figure appeared, shaking off the ushers. James rose. He was always terrified of assassination by the English. He said: 'Who the devil comes?' Joan looked frightened. The figure completed its illegal entry and came through the hall, the rumbling noise was explained. The harps, polished to a sheen, had been placed on a trolley, and this Owen drew behind him like an instrument of war. He came grimly, his face as white as Katherine's. Ushers ran after him, expostulating.

Katherine stood up. I am drunk. No, I am not drunk, far from it. I see a face from the past, from the happy and sad times. Now he comes, with my beautiful harps, mended anew, in his blue and tawny clothes, spashed with mud; he's ridden hard to bring them to me. She pushed back her chair. James said again: 'Who is this, that disrupts my feast?'

'A common man,' Joan said doubtfully

And Katherine said: 'No! a friend . . . a fine *chanteur* . . . he served my father, and Harry . . . he now serves me.'

Then she was down in the body of the hall with no recollection of having stepped from the dais. Drawn willingly by a mystery, seeing the harps, the proud gold birds, going lovingly to caress their graceful shafts while the proud gold man knelt beside them at her feet. The indignant ushers withdrew. For the first time in her life she had his name right, and called him by it.

'Master Owen Tydier. It's a long time since you were with the Household. Are you well?'

He looked at her, and she at him. He with his blue-gold look that she had called '*féroce*', culled from the years of passionate thought, and he rocked and held her on that look which contained her life and his, the sadness, the longing, the desires. She stepped behind the harps so that his face was masked a little by the strings and she could study it. She knew it far better than she had thought. He was older (as they all were); he looked tired, there was a new crease between his brows. The rest was the same, the smooth honey skin, the bright hair, the mouth. As if without thought or knowledge she had stored him in her mind. The blazing blue-gold eyes never wavered, they locked on to hers and drew her in.

The dream is very slender, thinner than I remember. So pale, but she's flushing now, she sees me, she almost knows. She's so weary, so sad. She's not as tall as I remember – perhaps she was always wearing pattens when we met before, I judge that her head would come up to my eyebrow if I were standing. I love her. I'd like to make her laugh. I'd like to make her cry. I love her. I'd like to kiss her until she fell unconscious. I'd like to have her tread on my face. I love her. *Am byth.* For ever. She could put a knife right through my heart. She already has. I love her.

The dream is mortal. It is moved by my look. The colour deepens. The dream is flesh. The perfume is real. Look at me, Cathryn. Look at me. I am stronger than you, dearest dream. Soul of my bliss, *cariad*, I never thought I was so strong. You may look away now. I'm happy.

'Are the harps in tune?'

'Perfectly in tune, your Grace.'

Jacqueline had called him the handsome one, and so he was, and more than that, and she could not stand here still scalded and shaken by that look, in full view of James's guests.

She said unquietly: 'Gramercy . . . Owen. Are you to entertain us today?'

He would sing her a sad love song, no doubt of that, but the urge for it had gone, vanished into his look, and enough for now, more than enough, for he was looking at her again, a look like honey on steel.

She heard herself saying: 'You could . . . you will, perhaps, accompany us. You might . . . you may . . . you *will* accompany us to Windsor, where you will entertain. Sing . . . dance?'

He said very calmly: 'I am honoured, Madame. There's a dance I have composed – it has never been performed.'

'*Bien,*' she said. She broke at last from the gold and blue; she had to turn away to do so. She walked back to the dais. He rose, bowed and left the hall. The ushers wheeled the harps to safety. Katherine sat down and began to eat her supper.

Bishop Beaufort, leaving the Queen-Dowager's apartments, had no idea of how narrowly he had missed being embraced by her. That would have created a fine scandal, she thought, smiling into the austere grey eyes. He's given me my heart's desire, if only for a season.

'I trust the King's Grace will enjoy his visit to you, highness,' he said. 'On your coming birthday – for which, *félicitations* – ' he wagged a princely finger – 'let him not be overtaxed. He should be in bed by five at latest. No doubt his good governess will see to it.'

His good governess, she thought with glee, will do as I say! This is my household. It will be my birthday. And, most wonderful of all, there is no Humphrey of Gloucester to interfere! He shall stay up as late as he wishes, I shall do exactly as I please. Meekly, she said:

'I am sure the King would be honoured by your presence at the feast, my lord.' Beaufort, standing flanked by his sub-servient clerks, answered sternly: 'Madame . . . I regret . . . I have much to occupy me in my diocese. For one week I leave the King's Grace in your care. I trust the purse will be sufficient for his entertainment.'

Sufficient! She had seen the coffers of gold coming in. It

was enough to keep her household for a year. Another worry over. Blessed Bishop Beaufort!

'God's blessing be on your festivities,' he said. 'May they be holy ones.'

As he made his measured exit she thought acutely: he is enjoying this added power now that Humphrey has gone to Hainault. He relishes bestowing the Council's favour without let or argument from his *bête noire*. Doubtless he hopes that Philip of Burgundy will ride after him and slay him on the road. She smiled radiantly. Humphrey is gone. It was like music. She had the feeling that Humphrey was doing more or less exactly what the Bishop wished. For surely, had the Council wished to prevent his going they would have stopped him with swords . . . He's gone, and he's taken an army with him, paid for from the Duchy of Lancaster. No more of his misery-provoking presence, for weeks, or maybe months! Now, would that I could hide my little boy away, as Belle hid me at Poissy. No. He is to rule England, and I must not rob him of his destiny. There are others who would gladly take his place.

What a birthday gift! October 27th. I shall be twenty-three. I feel so young. Unprotected (for Beaufort isn't really my ally, he is too self-seeking) and Bedford has yet to give me the support that Harry asked of him. *Ça ne fait rien!* I do very well. I am sheltered within this new pavilion of brightness.

Owen ap Meredyth ap Tydier. He is my good luck. From the moment he knelt before me at Hertford I began to heal. They say the Welsh are magicians. Belle called Glyn Dŵr 'matchless', yet he had a great reputation for sorcery. Benign sorcery. I am happy. She rolled the word carefully around her mind. Owen has changed my fortunes. I now recall all the times he roared singing through my life; I did not register him as the talisman he was . . .

Her ladies came into her bower, to talk about dresses and discuss the menu for the birthday feast. They were relieved by her new mood. Some who were themselves widowed were jealous of her gaiety. She coaxed a tune out of one of the harps, laughing and cross when she discovered she had almost forgotten how to play. We're going to enjoy ourselves, she told the ladies. All that day and the next, her birthday eve, attendants scampered from the Upper Ward to the pantry and buttery, to the Wardrobe and the quarters of the Revels Master. Sire Louis de Robsart was supposed to be in charge of the proceedings, but found himself overruled by a bursting tide of ladies all giving contradictory orders. So he took himself off with his escort to fetch the little King.

'There's scarcely any Bordeaux left!' cried the Duchess of York, returning exhausted from a domestic foray.

'Rest, dear Philippa,' said Katherine. 'Who needs wine?'

'I do,' muttered the Duchess of Clarence.

Katherine sat before her mirror, her face smooth and beautiful. Margaret of Clarence began to comb her hair. The Countess of Kent slipped the robe from the Queen-Dowager's shoulders; the comb moved down through the dark, endlessly shining cloud, and caught on a tangle. No one could dress her hair like Eleanor Cobham, although little Guillemot, being ordered about now by the Duchesses, was the next best. Jacqueline too was skilled, but she was gone. She had wept. Looking ill, and talking wildly. Sweet Kéti, I'm so afraid.

'You must go with your husband.'

'But if Philip and Brabant should take me . . . they'll punish me. I feel' (shuddering) 'that you and I will never meet again in this life.' Whispering, looking demented: 'I am afraid. *That black one goes with us.*'

'Who?'

'*Kitten Cobham,*' said Jacqueline through her teeth.

Eleanor had come to bid farewell, quiet and solicitous.

'Your Grace. I was anxious that your cough should not worsen while we are away. I have a little leech book – may I lend it to you?'

Katherine was touched. She kissed the small pale face.

'Keep the book safe, your Grace,' murmured Lady Cobham. 'There are certain nostrums that might not find favour with the Church . . . but the cough remedy is most effective.'

There was nothing startling in the book save for one charm purporting to have been used by the ancient Egyptians. Simple herbs, when combined with the phases of the moon – to prevent conception. No, the Church would not approve.

Smiling, she locked the book away, wondering what old Dame Alphonse would have made of it all.

'Which gown, your Grace?' the Countess of Kent said. 'I have been to the Wardrobe, but they all seem half-witted down there.'

'Then bid them mount above!' said Katherine impatiently. She drew on a velvet robe.

Owen came, with two small pages. All three were laden with gowns. The ladies pored over silks and sarcenets. Philippa of York held up a green dress. 'This is exquisite, your Grace.'

It was one of the gowns bought by Isabeau in the campaign to woo Harry. It was almost unworn. She had never liked it. Owen was kneeling quite near. The ladies' voices faded. Katherine said suddenly:

'What's *your* opinion, Master Tydier?'

He got up slowly. Into a disapproving silence he said: 'Never green, your Grace. It is the worst colour for your highness. This . . .' Silk, soft-coloured as a fallow deer, starred with roses, swirled over his arm. 'This one.'

'I'll wear it,' she said. Owen bowed, the pages copied him jerkily, and they withdrew.

'Servants,' said Philippa of York, 'given encouragement, become very bold.'

'Well,' said Katherine carelessly, 'he is *au fait* with fashion, being in the Wardrobe service.'

'I thought he was a singer,' said Margaret of Clarence. She pulled a little face at the Duchess's back.

'He is,' said Katherine. 'And a dancer.' I should have mentioned the dance he promised me. 'Please fetch him back,' she said to Philippa of York, who departed, none too pleased.

Margaret took the comb again, bending close to Katherine, whispering, as usual of family feuds.

'She need talk of the boldness of servants! What of the vainglory of lords! Just because her husband was killed, like my poor Thomas, in Harry's service . . . she forgets her brother-in-law Richard of York once tried to kill the King and was executed for it. *There's* boldness! the boldness of the House of York, who pride themselves on having better claim to England than we of Lancaster!' She talked on and on of

354

Edmund of Langley, the female line, John of Gaunt, and caught the comb in Katherine's hair again, hurting her. Katherine made no comment. All this was foreign yet hatefully familiar. Burgundy and Armagnac. King versus cousins.

'There'll be blood, in a few years, as a result of such vainglory,' said Margaret darkly. 'I was surprised to learn that the assassin York's son is close companion to our little King.'

'Richard of York is fourteen years old,' said Katherine, taking the comb from the Duchess. 'I don't care who his father was. He's kind to Henry.'

Then Philippa of York came back, a little crowd behind her, all smiling.

'I couldn't find the esquire,' she said breathlessly, 'but see who I have found!'

Katherine flung herself from the mirror and down on her knees. She held out her arms; the little King ran into them.

He had needed no reminding. The dance was ready, perfect and polished, untapped and matured like the war-longings of his youth. He had every nuance, every transient theme, every intricate step. His flame-coloured tunic and scarlet hose had been carefully chosen. He wore his tawny cloak caught at the shoulder with a dragon buckle, and he had on elegant dancing shoes. His gold hair shone, his eyes were full of light.

John ap Meredyth and Howell ap Llewellyn of Gwydir were to accompany him. Tough mountain men, they had come as envoys from a Welsh protectorate of the Crown; uneasy and isolated, they were longing to return home. Their appearance was a rude contrast; Meredyth in particular looked a disgrace, sporting a beard longer and dirtier than Gruffydd Llwyd's had been. Their sweet mockery drifted about Owen. They could not help but admire him and stayed close, glad to talk in the only tongue they knew. There is a fine, dressed-up monkey, they said, and Owen warned:

'One wrong note, and I'll brain you, cousins. You do remember the awdl?'

'From the cradle,' said Howell with disgust.

'Sing it in Welsh, is it?' asked Meredyth.

'No, French. For the Queen.'

'French!' they cried. 'How shall we know when to come in, boy?'

'You'll know. Watch my eyes and my steps and hear the colour of my voice. You'll know. Play as you've never played.'

He gleamed, standing between them, and they shook their heads, a little alienated, but still loyal and loving, part of the great family that was Wales. The Revels Master was beckoning around the screen which divided entertainers from hall. The feast was over, the minstrels had finished playing French *chansonettes*. Owen drew a long breath, and entered. He strode up the hall, his cloak lifting behind him. A slight rustle of amusement greeted the entry of the men from Gwydir who followed with their little harps and their fierce faces, but he did not hear it. The torchlight wavered sleekly, the scores of candles cast shadows like moonlight. As he walked towards the dais he thought: let my performance be to the glory of God, but first, to the glory of *her*.

The harpists moved left and right towards the walls, to give him space. He unclasped his cloak and flung it out of the way. His tunic took flame from the candlelight and there was another rustle, this time of admiration. He looked for her, knelt in homage. She was nearer than he had imagined, sitting on a low chair below the dais; the high table had been dismantled. The little King sat on her knee. The dream was pale and rosy and vivid. She was wearing the dress he had chosen for her. The Revels Master stamped the floor with his rod and cried: 'Let the entertainment begin!'

The harpists struck one fierce opening chord laced with weird harmonies, and Owen was no longer Owen, slender and pliant in his suit of lights, but Ysbaddaden Chief-Giant, the terrible, growing taller and broader before the watchers' eyes, undergoing a frightening metamorphosis, his tossed head and upraised arms flinging the shadows about like baubles, his legs rousing a storm from the rushes as he roared his song of defiance to the world. Thickwaisted as the boles of twelve oak trees, he kicked mountains from the earth, his tawny-gold head became the head of twenty lions, the nest of a thousand serpents. Here was Ysbaddaden the ungovernable, who lived outside the peace, greater than God! with steel crumpling at his touch and fire quenched beneath his spittle, the ultimate challenge, seen by King Henry as France, and Glyn Dŵr as England. The worthy foe, the prize, the raging splendour of the world, the deathly mirror of all greatness ... Ysbaddaden's feet stamped and he rose mightily in the air. His brassy lungs carolled of his own vigour. The harpists (at whom none laughed now) thrummed out a clamour in time with the giant wildness, and blood sprang from beneath their fingernails. Transfixed, the company sat, some with goblets halfway to their lips.

Then under the fading storm came Culhwch with his tenor-bell voice lifted sweetly in chaste French and his prince's face smooth and beautiful, and his body flamelike and lithe in the caress of the candles, so that more than one lady in the hall leaned to see him better and felt her flesh prickling warm and cold and forgot that this was only a barbaric dancer without land or privilege; for this was Culhwch, cousin to Arthur, with a king's brave and noble mysteries inherent in every gracious twirl and posture, and the men of Gwydir beat out the rhythm of the shell-hooved horse curvetting in his voice and the rich flame of his dancing.

The star-bright armour took shape from his lips and shivered in the minds of his audience. Fleeter of foot than the magic deer of Powys Fadog he pranced and spun, as he showed off the two silver spears and the sword with its jewels mined from the sacred mountain. And the spears drew blood from the air, and the serpent-headed horse reared to cry its own challenge underlined by the harpstrings and its breath sucked men in and blew them out again as it flew faster than light ... while the mask of Culhwch covered the mind of the man who found an instant to think: *it goes well in the French, it pleases her*, and one second to look and confirm – the tight hands, the excited flush on the dream's beloved face ... and I, Culhwch meet now with Glewlwyd Mighty-Grasp whom none has ever passed alive, and the watchers cringe at the danger of my quest. And come! Cei! chief of my little army, make fire from your belly, and come! Bedwyr the One-Handed, and Cynddylig the Waymaker to find me my path. And Gwalchmei, best horseman in the world, and Gwrhyr the Translator, and Menw, who makes us all invisible . . .

And they come, through my voice and my steps, and all is clear and bright with no sound save for their cries and the galloping harps. The blood flows from the fingers of my kinsmen and gathers in my own shoe where my toes split on the last leap. Pain in legend, pain in perfection, that shows all too cruelly the shortcomings of reality. And the spirits he had captured drew form from his art and came running, hermits, seers, monsters, invisible doves fluttering from his fingertips, ghost-flames starting about his head. Built of music, the stones of Ysbaddedan's castle sprang up. The giant and Culhwch faced one another, roaring, belling, while the little harps on either side faithfully reproduced the challenge and the giant's dreadful coiling hair sprang singing from Owen's mind and lips and hands and feet. And, compelled, the watchers sat still, though the candles were burning down late to form the shadows that housed the last enemy, the Twrch Trwyth, the Great Boar.

From crown to soles he was soaked with sweat as if he had stood in a river. For the first time during the long dance he felt a pang, no more than a bee-sting, in his wounded thigh. One of the Boar's tusks had speared him. He began to whirl faster and faster to confuse the beast. It came for him, snorting, and his eyes slitted, so that the watchers gasped at this dervish-man who sang of a monster and briefly looked like one. And at that moment they were all believers and his enchanted slaves, and when Culhwch, pure as a singing mountain, snatched the comb and scissors from between the ears of the Boar, the gasps changed to the fluttering laughter of relief. And Ysbaddaden died, shorn by the magic tools, with groans to shake the hall . . .

The sweat was drying cold upon him as Olwen came. She had never been lovelier, in legend or in life. He heard the harp-note change to the haunting minor key that was the Princess, with the gown of fire-coloured silk about her and the heavy golden torque about her neck, her head more yellow than the broom-blossom and her skin whiter than the bog-cotton where it grows beside a river. He danced and sang, sang of perfection.

358

'. . . and her eyes! their look
Was lovelier than the thrice-mewed hawk
And her breast was softer than the sun!
Where she trod, four white clover flowers
Grew behind her feet . . .'

Nearer to the dais, to the dream. The last adventure of all
– to be man and woman in one, potent yet yielding, gracious
and virile, to deliver the chant in time, to look where the holy
blossoms sprang . . . to know that Olwen was Culhwch's at
last . . . most difficult of all – to sing her name.

'All were longing-filled when they beheld her . . .'

Nearer, still nearer to the dream. The lily, the rose, the
honey, the scent of her joy in his meagre gift of perfection.

'And therefore she was called . . .'

He was Culhwch of stainless valour, with whom King Harry
had sought identity in the dark tents of Harfleur.

He could see the eyes of the beloved dream, intent, entranced.
They met his without reserve. And then the pain left by the
Boar's tusk seized him, crippling his thigh, and all strength
left him. I'll never dance this dance again, he thought, and he
fell, right across the low chair where she sat.

Her silken lap took most of his sweat-soaked weight.
Rather than risk injuring the little King he reeled sideways
and let himself rest on her, snatching the child into his arms.
Henry's small velvet-clad body hampered him entirely. They
both lay helplessly across Katherine. Owen felt the blood
leaving his head, and faintness gripped him. Then he heard
the laughter beginning, fuzzing his ear, drowning the shocked
whispers of the courtiers. The King's little face was crushed
against his cheek, he was laughing like a jay, delighted at
the antics of this man who lay across his mother, his head on
her breast. The soft breast moved warmly under him, he
jerked, found his hair entangled in her necklace. The breast
rose and fell in wave after wave of shuddering laughter that
burst and mingled with the glee of the child. He tried to claw
his way free. The silk of her dress was like a glass mountain
and Henry's weight pinned him down. *Duw annwyl!* this is how
men died at Agincourt!

'Madame,' he whispered, 'if you could only remove the

King's Grace!' She was laughing too much, she laughed and laughed, beautiful, rich gay laughter, and only when the Duchess of York swooped to lift Henry away could Owen extricate himself. He slid to his knees. She was wiping away tears, her face was pink. He looked then at the breast on which he had lain. Its memory burned his cheek, his mind kissed it, and something of the dance's mystic power must have remained, for she sobered a little, looking down at her own flesh as if for the mark of his lips.

Yet again his eyes drew hers back. They hung on one another's face, learning, knowing, recognizing that there was nothing to learn, for all was known already. She said, her voice trembling:

'And the Princess . . . what was she called? you left it unfinished . . .'

Over his choking beating heart he answered steadily: 'Cathryn. She was called Cathryn.'

He could see her heart beating too, it moved the fawn silk like a wind-tapped leaf. He held the hem of her gown tight between his fingers. He looked at her; his eyes said: '*It is unfinished* . . .'

'Do you love me, Guillemot?' she asked softly.

It was the wrong thing to say. Guillemot burst into sobs. To Guillemot, Katherine was kin to the angels and always had been. But Guillemot lacked the wit to express herself and moreover did not dare. Katherine was the one person who had been invariably kind to her during the bewildering four years in the royal service. Unlike Jacqueline of Hainault, who slapped Guillemot when she was herself unhappy, or the Duchesses who bullied her; or Lady Cobham, whom she feared most of all. Love? Love can make you cry, thought Guillemot. Worse than fear.

'Don't weep, you silly infant. Answer my question.'

'More than life,' muttered Guillemot.

They were alone together. It was nearly midnight. Katherine was lying on her bed, in her long linen shift. She felt very hot. Her heart was beating fast. She had drunk no wine tonight, but her head was spinning.

'Guillemot, why are you called Guillemot?' The voice was teasing. 'It's a bird's name.'

'My father's name,' whispered the little maid, 'was Guillaume.'

'No,' said Katherine. 'You're a seabird. My little seabird. Come here, and tell me how much you love me.'

Guillemot crept over to the bed. Only a tiny nightlight burned. She could see the Queen-Dowager's eyes shining.

'Now,' said Katherine, 'are we friends, you and I?'

Guillemot nodded her black head vigorously.

'Can I trust you?' The voice teased no longer.

'Madame . . . I'd die rather than betray you.'

'No need to die,' said Katherine. 'All I wish for is a friend. Is that your cloak, hanging there?'

Again, the nod. Katherine slid from bed, pushing back her long heavy hair.

'Why do you love me?'

'You're so kind.' A whisper. 'So kind, your Grace.'

'I wasn't kind tonight, Guillemot. I lost my temper!'

With the Duchesses, serve them right, thought Guillemot. Yet Katherine's voice had still been soft, as it was when she asked whether Guillemot were tired or cold, or if she had enough to eat . . .

'Will you lend me your cloak?'

Wordlessly Guillemot brought it. It had a big hood like a friar's cowl. It was rather too short for Katherine, she laughed as she put it on. But the hood almost concealed her face; her eyes gleamed from its darkness.

She had sent the Duchesses away, bidding them attend the little King, whose chamber was already full of guards under Sire Louis de Robsart. Philippa of York had begun the nearest thing to a quarrel Katherine had ever had with her ladies. It had started immediately they retired.

'In all the courts I have attended, your Grace, never have I seen such barbarism. Were you harmed by that wretch?'

'Not in the least,' said Katherine smoothly. 'But I fear he may have hurt himself.' She'd seen him limping slightly as he went with his kinsmen from the hall.

'Such a common man, your Grace. Like all the pagan Welsh. No wonder they're allowed no privileges – with respect, I marvel that he should have been employed to entertain – '

Margaret of Clarence said quickly: 'I thought the dance was wonderful. I was enchanted.'

'You were lucky to find him,' said the Countess of Kent, taking sides.

'Harry found him,' said Katherine.

'But,' the Duchess of York said, 'those minstrels! So uncouth! When they were presented to your Grace, I was appalled. Speaking no French! They were scarcely better than dumb creatures!'

That was when her anger had started. She couldn't remember ever being really angry before. It was refreshing. She said, very slow and soft: 'Then, Madame, they were the nicest dumb creatures I ever saw!'

But Philippa, in full spate, was riding her hobby. 'The trouble is, one gives encouragement to these people and liberties are taken, lordlings aped. Your Grace should have punished his rudeness. Common men have their place and should be confined to it.'

The anger grew, taking vigour from her restraint. She had liked very much having him lying across her lap. He had been quite light, cleverly taking his weight from her, but she had felt his strength, had smelled the fresh sweat on him – a pleasant healthy scent. She had liked having his face against her breast. She had liked it inordinately.

'I do not know what our late sovereign lord would have said, I am sure!' said Philippa of York.

The anger clawed free. Katherine said in a voice like frozen rain (remembering kind Bet at the tavern, remembering even the bastard stableman, Gaspard, who had hanged to help her father all those years ago):

'*My lady. Madame. Your Grace.* Our late lord and sovereign, my dear husband, thought much of common men. Before battle he toured the lines giving cheer to them. Common men fought and died for him in love and gratitude. Speak not to me of common men, Madame! Harry loved them.' Her voice began to shake, but not to rise. 'The most ragged, the most uncouth and unlettered, were cherished by him for their loyal and faithful hearts. And what better example should we follow than of that great soul?'

Philippa had wriggled about, beginning to apologize, but was cut off short.

'Leave me, all of you. I will sleep alone. My maid here shall attend my wants. She is of no great family and knows when to hold her tongue. So look to my son if you would serve me!'

They had gone, but at the door Philippa had loosed one more shot.

'I still say servants should have their place, highness. And that man should be reprimanded. Even now he loiters in the Upper Ward; he is everywhere. One cannot get away from him!' Then she had made a strange outraged noise – *Tchah!* and Katherine was left alone, with Guillemot.

She wrapped the cloak around her. Guillemot was even more slender than herself; the cloak kept coming apart.

'Guillemot.'

'Yes, your Grace.'

'Do you know who the Duchess was talking about?'

'Yes, your Grace.'

'Is it true?'

Guillemot worked her wits frantically, and came up with the answer.

'Yes, highness. He is there. In the East Gallery. He spoke to me earlier.'

'What did he say?'

'He asked if you were well. He said something about it being a special guard duty.'

'He's not in the guard.'

'No, highness.'

Katherine stood silent for a moment. She said: 'What time is it, Guillemot?'

'They haven't rung Matins yet, your Grace.'

So it is still my birthday. I can do as I please on my birthday. The flame-figure leaped singing in her mind. It shivered her skin. Just for a few minutes, she thought. And I won't lie, not even to Guillemot. I could say I was going to see how the

363

little King is, but it would be bad luck.

'Listen, Guillemot.'

'Your Grace?'

'I'm wearing your cloak, Guillemot. I am you, and you are me, for a few minutes. Do you understand?'

'I understand, your Grace. Will you be safe?'

She didn't answer. She stroked Guillemot's black head; it was like the smooth poll of a bird. Guillemot turned her face to kiss the Queen-Dowager's hand.

'Only a few minutes,' Katherine said. 'Bolt the door. Let me in, in a few minutes.'

It was very quiet out on the gallery. She went quickly, softly. The starlight was shining through the high embrasures and it picked out her dreaming face within the deep cowl, making her more beautiful even than Isabelle of Valois had been, although, lost within herself she was cheated of this knowledge. It felt cold on the gallery. I am now one of the common people, whose pulses run, whose blood is rich and uncorrupted by the enmities of power. She reached the East Gallery. It seemed deserted. Then from behind a pillar a shadow moved, making her heart jump and pound. It stepped out into the starlight.

'I knew you'd come,' the shadow said. '*I willed it so.*'

She pushed back the cowl, and as she did so he remembered the night behind the lines before battle, when Gloucester's Frenchwoman had kissed him on the mouth and laughed at him. He had thought she was a friar at first. That was no memory. That was a precognition.

'Do you know me?' she said.

'I know you. Should I kneel?'

'No, no.' No more kneeling, no grovelling. Not on this common person's birthday. 'You must be tired. Your leg must hurt you.'

She heard him laugh very softly. 'That's nothing. And I'm not tired. I've been waiting a long time.' And then he said, even more softly: 'Cathryn.'

It was quite different, the way he spoke her name. Not Kat-air-een, as she was accustomed to hear it. But *Cathryn*, the last syllable slipping down quick and heavy, definite, final, as if at last she had a place in the world. She could see his face at last. He did look tired. She saw that he had changed, and washed off the sweat, and combed his hair. He was waiting for her to say something.

'Thank you for the dance,' she said awkwardly. 'The King loved it all. He talks of nothing else. He will not sleep tonight.'

Neither shall I, he thought. Nor did I last night.

He said: 'And you? Did it make you happy?'

He spoke a strangely accented French; each word curled up at the corners.

'I was very pleased,' she said. 'I thank you.'

'If your Grace was pleased, then I have my thanks.'

She gave him her hand. He took it to his lips, formally, then turned it over and kissed the palm. His mouth was warm, it breathed warmth into her, up her arm, down into her blood. There was a great chasm between them. Standing on its brink she felt dizzy. She took a step forward, then another, across the chasm of race and birthright and discovered it to be no more than a little gap, the shortest journey of all, into his arms. He was trembling.

He bent his head and began to kiss her. She would never have believed that anyone could kiss like this. The kiss went on and on. He seemed to be all heartbeat, it shook her through. Then, kissing her, he drew her body hard against him, deliberately honest, so that she should know the force of his desire. And for a moment she was afraid; that force had grown powerful and impatient in its long captivity; she too trembled. Then while he held her still within the kiss and the awful longing, he began to touch her body, with no haste or lust or greed, but more as a blind man explores an unfamiliar room. He held her warm within his arm, his free hand moving over her. She was naked beneath the shift, and now the warm lover's hand knew it too . . . a small convulsion shook her. Under his mouth she made a choked sound, and he released her at once. She saw the tears in his eyes.

She tried to speak. It was almost impossible. They stood apart. She whispered: 'Why do you weep?'

'The dream . . . the dream. It's too beautiful. I cannot contain the dream.'

The tears distressed her. So did the gap that was between them again. She put out her hands.

'Must the dream end?' Her softest whisper.

'It is for you to say . . .'

But he gave her no chance, he held her more tightly this time, and, silenced, she put her arms about him, her turn to learn him now, his strong shoulders, his slenderness, his thick crisp hair, smooth cheeks under her fingers. She pressed delicately against him, and his gasp made her aware that something in him had snapped, that this guard-haunted gallery was neither the time nor the place but that in a moment it might well be. He was whispering to her now, she couldn't understand a word – half of it might have been swearing – he was extremely strong, her toes were off the ground. There was a little blind arcade behind the pillar and somehow they were in it, she was falling, slowly, and he came down with her on one knee, his hand supporting her head so she shouldn't hurt herself. Her hands touched the freezing floor. His face was between her breasts; he drew up her gown.

'Not now,' the words came out just in time. 'Not here.'

'When?' He lifted his face; even in the gloom she could see how deathly pale he was. '*Annwyl Crist!* For the love of God, when can we lie together?'

'Next week. Next week, when the King returns to Eltham.'

'And where? In Christ's mercy, where? I can't come to your chamber . . .'

They struggled upright, clinging to one another. He wiped his eyes.

'I will arrange it.' Her teeth were chattering.

'But where? For God's sake, tell me . . .'

She choked back a sudden hysterical laugh, crushing it against the back of her wrist. An idea had come to her, mad, mischievous, devilish. A good satisfying gesture against someone who had brought her much misery. He thought in terror: this is only a light adventure to her; she came tonight to torture me. *Elle s'amuse.* He said wildly:

'If this is a game, I'll kill myself.'

He meant it. She could tell. She said swiftly:

'No, no. All will be arranged. I promise. I promise you'll

laugh too, when we . . . next week.'

Next week. 'How can I wait? How shall I know?'

'I'll send word. My maid. The time and place.'

She started to move away. Further down the gallery a guard's halberd chinked on the stones. Perhaps the dream was only a dream after all. He knew better than to try to stay her going, but he caught her hand and kissed it as she passed. The perfume was fading, lilies and roses and honey, but he had her secret scents within his palm. The cloaked figure became a shadow, darkness, gone. He stepped back and leaned against the pillar. He needed that pillar very much. It was a long time before he could move away from it.

Guillemot loved her. She was herself in love with Lord Audley, a married man who didn't know she existed. But Guillemot was a virgin. She could not really understand, but she had been to the Wardrobe. He had been alone, waiting for her, had kissed her on both cheeks, frightening her half to death, after she had given the day, time and place of the delivery to be made. The Wardrobe delivery. The other maids had been sent to Eltham with the little King. Likewise the Duchesses. Philippa believed she was really out of favour. When the King was ready to leave, she had agreed to follow him, serve him with her life. Margaret of Clarence and the others, not to be outdone, had followed suit. They had left on the Thursday.

The week would have been impossible without the leavening presence of the little King. Katherine had enjoyed him with gratitude and fervour, but part of her was away, back in an unreal, unforgettable moment. She wondered if she had been a little mad. But time and place were set. It was arranged.

She thought: Louis de Robsart must love me as well as Guillemot does. He was so willing when I asked for the keys of Gloucester's apartment. Humphrey is gone, with all his servants. His chambers are shut up until his return. It was to be a jest, but somehow it does not seem so now.

'My lord of Gloucester's apartment, your Grace?'

She had smiled at him. A long time, over two years, since he had seen that smile. The Comptroller had grumbled at

367

him, saying this was the only set of keys. It had been worth a slightly humiliating argument just to see the smile again, when he returned triumphant.

The Upper Ward seemed silent without the Duchesses' chatter. It was as if she and Guillemot were the sole inhabitants. Except for the guard, strung out like beads along the corridors. But the stairway and gallery through which she would need to pass were comparatively deserted. It was Friday now. The day. The night. Waiting for the Matins bell. Only the most devout would be at that midnight service.

The strange difficult week had brought with it distortion of emotions. She began to feel unhappy. It was worse when the King had gone, little Harry, whose face looked less pale after his holiday. She warned the Duchesses to watch him well. There had been no more opinions from Philippa of York on the common man.

She had seen him once only during the entire week. She had been passing through to the great hall with her ladies. He was in the corridor with the valet Waterton and two other household servitors. One of the men had his arm about Owen Tydier's neck for a murmured conversation. He had laughed, flinging back his head. Then he had murmured something in response, and thumped his companion on the back and laughed again. He had very good teeth, a rarity in someone who had been in the wars, involved in sieges. That laugh had shivered her spine. As soon as they were aware of her approach they all became sober as priests, stepped back against the wall, bowing low. She stared ahead, walked on, shielded by her ladies. Then she knew he had lifted his eyes; she felt his mind upon her, his hands, his mouth. And he had been laughing.

He had been laughing at the tale of Thomas Harvey's miserly grandfather, who had lately taken a very young wife, and what that wife had proposed to Harvey. He had also been laughing because he was happy.

The November evening seemed to come down quickly. Supper went in a flash, though she loitered over it. The cup of wine she drank tasted foul. Not so foul as other tastes, in her mouth and her mind, when she was at last alone in her chamber with Guillemot.

Cobham's little leech-book. If this thing was to be tonight, there was one risk she could not take. It was almost as if Eleanor had forecast the future. The Egyptian herbal, drunk in the dark of the moon. Guillemot brewed it to her instructions. It was dreadful. She thought: I do not conceive easily. But this man looks as if he could easily get someone with child . . . A wave of heat filled her. She sat naked and trembling while Guillemot, silent, combed her hair, sponged her body. Wash my guilt away, little seabird. Anoint me with my rose-water and lily unguents, to cover this awful scent of lust.

I must have him. I must. I am like my mother. No, I am not. I have been chaste, despite my terrible hunger. In the moment it overwhelmed me he was there, shining and undeniable, with the right words and the music. A sorcerer. I cannot do it. I must. But I am a Queen. Another French Queen of England once took a lover, Mortimer. But Mortimer was lord and knight as well as adventurer. This is a landless esquire, a common man, a barbarian. In secret I shall rock the whole fabric of English royal protocol. That should make me happy, with my talk of equality, but it doesn't. Pray God that dreadful potion hasn't harmed my woman's parts. My heart beats so fast. Guillemot's eyes are troubled. When he touched me last week I felt the scars on his fingertips. That's from the harp. I am like my mother. No, I am chaste. I am a woman. She stood up before the mirror. Dark hair against ivory flesh. Long thighs, long eyes and lips, dark, secret, gleaming. The hunger growing, edged by guilt. He willed this so. I pass the guilt. Sorcerer. Lend me your cloak again, Guillemot.

A loose cream silk gown, with little hooks and eyes to the throat. Guillemot looked at her with love. Love. The only candle in this dark old world. Ah, my love. The words came unbidden, undirected. He had had tears in his eyes after kissing, touching me. He was limping when he left the hall. He was laughing when I saw him last.

Just once, then. Just once. I'll let it happen and then I'll send him away. Dismiss him from the court. I wish I could stop trembling. The Matins bell sounded.

'You can sleep in my bed tonight, Guillemot. You'll be lost in it.'

Guillemot was trembling too. The three candles in their sconce wavered as she handed them to Katherine. Humphrey of Gloucester's keys weighted the deep pocket of the cloak.

Not a soul on the gallery, or the spiral, or the walk to the apartments. Round the corner the rasp of the guard's halberd on stone, as he shifted his sore feet.

It was frightening to be alone in Humphrey's apartments. Her candles brought up the shadows and lit the beautiful ceiling, embossed with blue and gold. His great goosefeather bed took up most of the chamber. Near the bed was a little image of the Virgin, and a prie-dieu. She lit the votive candle, blowing out all the others. She knelt. She watched the candle begin to burn. She had marked off the candles at Poissy, waiting for Belle's visits. Belle, who had died and left her. The Virgin's face smiled down, benign. But the candle was burning, burning. An inch, then another. An inch of guilt, and one of fear.

He's very late. Then danced the demons, as never before, an inherited instability that almost tipped her mind off balance. It was all an unspeakable jest. Even now he boasts in some tavern of how he kissed the Queen and had his hands all over her body and, with a laugh – she was just as other women! stark bare she was for me, my friends, I could have taken her but she put me off at the last minute – let's drink to her Grace, to her hot bare body. Starved, she is, poor creature. But afraid of it. We even made an assignation . . . Keep it? Devil damn the thought! I'd not risk my neck – wouldn't it be treason?

He isn't coming.

She began to cry. The Virgin looked down with great severity, no longer smiling. She put her face in her hands. Such frail hands. So much guilt. So much love. Harry is dead. Harry lies lapped in silver, his spirit wandering on the North side of Paradise. What would he have said? That's easy. For a tenth of what has already passed, he would have burned him alive, and watched him burn.

She struggled to rise from her knees. The Virgin looked down with great disapproval. The door behind opened and closed softly. She felt arms about her, tight, he knelt beside her, stroking her back, whispering in his own language and hers: *Paid a llefain, cariad. Ne pleurs pas, ma bien-aimée.* Don't cry, my darling. She turned and clung to him and he drew her up. Her cloak fell to the floor.

The weeping and wondering were finished. Too late now to draw back, with the kiss, doubly desperate and desperately returned after the week of waiting, going on and on. Some lovely lightness entered; he was trying wildly to undress her and himself at the same time, still kissing her, half in and half out of his doublet, struggling with the little hooks and eyes on her gown, taking his mouth from hers for an instant to swear and say:

'Tonight of all nights! *Y diafol!* Old Feriby . . . kept us late . . . some laundry gone astray . . . oh, *cariad*, where are you? I thought I should go mad . . .'

The gown was off at last. She saw his face turn quite white as he looked at her body. Still in his shirt and hose, he knelt and embraced her thighs, laying his face on the softness between them, while she put her hands gently on his head, as if she blessed him.

Over the years they had been nearing one another in all innocence, drawn gradually together by an inevitable movement outside the spheres; he, a faint song in the distance, she remote and shadowed by pomp and tombs and intrigues. Now the final threads were linked, the span was bridged.

'Ask me,' she said softly.

He rose to his feet.

'Ask me, as you asked the others.'

Instinct told her there had been others, dozens of them. For he too was naked now, and he was beautiful.

He said: 'Come to bed with me, Cathryn. I want you so much. I love you.' (And thought: that last, I never said.)

He laid her snugly in the centre of Humphrey's great bed. There was a dip in the middle where the Duke had lain, alone or lusting with his lemen. He thought of making a jest about it, but he had never felt less like jesting.

There were a lot of covers on the bed, a heavy wolfskin and two or three brocades. He thought: Humphrey must feel the cold – we shall not be cold. He moved over on to her very carefully, she put her arms round him and lifted her head from the bolster to kiss him; for a moment he swam in the long dark eyes with their last vestige of anxiety. He had the dream in his arms, under him, holding him, and still he did not believe it.

He sheathed himself in the dream. It yielded tenderly. His mind reeled. Fire and silk. It has a core of fire. And something else . . . the two years of honey within me are screaming for release. *Duw!* don't let me disappoint her! . . . think of other things, quickly. At the training school at Smithfield, there was a terrible sergeant – he always had it in for the archers. The drill had to be so closely observed . . . her lovely throat, her mouth . . . if one unfortunate bowman loosed his fire before the signal the sergeant would go round behind him, cursing, and deal him a blow on the head with his baton . . . her soft breasts beneath me . . . that was when I learned to swear in English – you had to hold the sixty pounds of notched tension until he gave the sign, until your spine cracked, the sweat ran into your eyes, loose before then and you were for it . . . *Annwyl Crist!* her little moans, the feel of her smooth thighs . . . Erpingham was pleased with us at Agincourt – with the Notch! Stretch! Loose! the discipline . . . *Oh, Cathryn* . . . but the training school hadn't broken us, it had made us into artists . . . not yet, not yet, hold the notched arrow, damn you boys, hold, I said, hold fast! . . . hang like death on to the honey of the loose . . . but she moved under him, raising her hips so he could thrust deeper into her, she muttered something old and secret. He stroked her sleek lips with his tongue, her hands clutched his back, his flanks, she threw back her head. He thrust deeper, deeper still, and the hold broke, loosing the honey of two years, flooding her. He groaned as when the sergeant's baton knocked him almost senseless . . . and his voice and mind broke up too as he covered her face with kisses, using the language of home, of deepest love . . . *R'wy'n dy garu di, cariad, fy nghariad annwyl, r'wy'n dy garu di, fy merch fach, lili'r môr!* I love you, my beloved, lovely darling, I love you, my little girl, my lily of the sea!

He lay beside her, supporting her head on his arm, looking down at her. He said sadly: 'I didn't pleasure you enough. I wanted you too much, for too long.'

She smiled. It was done. No more fears. Ah, my love. The candlelight from the Virgin's prie-dieu was very strong on his face; it lit jewels in the shadows of the blue-and-gold ceiling. He was paler still, his eyes downcast as he looked at her. He had pushed the covers back so he could look.

He has the most beautiful mouth in the world. The top lip is very sharply defined, both lips are the same width and fullness, curling at the corners, turning up as his eyes and eyebrows do, and his voice. That mouth is tender and wicked and vulnerable. Now it's on mine again, that mouth is on mine. *Sainte Vierge!* one could die of this. It would be good to die so, in his arms. I would never have dreamed anyone could kiss like this. Ah, my love.

He thought, half-insanely: the dream is better than the dream itself. It need not have been like this: she could have been cold, arrogant, she might have made me feel ashamed of my gross encroachment of privilege. She might have made it clear that I was here at her command, that she was merely using me to service her . . . but no. She lies there, so lovely, with that kind and wanton little smile, her hand stroking my neck, so loving, so gentle, with her fiery generous heart and her noble blood. She might even (and here he chuckled aloud) have insisted I call her 'Your Grace' in bed!

'What is it?' she whispered, and he told her. They stared deeply at one another.

'I could command your death!' she said wonderingly.

'Of course you could. You could say I'd raped you.'

'What would be the penalty for that, I wonder?'

'Unimaginable . . .' They both shivered. He held her tight.

'Have you ever – raped anyone?' she said curiously.

'No. I never thought there was much to be had from hurting . . . but I've seen it done, many times. After a siege.'

'Last week, in the gallery . . .'

'Forgive me for that, *cariad*. Forgive me.'

She put her hand over his lips.

He moved a little away so he could watch her heart beating. It shook her left breast with its rhythm. A faint line of sweat lay on her neck. She was much thinner than he had remembered. He stroked her flat belly. None would ever think she had borne a child. Would to God it had been mine. I would like to have been first with her. If I could get her with child it would be the most wonderful crown to this glory. I may already have done so. He lowered his head and kissed her breasts and then her belly, slow kisses from hip to hip and then up again under her ribs. He heard her sighing breaths and felt her fingers in his hair.

How frail flesh is, he thought. It only just holds in our vitals and our souls. He felt suddenly afraid.

'Tell me you love me,' he said, and smiled at the ironic demise of his old self. The times he'd heard those words, and never once asked them.

'Say you love me, Cathryn.'

He raised himself and set his mouth on hers again. You'll say it, before the night is done . . . *Annwyl Crist!* a thought struck home. Let it not be only for one night! To lose her now would be worse than death. It is *am byth*. For ever. Someone will make you weep one day. They'd said it. Yes, he was afraid.

She thought: I must contrive to keep him with me always. It can be done. It must be done. Not here at Windsor, but there must be a way. Folk have lost interest in me since the King . . . since Harry died. Somewhere fairly near London, so I can attend Parliament when necessary and keep watch over my little boy . . . but this is paramount. I must have Owen with me like this, always, or give up life itself.

He said, against her lips: 'There's no escape, Cathryn. I shall give you no peace. I shall hound you and haunt you until you have me killed or send me back to Wales. There's no escape from me now, *cariad*.'

And she said: 'But I love you. I love you, Owen. *Owen, comme je t'adore!* We must leave here. We will go together . . . to Hadham, or to my manor at Hertford. I am very fond of Hertford. I will gather all the servants I can trust. I'll spin some tale to keep the Duchesses away. We will establish our own ménage there, and be together always. I love you. I love you. *Je t'aime*, Owen, *mon amour*.'

Tears came to his eyes. He could not move or speak.

'I can't lose *you*,' she said. 'Not you. It's unbearable. Once I loved someone dearly and lost them . . .'

374

'The King,' he whispered.

'No, not only Harry. I was speaking of my sister, my Belle.'

He knew she had been ill and lonely and starved and afraid and disappointed. Deep were the fragile clues. The day would come when she would tell him all. Meanwhile he could mend the damage so expertly that there might be no need, yet if she wished, he'd listen . . .

'She was everything. A mother, father, protector. She saved my life. And she loved and lost someone too. Yet she was virgin when she wed her second husband . . .' She smiled, the smile stopped his heart for a moment. 'Love, ah, love is strange.'

He said softly: 'Cathryn, *fy nghariad*, my own darling. I will be brother and sister and father and protector to you. But I have no lands, no money, no estate, no fame. This – all this, is the only treasure I have for you. Take me. Take my love.'

He thought: and you, in your way, were virgin when you came to me, and I am now your husband. And now your husband will pleasure you.

He did all that he would; things that she had never imagined even in her wildest lonely longings. She turned her face into the bolster to stifle the sounds he brought from her.

Dere yma, fy merch fach. Come here, come to me, my little girl. Open your mouth, Cathryn. Now kiss me. Touch me. Here . . . and here, ah, Cathryn, Cathryn . . .

Near Llangollen Vale there is a mountain. There are flowers at the hill-foot and birds nesting towards the summit and on top is the snow . . . in the morning the sun strikes the peak – sometimes in summer the snow melts on the peak – it's so beautiful . . .

Now these, these are the flowers that grow at the hill-foot, so soft, I feel the dew on them and the little streams that flow among them . . . and here, much higher, the birds are nesting, I feel their fluttering wings, they're frightened. No need to fear, little birds. He kissed the fluttering, the hard rosy tips of her breasts, the hard pulse beating at the base of her throat. The sun begins to rise up the mountain. It is a very fierce sun today. At the top the snow waits. You are the snow. This is your mountain. Now the sun begins to touch the peak.

She rubbed her long neck against his like a courting swan, she moved her hands ceaselessly up and down the muscles of his back, feeling their graceful ebb and flow; her eyes tightly shut, she arched yearningly to meet him. She could see the flowers and the birds and the mountain. His voice was fading, she could just hear . . . it was like death, it had the power of death . . .

Ah, feel the sun, now the sun is on the peak . . . it melts the snow . . .

'Quickly!' he cried. 'Look! See the sun on the peak! Feel it melt! Cathryn, my beloved *Cathryn* . . .'

She opened her eyes straight into his – they had changed, all the blue was gone, they had darkened to gold, ardent gold in the little candle's light – the sun was in them, in her, the snow melting, the sun bursting on the melting snow! He stemmed her terrible wild cry with his mouth. The silence became profound. Very faintly outside came the chink of the guard's halberd on the stones.

'I hurt you, *mon amour*,' she whispered.

'No, no. You cut your nails too short. There, *cariad*. There, my darling.'

The silky dewy dream with its core of fire. It had been like trying to hold a whirlwind. The valley in the bed was deeper now, a wonderful place to be thrown, pressed together, skin and limbs and lips and heartbeats. Her pulse was so fast it frightened him, he kept his hand on it until it slowed a little. Her long thick hair was falling over her face and clinging to her wet body. He sat up and quickly made it into two long braids, to ease her. The little flame was burning low, beneath the Virgin.

'Have you ever lost anyone you loved?'

He said: 'I never really knew my parents. I have never been married. I have never been in love. Oh, how glad I am I have never been in love! I am changed. Are you changed, Cathryn?'

She whispered: 'I am changed.'

He thought briefly of the past. He realized he had always been jealous of Harry. Yet she had loved Harry, and that was good and right. He thought with bitter regret of Alys, Blanchette, Ghislaine, Jeanne, and all that company, wishing them out of existence. Then: without them I would not have had the knowledge to pleasure her so, to see and feel her lost eyes and her wild body. The man I now am is their gift to Cathryn. Thank you, ladies. God send you good husbands.

She thought: I'll have to maintain him; he shall want for nothing. He has nothing save for his Wardrobe salary. She suspected he was extremely proud in these matters, and accurately forecast storms. Any storm was worth it. But we must leave Windsor. Near this room they change the guard every four hours and someone may have heard us. I loved Harry, I loved him dearly. *Requiescat*. It was never like this.

She caressed the knife-scar on his thigh. He discovered a vein between her neck and shoulder which, when kissed, made her shudder and gasp; he went to work on this for a long time. And at last he found the words to tell her of the duration, depth and truth of his love for her, and this took longer still. She kissed the crease between his brows and ruffled his hair. He turned her over and kissed all the way down her spine, stroked and squeezed her soft round buttocks. She lay still. Thoughts tripped by, weightless as clouds. No shame, no guilt, no fear. Could Philippa of York only witness this scene! The thought was too much, she twisted back into his arms to hide her mirth against him, embracing him with her silken limbs. He became extremely excited.

'This is a rape, Cathryn. You are my poor hostage and I am a great lord. This is how it's done. This is rape. Does it hurt? It should, Cathryn. I must lack the skill. You shouldn't be holding me like that, Cathryn. You should be struggling, screaming for mercy. This is rape. I'd better put more vigour into it . . . you shouldn't be kissing me . . . you shouldn't . . . kiss your ravishers . . . it encourages them . . .'

Their kisses and cries mingled. They came apart gasping.

'We shall break Duke Humphrey's bed,' he said.

They began to laugh. The more they tried to quell the laughter, the wilder it became. He hauled the furs and brocades over their heads. They lay in a hot cave, laughing and kissing, half-mad with joy in their private dangerous Paradise.

Then, breathless, he threw the covers back. He got out of bed to light a fresh candle. She looked at his golden body in the soft light, heard him swear as his trembling fingers burned themselves on hot wax. She looked at his slenderness, his strength. Since he had been out of the wars he wore his hair rather long, its tawny gold had a thick curl in it. She stretched her toes down the bed. Her loins and back were filled with a beautiful ache. She thought with certainty: if I am ever parted from him, I shall die.

He came back and held her tenderly. He began to think very seriously about their future together. About the shattering possibilities. Would it be possible to marry her – the Queen-Dowager? If I applied for letters of denization – became an Englishman? The Lord Glyn Dŵr would turn in his grave, wherever that may be. It doesn't matter. There is nothing but this. *Am byth*. For ever.

'There is something I can give you.' He tugged at a ring of heavy Welsh gold he wore on his little finger. He slipped it on her hand.

'Owain Glyn Dŵr gave me that ring when I left home,' he said. 'He was furious with me but he gave it me for protection. It's supposed to be magic. I don't know. Only wear it for me, for love.'

'I will always wear it. Are you ever homesick for Wales?'

'How could I long for anything now? I haven't been back for ten years. I miss the language sometimes.'

'Are there servants you would like to take with us to Hertford? Your two kinsmen?'

'They have two young boys, seeking service in England. Huw and Caradoc. Perhaps.'

'Can they be trusted?'

'Oh yes,' he said instantly. 'They're children of my race. They'd die rather than be false to a fellow Welshman.'

'Then they shall come.' She closed her eyes. He laid his face against her hair. Dawn would soon be here, damned dawn.

'Shall I see you tomorrow?'

'You must not look at me,' she said.

'It will be difficult.'

'Almost impossible.'

'My darling. I wonder if they'll be able to tell? You look like a flower.'

She opened her eyes. 'You're so pale. You must rest. Hold me in your arms.'

'Ah, Cathryn. I love you. For ever.'

She began to drift. He had re-baptized her. She was no longer Kéti, the anguished, frightened maiden. Nor Katherine, bereaved and lonely Queen. Both those beings were dead. She was Owen's beloved Cathryn, and she was safely home at last. And strangely, she was still chaste, as was he. Love had made certain of that.

He didn't sleep, but waited until dawn made it impossible to linger. He lay cradling her head, and with his other hand held her hand against his heart. He eased himself half underneath her to support her while she slept. He kissed her closed eyes without waking her. Under the braids he had made her neck looked like a child's. *Fy merch fach.* My little girl. Her lips were swollen. There was a long rosy mark on her neck where he had kissed her too hard, and a bruise inside her arm. He would send up a high-collared dress for her to wear today. The brown velvet. I'll be good today. I won't look at her. It will be easier now. Knowing we are going to Hertford together. Let it be soon. Soon. And another thing. When we are safely there, there'll be no creeping in secret to her bed. We shall sleep together every night, without shame, openly. Man and wife. And she will bear my children. *I will it shall be so.* He turned her hand over and looked at her palm. Megan at Glyndyfrdwy used to boast she could read hands; she always marvelled at his own long life. Cathryn's lifeline stopped short halfway. Megan was a lying, crazy old witch. He turned the hand again on to his heart. He laid his head back, holding her sleeping face against his throat. Then at last he shed tears, they rolled into Duke Humphrey's bolster. He thought with great humility: thank you, sweet Christ. Thank you, dear God. Thank you, Drwynwen, love-goddess of Anglesey. Thank you, whatever forces brought me to this time.

Part Six

THE TOLL
England, 1430-38

Western wind, when will thou blow,
The small rain down can rain?
Christ, if my love were in my arms
And I in my bed again!

Anon.

John, Duke of Bedford, sometime Regent of France, paced the audience chamber at Westminster. He was awaiting the presence of his sovereign, now a growing boy of eight years old. Spring sunshine poured through the windows. Bedford was too preoccupied to notice or enjoy it. His brown, slightly protuberant eyes were veined with worry. He paced as a soldier does, to loosen his muscles and let his mind run free. He grudged even this brief but necessary visit to England, with its accompanying sloth. France called him; battle called him, even after the years of fighting and achieving nothing. One step forward and two back. He realized it. And now this latest curse, unprecedented perhaps since Boudicca of the Iceni. A woman soldier. A living inspiration infusing the blood of the jaded French. A village wench with a mind like a seasoned warrior. A parody of all womankind. A vile blasphemer, with her saints and her secret voices. *La Pucelle d'Orléans. Jeanne d'Arc.*

Bedford was more slightly built than his brother of Gloucester, but less delicate than the dead king his brother. He was a mixture of gentleness and ruthlessness. At this moment his kind mouth was thinned with trouble. He slapped his thigh as he paced, as if goading a horse. His regency was in ruins. Less than a year ago, the Dauphin had had himself crowned Charles the Seventh of France at Rheims, in direct contravention of the bloodily won Treaty of Troyes. The witch had been there with him in the Cathedral. Had her black wings been folded? No, he thought; no ordinary devil she, but a monstrous travesty of womanhood. They said she had no female parts. Only a mind tuned to her diabolical visitors. Blaspheming her way through the steely pastures of triumph, swearing that her voices came from blessed Margaret, Catherine, Michael. When, in truth, they were from Lucifer, the fallen and glorious.

He chewed absently at a handful of little wild strawberries the Queen-Dowager had sent him in a gilded basket. He was looking forward to seeing her properly for the first time in nearly seven years. A pity that Harry had died, for many reasons, not the least being that he and Katherine were happy together. He regretted having failed so far in his promise to Harry – he had promised to cherish her. And yet – a reluctant smile touched his lips – since her retirement she seemed to have been compensated . . . but there were problems in England too. The strawberries tasted sweet. He had not forgotten the autumn of 1425, when armies belonging to Humphrey of Gloucester and the Bishop (now Cardinal) Beaufort had been arrayed in opposition on Tower Bridge. Humphrey had wanted sole possession and jurisdiction over the little King, and Beaufort, wanting exactly the same, had removed the chains from the southern end of the bridge and had occupied positions for firing from the houses built on it. But Gloucester had been the victor on that occasion. He had taken the King under guard to Westminster. And now these two great lords held an uneasy truce. Bedford had made them swear friendship. A grant of 5,000 marks from Parliament had sweetened Humphrey. With this he was supposed to have rescued Jacqueline once more from the grasp of Brabant. Poor Jacqueline.

Jacqueline had been left a virtual prisoner of Brabant and Philip of Burgundy. Humphrey now had a new wife. Eleanor Cobham. Perdition have him, Bedford thought. He nearly wrecked my own alliance by his wild provocations. Christ be praised; I am wed at last to Anne of Burgundy. We love one another, very much. A bonus in these times of policy and gain. Humphrey had declared that the Pope had never recognized his liaison with Jacqueline. By sleight of hand, bribery, and God knew whatever chicaneries, he had extricated himself from any charge of bigamy or other crimes. Very clever, thought Bedford in disgust. He would be a fit companion for *La Pucelle*. Although she would not suit him, having no female parts . . .

His mind fretted again over the witch, as one probes a sore tooth. At Chinon she had infected Charles of France with her blazing zeal. With Alençon as her commander she had relieved Orléans (which Salisbury had died to capture earlier) and then had taken the river-fort of Tourelles from the English.

She was a thing against nature. She had the heart of a man. She had attacked St Loup as a diversion, and then stormed in to secure the fort of the Augustins which Bedford had deemed invincible. Then Patay was hers, and Auxerre, Châlons, and Rheims, where her victories were consummated in Charles's coronation. She had tried for Paris next and had been wounded near the Porte St Honoré in a skirmish with Burgundian and English forces. That had cheered Bedford a little. He feared her, he was not ashamed to admit it. She was a thing of the Devil, with her inspired expertise in campaigning. Philip feared her too. But we'll have her, Bedford had assured him.

His visit to England had a twofold purpose. First, to borrow troops from Beaufort, troops originally levied for the Cardinal's forthcoming Bohemian crusade. Beaufort had acquiesced, albeit grudgingly. Second, to take back the little King to France. Henry must be crowned King of France, in the hope of stimulating any latent French loyalties; remind them of the Treaty, and of Agincourt.

'A pox on necromancers!' he said aloud, and finished the last of the wild strawberries. On Jeanne, the devil-haunted goat-girl of Domrémy, and also on Eleanor Cobham. The black one. She had turned Humphrey from a mere nuisance into a positive plague, and how else but by witchery? Nothing could be proven against her; she was so clever. I'd like to burn them both. The door was tapped. His wife Anne entered. As always, he was enchanted by her douce gentleness. Some of his care evaporated.

'The King is coming, John,' she said. 'With his mother.'

They knelt, and waited, and Henry entered with Katherine behind him, escorted by Louis de Robsart and Richard of York. Bedford kissed the royal hand. Such a thin hand. Such an old-looking child. More like eighteen than eight. Those long eyes, so dark and far away, the straight thin figure, the gentle, weak mouth. He had a priestly look. All spirit. Then Bedford looked at Katherine, and for a moment was quite lost.

She had a light about her that was nothing to do with the spring sunshine through the blazoned window. Either he had never looked at her properly before, or war, worry and sieges had muddled his memory. She wore a full-skirted gown of saffron and rose. Even her strong features seemed to have softened, grown tender. Her eyes were beautiful beyond words. Her skin had a seashell glow. She moved sensuously, even in her curtsey, like a lithe dancer. You could warm your hands at her. Her smile shattered him. For a full minute he was deeply in love. *Katherine la Belle*. A true woman. Not a rabid, sexless witch.

The King put his arms about the kneeling Duke's neck.

'We are graciously pleased to see you, good Uncle. Are we for France? I'm told I am to be crowned in Paris.'

'Then Paris it shall be, your Grace. If God wills that we come through all our trials.'

'Amen.' The child spoke so devoutly that Bedford was moved. 'My trust is in Our Blessed Saviour. He has sworn to look after us.'

Someone has influenced him well, thought Bedford. His mother? But he hardly ever sees his mother. It was scarcely likely to be Humphrey of Gloucester. He noticed a young priest hovering in the background, praying silently, constantly, his lips moving, his eyes fixed on the young king as on a saint's image. A pity that the time has come for him to leave home, Bedford thought. He could do worse than remain here – under such holy influence. The occasional presence of that beautiful mother could do him no harm either. But I need him in France, as a buckler against that daughter of Hell . . . He rose to his feet.

'I have prepared a psalm for our voyage,' Henry said, as practically as if he spoke of baggage. 'Master Tydier has set it to music.'

The blush, like a kindling beacon, caught Bedford's eye. It rose from the neckline of Katherine's dress, swept over her neck and face and was gone. Not an unhappy blush; more like sunrise through a seashell. Bedford said gently to the King: 'Will you make ready? Choose your favourite companions. Our army is all set to move.'

'I will take Richard.' Henry glanced back to where Richard of York stood quietly listening. 'You'll come, won't you, Richard?'

Katherine said: 'Go, Harry. Make ready.' She bent and kissed him. Momentary sadness stole some of her glow.

'Assist them, my lady,' Bedford told his wife. 'I wish to speak with the Queen-Dowager alone.'

Outside the gay glass window the concupiscent birds carolled of springtime. Bedford and Katherine sat down together in the window-seat.

'Well, my dear sister,' he said. 'Are you glad to see me, after this long time?'

'John,' she said, dropping all formality. 'Many times in the past I wished you were here. I prayed you would return safely and for good.'

I wanted your protection, she thought. Not now. You are a little too late. She looked at him with her radiant eyes.

'I'm safe,' he said. He could not take his eyes off her. 'But I may not stay. How do you, Katherine? Do you need my assistance? In any way?' Then he said acutely: 'Does Gloucester harass you?'

She looked down, smoothing her saffron-and-rose skirts.

'No. No. I keep my household well away from him. I see him occasionally. I fancy he is more objectionable since he married Lady Cobham. Have you news of poor Jacqueline?' And Bedford told her what he knew; her face grew sad.

He said: 'Does Humphrey still keep you from the presence of the King?'

'Yes, when he can outwit Cardinal Beaufort. I am with my son when Parliament is prorogued, and on feast-days. With this I must be content.' Smiling her unbelievable smile, she sighed, and Bedford studied her. He wondered; there was a delicate fullness about her breasts, the sheen on her skin was something no creams, no maquillage could invest. He had seen that look before, in his own wife. Yes. He was right. He was neither offended nor shocked.

'And otherwise you have retired,' he said gently. 'You live in seclusion, at Hertford, with your handsome esquire. And I see that you are *enceinte*. When will your child be born?'

She was speechless. She turned pale. Then she saw the kindness in Bedford's eyes.

'So you know,' she said faintly.

387

'I've known for some days. Unfortunately so does Gloucester. I refused to listen. God knows what he expected me to do about your liaison. There's nothing. It's done. How long is it now?'

'Over five years,' she said. 'Who told him?'

'It appears,' said Bedford, frowning, 'that Lady Cobham – I should say the new Duchess of Gloucester – had it from your little maid. I gather some duress was involved.'

Now she remembered. Some months ago. Guillemot crying and crying as if her heart would break. They had only just returned from a brief visit to Westminster. Guillemot had had a great angry wound down the length of her arm. As if it had been held in a fierce flame. None could get from her the reason for her anguish. Not even Owen, who could draw things from almost anyone, just by looking at them and speaking softly. Katherine felt sick.

'Damn her,' she said violently. Troubled, she looked at Bedford, said uncertainly: 'What now?'

He took her hands, kissed them, patted them hard.

'Nothing,' he said. 'But be discreet, Katherine. And remember the decree . . . that none shall aspire to marry the widow of King Henry the Fifth.'

'I thought that decree was made to discourage Edmund Beaufort!'

Bedford looked out of the window. Roses and ivy twined richly against the ancient stone.

'When I ransomed Beaufort from France, he told me that he wished to marry you. He had heard of you through his sister, Joan of Scotland. I knew then that Humphrey would do all he could to prevent it. Thus he robs the Beauforts of any further enhancement of power, and likewise your . . .' he was lost for a fitting description. Very difficult.

'My lover,' she said. 'My husband in all but name. My life.'

'Of course, the Welsh,' he mused, 'are excluded by law from marriage with any Englishwoman.'

'I am no Englishwoman,' she said tightly.

'You are English now,' he said.

'Y *diafol!*' she cried. Bedford's eyebrows shot up. 'I'm in love with Wales! He took me to Wales. We stood upon a golden, singing mountain. It's a land of love and passion and courage. And if they say that Owen is a landless upstart, they lie! His father and his three uncles, Goronwy, Gwylym and Rhys descend from Sir Tudor of old Goronwy's great line, and his grandmother from Thomas ap Llewellyn, kinsman to the greatest of Welsh princes, and to Owain Glyn Dŵr. The senior line of Theodor is related to the great Gwylym ap Griffith of Penarth, and . . .'

Bedford was laughing.

'Katherine, Katherine. I didn't ask for his pedigree.'

'The King is very fond of him,' she said quietly.

'Then that is well.' Bedford spoke with great gentleness. 'Katherine, listen to me. I am your friend in this. I only beg your discretion. Humphrey of Gloucester knows nothing of your coming child, and I shall not tell him. But I must speak truthfully. There is more than a possibility that Parliament will repeal the Act barring Welshmen from privilege. It's an obsolete Act, and stems from the Glyn Dŵr rebellions. Maybe in a year or so your – ' he struck the right note at last – 'your *bel-ami* will be regarded *sicut verus anglicus ligeus* – a true English subject. But put marriage with him from your mind. There would be heavy penalties, in unforeseen ways. Humphrey can be very spiteful. I beg your discretion.'

For a moment she looked very sad. Marriage. Marriage. That was all Owen ever thought about, when he wasn't making love. He was obsessed. Never a day went by when he didn't bring up marriage to her in some form or another. Again, he would be disappointed. She would make it up to him.

Bedford watched her affectionately. A real woman. Not like that creature in France, that armoured limb of the Fiend . . .

'I am arranging for you to have extra funds for your Privy Purse,' he said. 'Is there anything else you need? Are your servants loyal? Have you a good midwife? And where will you bear your child?'

'Hadham, I thought,' she said. 'We stay there sometimes, as a change from Hertford.' Her sadness had gone, her dark eyes were full of mischief. 'I think I shall call him Edmund,' she said, 'in memory of poor disappointed Edmund Beaufort!'

Bedford laughed. He kissed her on both cheeks. No wonder

Harry, and this Welsh wonder, loved her so.

'God be with you, Katherine. I must go to oversee the levies. The King will be well looked after with me. Remember I am your friend.' He got up. He said suddenly: 'Young Harry clings very close to Richard of York. There's proud blood there, an ambitious family. Do you approve, Katherine?' but she shrugged, uninterested, and again he gloried in her woman-liness. Never, never, could *she* lead an army . . .

She took her farewell of the King. God keep you, in France, my son. He vowed he would pray for her. The young priest looked on severely as she kissed him. She would like to have held the child close, but he was on his dignity, and it was a painful moment. Beneath the concealing gown, Owen's child gave a hefty Welsh kick.

On her way back to Hertford, she felt great relief at Bedford's attitude. She was glad he knew, although surprised at his liberal attitude. But he had a lot on his mind. And he didn't know about her two miscarriages, one occurring quite soon after the move to Hertford, the other two years later. She would never forget that second miscarriage. She had been in bed afterwards, still bleeding, out of danger but sorry for herself. Owen had been lying on top of the bed beside her, holding her, bathing her forehead, and she had fallen asleep in his arms. That was when she had had the dream. More like a vision, very strange. She had told him.

'A woman, *mon amour* . . . a woman with long red hair and a fox cub in her arms. She was weeping so dreadfully. She was more distressed than we are . . . it was strange . . . all mixed up with the herbal potion . . .'

And he had said, very carefully, his body becoming rigid:

'What potion was that, *cariad*?'

'Oh, some stuff that Cobham advised . . . I took it once or twice.'

He had left the bed. She had never heard anyone swear like it in any language. When he was in control he came back and told her all about Cobham. So notorious a witch that even when he was in France she had been talked about. Yet so clever none could pin down her evils.

'So it is she who has killed my children,' he had said.

She could not look at his eyes; he frightened her so. She wept; he became calmer, tender again, telling her it was no fault of hers. I will make you another child, he said. When you are strong again. Sweet Cathryn.

She came back to Hertford. The sun was shining. He was waiting for her. Standing in his embrace, she felt a scratching at her gown. A fluffy white dog grinned up at her.

'I remembered,' he said. 'Your little dogs – your Beppo and Jacquot, who died. Page got this one for me. A sailor at Southampton brought it home. White dogs are hard to find. Don't ask me what breed he is.'

He was a mystic. He could cut down into her most secret past and heal wounds none other had ever seen or cared about. He picked her up and carried her into the hall, and up the stairs. She had been away for a week. She kissed his neck. She knew his mind.

'Bedford knows,' she told him. 'Gloucester knows. But there's no need to worry. John was so kind . . .'

While she told him he walked to the solar window and looked out. Huw and Caradoc were in the yard. They were good little hardworking boys, though he thought Huw not overblessed with brains. They had settled well, they were not homesick for Wales. It was good to talk Welsh to them. Cathryn could speak quite a bit of Welsh. He thought like this to blot out a retrospective pain.

Bedford knows. Huw was grooming a horse. Caradoc was tending the roses. Red roses. He could have told Cathryn himself that their bliss was no secret. Two months ago, was it? No, it was near Christmas. He had gone with her to Windsor, as part of her entourage. Careful to keep away, not to speak or touch or look. She wanted a fur cloak that had been left behind. He had gone down to the Wardrobe, and just outside the door, had heard the voices. One of them was Robert Waterton's. But the first was Thomas Harvey – one-time friend.

'I see we have his Grace with us today.'

His Grace. That could mean anyone. Several lords and bishops were at court.

Someone laughed. 'We're honoured.'

Another voice: 'Who?'

'The Queen's creature. Katherine's tame stallion!'

Loud laughter. Then he heard the voice of Waterton, who had loved the King. It was full of grieving rage.

'Sweet Christ!' Waterton said. 'Would that King Harry could return, *for just one day* . . . he'd have the bowels from that . . .' An unspeakable name.

He had felt the blood leaving his face. Of its own volition his hand unsheathed the baselard at his belt. He touched its wafer edge, cutting his thumb, watching his own blood spring. Harvey first, up under the ribs, straight into the heart. Then Waterton. Then the others.

'Fell on his feet, didn't he?' said another voice. 'The post's no sinecure, I'll wager. But he was always a good cocksman, from what I heard . . .'

'I'd not complain, to be in his place!'

'Sweet Jesus, yes. She has the look . . .'

'I wonder if she pays him by the hour, or by the deed!'

They all burst out laughing again. Except Waterton.

His father Meredyth had killed a man in anger. For the rest of his days he had lived a fugitive, outside the peace. It was the hardest thing he had ever done in his life, to sheathe that blade, to walk in to the sudden awful silence with his face and lips chalk-white, to go to the chest and take a fur cloak, any cloak, and walk out again under Waterton's loathing eyes. But he did it. Kill, as he should have killed, defend her as she should have been defended, and he would never see her again. He felt as if they had all had their hands on her. He felt himself defiled. Riding back to Hertford behind her equipage, he shook all over. He felt dirty. Bought and sold. Her tame stallion.

As soon as they reached home and were in their chamber, he threw her on the floor and raped her. Not in play or in pretence, but hurting her. It relieved his feelings somewhat. He took a long time over it. As far as he could judge, that was when the child she now carried was conceived. It should be a strong fierce child, got in such anger. She had kissed him, kissed away his shame. He did not tell her. Demons could not have dragged it from him. Now he put the memory away. But he would never accompany her to court again.

Now she was leaving the solar, going towards their bed-chamber, looking back at him once over her shoulder. The white dog trotted beside her. The back of her neck shone like a pearly crescent. She swayed like a young tree as she walked. He went after her, managing to shut the dog out of the bed-chamber.

He turned her to face him. She had been away for a week. All of her was so lovely he didn't know where to start. Five years with her! It could have been five weeks. Five days. The passion was brighter, hotter. At times it reached peaks of intensity that awed them both, almost frightened them.

'Be careful. The child.'

There was no need to remind him. He wanted this child desperately. Nearly as much as he wanted her.

'I have decided to call him Edmund,' she murmured.

'Whatever you please. Oh, my Cathryn . . .'

'Do not punish me so, Uncle.' The King spoke quietly through a bleeding lip. 'You do ill to strike the Lord's anointed.'

Despite these brave words, he bowed his head like a beast to the slaughter before Gloucester's massive menace. It was wrong for his uncle to chastise him; there was nothing in the edicts of the Privy Council to approve such acts – he was almost sure of this. On the other hand he was guilty. Guilty. He should be punished. His guilt had been revealed to him clearly during the last dreadful, dreamlike eighteen months in France. Before his eyes men had burned a woman, a woman who had cried on the Holy Name at the last. Jeanne d'Arc was always with him, in dreams and daylight, her sad eyes looking into his. She had come from God. They had burned her, and he had done nothing to assuage her doom. Therefore he was guilty. His guilt blurred any perception that Gloucester tormented him now from any motive save his own foul humour. He sighed. Humphrey of Gloucester thought: I hate the sight of him. That frail, black-clad figure, heir to all the greatness I could have worn so much better. This diademed infant so lost and holy . . . he irks me, oh how he irks me with his tiny omnipotence . . .

'Anointed!' he sneered. 'You call that makeshift mummery in Notre Dame, where you were sacred by a mere *Bishop*, a true coronation? Charles of Bourges is crowned King of France. Your father died in vain. Are you not ashamed?'

'I am ashamed,' said the King softly. From the tail of his eye he saw the woman, pretending to work on her tapestry. Her long silver needle rose and fell. He felt it penetrating his own nerves, delicate, relentless, sewing him to his own tragic future, tightening his guilt. Eleanor Cobham, Duchess of Gloucester. Watching him. She is of the Devil, he thought. His pliant mind registered the fact unerringly, but he was not comforted, for how could he be right in his judgement and the rest of the world be wrong? For *Jeanne la Pucelle* was of God, and he had watched what they did to her. Seeing her truth in that last terrible moment. Yet Eleanor is of the Devil, with her shifting, changing dark shape and the flashing silver needle that goes straight to the heart, biting, punishing, drawing his spirit's blood . . .

Gloucester was speaking of his mother now, saying dreadful things about her. Cardinal Beaufort had agreed that the King should go with her to Wales for a short visit. If he could get through today – he would look forward to it. And to seeing the children – he had never seen her children. Edmund, and the baby, Jasper. It was a secret between them. Gloucester was still saying terrible things about his mother.

'. . . make the most of your visit to her. It will be the last for a long time. She is an evil influence.'

Master Simon, his young chaplain, never said that, although there was a certain veiled disapproval in him when he spoke of her. He merely said that the King should pray for her, and for all sinners. Other than that he made no comment. Now the King felt himself moved to defend her. I love her very much, he said, and Humphrey raised his hand again.

'No,' said Eleanor. 'No, my lord.'

She rose and came to him, terrifying him with her gentleness as she wiped the blood from his mouth. She looked at her husband over the King's head, a keen black look like a viper's inclination. The Cardinal will notice if you mark him further, the look said. And more: give him to me. I have poisons none can discover, used in ancient Rome by Livia on Augustus, by Agrippinilla on Claudius. Also, I can kill without touching; my powers are strong. You should be King; you are next in line after Bedford, and Bedford cannot live for ever. Give little Harry to me. Almost imperceptibly Humphrey shook his head. There was the Cardinal to be reckoned with. There were subtler means of torment. He drew Harry between his knees.

'Your Grace must tell me again of your experiences in France. Tell me again,' he said. The King's white face became tinged with green.

'Tell me of the burning,' said Humphrey. 'How long did she suffer? Did she scream much? And her flesh must have reeked. There's a stench, isn't there? A stench, and a crackle, and the blood boils. It bursts the veins. You had a good view, didn't you? A front seat for princelings. Did her hair catch fire? Or was it shaven like a soldier's? Then her brains burned, eh? Did they run, and melt, what colour was her brain, little nephew? What did she say to you, tell me, tell me . . .'

Between his knees he held a cluster of frail bones that shook so that the chair and the man who sat on it shook in unison. The dark eyes cried silently for release, became unfocused. Eleanor drew the fainting child away.

'Don't talk so, my lord.' She was a little pale herself. Even behind the defences of her unearthly kingdom she feared the burning. Gloucester looked at her, knowing her kin to all witches. He was more afraid of her these days. Love had almost gone out of their relationship; she was mainly his counsellor. On countless nights they had lain in bed together, and he had touched her and found her icy cold and motionless, in catalepsy; at first he had thought her dead. Then later he understood; her spirit was out of her body, wandering, wreaking mischief near or far. That understanding terrified him most of all.

It was a new bed. Two years ago he had had the great goosefeather bed chopped up for firewood, after Eleanor had burned the truth out of Katherine's maid. That bed had been profaned. Humphrey had a vivid, lustful imagination in which rage and envy mingled. A whore, and a Welsh mountebank. Whore. But Bedford was her friend, and out of sheer perversity,

Cardinal Beaufort seemed to be turning a blind eye. You should have been King, Eleanor whispered in the new bed. You should be King. Let me have charge of the child. And always he said No, for the Cardinal still held mighty sway with the Council. And yet (the only comfort in his life at present) Beaufort was growing old. The last time they had met Humphrey had noticed it. The very slightest of tremors, the faintest hesitancy in the harsh, direct voice. All of a sudden his foul temper vanished. He said kindly to the King, now reviving queasily against Eleanor's arm:

'Make ready now to leave for your stay with your mother. Wales is very pleasant in summer, I believe, especially by the sea. My compliments to the Queen-Dowager.'

Henry left the chamber like a hare before running hounds. Along the devil-haunted corridors he raced, to his own apartments, where he fell into the arms of the young chaplain who had been waiting with prayers so fervent they had become almost unintelligible.

'Hush, your Grace, be still.'

'Father. Let us pray.'

'I never cease,' said the young man, dragged by Henry's hand towards the royal Chapel.

'We must pray,' said the King, lifting his tearful face. 'For all sinners, of which I am chief. Now and at the hour of our death, amen, amen.'

The surf crashed hungrily on the strip of crystalline sand, swirling away to leap against jagged rocks and fill the pools at their feet. Out to sea, above the zircon glitter, fulmars drifted against a sky pure as porcelain. Cormorants, like sentries waiting dourly to be relieved, sat on the ancient pinnacles of rock. The day was full of colour and change, wind and sun working subtle alteration on the red sandstone cliffs, the shining stones that littered the beach, the rock-roses and heather growing up the headland where the Bishop's Palace and the Cathedral of *Dewi Sant* stood. Both were built of the same indigenous stone, a breathtaking mosaic of lilac and saffron and dark grey. A lovely light fell over all: on the silken sand, the birds and flowers, the golden-haired man and the pale child who walked together, a little apart from the young priest and the servants going behind them beside the sea.

Here was a pebble of purple dolerite, almost perfectly round, and warm. Owen picked it up. A jewel for your Grace, he said, and laughed. Everyone thought them mad, to walk like this in the dangerous sea airs, but Henry had desired it.

Henry took the stone. At the same time he curled his fingers round Owen's so that they went hand in hand, the smooth orb chafing between their palms. The King exhaled, a long shudder. Safe, he thought. Safe, for a season. He glanced up covertly at the merry mouth, the bright, breeze-curled hair. The whole face so right, so comforting. Owen wore the Red Dragon of Cadwallader, the royal House of Wales, blazoned on his tabard, and a beautiful cloak. A few moments ago he had half-drawn this over Henry's shoulders lest he take cold. Safe. For how long?

Owen felt the jealous eyes of the young chaplain on his back. This priest had filled Henry with spiritual grace until it bordered on mania. Does he consider me a corrupting influence? A little smile touched his mouth. If he only knew! I'm the last in the world to harm this child. My life is his, if only for the blessed womb that bore him. That womb which I have twice filled and shall again. My lovely Edmund. My little Jasper. My beloved Cathryn. He squeezed the hand of Cathryn's son. He saw the dark eyes looking up, full of trouble.

'What is it?' he said softly. 'Your Grace is tired? Shall we return to the manor? You can play with my sons again. But beware Jasper. He may be only twelve months old but he's a monster. He bloodied my nose yesterday with his fist. He'll be a fighter, and Edmund a poet!'

Henry smiled dolorously. 'Jasper is a fair name. It comes from the Greek.'

'It's a stone,' said Owen, squeezing the hand again so that the pebble warmed between them. 'A hard, bright, crystalline stone, opaque and invincible. Jasper will grow up strong to serve your Grace.'

At thought of the future sudden irresponsible joy filled

him, shattering as the surf on the toothed rocks. And then he felt a tear fall on his hand and saw Henry's head bent. Joy was replaced by chill, glory by vainglory.

'I think your Grace *is* weary,' he said gently. 'I think you haven't yet recovered from that rigorous time in France.' He felt the hand in his grow icy. He knew that here, after nearly two years, was the nerve of agony, the canker that must be excised here on the bright sand and thrown to the greedy surf.

'They made you watch, didn't they?'

The black brimming eyes reminded him so much of Charles of Valois in his desperate madness. (*Ease my soul, Jacques.*) Silently they walked on and came to a broad flat rock, glittering with barnacles and veined with fossils. Owen sat down, and the King folded his trembling legs and perched beside him. A few yards away the escort hovered out of earshot, the priest's mantle blowing like a flag of doom.

'Talk, Harry,' said Owen. 'Talk it all away until it is gone for ever. Jeanne d'Arc is in Heaven now. Talk, and speed her on her way.'

'Master Tydier,' said Henry, trembling, 'you're the only one in the world who believes this. Save for that soldier – he cried out: "Before God, we have burned a saint!" A saint – ' he said bitterly ' – so that I could be crowned King of France! When all I wish is to enter the Church and be saved from my sins. *Mea culpa, mea maxima culpa . . .*' He hid his face, weeping. Owen longed to take him in his arms. The priest was watching. It would be unwise.

'Tell me,' he said, looking out to sea. Haltingly the dreadful detail unfolded. Everyone had expected to see a livid fanged demon brought into that square at Rouen. Instead they were faced by a pale young girl with the marks of torture and ravishment upon her. *La Pucelle* had female parts after all; several of her guards had discovered this fact, with some violence. She had gone to the pyre so bravely that many discovered shame for the first time in their lives.

'Not one sigh or cry. Only at the last when the wooden cross they had given her burst into flames, and then – *Jésus, Jésus,* and I longed to run away but my uncle held me still

398

and told me it was just and right and a sacrifice to my sove-
reignty in France . . .'

'Bedford was unkind?' said Owen, amazed.

'No, he's never unkind. Only full of policy. He said it was
expedient and unavoidable that the Church should have handed
her over to the secular arm, to himself and Philip of Burgundy.'

'Because she was a light and an inspiration.' Owen lifted
the King's hand to his lips. 'Harry,' he said tenderly, 'Harry,
bach! Bedford was right in his convictions. You see, she did
have power unknown to mortal man.'

'They said,' whispered Henry, 'that she could read men's
thoughts, that she picked out Charles in a crowded room where
he'd disguised himself – that she told him things none on earth
could have known . . .'

'Yes,' Owen said slowly. 'In my life I've known two people
like that. They're always either doomed or persecuted – or
else used. They can see beyond this world.'

'Where were they?' Henry lifted his face at last.

'Why, at home. At Glyndyfrdwy.' The Lord, with his dreams
and his horses of the wind. And Hywelis. Why do I still call
it home? My home is where Cathryn is. Yet I still call it home.

Henry was looking calmer. Owen went on: 'You must
remember always that Jeanne had to be discredited. Every rule
was broken to this end and there were, I believe, grave judicial
errors – provocation, fraud, false witness. Because she had
fired the morale of France to such a degree, coming as she did
from God, it was not enough to ridicule her power. She had
to be shown as a heretic. That's what I believe.'

Henry whispered: 'So . . . I was not the instrument of that
good woman's death?'

'Harry! You, who are without fault? Who told you this?'
Gloucester, he thought. He looked closely at the King's face.
'When did you hurt your mouth?'

'Gloucester speaks unkindly of my royal mother,' said
Henry with sudden wildness. 'I love my lady mother! I miss
her still, when I'm not with her. And I love you, Master
Tydier! Do you love me? Do you?'

Owen slid from the rock and went on his knees, spoiling
his finery beyond repair in the salt pool. He took the King's

399

hands between his and bent his brow, saying:

'I am your liege man for ever, most noble sovereign lord. I pledge you my life, and the lives of my descendants. To our last breath.'

'We thank you,' said Henry formally, and gave another shuddering sigh. 'Before we left London, I wrote a psalm, one night when I couldn't sleep. *Domine Jesu Christe, qui me creasti, redemisti, et preordinasti . . .*'

'Construe, your Grace, my Latin is inferior.'

'O Lord Jesus Christ, who hast created and redeemed me and hast brought me to that which now I am, Thou knowest what Thou wouldst do with me; do with me according to Thy will, for Thy tender mercy's sake. Amen.'

'Amen.' *Duw*, poor child, with such a fatalistic philosophy. He thought of his own sons: Edmund at two so fair and lively and already singing, and Jasper, brawling from the cradle. Sadness filled him, enhanced by the memory of those unstable Valois eyes. He rose.

'Look at the sea, Harry. If we could walk across that blue and green and white – what sights we'd see – mermen and dragons and ghostly ships and Neptune roaring up to salute us with his trident, and a million fishes swimming to form his crown –' he heard the rare, almost painful laughter beginning – 'and then of course' (ruefully) 'we should fall off the edge of the world.'

'It's time for his Grace's private prayers.' The young priest, crow-gaunt, was beside them, leading the King away. More prayers, thought Owen, relinquishing him. Prayers won't save that one. (What a heathen I am.) Only love. Then he heard the sound of more laughter, rich and glorious this time, and saw his Cathryn coming along the beach. Quite the carline wife, with her skirts held up, her hair blowing. The most sparkling thing on the shimmering bay. The little white dog was leaping beside her, and her women were panting to keep up. Edmund, blue-eyed, golden-haired Edmund, rode high in Guillemot's arms. Jasper, with his fierce little dark face, was, against Joanna Troutbeck's agitated breast, trying to wriggle out of a fur robe. Owen went forward and took him. The women's protests rose like the seabirds: it's too cold, against nature, they will die from these airs! And his own woman, crying: 'Pouf! Let them breathe deep, it's wonderful!' coming closer, now leading Edmund by the hand. The entourage drew away with disapproving shrugs at this madness. Edmund's eyes were fixed wonderingly on the myriad shells at his feet. 'Play, then, *bébé*,' she said, releasing him.

He hadn't seen her all day. He hadn't been with her as much as he would have liked lately. Not half as much. A further discretion had been forced upon them by the presence of the King and his servants. He set Jasper on the flat rock. He kissed the tiny furious face. He took Cathryn's hands. He looked down at them. She still cuts her nails very short, he thought. He remembered the hands, the nails of Charles of Valois, like talons, the talons of a wild injured hawk. He understood this severe cutting of her nails.

'*R'wy'n dy garu di*,' he said. '*Je t'aime, mignonne.* I love you, my sweet darling.'

'Your hose is all dirty,' she said. 'You look a villain.'

'I've been kneeling. A private oath. Nothing to do with you, Cathryn. What mischief have you been up to?'

The little dog frisked at the edge of the waves, leaving tiny trefoil prints instantly smoothed by the sea's soft iron. Jasper crawled along the rock.

'I have been to see the Bishop of St David's. He is *gentil*, we talked of Archbishop Chichele and he showed me the building that Chichele did for Harry. The carving's beautiful. And he told me the legend of *Dewi Sant*. Did you know that St David brought little fires from heaven? To shine round those who are soon to die?' And she laughed. 'To remind mankind of their mortality!'

Owen said: 'Yes. I know.'

'Also we spoke of the Cardinal. Beaufort told the Bishop I was coming here.'

'Beaufort approves,' he said. 'This *congé* was one more little shaft against Gloucester.'

Gloucester. They had kept away from Pembroke Castle; it belonged to Gloucester.

'We're far from home,' she said.

'But we must go back.' Back to Hertford. Privacy. The

maids were coming to take the children, still convinced that they would meet their death through the mad sea airs. Soon we'll be going home. Not Glyndyfrdwy. *Home.* He drew her behind a great rock. Out of the sight of the others.

'Our home is in one another.' He held her very tightly; she fitted her body to his. He drank the salt from her lips, kissing her until she sighed for breath. The maids were bearing away the children. She twisted in his arms to look after them.

'They are the most beautiful children in Christendom,' she said.

He released her for a moment. He must speak to her about Harry. Poor tormented Harry. Gloucester had struck him. But not now. Not today, when she was so happy. Later. Much later. He came back to embrace her again, touching her soft breast, closing his eyes against her sea-scented hair, wrapped in the essence of the deathless dream. The entourage was disappearing – the children, the priest, the servants, the King. This was such a lovely little sunbright cove, flanked by the great purple and saffron rocks. A cave, made magical by shadow and sunlight. He took her hand, began to walk with her towards the mouth of the cave. He looked back at her once.

'You are mad,' she said.

'See, the sand is dry. My cloak's warm. Everyone's gone.'

'You are truly mad, *cariad*,' she said. The sand was dry, silk-soft.

'Yes,' he said, straight-faced. 'I was kicked on the head. By a horse. At Corbie. Ah, lie back . . . Cathryn . . . *fy nghariad.* My sweet love.'

Such a beautiful place, he thought, lost in the dream. This will be the most beautiful of all our children. He laughed softly; the roar of the surf tore his laugh away and flung it into the teeth of destiny. Tempting it.

Hywelis dampened the fire. The smoke rose ochre and ebony, diminished to pearl. It wafted about the ruined chamber. Madog, fourth of his line, was irritated by the fumes – he got up and strolled away.

'My father,' she said softly, kneeling. 'Are you pleased with me?'

His face appeared. He looked so young. Davydd ap Llewellyn ap Hywel was with him, both eyes clear and bright. He was smiling. Owain Glyn Dŵr was smiling. She had to bend very close, her own eyes streaming, to hear their words. The barrier between the spheres made them very faint.

'I am well pleased. Have I not returned to you the torque of Maelor?'

She touched her neck. The feel of the heavy gold was reassuring. She had found it in moonlight, washed, after all the years, from the mountain stream into the peat-hag. She had needed it last night; the black one had come again. Furious beyond belief, strong as a thousand devils. So far Hywelis was the stronger. The black one was envenomed by Edmund, by his health and beauty. This morning Hywelis had noticed a few white threads in her red hair. The black one had come in the form of a furred serpent. So strong.

'Father,' she said. 'My father.'

'Continue, Hywelis.' The fine falcon's face, so young, smiled at her. 'Breed your foxes, girl. Draw your pentacles and say the charms I give you. Have I not returned the torque of Maelor?'

'Never lose sight of the aim,' said Davy Gam. Both eyes so clear and bright. 'Edmund is the one. *Duw a'n bendithio*. God bless us.'

Wales shall rule England. They said it together. The smoke swirled and filled Hywelis's eyes with pain.

'Help me,' she said. 'Help me, against the black one, Eleanor of Gloucester.'

'We will help you.' Their voices were faint. 'Be brave.'

'I don't want to die!' she cried. Madog started to howl. 'I want to live, until he comes to me again!'

'We are with you,' the faintness said. 'He will come, but not yet. Be brave.'

Summer came. Summer passed. And in summer, Humphrey,

at Windsor, stood admiring himself in the reflected twinkle of the mullioned window. He wore a new velvet jupon and mantle so richly red it pained the eyes. His soft black hat was powdered with lilies; across his chest was the gold Lancastrian collar of SS's. All this elegance was marred somewhat by an uncomfortable tightness at his waist. But let who dared say he was becoming stout! His valets, in any event, had all but swooned with admiration. It was a day for careful rejoicing. Oh, Beaufort, Beaufort, he thought. As I wax, so shall you wane!

The long feud had burgeoned, a black growth, and Humphrey had applied the clyster, flushing out Beaufort's treachery and greed into the sight of men. He thought: I have actually called him traitor before the Council, and have heard the murmurs of assent. How are the mighty fallen, Beaufort! It was I who made the Council aware of your monstrous acquisitiveness. It was I who, while you were away in Calais, drew attention to your misuse of the Statute of Praemunire, your angling for Papal Bulls so as to retain all your ecclesiastical preferment in England. Your discontent with the red hat, your illegal clinging to the See of Winchester . . . not to mention the Crown jewels! He laughed at his own thoughts. The young man who sat reading at the table behind him looked up, smiled a faint, cynical smile, and resumed his book.

The joy and satisfaction it had given Humphrey to snatch the greater part of the royal gems and plate from Beaufort's cache at Sandwich was past telling. How eager the Cardinal had been to lend incalculable sums to Parliament in a desperate measure to redeem and ingratiate himself! but Beaufort would never again be trusted. Most wonderful of all: Humphrey of Gloucester now led the Council. I waited, he thought. Though my impotent fury half wore me out, I waited. Just as Harry did until cities fell. Attrition never fails. And now, save for my brother of Bedford, I am the most powerful man in the realm.

'Beautiful,' said the voice behind him, as if the mind to whom it belonged had been accompanying his bubbling thoughts. He turned. Richard of York closed the book and carefully folded it in layers of silk.

'The *Astrolabe*? Or the *Legend of Good Women*?' Humphrey could again, at last, appreciate Chaucer's work.

'Both,' said Richard. 'Weren't they inspired by his travels in Italy?'

'You may borrow them if you like,' said Humphrey. Richard of York bowed. The reflected glow of Gloucester's mantle rosied his face. It was a short strong keen face with fine bones and an unusually hard jawline, as if his teeth were permanently clenched. The eyes were a bright light blue, forceful and direct.

'You'll keep them safe,' said Humphrey. 'Are you going up to Westmorland? Your betrothed lady will enjoy reading them. They get little in the way of culture in the North, I imagine.'

'Yes,' said Richard. 'I wrote to her from Calais.' His hard face softened for an instant. 'But naturally my main purpose here is to see your Grace, and to return the King.'

'How was he in Calais?'

Richard said: 'As usual. Everything seems rather too much for him. But he's safely back, and at his prayers.'

'Let's have some wine,' said Humphrey. Richard poured two full goblets from a tall gold flagon. Gloucester sat down opposite him, and raised his cup.

'Sink our enemies,' he said, and drank.

'From what I hear,' said Richard with a little smile, 'most of yours are already *en perdition*!'

'Ah, have a care, Dick,' said Humphrey. 'Some. Not all. Beaufort has lost face greatly. But de la Pole . . .'

'Oh, Suffolk!' said Richard of York. 'Yes, indeed. He's the Cardinal's man and trades on his long history of martial closeness to the crown. My lord, I saw him in Calais. He advocates the new Treaty – this Treaty that is planned for Arras, if Burgundy and Armagnac keep the promises they have sworn together.'

'Is it possible?' said Gloucester incredulously. He refilled his gold goblet and took a great swig. 'Did that witch-woman do so much damage that the feuding nobility of France cluster together like children frightened of the dark?'

'France is sick,' said Richard cryptically. 'The *écorcheurs* still roam at large. Thousands of mad ragged wretches – some scarcely out of childhood – burning and looting and raising havoc, all in Jeanne d'Arc's name. The poison's within. The country's crazy. Even Philip and Charles realize that unity is now the only hope.'

'And the Treaty of Troyes no longer exists!'

'Ay. Pope Eugenius declared it null and void, and the Fathers of Basle now recognize Charles the Seventh as rightful King. Only a marriage between the nations will give us back our foothold . . .'

'How history repeats itself!' said Humphrey bitterly. 'Drink up, Dick. Tell me more.'

'Philip is mellowing in his age,' said York. 'I wouldn't say he has forgiven Armagnac, but he's ready to forget. He demands reparation – thousands in gold spent on Masses for Jean sans Peur, his assassins found and punished (most of them are dead anyway) – and full expiation made for that day at Montereau. Charles attempts with some success to exonerate himself. He says he was young and led astray by false companions. And Philip is not the man he was. He bestows his new Order of the Golden Fleece willy-nilly – even on some Armagnacs. The Ram no longer butts and batters. All the lands that England and Burgundy won together will be thrown back into the common pool. Sweet Jesus!' he said in sudden disgust. 'All those decades of war, those mighty families decimated, for nothing.' He spat on Humphrey's fine Turkey rug, apologized, and said: 'It'll kill my lord of Bedford, all this.'

'You think so?' said Gloucester slowly.

'Well, it's trouble on trouble. He was most distressed over the death of Anne, his wife. We couldn't comfort him for months.'

'And with her went our last link with Burgundy,' said Humphrey morosely. By now he was slightly drunk, his mood went up and down. He said, after a moment:

'You're a good and useful subject, Dick. How would you like to be the King's lieutenant in France? He favours you, doesn't he?'

'It's more honour than I deserve, your Grace. And yes,

he does.' And he trusts me too, he thought. Because I have the wit to be kind and sympathetic to his fancies. Not like you. You old devil! Then smoothly he returned to the topic of French policies.

'They're desperately concerned to have Charles of Orléans back – God's life! – ' he laughed – 'it will be twenty years since he was imprisoned. Suffolk says . . .'

'What does Suffolk say?' said Humphrey heavily. The flagon was almost empty.

'Suffolk, as chief warden of Orléans's captivity, declares it will need the ransom of five kings to secure the Duke's release. Though Orléans, I gather, is far from unhappy. He has at least two high-born mistresses, and writes poems to them. Let's hope he doesn't get their names mixed up.'

'Dick,' said Humphrey, no longer listening, 'about the King. Henry must marry – ' he belched – 'one of Charles's daughters.'

'I'd already heard that was what you had in mind. But,' he said delicately, 'Prince Louis is still heir to the French throne. Ten years old, ugly as sin, but strong. However, you know best. My lord of Bedford will hate the thought of such an alliance!'

'It will kill him,' said Humphrey thickly. He tipped his winecup over, cursed, and rang a little silver bell as if he loathed it. A page mopped up and brought more wine and withdrew. The two men sat silent. Richard of York watched Gloucester closely. Yes, my lord. I know well how much your mind frets over thrones and kingships. How much you've craved the crown of England for yourself. And, by sweet Christ Jesus, so do I!

Soon, he would come into his vast inheritance, the proud acres of York, the dukedom's northern holdings and his father's entailed lands not to mention the vast Mortimer estates due to him through his mother Anne, whose brother had died childless years ago. His square jaw tightened as he looked at Gloucester's lax scarlet form. I am a king's councillor. I shall be king's lieutenant. But by right I *am* a king. Through my undeniable claim which none has ever taken seriously. They will. I am the direct descendant, on the distaff side, of the third Edward. Now I pay lip service to this bully of Lancaster. But I'll stake my claim or die in the attempt. And I have a woman behind me. Once again the taut Plantagenet face softened as he thought her name. Cicely Neville. The Rose of Raby, waiting for him now in Westmorland. Cicely with her panther's heart and her mind like finest Nuremberg steel. Centuries of high Norman blood roaring in her veins (and his); beauty to make the pulse of even the blind beat faster. His true and chosen mate. The future mother of kings. Of this he was as sure as if a sybil had spoken it. With Cicely, he thought for the thousandth time, I can achieve the world. The thoughts made his face hot. He said lightly:

'This is good drinking and good company, my lord. Is there more you wish from me? You've seen the despatches?'

But venom was creeping over Gloucester; the wine worked in his brain.

'So, Dick,' he said with contempt, 'you think the King is old enough to take a wife?'

'He's in his twelfth year,' said York, and shrugged. 'Though he's passing fond of his mother still. We came by Hertford so he could call on her.'

And he smiled at the remembrance of what he had seen. The strange, secret ménage at Hertford, a little world, fraught with tremors of an unstable ecstasy that one could almost touch. He had been fascinated, loath to leave, especially with Henry in tears again, clinging to the Queen-Dowager and to Master Tydier, and the tumultuous ambience of love had made him think of Cicely, his Rose, his own lieutenant in the cause . . .

'You saw his mother,' said Gloucester. In his hand his goblet felt pliant, as if he could crush the soft gold shapeless. 'What of her?'

Richard didn't answer for a moment. Master Tydier seemed on very familiar terms with the King. '*Paid a llefain, Harry, bach!*' he'd said, looking at the boy with those strange eyes, and the tears had ceased. As for Katherine . . . he smiled again.

'Well,' he said. He shot a little glance at Gloucester under his lashes, man to man. He laughed. 'Totally given over to the pleasures of Eros, I'd say. The children are very comely, the two little boys . . .'

The winecup did bend. Two dents appeared on either side. Humphrey said hoarsely: 'Two boys? She has children?'

Richard swallowed his surprise. He said with great diplomacy:

'I know that your Grace sees nothing of the Queen-Dowager these days . . . that would explain . . . I was aware, however, for the King speaks often of his half-brothers, to whom he seems attached. There was, I believe, another child, a girl, Margaret. About a year ago. But she died soon after birth.'

A long silence, during which an unkindness of ravens set up a barking in the trees outside, and Gloucester studied his winecup. Richard watched. He felt the quivering indrawn rage, as surely as he had felt the tremors of passion at Hertford. Now why? he thought, intrigued. Spleen at being made to look ridiculous? Fear that two little bastard boys find favour with our future sovereign? Or – and this perhaps unlikely – mere male jealousy? For Katherine is a peach, a prize. I'll try that one, just for bravado. Like poking a stick into a nest of hornets.

'I must say,' he remarked casually, 'that Master Owen Tydier looks very fine. Welsh wildman he may be, but, by Christ's bones! I swear he must be the handsomest man in England!'

And sat back and waited, holding his breath, and would have been disappointed save for the sight of a vein galloping uncontrolled in Humphrey's temple. Christ! he'll have a stroke, thought Richard with interest. Gloucester rose, and walked to the window. He said, looking out:

'The woman is a disgrace. She profanes Harry's blessed memory. She must be mad, like all Valois.' Then he said: 'How does she seem?'

Richard had also risen from his chair. 'My lord, you'll soon have the opportunity to see for yourself. I passed her equipage on the road.'

And took his farewells and bowed out, graceful, hard as a diamond. He listened for an instant outside, to hear the little oath and the flung goblet's tinsel note. Then made his way swiftly from the palace. Time I was away. Westmorland now,

409

and the face and voice of the Rose, and beauty and strength in the plans for the House of York to live for ever.

Gloucester kept Katherine waiting for half an hour after her arrival. The Duchesses flitted in and out of the antechamber, greeting her with light kisses and meaningless courtesies. She had seen none of them for a long time. She felt the vibrations of their subtle curiosity. The gown, your Grace, the azure and gold, *ravissante*. But your Grace still has the cough, *hélas*! She wanted to say: this is the first time I've coughed in months and months. It's because he keeps me waiting. The longer I wait the more I cough. Silently she rehearsed the conversation, wondering how best to put him off balance when he came. My lord, I have tried seven times to see you. My lord, what are these rumours I hear of a match for the King with his cousin of France? My lord, I understand it is your custom to persecute my son; he weeps overmuch. I command that this ceases forthwith . . . *He struck him. Owen told me.*

The dry spasms in her throat continued. One of the Duchesses brought her a drink, admiring her headdress, a little pale-blue cap crowned with two snowy horns of veiling. Owen chose my dress for today. He didn't want me to come. I started coughing, it worried him. He had Guillemot brew me some elecampane, the yellow flower. The leech-women at Glyndyfrdwy call it *marchalan*. Now, how to begin with my dear brother-in-law? Do I still fear him? Yes. No, I fear nothing these days. Owen has taught me not to fear. He has taught me to show passion, and anger; he has released my inner self. Yet I still cough, waiting for Humphrey. Think of something else – quickly. That's what Owen always says. When you are in a difficult situation, a static situation like this, think of something interesting, or challenging, or beautiful. There are so many beautiful things I can think of, while waiting for Humphrey.

Owen's body. He must be nearing forty, but his body has cheated the years. It is still as strong and slender, as the first time I ever set eyes on it. Last week he had come to the chamber where she was to ask her something; he had been rather carelessly attired, in a green robe tied at the waist and little

410

else. She had untied the robe and put her hands round his waist. The light had touched his honey flesh against which her own always looked so pale. The supple dancer's thighs, with the old knife-scar like a personal insignia. The broad singer's chest upon which the gold hair grew lightly in the form of a cross, and at its base the flat belly with two hard bands of muscle like those in the long smooth back. She loved his back. On either side of his spine there were two tiny indentations. She had stroked them, inside the robe. His immediate, searing response. The shining mountain – he took her there at once. The flowers more beautiful, the birds more eloquent, the snow melting. She had let out such a cry that Huw and Caradoc had come hammering on the door, thinking she was taken ill. They were utterly loyal, those two, good boys. Always merry. Unlike many here at Windsor. On entering the precincts she had met Waterton, the late King's valet, and he had looked at her even while he knelt in duty, with a look of extraordinary venom. Poor Robert, she thought. Being in Humphrey's service, as he now was, was enough to embitter anyone.

The ménage at Hertford was some days like a madhouse. Everyone went about singing. Olwen and her four white clovers. A funny ditty Guillemot had on her mind – The Wife of Usher's Well, who had three stout and stalwart sons and sent them o'er the sea. They returned as ghosts, dressed in the bark from the tree that grows in Paradise . . . not a funny song, a sad song. Guillemot was the best nursemaid anyone could have – she loved Edmund and Jasper as her own. They were safe with her. All the servants were trustworthy, happy. The steward was very old. The chaplain older still. The maids were young. There was the infection of romance throughout the manor. Some of the servants called Owen 'My lord' – much to his disgust. Many of the servants thought that Owen and she were married. Nothing was said to discourage them. Owen had a fierce temper. It never lasted. They quarrelled over two things only; marriage (Marry me, please marry me, Cathryn!) – and money. Last week he had discovered her ploy of giving Huw money in secret to meet his master's expenses. He had shouted at her. She had slapped his face. I knocked him down, she thought, and bent her head to hide a smile. I caught him

411

off balance. He fell in the hearth. Happily the fire was out. He pulled me down into the ashes and rolled on me. We quarrelled no more that day.

He was worried lest I conceive too soon after the death of Margaret. Poor sweet little Margaret, the baby bud. He wept more than I did over that. I comforted him. I comforted him too well. Another miscarriage. The midwives are shocked senseless when he insists on being with me. No place for men. Unprecedented. But he never stays long; it frightens him. He says it's worse than Agincourt. That's strange. Love is strange.

I love the winter, the nights when we retire early and bolt the door. We leave the servants to their own devices. So long as they build a big fire in our chamber. Then I sit in my low chair and he sits at my feet with his lute. He sings all my favourite songs, the sad ones, the merry ones, the songs of love. Then he puts his lute aside and lays his head in my lap. I stroke his beautiful hair. The wolfskin in front of the fire is becoming worn. Our one side is scorched by the fire, our other side frozen by the draught. All the warmth lies in between. And he holds my head and strokes the hair at my temples and again and again we reinforce our private oath. *Am byth*, Cathryn. *Toujours*, Owen. For ever. For ever. Beyond life.

These last ten years of my life are worth all the rest. If I had to give up the rest of my life for these last ten years, I would sacrifice it, smiling. The years go by so swiftly.

We are trying to make another child. Perhaps next winter in the naked, flickering, wolfskin firelight . . . not his fault. Mine? Did Cobham's elixir really harm me, I wonder? No, think of something beautiful. The precious summers and springs and winters, the shining mountain top, the flowers kissed by the melting snow . . . the shameless tenderness and lust. Ah, my love. Her heart was beating rapidly. She lifted her face, thought-enraptured, as Humphrey entered the room. He caught the full force of her look, and was filled with heat and hatred.

He was flushed, wine-belly rolling, splendidly scarlet, smiling, holding out his hands, greeting her: '*Ma chère sœur!*' He drew her with him into the inner chamber. Dismay at the realization that they were completely alone together robbed her of her proud opening gambit. She said, her voice thin and uncertain:

'My lord, I must send for my servants. They can attend us.'

He laughed. 'I've sent them below, dear Katherine. To get some food into their bellies. They look a meagre company!' Her heart dipped. Huw and Caradoc would be teased by the English pages, and the women intimidated by the Duchesses. Humphrey's eyes moved over her. She was wearing a double string of pearls. Little Harry had brought them for her some time ago. Gloucester touched them with one finger, admiringly.

'Ah,' he said, squinting at them like a gemsmith. 'A gift from the King's Grace!' His eyes, she noted, were pouched with fat. Suddenly she thought: he looks *enceinte*! at least five months gone. She smiled irrepressibly. Humphrey's expression changed.

'A million pardons, I kept you waiting. I've been delayed in the stables. I have a horse running next week at Smithfield. A beautiful beast; its trainer is an imbecile. You should come to the races, Katherine, you'd enjoy it.'

Her smile vanished. 'My lord,' she said, and out it came, though by no means as forcefully as she had planned, 'I have tried seven times to see you.'

'*Dommage!*' he answered. 'The pleasure I have missed. But you know I've been to France again, and then there was the endowment of my library at Oxford University . . . various affairs. I'm flattered you wished to see me.' He moved to the table to pour wine; she could no longer see his face. The cough threatened again; her next words were cut off by the dreadful itch. Humphrey came back and set a goblet near her hand, with a little dish of comfits.

'They really are magnificent pearls,' he said. 'Aren't they part of the stolen revenues . . . Cardinal Beaufort, that misguided prelate!'

To fight the cough, she sipped wine. It was so strong that she wondered whether Cobham had been at it with her herbal additives. She said: 'Cardinal Beaufort has always been a good friend to me and to the King's Grace.'

To her amazement Humphrey went on his knees, kissing

413

her hand. 'Oh, Katherine!' he said. 'Once you and I were such good friends!'

I remember none of that, she thought. I remember how you stole my confidence, with Harry in France, and Eleanor your accomplice, how you stole and misused my little son! She glared down proudly at him. Unperturbed he continued, each word more outrageous to her ears.

'You should have more than mere pearls, Madame,' he said thickly. His hot hand clung. He's drunk, she thought. But this is more than drunkenness. I don't like it. 'Jewels to befit you, bestowed by a rich lord who I may not, in modesty, name . . . oh, Katherine,' he said, like a confessor heartbroken by the hearing of some ghastly crime: 'Why do you hide yourself away with evil companions?'

She snatched her hand away. He pursued her, ridiculous on his knees, talking, eyes and voice hot, his scarlet gown a heavy blaze.

'This Tydier!' as if he scolded a child. 'He cannot have more than twenty pounds a year. Do you still maintain him from your Privy Purse?'

Unease gave way to anger. She said, her lips tight:

'I give away what is mine. I still have my portion from the late King's dower. You have no jurisdiction over that!'

'But I could augment that portion,' he said softly. He stared at her thighs. The blue gown was quivering under her tension and anger. 'You would want for nothing. Return to court, Katherine.'

Wildly at last she found her original purpose, the high words that should have crushed him at the start.

'We are away from the subject. I have come to demand full knowledge of the King's proposed betrothal. And more, I've come to demand that you cease persecuting my son!'

He rose. He smiled. His scarlet mantle pained her eyes. He said:

'But which son, Madame? You cannot mean Henry, for my protectorate has lapsed. Which son? I gather you have two!'

Shock launched the cough. Shock gave it vigour, it shook her as a hound shakes a rat. It weakened her bones; she trembled. Humphrey came near, his intent unmistakable. He said softly: 'You see, I understand. You are very foolish. But I forgive your folly. You were married, you were bereaved. You felt a certain lack. You were young. Return to court, *ma chère sœur*, and you will lack nothing. Nothing.'

She stepped back. He came on, a billowing scarlet hill. She thought: this isn't happening. The words of James of Scotland came back in a flash – 'Has he ever paid court to you, Katherine?' He pressed her back as far as the window. Gasping, coughing, she said: 'I shall complain to my lord of Bedford about this. I shall speak to the Cardinal . . .' and heard Humphrey laugh in a kind of pity, and smelled his winey breath, and felt the window-seat behind her, and then his seeking mouth on hers and his hands primed to grope and ravish. Unbelieving rage took her, brilliant cleansing rage, and she thought: this is how women hostages suffer in war, and was at one with them and reacted as they did, wrenching her mouth away and striking with a clenched fist, straight to the mark. She always wore the ring of heavy Welsh gold that Owen had given her. It split Humphrey's left eyebrow to the bone. And she swore: French gutter-language learned from Gaspard the stableman through Louis her brother all those years ago and suddenly resurrected; obscene Welsh insults taught her by Owen in play. Blood jetted and ran into Gloucester's eye and trickled richer than the scarlet robe.

He let her go. 'Harlot!' he said. 'You are truly your mother's daughter!'

And she screamed at him, aiming another swinging blow: 'I strike you, my lord! As you struck my son!'

And he said, dabbing his face with a linen square, looking suddenly old and dangerous beyond words:

'Look to all your sons, Madame. And to your baseborn paramour. And to yourself. Sweet Christ! you have made yourself a deadly foe this day!'

She stood still, trembling, with a deep sickly pain inside her. Humphrey gulped down a cup of wine, turning his back, still pressing the linen to his eye. The door opened and Eleanor Cobham came in.

'Your Grace. My lord.' She doubled her dark weasel body in obeisance, as cool as if she had found them in cordiality.

She gauged the throbbing anger and its cause immediately. Others might have been jealous. Eleanor Cobham cared nothing for the flesh, unless it were the carrion of an enemy.

'Dinner,' she said. 'It's past the hour. Will your Grace permit . . .'

Katherine walked from the chamber without a word, steadily enough. It was only when she reached her carriage waiting in the courtyard, that the rage ebbed into weakness. She rested in Guillemot's arms all the way back home. A small splash of Humphrey's blood was drying on her neck.

Gloucester said: 'I'll have them. I'll have them. By Christ's blessed crown. That crazy whore to a nunnery, and the Welsh scum thrown in the deepest jail in England.' He turned on Eleanor. 'You! You once promised me kingdoms! Now give me vengeance!'

'You shall have it. That I do promise.'

His head ached from Katherine's blows. Jangling thoughts raced repetitively within. Bedford had warned him long ago never to harass the Queen-Dowager. Beaufort turns a blind eye to her heresies, her fornications. But Beaufort's star is falling. And Bedford . . .

'. . . is mortal,' he said aloud.

'I have a little news of Bedford,' said Eleanor, biting into a comfit. 'He is assuaged of his grief over Anne. In Calais he has met with Jacquetta de St Pol, who, although in love with the commoner Sir Richard Woodville, would be willing to advance herself through marriage with the royal house. And then . . .'

'Then what?' He ached with fury, was curious and confused.

'And then my lord of Bedford may begin to count his days,' said Eleanor. 'For Jacquetta and I are sisters.'

'Sisters?' he said dully. 'How can that be, Nell?'

'Sisters in skill.' And Eleanor showed her little teeth in a terrible smile.

She had never seen anyone turn so white as he, when she told him. With all colour gone from his mouth and cheeks, his bones stood out clearly, and for a moment she saw how he would look when he was old, and they would still be lovers.

Two ancient lovers. He's going to faint, she thought. But he did not; he was controlled, and looked after her, taking off her headdress and loosening her gown so she could breathe more easily, soothing the cough with medicine, then holding her to him until the trembling became intermittent. Only then did he draw the covers over her on the bed and get up.

'Where are you going? Don't leave me.'

He smiled. A ghastly, pleasant smile.

'I'm going to kill him.' He went to an arms chest and took out a sword. It was once the property of Davy Gam and had been willed to him. He kept it oiled and cherished. It had not been used since his brush with the Lombards when he was wounded, the same year that he and she came together. He took his baselard from his belt and carefully felt its edge. He went to the door; he shouted for Huw to saddle his horse.

She found herself able to rise from the bed, and cross the room, and close the door and put her back against it. She pressed hard against the door. He frowned at her.

'Get out of my way. Out of my way, *cariad*.'

He took her shoulders and tried to prise her away from the door. She stood firm, gasping a little as he hurt her. She suffered the hurt like a caress. She stared into his eyes. He looked at Gloucester's blood splashed on her neck, then back to her eyes. For the first time she was the stronger of the two.

'They'll hang you within a day,' she said. 'Leave this house and you take my life with you.' He drew his sword.

'I'm going to kill him,' he said. 'Let me end him. *Annwyl Crist!* Let me drink his blood!' He bent and deliberately licked the blood from her neck. She shivered; she thought – it's turned him mad. She put her arms round him. She unsheathed the baselard and threw it on the floor. The sword drooped in his hand.

'I'm going to kill him,' he said with great misery.

'No, my love. Stay with me.' She called him *bach*, little one. His face was still ghastly.

'I shall challenge him then,' he said. She took him across the room, forced him to sit with her on the bed. He was as rigid as a corpse. But she had stopped trembling.

'No harm was done to me,' she said. 'You cannot challenge him. Only knights can meet in chivalry.'

She took his head against her breast and stroked his hair and felt his tears. She became frightened again. He was so strong; how violently the strong are shattered. They break, but they do not bend. My love. This awful truth, hurting him so.

'He's not worth your steel! Someone will kill him one day! He collects enemies . . .'

He raised his face. 'He is *not* worth my steel! I may be no English knight, but I am of a race of great Welsh princes.' It was not often he talked like this. He laughed bitterly and swore. It was a relief to hear him swear. 'To think that Davy died on Artois plain and I risked my life, to save that swine!'

She stroked his face. As he grew calmer, she became less calm. Her own stroking hands looked so frail, as if she could almost see through bones and skin.

'There's something I would rather be than the greatest knight,' he said. 'Your husband. With rights to defend you, my wife. Cathryn. Oh, my wife.'

'I am your wife. You know it.'

The firelit oath. The feather bed. The flowery mountain. The words repeated over and over. The pact and pledge that none could break. *Am byth. Toujours.* For ever. For ever.

'Lie down with me,' she said.

'I always envied Harry,' he said, in her arms. 'God rest him. You and he were man and wife.'

'None shall marry the Queen-Dowager. You know that, too.'

'*Y diafol!*' he sat up violently. 'Devil damn that! Once you spoke of risks, hazards. We've gone beyond risk and hazard. We've gone beyond everything. The Act against the Welsh has been repealed. I am regarded *sicut verus anglicus ligeus*. I can hold privilege. You are the privilege. Nothing else.'

'I promised Bedford. I swore discretion. He has befriended me. He spoke of ruin and danger to us both if I disobeyed. I am your woman. I bear your children. I belong to you. What more is there?'

'A legal ceremony,' he said stubbornly. 'If only in secret –

better than nothing. Your chaplain . . . Cathryn, please.'

She was looking very tired, lying there. She said: 'I feel . . . Owen. Do you see anything strange about my hands? They look . . . *translucides* . . .'

He was alarmed. Charles of Valois. Shocked into mania. He said quickly: 'No. Beautiful, strong hands. Fierce hands. Full of temper and grace. Look at their perfection. Give me that hand in marriage. That one.'

The envy of Harry had been strongly re-awakened, this awful day. She was silent. An almost mortal bitterness gripped him. He said:

'Cathryn. I must ask you. I've never asked you. I don't ask if you loved Harry, I know you did. But did you love him better than me?'

Still she said nothing. Thought and memory lapped her. She made no conscious effort to seek conclusion. It was there, final, blinding.

King Henry Plantagenet of Lancaster, descendant of the most ancient Norman line. Owen ap Meredyth ap Tydier, Esquire, whose mystic line stretched back even further. The only two men she had known, and one of them unique.

She thought of the jewels, the words, the eight white horses. The raging welcome ashore at Dover, the close-held nights, the pain, the pity, the long absences, the silver effigy. The promises, vows and confidences. The security, the loss. And the flame of Culhwch, dancing in her soul, something not of this world, incomparable.

She said: 'I loved Harry dearly. He was my harbour. But you are my storm. He was a distant beacon. But you are my light, my star. Beyond life. Beyond death. Beyond time.'

They lay quiet, embraced. A perfect moment; something far outside the spheres mocked it and marked it down.

The door opened. Edmund appeared, weeping. Golden Edmund, who never cried. He had the torn body of the white dog in his arms. One of the big hounds, he said, had mistaken it for prey.

On the Feast of St Augustine, 1435, the merest hint of autumn

419

was crisping about the walls of the White Tower. Within its Chapel of St John, the King knelt in prayer. The holy rites had long since finished but he remained, his figure dwarfed by the creamy Corinthian pillars and high barrel vault with its two tiers of arcaded windows through which a gleam from outside filtered and was blocked by shadows. He had much private praying to accomplish. He hated the Tower of London, where he was temporarily lodged; he sensed its macabre implacability. But he was no longer a child; he was nearly thirteen, nearly of age. And he loved the chapel, its rich-garbed credenza reflecting the solid milky stone, the magical high altar above which hung Life in Death, with wounds of garnet blood. He tugged away the faldstool and knelt on cold flags, rejoicing in the ache that attacked his knees. He looked ardently towards the altar.

'Sweetest Lord Jesu!' He bowed his head.

From his doublet breast, a distracting odour arose. It was the perfume from his mother's embrace. She had been gone some hours but her essence clung, softening the acrid incense that hung about the chapel. She had held him so tightly, kissing his forehead. For the first time he had felt that he was her champion and protector, not the other way about. He would pray for her first. 'O Christ, redeem her sins with Thy Precious Blood,' he began, and even to him this sounded false, presumptuous, wrong, as he remembered her kindness, her pure and loving eyes. 'O sweet Christ Jesu, protect her from all evil,' he said instead. 'Deliver her from all sorrow, sickness, distress of mind or estate, and from all perils in which she may stand.'

She had been so pleased with the magnificent ruby ring he had given her. Bedford had sent it by courier from Rouen with instructions that the Queen-Dowager should have it – as if there was any danger of Henry keeping it for himself! Before visiting him at the Tower she had written to ask if it was convenient. That was their little code – was Humphrey in London? And Humphrey was in France again, so all was well. God be thanked, thought Henry, and was instantly so ashamed that he prostrated himself before the altar.

'Almighty and most merciful God, I ask thy blessing upon the person of my uncle, Humphrey, Duke of Gloucester.

Bestow upon him all felicity, pardon and peace. Preserve and deliver Humphrey thy servant from all trouble and adversity, for the love of Thy blessed Son, our Saviour and Redeemer.'

Had not Christ said bless them that curse you? He reared from his prone posture and stared at the livid face, the eyes full of painted tears and blood, the agonized twist of the mouth. He felt in his own hands and feet the insupportable hurts of the nails. The figure swam in his sight, became three-dimensional and began to swoop and descend through shadows from its apogee of pain . . . he closed his eyes in ecstasy and fear.

His mother had petitioned a private audience. He had seen her in his little chantry where they had knelt shoulder to shoulder, their voices masked by the thin ethereal notes of the choristers. It took a little time for her to reveal her request, all the while addressing him formally. My liege. Scarcely anyone called him Henry now, let alone Harry, and certainly no one ever called him Harry, *bach*! Yes, he had asked her, with uneasy tenderness, how Owen was, thinking that all whom he loved seemed to vanish from his life. Even Richard of York was seldom seen these days, being most of the time in France, or posting pell-mell north to visit the Nevilles. And Cardinal Beaufort, whom he saw as something next-door to a saint, was nearly always in Bohemia where he was Papal legate. His mother's rare visits were like drops of rain in a desert.

'Sire. I would like your advice regarding your half-brothers.'

'Edmund and Jasper?' He brightened at the thought of them. He was flattered by her approach. 'They must be growing up.'

'They're five, and four. They salute your Grace. Yet . . .' She looked fully in his eyes, intensely anxious. 'There's the possibility that they have made enemies . . . an enemy, you understand?'

He took her long ringed hand in his small bony one. He whispered: 'I understand.'

'The day might come when they require sanctuary. If that should be, where would your Grace suggest they be sent?'

He pursed his lips wisely, he groped in vain for a solution, and was so long silent that their clasped hands began to tremble from a mutual source.

'It's difficult,' he said lamely, then suddenly remembered something told him by the young chaplain, Father Simon. A house of the most excellent order, full of the dedicated religious.

'The Abbey of St Saviour, at Bermondsey!' He was surprised when she emphatically shook her head.

She had heard more of Bermondsey than he knew. It was by repute more like a house of correction than one of peace. Even in Harry's day political prisoners and folk who for one reason or another had become an embarrassment were immured at Bermondsey. It was a place of incarceration as sure as Fleet or Newgate. No, my liege. Not Bermondsey. Lost again, he had said: 'I will give the matter thought, Madame. Trust me.' He had looked so unhappy at having disappointed her that she had taken him in her arms, invading him with the perfume which he inhaled with a mixture of disapproval and delight. I will speak to my Council, he said proudly. She answered swiftly:

'Oh no, my liege. This is a secret matter!' and he'd thought: of course. How stupid I am!

Now, kneeling upright, grasping his rosary, he whispered: 'Most merciful God, protect and strengthen our dear mother the Queen, and find me an answer to her plea!'

Time was precious. He thought quickly down his list. Who now?

'. . . and for our dear friend and counsellor, Richard, Duke of York, that he may have protection and guidance throughout his travels in this life and thereafter everlasting bliss.' (And that he may think of me, sometimes, with love.)

'. . . and for that most high and mighty prelate, thy servant Cardinal Henry Beaufort, that he may perform thy work ever to thy greater glory, O Lord . . .'

He squeezed his eyes tight. A draught of moving robes blew beside him and he froze in terror. Cautiously he looked and sighed with relief. It was only his steward, William de la Pole, kneeling reverently at his left, crossing himself, then turning to smile at him.

'My lord of Suffolk,' said Henry, and smiled back.

'I startled your Grace, I'm sorry.'

He had for a moment forgotten Suffolk, forgotten that he

was not after all completely isolated in his high estate. William was kind, and being fairly tall and slim, looked a little like Owen, although his thick hair was quite grey. But then, he didn't. Nobody looked like Owen.

'It's very cold for you in here, Sire,' said de la Pole.

'What?' said Henry, nodding towards the Christ. 'With *Him* to warm me?'

Suffolk bowed his head. Henry thought: I'll ask him! He is discreet, and he loves me. I *think* he loves me.

'My lord, your counsel, please,' he said softly. 'There are two children . . . friends of mine' (no lie, dear Jesu!) . . . and he went on, haltingly, to explain the predicament. Suffolk listened intently.

'They are wards of your Grace?' he asked. 'A place of safety, you say, should the contingency arise . . . That's easy, Sire.'

'But not Bermondsey,' said Henry quickly.

'No, no, of course not Bermondsey. That's no place for the innocent! Not even for the health of their souls. Not Bermondsey, but Barking. My sister is Abbess there. I can vouch for her goodness and good sense. Would that serve your Grace's intention?' He saw the grateful eyes and congratulated himself. That will advance me in the Cardinal's esteem, and advance my sister, too. God's Blood, he thought. What fortune serves those who serve an infant king!

'I must pray now,' said Henry apologetically, and Suffolk said: 'One more matter, your Grace. I came to tell you at once, so you might light a candle. This news I only had today, from my lord of Gloucester's envoy. Your uncle of Bedford is sick, at Rouen. They say it's mortal.'

He left the chapel quietly and Henry knelt very still, tasting the news. The name Rouen awoke the faintest tremor, and then the sea of Pembrokeshire came in, washing his mind clean together with the sound of Owen's voice. Jeanne is in Heaven now. And Bedford is on his way. Will they meet, I wonder? Will they forgive? He rose, his legs half-paralysed with cold and stress, and went unsteadily to the altar where candles burned. He took flame and moved, frail and delicate in his black clothes, from one bracket to another, working deliberately, constantly praying.

He lit candles for the dead, the dying, the living. One for his mother. One for Master Tydier. One for Bedford. One for Cardinal Beaufort. One for Suffolk. One for Richard of York, and one for his own father, the great and glorious Harry, too marvellous even to wonder about save as the silver mask under the H-shaped chantry. Two smaller ones (he thought this appropriate) for Edmund and Jasper. A large, beautifully carved one for Jeanne d'Arc. He began to cry. One thick as his own arm for Humphrey of Gloucester. One for Father Simon, who had taught him to pray. The living and the dead. Had he missed anyone? Dare he light one for himself? And shakily he did so, looking up where the garnet wounds became more bloodily real than ever in the transient gleam, seeming to roll down the limbs. He lit a candle for each member of his Council, the six prelates, the two clerical ministers, the eight dukes and earls, the four knights. He lit one for his French grandfather, Charles the Mad, and for his own rival, Charles the Seventh. He lit one for the peace of the world. And then, white and exhausted, his face irradiated by the shining, blowing flowers of flame, he knelt again and said:

'*Domine Jesu Christe* . . . do with me according to Thy Will, for Thy tender mercy's sake. Amen.'

His personal psalm. It served only to enhance the thought of his own unworthiness. He got up and extinguished the candle he had lit for himself, there in the Tower of London.

As Humphrey, with his entourage, blown by the autumn wind, rode north-west along the Rue du Gros-Horloge into the *place* adjacent to the Palais where Bedford lay, he saw a wild-eyed man, festooned with rags, dart from an alley. For one moment he was afraid. But the wretch took no notice of him or his caparisoned escort. He loped purposefully across the square. After four years there was little evidence of where *La Pucelle*'s pyre had stood; only if one looked very hard the faintest darkening of the cobbles could be seen. The ragged man knew, however; he went straight to the spot and flung himself on the ground. He scrabbled to gather up handfuls of wind-whirled dust which he rubbed into his eyes. Then he crossed himself, leaped up and scuttled away back into the narrow shadows. Humphrey swore. He rode on quickly through the great studded oak door of the Palais, dismounted in the courtyard and mounted the spiral to his brother's apartments.

He had been away only an hour but he feared that Bedford might have died. He forced himself through the thronged chamber. Bedford lay propped on pillows, his face stamped with the milky, childlike glaze of mortality. He had been anointed with the seventh sacrament, and his brow shone with oil. Priests and monks droned ceaselessly. Four or five Norman knights were bitterly weeping. Here in this seat of English administration a just and temperate Constable was departing. To a man, they recalled his fair dealings. Humphrey averted his eyes from their grief; his own throat felt thick. He leaned and took his brother's hand. Bedford's lips fluttered. 'You returned swiftly,' he said. 'Was all in order? The library?'

'Eighty-nine volumes in all. The treasures of France, of Italy.'

'They're yours,' said Bedford faintly. A clerk scratched with his quill on the Duke's last will and testament.

'Damn the books!' said Humphrey, outraging two young priests effusively praying by the bed. 'John . . . no treasure could amend your loss. Is there nothing? I've brought Doctor Swanwyth . . . I know he didn't save Harry, but he is skilled. Have you pain?'

'I had a griping in my bowels and I vomited, but no more . . .' Humphrey felt the hand draw him closer. 'Is it fancy? to say one dies of a broken heart?'

'They say it happens.'

'I laboured so long,' said Bedford. 'So vainly.'

'You were valiant. A true and excellent knight.'

'We had some good days.'

'We did. John, is there anything? Anything?' I've wished him dead, he thought. He is the last of my brothers. Now I am sorry . . . Bedford laboured to reply, intimating that priests and courtiers should withdraw from earshot. He whispered, with his lips against Humphrey's face:

'I want you to stay in France for as long as possible. Keep a close eye on the military and naval arsenal in *le clos des gallées* here . . . vital. Control the garrisons. Stay until Richard of York is experienced enough to take command . . . relations between English and French here must remain solid . . . close surveillance, Humphrey . . . if we are to salvage anything from this wretched . . . shambles. Continue to woo Charles and Philip. If Paris falls . . .' He shut his eyes and breathed noisily.

'John!' Humphrey held his brother's hand tightly. He heard a feminine echo: 'John?' and drew away to look into the face of the new wife, Jacquetta. Even in his grief her beauty stung him. Red-gold hair, dark blue eyes, a perfect body. And near her Sir Richard Woodville, with his arch-angel's face and his arm supporting the Duchess. Neither were weeping.

'Go away, lady,' he said rudely. For a moment he recalled what Eleanor had said – sisters in skill! and hated all women, all witches, seeing no division between the two. Beautiful women were the Devil's handiwork, ever since Eve . . . Bedford said, his eyes still closed: 'Come near.'

'I am near.'

'Look to the King, Humphrey. Support him with the Council.'

'I am his loyal servant.' For a moment he believed himself implicitly. 'I'll guard and guide him like a father.'

Bedford, weakening, murmured: 'And my lord . . . promise . . . go gently with the Queen-Dowager, with Katherine. Let her live out her life in peace. She means no harm. I know that you and she have had your skirmishes. But she was Harry's joy and pride.'

Humphrey bowed his head, silent. He thought: my own promise came first, to myself, to see them ruined and damned, she and Tydier. Even for the brotherly love that tears me this minute, I cannot, I will not renege on this. I will obey in the spirit if not the letter. I will do Bedford's will in France. I will protect our interests. I will give them a little grace. A savage smile broke through his sorrow. It will be yet another exercise in attrition. This sojourn in Rouen will give me time to prepare the case against them.

Bedford was dying. He scrawled his signature on the will. Wax smoked and was crushed beneath the seal. His fingers opened, the quill rolled free. He whispered: '*In manus tuas, Domine*,' and very soon the vibrations of death sang in his throat. The priests moved forward, chanting softly. Humphrey stepped back. He moved against the wall. Through tears he saw the widow, Jacquetta, turning to lean in graceful grief against Sir Richard Woodville. They were on the edge of a lamenting knot of clergy and knights but Humphrey saw, for a clear instant, Sir Richard's hand slide round to caress, even in death's awesome eye, the woman's curving breast.

And renewed fury drove out sorrow, as two other lovers filled his mind. I will have them. They deem themselves gods, outside the law, outside the Church, outside morality. I will give them a little more time, but that is all.

There was now a broad white streak in Hywelis's hair. Like the streak on Madog's head and withers, the mark of the eagle, showing the purity of his line. Her body was emaciated, not so much by her anchorite's meagre diet as from the em-battled nights, the tearing strife with the black one.

It was over twenty years since the Lord had died. Lately Megan and the bard had joined him. Glyndyfrdwy was now almost completely a shell. The wind swept howling through its broken roof. Its battlements had succumbed to frost and gales, and parts had crashed into the courtyard. And here she stayed, seeing no one, living off the insubstantial fruits of the valley, sleeping beside her foxes on the floor. Tending the fire. In constant communion with the smoke.

The vapours whirled about her, densely grey. The Lord appeared almost at once, handsome and smiling, with Davy Gam looking over his shoulder. Faintly etched in the topmost billows was the face of Megan, all her bitterness gone, and Gruffydd Llwyd. Hywelis would never have known the beard-less youth that death had made of him. Another face filtered into the pearling, acrid cloud – Iolo Goch. Out of the ancient past he blessed her silently. Hywelis began to weep.

'Father,' she said brokenly, 'I cannot continue. I shall die. The black one becomes too strong.'

Behind her, within the pentacle drawn on the floor, the

427

little vixen whimpered. Madog's bride. Panting. Usually the vixens dropped their cubs with ease. This one was having a great struggle. Her sides heaved. She whined. Hywelis moved from the smoke and looked into the rush basket within the pentacle. She spoke to the vixen in its own tongue. The vixen raised tortured eyes. Panting. Crying. Hywelis went back to kneel beside the smoke. Today the barrier outside the spheres was fragile. The Lord's voice was very strong.

'Be still, girl,' he said. 'We are so pleased with you.'

Last night the black one had almost triumphed, flinging itself over Hywelis as she slept unwarily. It was a writhing suffocating mass of fanged and taloned slime, risen from blackest Hell. Hywelis had had to retreat, only just in time, coiling herself within the golden torque of Maelor. She could not stay there long; its heat and brilliance killed, as surely as the black one's power. The black one had spoken for the first time, in its voice unctuous from the Pit.

'Cease. Cease fighting. I claim my right.'

Behind her she heard the vixen moan. The Lord's voice mingled with the sounds of travail.

'It is accomplished,' he said. 'Edmund is the one. Wales will rule England. We love you, Hywelis.'

'*Duw a'n bendithio*,' said Davy Gam and Iolo Goch together. 'God bless us.' Megan and the bard echoed them.

'My daughter. My good girl,' said Owain Glyn Dŵr. 'You may join us now. Find peace. Watch the glory with us.'

'When is the glory to be?'

'In fifty years.' The smoke itself had a rapturous voice, sibilant and pearly. 'In fifty years. The greatness. Wales will rule England.'

The vixen gave a terrible groan. The cub's head appeared, blind and bloody. Such a tiny cub, marked with the blaze of Madog.

'No!' Hywelis cried. 'I want to live! You promised. He will come to me again.'

'Live then, girl,' they said. 'It is accomplished. You may cease fighting. The seed is sown. The dynasty is founded. Wales will rule England. Edmund is the one. We will protect him now.'

428

The vixen was panting, her eyes closed. She was expendable. The tiny cub was also expendable, but Hywelis let him live.

The smoke was fading. There was one more question. The Lord's face shimmered, young, triumphant, foreseeing the greatness.

'When? Father, father! When will he come to me?'

'Soon. Quite soon. Prepare for him to hate you. Prepare for him to hate the world.'

Winter had gone, and spring, and summer too; a year during which delicate negotiations were initiated in France, only to crumble inconclusively. France and Burgundy promulgated the Treaty of Arras. Charles yielded to Philip many of the coveted royal demesnes, giving visible assurance of contrition for the death of Jean sans Peur. And both parties ranged themselves side by side in the event of either being attacked by the English. In Rouen and Calais, Suffolk, Gloucester and York, with some of Beaufort's forces, held on doggedly in the lost hope of establishing the young King as ruler of France. And Paris, hub of diplomacy and destiny, declared its allegiance to Charles the Seventh and his descendants. Almost exactly one year after Bedford's death, a large proportion of the troops and their commanders prepared for home. The glory of Agincourt had become a faded vision, a tawdry myth. It was over. And at Hertford, within the ambience of stubborn affectionate loyalty and passionate love, autumn lost face to winter.

Fog filled the day. The trees were almost bare. In the filmed courtyard a fine bay horse chumbled and tossed its silver bit, flicking little excitements of foam over the bridle. Huw stood calming the horse. Huw was dressed for the road, his wild little Welsh face set in impatience. Another horse waited, laden with saddle-bags. Huw's pony wandered at will, tearing the last leaves from a rosebush. Owen opened an upper casement and shouted at Huw. He looked up and grinned.

'The boy's a fool,' he said. 'I wish I were taking Caradoc with me instead.'

'Huw adores you,' said Katherine. 'He would give you his

life. And Caradoc has gone to Carmarthen. To get married, I understand.'

She stood in her shift, her arms clasped about her against the chill. Owen was in his fine embroidered shirt and hose. Guillemot, humming her silly ditty, and seeming in a trance, wandered in and out of the chamber with armfuls of clothing.

'Marriage,' said Owen, looking hard at Katherine, 'is an honourable estate, and much to be desired.' To her amazement he left it there, instead of badgering and pressing her until she lost her temper and quoted her promise to Bedford. He's up to some mischief, she thought.

He was. Hence the waiting horses. Bedford is dead, he thought. There are no promises for her to keep. He had already found it useless to approach her own chaplain (a doddering old man who seemed scarcely to know what day it was), saying: Father, will you marry us? No hope or help there; the old man was not so witless. I take orders only from the Queen-Dowager, my son. The Queen-Dowager had said nothing. But there were other priests. Poor priests who would be only too glad to line their purses for his heart's desire . . . He was going to find such a one.

Katherine said, shivering: 'I must make ready. How soon the opening of Parliament comes around. I wish I weren't going. But Henry would be so disappointed.'

Owen closed the door. Guillemot had gone on some foray and had been deflected, for she now appeared in the courtyard below. Huw tried to kiss her. She screamed and ran behind the horses.

'Don't go then, *cariad*,' Owen said. 'Stay here and wait for me. I shan't be away for long.'

'I must,' she said.

'You're not afraid?' he said. 'There's nothing to fear, surely, at Westminster?'

'I've not been afraid all this year. Gloucester's in France. But I wish you were coming with me.' She looked down at herself. 'Does it show? If it shows, I shall stay behind.'

Never again, he thought. Not since the last time, when I heard the dreadful insults levelled against us both and could do nothing. He put his arms about her. He stroked her swollen belly. Not so much a swelling as a graceful curve. It was hard to believe she was in her seventh month.

'It never shows very much,' he said. 'And I have a new gown for you. It will conceal the world. Wait till you see it. The latest fashion. Monstrous.'

'The last time, Bedford knew I was with child,' she said. 'It was a good guess on his part, I imagine.'

'Try the dress, then,' he said. He went to the dower-chest and took out a gown. 'I had it made up at Taylor's in Chepe. The new style, the houpelande. From Burgundy.'

And Bedford's dead, he thought again. God rest him. When we meet again, dearest dream, I shall have a surprise for you. I will have a willing priest with me, and if force will be needed to have you to the altar, then force shall rule. Even if I have to knock you senseless and bring you round to speak the vows. He helped her into the dress. It was low-necked, tight-girdled beneath her breasts, with an enormous padded stomacher thrown forward in impudent pride. Long dagged sleeves trailed almost to the ground.

'This is the new fashion?' she said in amazement.

'Everyone wears it. Taylor told me. It's not pretty to my mind, but perfect for the purpose.'

She studied her reflection. She said, for the fourth time that day: 'Why are you going to Southampton? Who is in Southampton?'

Friends, he answered. He thought: the monk who tended my wound may still be there, and John Page. They will know of a priest to do my bidding.

'Oh, it feels tight!' she said, and wriggled out of the gown. She said: 'Have you enough money?' and became very intent on choosing stockings from a pile on the bed.

'Thank you, yes.' A little constraint grew between them. Already her gift of the fine bay horse had hurt and delighted him. She saved the moment quickly.

'I know. You have a woman in Southampton! Ha! She's welcome to you. At last I shall have some peace.'

'That's it,' he said. 'The secret's out. I'm tired of you, *cariad*. You are so fat!'

'Who made me fat?' she cried. He dropped to his knees,

and before she could protest, he whipped up her shift and began kissing her belly I did, he said. I did, my little girl. This is where my new son lies. The kisses moved downwards. And this, the soft gateway of his kingdom . . .

A convulsion moved in her, as if a tiny planet had shifted on its axis. She put her hands in his hair. She whispered: 'Ah . . . *mon amour*. Do you remember when we made this child? We had a lot of wine. Your kinsmen called on us. You sang for me. You made me drunk . . .'

He rose from his knees. He began to kiss her throat and breast. He said, 'Everyone was drunk. Howell ap Llewellyn misplaced his harp. A most wonderful evening. A more wonderful night . . .'

She slipped her hands under his shirt. She began to caress him as wantonly and skilfully as he had once caressed her. He tried to take her hands. Her long lips were smiling wickedly.

'No,' he said. 'No, *cariad*. There's danger in it. I want this child. What will we call him?'

'Owen,' she said. 'My little Owen.'

He was weakening. He took her shift off, and held her naked body hard against him. She kissed his eyes, his neck, his mouth. He could feel their hearts racing, exactly in time.

'Bolt the door,' she whispered. 'Guillemot . . .'

'We shall be late,' he whispered. He did as she said.

He tried to be careful. She was very reckless today, she swung him into rapture. He felt that part of his soul had flowed into her. Sometimes it made him want to weep. This was one of those times.

'That was very foolish,' he said softly. 'Forgive me, my love.'

Her closed eyelids were moist. She lay smiling. There was a delicate map of blue veins on her breasts. He touched where the child lay. He had felt it move, petulantly. She was so beautiful. Still the dream, the unfathomable, unbelievable, beloved dream. Oh, Cathryn, my dearest dream.

'Don't go to Westminster,' he said. She sat up, and kissed him.

'I feel well,' she said. 'I feel wonderful.'

Her skin felt cold. 'Let me dress you,' he said. 'I love to

432

dress you. The times I've dressed you, and undressed you. My little girl.'

She sat while he drew the fine woollen stockings on her legs and bound a garter about each thigh. What pretty garters, Madame, he said – who bought them for you, a lover? Yes, a lover, she said. From Hadham Market. He kissed the flesh above each garter. The strange little convulsion moved deep inside her again. I've never felt like this, she thought. As if a universe were whirling about within me. Lie still, little Owen. We are for Westminster. She watched the deft strong musician's hands, felt the corns left by the harp on each fingertip a little rough on her skin. He lifted kirtle and petticoat over her head and drew them down. Then the dress, which seemed less tight now. It was still a monstrosity. It made her look as fat as Bet, at the tavern . . .

'We never found it,' she said.

'What, my love?'

'The tavern, at Staines.'

'I think you set us on the wrong road,' he said.

She had wanted him to see the tavern at Staines, where the baby Henry had been so happy. She wanted him to see Bet. She had wanted, belatedly, to reward Bet herself. But the tavern was no more. They had looked for it for a day; there was no trace of it. It had disappeared, like a mythical halt on some faery wayside. Only the memory remained, an everlasting warmth.

'We'll try and find it again,' he said.

She sat before the mirror. He combed her hair, expertly, with no tugging or tweaking. His brilliant eyes were veiled over his task, the shirt was open at his strong throat. She watched him, sick with love. The pleasurable convulsion moved within her again, almost a pain. When every hair was free as silk, he made the two long braids, anchoring them about her head with butterfly pins. He placed her great wired headdress with its pinnacles of starched linen on her hair. He looked up and winked at her in the mirror. He bent and kissed between her neck and shoulder.

'Dame Alphonse used to tell me not to look in the mirror. She said I'd see the Devil. She didn't know I was worried because I was so ugly.'

He didn't laugh. He said simply: 'You're lovely, Cathryn. The loveliest woman I ever saw in my life.' He found it suddenly difficult to speak. He said: 'I must get dressed. We'll both be late.'

She left him. She went smiling, and glowing, below to the courtyard, stopping on the way at a small chamber where she unlocked the coffer of her Privy Purse. Huw had given up chasing Guillemot, who had gone inside to find her duties done. Huw knelt respectfully as Katherine approached, his eyes popping at sight of the new gown. Masking the boy and herself from the window, she gave him a leather bag. Owen would be furious. Let him be.

'There is two hundred livres sterling here, Huw,' she said. 'For unforeseen contingencies during whatever folly you two are about. Guard it for your master.'

'For my lord,' he said, his small dark face violently serious.

'For mine,' she said, turning away.

Her carriage was ready to take her to the Parliament. Winter was on its way. The lovely winter nights by the fire, with the lute and the loving, and the new baby. She breathed deeply. Even the fog tasted sweet, promising. The servants who were to accompany her were standing ready. Guillemot came running out, red-faced. Then Owen, in his tawny velvet cloak and cap. He drew Katherine aside. The carriage swung from side to side as the horses shifted their feet.

'Farewell then, *fy merch fach*,' he said. 'Farewell, my little girl. My humblest duty to the King's Grace.'

'Can't we ride a little way together?'

'Better not. I must ride fast. Too fast for your comfort. It will not be long . . .' He frowned, he looked closely at her. 'You're not troubled? There's nothing to fear. The gown is a sure shield.'

'Dreadful gown!' she said. 'And I'm not afraid. I don't think I shall ever be afraid again.'

'Well, long live the French squabbles,' he said merrily, 'if they keep Gloucester away!'

He mounted the bay. Huw sprang on the pony and took the reins of the spare horse. The keen bay reared and snorted.

434

Owen turned, and raised his hand.

'Adieu, Madame. Adieu, until we meet again!'

The bay's hooves struck a flash from the stones. The horses moved forward swiftly through the gate. Fog swallowed them and their riders. The strange little feeling moved deep in Katherine again. Not a pain. More like the sensation of an hour ago, when she had cried and twisted and trembled, cleft by love. The maids were holding Edmund and Jasper, ready to say their farewells, just inside the hall; Owen had kissed them before he left. She had forgotten the ruby ring. The King would be disappointed if she wasn't wearing it. She mounted once more to the little room where she kept her coffers. The ruby, usually a loose fit, was snug today. Her fingers were swollen; something that hadn't happened with any of her other children. The Welsh gold ring was painfully tight; it worried her. Any further swelling and it would have to be cut off. She tugged at it, removed it with difficulty. She locked it carefully away; her most precious piece. She recalled the night it had been placed on her finger. The night they both still talked about with joy and wonder, even in face of the thousand subsequent nights of equal joy. She recalled splitting Humphrey's eyebrow open with it. No need to fear Humphrey today. Yes, she thought. I think I have at last ceased to fear. I can strike back; I feel so well, so fine. Long live the French squabbles, if they keep Humphrey away!

She made good time to Westminster, arriving at evening when she heard Compline with the King in St Stephen's Chapel. Henry seemed pleased to be with her again, but now there was a certain detachment about him. He seemed at times lost within himself and when praying his whole body trembled frighteningly. His eyes flickered over the low neckline of her gown with the shrewd look of a little old priest. Yet he was sweet and courteous, although when she thanked him privately for the recommendation of Barking Abbey he merely nodded and didn't ask after his half-brothers. However, when it was time for bed, he thawed suddenly and spoke of them with eagerness, all the time looking over his shoulder as if for a judgement. She lay wakeful for a long time. She followed Owen in her mind on the Southampton road. It would take him four days, barring accidents. Supposing his proposed mischief there took two days – she would be back home to welcome him. She summoned his face clearly into her mind to hold as the last thing before she slept. *Don't love so much, Princess*, said old Dame Alphonse in the dream, *it is unfitting* . . . *Be quiet, old nun*, said Owen, laughing. *What do nuns know of love?* The white dog gambolled round them, its coat bloody . . . horrible. Katherine came up out of the dream quickly. The child was moving restively, as if it too disliked the dream. She lay awake until dawn, whispering softly to the child. Little Owen.

It was just as she had been told about the new fashion. Everyone was wearing it; everyone looked *enceinte*. During the service in the Abbey, all through the bidding prayers and invocations, the interminable plainsong of the monks, her spirits rose. She wanted to laugh. How many secrets like hers were concealed beneath the monstrous houpelande? The merry mood persisted even throughout the opening ceremony, with Henry's cold shaking hand in hers and the stiff hauteur of the royal arms bristling above their heads behind the great gold cross. Covertly she studied the assembly. There were many unfamiliar faces. Faces missing too. Philippa of York had been dead for five years, likewise the Countess of Hunting-don. Anne of Bedford was dead. Margaret of Clarence looked dowdy and faded. She peered through the press of knights and councillors, abbots and bishops and commoners. They were all girding themselves to petition the little King with a myriad private controversies. She saw how closely Suffolk guarded him, and was glad. Better Beaufort's man than Gloucester's. Then she saw Eleanor Cobham in the gallery of ladies, dark-clad as usual. She had made no attempt to follow the new fashion and looked her insignificant self. Well, no need to speak to her. Even if she descended with her counterfeit love. Did she miss her husband? It was hard to imagine anyone missing Humphrey.

Eleanor looked at her. She neither bowed nor gave any sign of recognition. She only looked, for about half a minute, a look of almost childlike opacity; it filtered through Katherine and out the other side. Katherine looked back. *Maudite* Cobham. Burning my poor little Guillemot's arm.

436

Katherine had been standing for a long time. Her back was aching a little. She shifted her feet for comfort. The child rolled about in sympathy. When the time came to withdraw her feeling of light-heartedness had vanished. Soon she would find somewhere quiet, send for her women, rest. But first there was St Edward's Chapel to visit. An eerie, inevitable duty, totally without sadness. Her only emotion a vague affection for something in another life. There was no quietness in the Chapel; it was full, people praying or gossiping while the chanting of the monks mingled with the chipping of a solitary mason, improving the frieze of the H-shaped canopy. As she approached Harry's lucent silver effigy she noticed the mason's face. Like one of his own gargoyles, an evil, leering little face. Her backache increased. She lit a candle for Harry. She prayed, sincere and brief. With half her mind she heard a commotion outside the door, and someone calling: 'Better late than never!' Men laughing.

Margaret of Clarence approached. She kissed her on the cheek. She said what Katherine had been thinking.

'There are so few old friends left, Katherine. You should visit more often. You look so well, so handsome. I used to quarrel with Philippa, but how I miss her! Have you news of James of Scotland? I hear he's in great trouble with his nobles. There have been two assassination attempts lately. At Perth, I believe.'

The strange little convulsive feeling inside Katherine sprang up again. It decided to become a pain. It gripped and worried her casually, then joined itself to the ache in her back.

'I wrote to James,' she said steadily. 'I've had no reply. That was in June.'

'How pale the light makes everyone look in here!' said the Duchess. 'I'm always pale. I've lost what beauty I had, and that was little – but you! How's it done?' She laughed; there was an edge of malice to her compliment this time.

Katherine did not answer. The girdle was unbearably tight beneath her breasts. She itched to tear at it. Owen would be halfway to Southampton by now. The bay was a good horse. He knew how to nurse a horse along. But he should not have girdled her so tight . . . But that was yesterday! she thought dizzily. Guillemot gowned me this morning. Foolish Guillemot, who loves me so. The pain roamed idly seeking a nerve to feed on. It curved down along her spine, inwards to her loins. Regular, like the drone of James of Scotland's bagpipers. A slow grinding beat that renewed itself at shorter intervals. It will pass. I've felt so well, so carefree, all these months. And it did pass, as if commanded. She straightened her back, sighing with relief. For a moment I thought I was . . . no, that wasn't how I remember the miscarriages . . . it was more like. . .

'I was so sad about poor Jacqueline,' said Margaret of Clarence. 'I have Masses said for her monthly. I blame my Lady Cobham for that!'

. . . it was more like giving birth.

'Jacqueline's dead?' Katherine said. Jacqueline dead. Lovely, silly princess, wounded to the heart. Betrayed, abandoned. Dead. And she was about my age. Jacqueline dead. The pain rose in celebration. Worse, heavy. Spreading back and front and down to . . . *my son's soft gateway . . . the flowers at the hillfoot, I feel the dew upon them, the little streams that flow among them . . . Sainte Vierge!* close the gates!

'But none dare cross or blame my Lady Cobham, she has such power.' Margaret's voice was a long way away.

Katherine took a step forward, away from the King's chantry, into the main aisle of the chapel. The exit was blocked by a press of knights and councillors. The monks of Westminster chanted on. The pain pressed downwards, urgent, demanding.

'Katherine,' the Duchess said. 'You look . . . Stay, I'll fetch your women.'

She tried to call Margaret back, but she was gone. The knot of men parted to let her through. Katherine took another unsteady step. She stopped abruptly, swinging round so that none should see her twisted face. There was a sticky warmth between her thighs, then a crystal rush that soaked petticoat and kirtle and stockings . . . *the snow melting on the mountain top . . . now the mountain gives forth its cataract* . . . a clear stain that seeped through the skirt of the new gown. She took another step. Blood spotted the floor. She leaned and grasped a carved bird's head on the capital of a pillar. She thought:

I can see the stonework through my own bones and flesh. Her legs were folding under her. She closed her eyes. She could see Owen's tear-wet, starlit face, white with longing – he pushed her down beneath him on the gallery. *It is my birthday. I can do as I please on my birthday. But I am chaste.* The child is coming . . . She heard one of the knights approaching from the doorway, heard and felt the swish of his robes and the sound of his mailed shoes on the stone. She thought, logical in agony: he has just returned from war. Better late than never. She stretched out her hand to him and said:

'Sir, I am taken ill. *M'aidez, je vous en prie . . .*'

He put his arm about her. She threw back her head with a tortured gasp, and opened her eyes. She saw a scarlet mantle, an eyebrow scarred from a savage blow, and on the face the ultimate flush of requital. From within her arose a whisper, a dreadful, conquering echo:

'*Do not touch me! I am made of glass!*'

But Humphrey of Gloucester held her fast. She felt herself yield, become crystalline, and shatter.

The young man pulled at the bell and shivered, stamping his feet. The bell-rope was stiff with ice and little cascades of snow, disturbed by the vibration, drifted on to his shoulders. More snow lay thickly on streets and sloping roofs, towers and crenellations, giving a weird unwavering light to the darkening evening. Blowing on his fingers, he tugged at the bell again. The square spy-hole shot back and a red face frilled by a beard surveyed him through bars. Keys clanked and creaked. He was admitted, into the wall of London itself, where in the gatehouse torches and a brazier lit up the gloom. The bearded man was tall and beer-bellied. He held out his hand.

'Your letters of appointment?'

These he read, holding them under the torchlight while with the other hand he adjusted the great ring of keys at his belt. The young man waited. He had never considered himself prone to fancies, but around him was four hundred years of pain and despair. His mind sniffed it out like a nervous hound. This was the start of what he had been assured was a career with boundless prospects. He was here through an uncle's connections with constables and justices too mighty to be named. The big man handed the documents back.

'Welcome to Newgate,' he said.

There was a cask of ale on the bench beside the brazier, and two pewter mugs. The big man poured, and thrust a mug into the young man's frigid hand.

'Cold out,' he said. 'I thought you weren't coming.'

'I'm sorry,' the young man answered. 'I had to wait for the boat from Southwark. They're having to break the ice on the river.' He swallowed gratefully and moved nearer the fire.

'Yes. Warm yourself,' said the turnkey. 'Then I'll show you my little kingdom. Yours, when I'm not here. You're not very old, are you? Are your wits in good order? By Jesus, you'll need them. Some of these devils . . . three jumps ahead before you can say kiss-your-arse. They'll offer their souls to be loose. Tricks you wouldn't believe.'

'Am I to be alone here then, when you're off duty?' The young man's voice was uneasy. The turnkey roared with laughter.

'No, lad. We've a good, small crew, but they can't be all places at once. Likely they'll look to you for judgement. It's Searching Time now, or near enough. So come, see the menagerie!'

He unlocked the inner door of the gatehouse. The noise and stench that had been sealed off by the oak now rocked the young man back on his heels. It was a huge communal chamber. The stone floor was scattered with straw so filthy that in places it was mere slime. Roaches ran about. The walls wept damp. In every corner and alcove fungi flourished in grotesque shapes. On the ledge of a bricked-up window a big toad sat like a bloated doom. A few torches lit the chamber. In it were about fifty people, several of whom rushed towards the turnkey as soon as he appeared, all babbling at once; a fat threadbare man demanding lawyers, a blonde whore in a ragged striped gown, screeching unintelligibly and clawing at the turnkey's sleeve. Smartly he drew a little cudgel and laid about him. The supplicants fell back, except for the woman, who crept close to the young man with a pallid desperate smile.

440

'Now, Alison,' reproved the turnkey. She turned and went away, to sit cross-legged in one of the cleaner corners. These were few. A channel clogged with human waste and urine ran alongside one wall to a vent in its base, and there rats congregated, nosing, skittering apart as a jailer threw a bucket of water at the course of the drain. A rat dashed over the young man's feet and he jumped, awed by its weight and size. The inmates had quietened somewhat after the first excitement. Two youths were casting dice. An old man prayed and groaned. Two more whores were examining their legs for flea-bites. But in a tumbled heap of straw someone lay recently dead, and the rats were busy there. Filthy, naked children wept against a woman's skirt. Lying with their heads almost in the drain, a man and a girl copulated frantically, as if liberty hung upon the act.

The turnkey yelled to the jailer with the bucket. 'I see the old Jew's dead. Move him out.'

He steered the young man through an archway and unlocked another door. They were in a torchlit stone passage lined with cells.

'So. Welcome to Newgate,' he said. 'This is where all the little felons end. The big ones go to the Tower of London, but you knew that, didn't you? That pack are mostly debtors, thieves, whores, paupers, vagrants. These, here, are no better. But you have to watch them. For divers reasons, they're dangerous.'

Each cell had bars halfway down its door, and was illuminated by the torches in the passage. A youth rose from his plank bed and smiled amiably.

'Sawyer. Apprentice carpenter. Murdered his master. Stand back.' He unlocked the door and entered to make a cursory search, turning the straw with his foot and feeling the youth for weapons. Sawyer smiled, mild as milk.

In the next cell a man was down on all fours, devouring his bedding.

'Watkin,' said the turnkey. 'He's been here so long even I can't remember why. He went mad last month. Thinks he's a horse.'

He laughed, slapping his barrel belly.

They moved on. The search became more and more perfunctory. A man and wife sat playing cards and greeted them with gracious nods. Their cell was better furnished than most.

'Fray, and Mistress Fray,' said the big man, but did not elaborate on their crime. In the next cell a man with a purple growth on his head was yelling and beating the bars. The turnkey roared back and dealt the door a blow.

'Houghton. Another murderer. Another madman. Swears he's innocent. Listen. Never argue with them. No one goes out and no one goes in, unless under the Constable's seal. And no letters. Some of these have money. They'll offer the world. It's not worth it.' They had reached the last cell in the passage. The new recruit looked in.

A tall slender man with thick grey hair was standing motionless, his back against the wall. A small dark youth sat at a table, his elbows among the remains of a meal. He was staring with utter misery at the other man.

'Meredyth,' said the turnkey. 'And by Christ's crown, if you thought those back there were mad . . . hey, Meredyth! what message for the King today?'

The man came forward to the bars. There was something in his eyes more frightening than anything the new recruit had yet seen in Newgate.

'What is your name?' the man said softly.

'Nickson,' he stammered impulsively. 'Nick Nickson.'

'Nick,' said the quiet voice. 'Have you news for me of the Queen-Dowager?'

He could not look away from the eyes. Their blue and gold, their pain, appalled him, sucked him in. He opened his mouth. He was suddenly almost lifted off his feet by the turnkey's arm and indignantly hustled away back along the line of cells.

'I told you he was mad! I've had my bellyful of him for the past twelve months. It happens all the time. Some claim blood kinship with the King. Some think they *are* the King! With him, it's mostly the King's mother!'

'Queen Katherine? But . . .'

'Jesus!' said the turnkey in fury. 'I told you. Don't argue with them! Don't get embroiled! Say nothing about anything! He is nobody. Neither of birth nor fortune, though he's enough money to pay for his victuals and his servant's . . . he writes quite a few letters. He'll ask you to take them out. It's your living gone if you do.'

'Would he hurt me?'

'I don't know. His servant might. All the Welsh are mad. When he first came in, he was like that one' (they were nearing the cell of the banging, raving man). 'But that's a year ago. I remember he had a safe-conduct in his pocket; there was some question of whether his arrest was lawful. But the Duke of Gloucester, no less, asked for and was granted a declaration under the Great Seal. Strange, Meredyth should have been sent to the Tower. So much more comfortable . . . but then, he's nobody!'

'What's his crime?'

'Inciting a rebellion in Wales. And yet . . . I sometimes wonder. He was quite alone, save for that boy. His hair was gold then.' He laughed. 'Grey now. Did you see? It's the air here that does it.' (Knowledgeable as an alchemist.) 'The foul air. The lack of light.'

'When does he come to trial?'

'When does anyone? He talks of seeking security in Chancery to appear in person before the King's Council. He has grand ideas. Listen – ' he took Nickson by the shoulders – 'I saw your face. Don't let him soften you up. He's cunning. Or we'll have my lord of Gloucester to answer to, let alone the Constable. No confidences. There's a good fellow. If you must talk to him, get him to tell you about the war.'

'I wonder what he thinks about, standing there?' said Nick Nickson.

Annwyl Crist! Sweet loving Jesus! this new little warder could never conceive my thoughts! He's young, I thought, he's malleable, I looked in his eyes and I nearly had him. News. Ah, sweet Christ give me news of her. I think as little as possible, or I should be truly mad. I must not go mad. When they brought me in, so long ago, I broke two of my fingers against the wall. It took four of them to bring me along that passage.

My fingers; my right hand. So farewell to the harp. The least of my cares. Huw is a comfort. We speak Welsh all the time. It drives the jailers wild. The blood dried dark on the wall, it's there even after all this time, that's where I hit my head. Huw stopped me. Huw should not be here at all. But he loves me. Who knows better than I what love can do?

How clever of Gloucester to have me committed to this common jail under the name of my father, Meredyth. A ticklish business for him altogether. Curse him, rape him with white-hot irons, like Mortimer had done to the English king.

Oh, my Cathryn.

The dreams come. I hold on tight and let them in. It's vital I remember every detail of the worst day of my life. I thought I had had bad days before. When every Englishman's hand seemed against me, through my race and my pride and the preferments I received through my art. Battle, siege, the terrible time when her mourning had taken even her essence from me. No. I've had no bad days. Until I returned, riding light, hot of heart, with Huw and the priest whom I had bought of all places in Warwick. The priest was the thinnest man I have ever seen; a skeleton.

The Southampton monk told me of him. This costly, cunning priest, whose trade it is to perform marriages with no questions asked. I rode to Warwick and added three weeks to my errand. It was the longest time she and I had ever been apart. Think of something else. Quickly.

The bad day. I start over and over, from the moment we left the tavern where the three of us had indulged in premature celebration. The thin priest could drink both Huw and me under the bench. Hertford; through the park and gates and into the bailey. Chaos and nightmare. The horde of servants, that funny loyal little crew who love us so much – running to meet me, world fragmented. The old steward in tears. Guillemot flinging herself into my arms. I couldn't stop her weeping. And the bailiffs, moving about the courtyard and in and out of the manor, taking inventory.

When I was young I used to drink the snow from the lower slopes of Eglwyseg Mountain just for the pleasure of shivering. As I looked over Guillemot's head at the open doorway, looked for *fy merch fach*, my little girl, my Cathryn, saw no Cathryn, the shivering deepened on me, colder than that snow. Then I looked for Jasper and Edmund who always came to meet me. The shivering grew. I picked Guillemot up and carried her in. I sat her on my lap and gave her wine. Day after day, month after month, I try to recall her exact words. I can't. I'm so lost. I'm so wounded.

Yet I know she told me I had another son. He came forth before his time. So frail that he was instantly baptized Owen by the monks of Westminster, in whose care he now was. Eleanor Cobham had sent her own midwife and a wetnurse. My blood became icy. Gloucester had returned unexpectedly. Guillemot held me while I shivered and shook. And when she told me where they had taken Cathryn, she had to give *me* wine, for she thought I would fall dead where I sat.

The Abbey of St Saviour, Bermondsey. I thought: it is only a name. Bermondsey. A dour place run by the Church. The rumours surrounding such places are often exaggerated. Still I shivered. A place of retirement for ladies in poor health. Like Queen Joanna. (Cathryn, when last I saw her, was in superb health.) No. A place of savage penitence, and Gloucester had put her there. I thought: they can't misuse her. She is a Queen. Little Harry will oversee her fortunes. Then I saw that the men who were turning our home upside down among the wailing servants wore the livery of the King's Council, and I remembered that little Harry was little indeed, and a refugee within his holy disposition. And I remembered who the leader of the Council was . . .

The manor is to be closed up, Guillemot said, at the Council's orders. They sent me home with all the others. They would not let me touch her. (Or, did she say: '*She* would not let me touch her? . . . I, who love her as my life . . .?') I know your feeling, Guillemot. Oh, sweet Christ, I know. I asked where my sons were. The old steward came with a parchment in his hand.

'My lord of Suffolk came and took them away to his sister at the Abbey of Barking.'

My heart lifted the barest inch. Suffolk is Beaufort's man, and the King's favourite councillor. Cathryn first, then. We

445

should soon see what kind of a place Bermondsey is. I got up.

'The bay is done. Saddle me fresh horses.'

The servants, crowding, were looking to me for all the answers I couldn't supply, Huw in the forefront. And Caradoc with his little new bride Angharad wondering what madhouse she had come to and weeping with the rest. And the priest, looking somewhat detached from it all, with £90 in his purse. I told Huw to come with me and he sprang forward, ready to put his life in pawn. And the priest too, I said. I don't pay money for nothing, and I need no Masses yet! and he nodded and made ready.

Then the steward said: 'There is more. You are summoned to Westminster to answer to certain charges.' And when I heard what the charges were I burst out laughing, although the laughter hurt my chest. I thought: how typically devious of Gloucester to feign a charge! How could he say to the face of the Council: I charge that man with having lain with the King's mother? We're no adulterers. Theirs is a secular court of justice. Hence the accusation of having initiated a Welsh rising. I, who haven't set foot in rebel country for years! The steward gave me the parchment, saying he'd taken the liberty of paying 12s. 6d. for it.

'It's a certificate of safe-conduct to Westminster.'

I thought then: better to go straight to Westminster. Leave Bermondsey alone until I have petitioned little Harry. I remembered us walking hand in hand on the Pembroke shore. *I love you, Master Tydier.* Harry's signet would open the gates of Bermondsey or Hell. I had again forgotten he was only *Little Harry.*

They were waiting for me outside Westminster Hall. I went forward, leaving my horse half-dead behind me. The Judas Waterton was there. He had grieved for King Henry for too long. He spat in my face. *Fornicator,* he said, then stood back so that the guard could take me and bring me to this living death. So much for the charge of rebellion. So much for the safe-conduct.

I came to my senses on the floor of the cell. Huw said there was blood all over my face. He was weeping over me, trying to wipe it off. I felt nothing. The pain took root in my heart.

It grows, and flowers, and I am lost.

Oh, my Cathryn.

The new turnkey seems drawn to my cell. Time and again I
ask after Cathryn and he turns away. But he always comes back,
wanting stories. He was wetting his baby-breeches when I was
standing at the Harfleur palisade. But I tell him, because it's
the only thing that keeps me sane, and I tell it well – the smoke
and flame and the quarrels spitting men like chicken against
the planking, and the coloured beasts and birds of the great
tower falling . . . then I look deep in his eyes and pour my
strength into him, whispering: 'Is she still at Bermondsey?
Take this letter to her. Where are the letters she has written
me?' And he shakes his head, silent, and goes away.

But how could she have written to me? My guess is, she
doesn't know I'm here. She wouldn't think to look for
Meredyth, an anonymous Welsh rebel . . . *Annwyl Crist!* a
most terrible thought: does she think I've deserted her? Think
of something else, quickly.

The priest escaped. He took a look at the situation outside
Westminster Hall and was off, a flying black skeleton, taking
a good horse and the £90. I had told him to lodge at John
Bore's, and as far as I know, there he still is, among the harps
and clarions, living like a prince. Avarice has its uses, for
sometimes, only sometimes, I feel that he may be a gateway
out of this stinking hell.

We're so lucky. Out of the money she gave Huw in secret
we are allowed certain facilities in here, but the stench that
filters from the main jail, even through the locked connecting
door, is indescribable. It is compounded of rottenness, wanhope. I've heard the children crying. The saddest sound in the
world. Oh, Edmund, Jasper! And my littlest, new, importunate
son, my little Owen. Does he live, my love?

It seems yesterday that I knelt and kissed her white fragrant
body. I couldn't resist the fiery, silky, dewy dream . . . poured
my life into her . . . felt the child quicken . . . now the real
torture begins. The dream is a mighty adversary, fleshed in
untouchable splendour. My loins ache. It seems yesterday

447

that we first lay together. I have all but had her soul from her body and kissed it. I have never felt guilt, not for a moment. I would never confess, as sin, all we have done together. Our bliss is given by God. Or if not by God, by the old gods of the singing mountains. My gods. Hywelis's gods.

I dreamed once of Hywelis, in this place. One night, early January, colder even than now. I think I'd been here about six weeks. A passing-bell began to toll, outside in the City. Its burden was taken up by other bells. My broken hands were hurting. The bell throbbed with each surge of pain. I dreamed of Hywelis; she looked sad, and nodded in her fateful way. She had her fox on a lead. This proves that dreams are nonsense. Madog has surely outlived his span. I dreamed that the passing-bell was for Madog.

I must keep still, to outmatch these ills of love. There's a part of me that has its own life and memories. It remembers how we never lay apart, save on her brief absences. Early dawns when she'd sweetly break my sleep, rolling to lie on me, whispering, her mouth on mine, her flesh like silk making me fire all over . . . and it was I, not the King, who taught her how to kiss.

Well, we shall kiss again. The dream will be dragged from its idleness and worked within an inch of its life. I'll kiss again, those blue-pale veins on breast and thigh, those threads of mother-of-pearl where she has borne my sons. And, within the dream, again, again, again, I'll embalm these long months of wasted love in velvet, not hastily, but building for us both the shining mountain to its sunburst, from the deepest dominions of tenderness that are mine and therefore hers. Cathryn. *Cariad*, my love, my little one, where are you? Do you pray for me? Are you still at bloody Bermondsey? I'm so lost, *fy merch fach*. I wanted to buy you beautiful presents, but you bought them for me. A lovely bay horse. A silly pair of garters. I always fancied myself your protector, now I know that you are mine. Help me, Cathryn, help me, dearest dream. We're split, we're halved. This is me, Meredyth, with the grey hair and the broken hands. Still in love. For ever in love. *Am byth*, Cathryn. *Toujours*, Owen.

For the strangest reason I feel slightly more hopeful. It's

to do with this new jailer, Nickson. I've heard nothing about my plea to Chancery. But there must be a way out. *There must.* I'm going to try to work my will on Nickson. I'll fathom how I may use the priest. The answer's there somewhere. And when I've worked my will, I'll be from this Hell, and I'll have my little girl and my three sons away and, by *Dewi Sant*! we'll start a small rebellion of our own, in Wales, in the wild country.

The whore came and looked at me today. Nickson lets her through to ply her trade with someone in a cell down the passage. I think he takes a cut of her earnings but I'm not sure. He's not interested in money. I've discovered this myself.

She looked at me so intently. We talked for a few moments. She asked me how we kept ourselves so clean. Somehow I feel she too could be useful. It is far from clear in my mind, but I wonder. She and the priest, and this uncertain young jailer, Nickson.

My love and I will be safe in Wales. I will it shall be so. Everything will come right.

My sweet darling. Christ! send me news of her.

Nickson's was a narrow life. He had no friends, no wife, his parents were dead. He had done nothing and travelled no-where. But he could read, and write an ill hand which made him something of a prodigy in the other jailers' eyes. He particularly looked forward to Searching Time on Fridays, when the head keeper was away, and the other staff were hugging the brazier in the gatehouse, or teasing the harlots, or scoring hits on the fleeing rats with lumps of wood. Then he would go quietly to the end of the passage and lean against the bars (careful to keep his keys out of jeopardy) and watch the eyes and listen to the voice. He could never have enough. Harfleur, the Somme crossing, Agincourt, Rouen, Verneuil. He had the glory without the danger.

He wasn't afraid of the Welshman now; the man seemed placid, no longer harassing him with enquiries after unlikely acquaintances among the nobility. Very occasionally a letter would be handed through and these Nickson took, to humour Meredyth. The last had been to King James of Scotland; it

449

followed all the others into the brazier flames. He hurried to the cell. Friday again; bitter cold outside, the black sky full of whirling motes of ice. For once the Welshman was sitting down. He didn't seem to feel the cold, but the little one was hunched and glowering. Nickson thought: I could bring them a few live coals, but no. Before his time a felon had set fire to his bedding, himself, and had nearly incinerated the entire jail delivery.

He nodded affably against his own huge shadow on the torchlit walls.

'I've brought you some mulled ale.'

Huw rose and held out two mugs. Nickson tipped the contents of a flagon into them through the bars.

'Pay him, Huw,' Owen said.

'No, no,' Nickson said hastily. 'There's plenty. It'll warm you.' Owen said to Huw, in Welsh: 'I may be wrong. But I think he's softening.'

The head keeper would have roared at them to speak English. Nickson said wistfully:

'Could I speak your tongue? Could you teach it to me?'

Owen came to lean, mug in hand, against the bars.

'None can teach it, but some can learn. It's the ancient tongue of the gods.' Then he said: 'I've something to ask you, Nick.'

'Christ, no, Master Meredyth!' said Nickson impatiently. 'I can tell you nothing!'

'Why, Nick! This is nothing. I'm over my madness. No more royal delusions for me, boy. This concerns my servant. He's blameless. You realize he should be at liberty?'

Huw said, sharp and quick: 'I'll not go! I'll never leave you!' and Owen rapped back: 'Quiet! You'll do as I say!' while Nickson looked from one to the other, yearning to understand the strange quicksilver speech.

Owen said: 'He's quite innocent. He was never charged.'

Nickson felt bemused. *No one goes in, no one goes out.* Yet . . . the Welshman was right. The other jailers will look to you for judgement, the head keeper had said. Maybe now was the time to use that judgement.

Owen smiled at him.

'Tell me again,' said Nickson, 'that final charge . . . where the old Duke of York was slain . . .' but Owen turned away and sat down.

'I'm weary tonight,' he said bleakly. 'Too many war memories. It's not good for a man to dwell on these things.'

'Oh!' Nickson revealed his bitter disappointment. 'Well then. A good night to you.'

He stumped off, great wavering shadow, shoulders drooping like a child ousted from a game. Owen called after him softly.

'Think on what I said!'

He got up. Always pale these days, now his face was drained. Sweat rimmed his lips. He went to where Huw sat shivering, and clasped him round the neck.

'Drink your ale. You young fool. I have him. You nearly wrecked it. You'll be going out, you see. You're my way out, boy.'

'Oh, my lord.'

'I'm not your lord. Now listen. You'll be going out, and soon. But you'll be back, *exactly* four weeks from tonight, before the City gates are closed. You're my key, you and the priest. God grant he's where I think he is still. And the woman – I've yet to talk to her. And all the others. Now sit still. Listen, and then, let us pray . . . now first, when you return, you'll find me dying.'

The first week is gone, and so has Huw. Christ be praised. Nickson is puffed with pride that he has got away with taking his momentous decision, though I doubt the head keeper even noticed Huw's departure. Nick has earned himself more yarns from me. He also has a new toy. He tortures the gods with his filthy English tongue, and the brainwork is nearly killing him.

'*Telyn*,' he says. 'Harp?' That's right, Nick. '*Mynydd* – mountain. *Carchar* – prison!' And looks at me with furrowed forehead and I say: '*Da iawn!* – good boy!' and he smirks. By tomorrow every word will have flown his thick pate.

The difficult part is to come. For my death will need to be convincing and dramatic, in this place of casual death. Nick

451

leans convivially close. He retains sense enough not to enter, though did he know it I wouldn't lay hand on him. Not yet. The lesson's over for tonight. What now? Ah yes. Killing the prisoners at Agincourt. King's orders, Nick, I say gently, and his eyes are avid. There's something unhealthy about this, but I must give him what he wants, then I can have . . .

My head in her lap again. The softest lap in the world. How often I've lain there, feeling her heat, and she bends her beautiful patrician face and cloaks me with her hair and kisses me . . . *Annwyl Crist!* she'll find me changed, with my grey hair and twisted, crooked hand, and will she love me still? I must be very down tonight, to think like this. She will always love me. She called me her light, her star. *Am byth*, Cathryn. *Toujours*, Owen.

I'm worried about Huw. Is four weeks long enough? Will he be able to buy good horses with the money? Will he find the road to Glyndyfrdwy, to Gwydir, to Sycharth? He has a marvellous sense of direction, though, he can ride by the stars. And the priest? The thin priest is fleet, and a renegade, but *is he where he should be, by now?*

There is silence. I have been talking all through my private thoughts, right up to the killing of Brabant, clad in a tabard made from a herald's banner and mistaken for one of no account, and I must have told it well. Nick is full of gratitude. I think he wants to give me some kind of reward.

'You must be lonesome without the boy,' he says, and, God curse him, closes one filthy eye. I clasp my hands behind me or I should be through the bars choking him and spoiling everything. I say calmly: 'I was never one for boys,' and here's the time and moment, fallen into place.

'A woman, though,' I say. 'It's been a long time.'

Y diafol! The last time . . . my darling, you were so impassioned, you swept me away, *and the child came forth before its time* . . . oh, Christ! was it my fault? Forgive me, my little Owen. It will all be put right.

'Alison is the cleanest,' Nick is saying.

'I haven't much money left,' I say. 'I gave most of it to the boy, to make his way in the world, alone he is now.'

He laughs. 'She's cheap.' And he goes to fetch her, while I

sit down, completely awed by luck. Alison was the one I had planned for.

She entered full of a trembling curiosity. On London Bridge there was a foreign alchemist's shop, full of strange charms and amulets, where men worked with the Philosopher's Stone, trying to change base metal into gold. Peeping into that shop she'd had the same feelings as now, entering Meredyth's cell. She was a little afraid. Once she had been sent to one of the private cells on the eve of the occupant's execution. The man had nearly killed her. She had looked into Meredyth's eyes before, studying their extraordinary colour and expression as a fisherman gauges the sea, the different currents and changes, sometimes full, sometimes grievously barren. The eyes of the condemned man had been like that. She had never had much to say to Meredyth, had merely looked and gone away, combing her matted blonde hair with her fingers as she did now and Nickson locked her in with him.

She was seventeen. Her name was not Alison at all, but Annetje, which none could be troubled to pronounce. She had come to England with an elderly wool merchant who had admired her blonde virginity on the quay at Bruges. He lived with his sister in a mansion near Temple Bar. There she had spent two happy years, sharing the merchant's soft bed. Within ten minutes of his abrupt demise she had been thrown out into the street by the sister. The teeming maw of London had swallowed her and she had been arrested for soliciting in Candlewick Street. She knew men, but the like of this one she did not know.

He drew her to him, calling her an endearment in a strange tongue. His hands were cold, yet warmth wrapped her round as she stood on dirty bare feet bloody with vermin-bites, chapped from the chill. She looked up at him uncertainly in the torchlight from the passage. His eyes were wild, secret on hers, with a transient veil of exultation replacing earlier pain. She saw again how clean he had endeavoured to keep himself and his dwelling. He led her to the corner of the cell where there was straw. The corner was almost out of sight. Nickson watched them lie down. Then out of an uncharacteristic sense of respect that did him credit, he removed one of the torches from the wall and went away, leaving them the privacy of gloom.

They lay very still. She put her arms round him. He was completely unaroused. He made no attempt to take her. Fear sprang; she had been beaten before for men's impotence. She struggled. He lay on her lightly, but she couldn't move. Lie quiet, he whispered. Don't be afraid. Together they listened to the jail-noises; the screams of someone fighting, a child wailing, a man coughing up his lungs. Nickson's steps and the tiny music of his keys, diminishing. The man's tense slender weight left her. He lay propped on his elbow. She could see his eyes, faint mysterious gleams. He murmured: 'He's gone!'

'Back to the fire!' she whispered. 'Back to his sty!'

'You're French? No?'

'Flemish,' she nodded, and shivered.

'That's good. I'm against the English now.'

'So am I,' she said. 'Now.'

She smelled bad, sickly with hopelessness. Her feet touched his ankles like shards of ice. You're cold, he said, and drew her close, rubbing her feet with his own. Not now, she said, after a moment. It's the first time I've been warm this winter. The lovely warmth of him poured into her, making her sleepy. He wasn't going to hurt her. Relief reminded her of why she was here and she moved her hands deftly down his body. He caught them and held them against his chest. Lice, brought forth by the warmth, moved to torment them both. The madman down the passage let out a terrible yell.

'Once,' she found herself saying, 'I lived in a beautiful house, with someone who loved me and cared for me.'

He laughed, an awful bitter laugh. It frightened her again. Then he said: 'So did I, *cariad*, so did I,' and patted her, and her fear fled. He scratched himself and cursed the lice, and she did likewise, and they laughed, friends in trouble, and he said: 'What would you like?'

'I?'

'You're hungry? I've a little food.'

'I'd like to wash my feet,' she said hesitantly.

'Then you shall.' He rose, moving confidently through the semi-darkness. She heard him pouring water and tearing cloth, then saw him as a vague dark shape, kneeling.

'I'll be your valet.' She felt him gently laving her feet with the wet cloth. 'I'm good with feet.' No, she said faintly. 'The King does it for the paupers,' he said. She winced as the cloth touched a rat-bite. Poor child, he thought. A very faint light fell on the foot he held. And suddenly it was Cathryn's foot, Cathryn stepping from the chariot at Leicester, holding out her innocent unknowing foot for him to shoe long ago; Cathryn's foot that he had spent the whole of one hour kissing and holding against his face in the firelight not so long ago . . . not now, he thought. I haven't wept for months. Nickson may come back at any minute and take this girl from me. But Alison, feeling kindness, remembering warmth, would already have done more for him than he was about to ask.

When he had dried her feet she took the cloth and washed her face and lifted her dress and washed her body. Then, refreshed but damp, she lay down again. She did not offer herself to him again, but for her own comfort pressed close, feeling his rapid, listening breath, and the tumult of his mind. She whispered: 'And you? What would *you* like?'

He bent very close and whispered:

'I must escape. But I need your help.' Then, softly: '*Y diafol!*' as shuffling steps and a light began along the passage. He rolled on top of her again. Instinct made her clasp him and moan. Nickson gave a hoarse guffaw.

'Go to it!' he said. 'And a good night to you!'

The light died, the steps faded. They drew apart, hearts pounding. Tell me, tell me quickly what you want, she whispered. But hold me while you tell.

'There's danger in it. I must have a diversion, to draw off the other jailers. In battle, while the main strategem goes forward, there must be a flank attack to diffuse the adversary. You understand?'

'Tell me what I have to do.'

He told her. Then he said: 'I wish to God I could remember what the main jail looks like. We'll need to go through there like hares,' and she described the structure of the awful room and the gatehouse and he fixed it in his mind, holding her close, while she wished for that day on the Bruges quay back again, and Meredyth coming ashore instead of the wool-merchant . . .

You'll need dry straw, he said, and she answered: a fresh bale comes in next week. Conserve some, he said. But the time and day are most important. *Three weeks from tonight.* The moment you hear us coming through, begin. I'll give you enough money to bail you and perhaps get you back to Flanders . . . and she said tearfully: 'I want no money. How do you say *I love you*, in your language?'

'R'*wy'n dy garu di*,' he answered absently, and she repeated it, her accent almost perfect, sad that he did not notice or understand. She fell into a doze. He woke her asking:

'What became of your protector, the one with the fine house?' and she told him of the old man's death and her own subsequent disgrace. He said: 'Tell me how he died. Was he sick for long?'

'Barely a week. He complained of his chest and his left arm. He held his heart.'

'Gasping, was he? How soon was it after he held his heart?'

'Yes, gasping, groaning. About an hour.'

'Thank you. Sleep now, *cariad. Diolch i Dduw*. Thank God.'

He slept. Stealthily she pressed her head against his neck and wrapped her feet round his ankles and held him close. R'*wy'n dy garu di*, Master Meredyth. She was awakened by a soft muttering. She leaned to catch his dreaming words.

'. . . the priest. The priest.' He was grinding his teeth.

'You want a priest?' He was instantly alert.

'It must be a certain priest. None other will do.'

'I know of a priest,' Alison said. 'Someone came in tonight, a thief who's been working close to Newgate. There's a priest who comes to the gates every night just before Searching Time. It's a special act of intercession . . . to pray for all captives within.'

He sat up violently in the rustling straw. 'Describe him!' She told him what the new inmate had said. The priest had spoken to him just before he was arrested, telling him to mend his ways. A very thin priest, swift, like an arrow.

Meredyth bent and kissed her. She wept, for all the lost hours and kisses such as these, and very soon Nickson came to take her away.

Only three more days left. Nick and I are both nearly out of our minds. I through this fierce hidden excitement and he at sight of my mortal sickness which means the loss of his bed-time story.

I fell sick four days ago, in the middle of the old tale about the Lombards and my leg ripped open by a dirty poignard, and Nick saying, in his usual vein – did it hurt? and I answering, no, it was the sweetest pleasure, try it some time, Nick, my irony wasted on him. Then suddenly I clawed at my chest. I know I turned pale; I felt cold sweat on my face. He saw it; he started dancing about not so much at my seizure but at fear of being cheated of the tale's ending. I took to my bed then. It's a wide plank suspended by chains from the wall. I began to groan. I remembered how John Fletcher rolled his eyes in the tent at Harfleur, crying something about Hywelis having wished him to death . . . I rolled my eyes. Soon I crawled over to the bars so Nick could see my agony.

It's weird, this feigning. I know that if it went too far it would take hold, Death misliking to be mocked. I'm like the dragon-lizards men bring back from the East; when I choose I can become any shape, any colour. It has to be inspired by wanting something badly enough. As in that old dance, which ended in her lap. Her soft lap. She often calls me a sorcerer, in play. It was my sorcery, she says, that willed her on to the gallery that night. If so, it's my inheritance from the Lord, Glyn Dŵr.

My sorcerer's luck is holding. Alison managed to get through to see me yesterday. I was alarmed and told her to go away, but she brought me staggering news. *The priest has been into the main jail.* Some poor Christian wretch did die the other night and was shriven. They only had to open the main gate and there was Holy Church, ready and waiting, and now he has an *entrée* to Newgate! Bless you, Father. You'll be rewarded next week, both for your work this coming Friday

457

and for something else. When you marry me to Cathryn, my soul.

I've been up from bed again to tell Nick where the pain is. Clever Alison told him: 'I saw someone die just like that!' God protect Alison from being harmed in the mêlée. I think of her as a dear daughter, and wish her well. I had a daughter once, conceived in that beautiful sun-silken cove, and too beautiful to stay long in this rotten old world . . . tomorrow I'll lie down for the last time. My resurrection shall be on Friday. *Annwyl Crist!* On Friday my love and I will be together again.

Bermondsey *is* a fortress. I remember now; she mentioned the fact when we were trying to think of somewhere safe to send the boys. There will be menservants. Force will be needed, force, to be provided by Huw. To think I ever thought him lackwit. Just see how well he's instructed the priest. Everything still hangs on him.

I trust there won't be too much violence at Bermondsey; I don't want Cathryn upset. I want her alone with me, somewhere quiet, over the border, safe, in some hidden hostel or a kinsman's house. I want to say many things to her.

I've prayed. To Christ, to Almighty God, to the Virgin Mother. But I've also prayed to the old ones, Drwynwen the White One, the love-goddess of Anglesey. And also Aerfen, the river-goddess. The fighter. It's damp enough in this place for Aerfen to feel at home. Greedy, faithful Aerfen needs a human sacrifice. Perhaps she will waive her need for once. I wonder if Huw met up with Hywelis, that is, providing she still lives. But then I would always know if Hywelis had died, and that's a mystery I've never been able to fathom.

I've decided we shall leave the boys at Barking for the time being. I am not so worried about them. It's a good place, and little Owen too should be safe at Westminster, unless Suffolk has taken him to Barking too, which is likely. My little girl, my love, comes first.

Nick has offered me a doctor. I told him I had scant faith in doctors, that from all accounts a doctor hastened King Henry's death at Vincennes. Then Nick wanted to hear about Vincennes, and the river-journey (which was mostly hearsay to me anyway), so I started, lovely and poetic, and had another seizure at the best part, and fell gasping to the floor. Nick is demented. He must love me very much. Soon he will see what love can do.

Now it's night. I can rest. I am going to indulge my mind, and think of her, and of our next embrace. It's like going to Hertford with the harps; the very first time I set foot in that beloved place. The dream is near.

Where shall I begin, *fy merch fach*, my love, my own, my dear delight? At your toes? No – too soon after poor Alison's raw feet . . . I'll start at your hair. In the centre of your brow where the parting begins the skin is whitest and shines like a star. I've spread your hair out, in its great darkness, rippling with a few prisms of copper and blue in fire or sun or candle-light. One or two tendrils lie across your neck and breast. I'm going too fast. You pluck your brows very fine. Perfect high crescents, they give you an imperious look at times. The little scar above your left ear, that's where you fell down the stairs at Poissy and cut your temple on a holy-water stoup. Dame Alphonse cried for an hour because you'd hurt your-self, and because Belle would be furious. Your beautiful elegant nose. There! I've kissed it, once more. Your long glossy eyes, I've seen them filled with tears, loving you, I've opened my eyes and seen the snow melting when we reach the peak of the mountain. Oh, Cathryn, you're fire and silk . . . I didn't mean my thoughts to go this far. I only meant to look.

I can taste the smile on your long shining lips. When you walk away and look back once with your long neck arched and that smile and the sad, gleaming, wanton eye, it turns my heart over. And nothing can keep me from you, not locked doors, nor bars, nor chains. Your eyes, more beautiful than the thrice-mewed hawk, your breasts whiter than the bog-cotton where it grows by the river . . . my Olwen. My Cathryn. I love you. Be patient. Just a little longer. The dream is near.

Put your arms round me. Your left arm round my waist, your right arm round my neck. My right hand in your hair, my left hand pressing you to me low where your back arches – they say that's the true sign of a loving woman, that deep arch in the back. I should know. Now let me kiss you. Very slowly, I'll melt open your lips, then take your whole mouth within my own. All kiss now, we are. You love to be kissed. I love kissing. My face must be very pale. Good. If Nickson looks in he'll think me worse. We hang on this kiss, it makes us shake like wind-shocked trees. Time is slowing down. Where's that place on your neck . . . I think I've made a permanent imprint there, like a strawberry. And the place just below your right breast, where your keen ribs begin. Down, and down, you're so sweet all over, like the taste of the sea in the cove. Don't tremble so, my darling. It's only foolish old Meredyth, your renegade jailbird lover, a common felon. No! It's Owen ap Meredyth ap Tydier, Esquire, your tried and chosen mate. Your husband. *Am byth*, Cathryn. *Toujours*, Owen.

I can see you clearly. Cathryn, you're here! I've brought you into this cell, my dear dear child, my beloved wife. Soul of my bliss. *Cariad*. I love you. Soon, now. Soon.

My death will be well-timed, for I'm running out of tales. When you and I are safe in Glyn Dŵr country I will send a letter to Glewlwyd Mighty-Grasp, telling him he has missed the best story of all.

God keep you, dearest dream, until we are in each other's arms, when we shall have need neither of gods nor men.

Oh, my Cathryn.

The seabird was flying east, seeking a harbour inland from the storms blowing up off Bristol; the pattern of its great white wings was leisured and confident. It dipped to rest and feed at the Wye and the Severn, then flew steadily on towards London's great river. The keen wind spurred and deflected its flight; at one time it converged with and followed the small company riding south-east through the late January day. There were about a score of men, with spare horses galloping alongside on leading reins. It was a hard, quiet, dedicated ride. The hoofbeats were softened by the thin powdery snow. The only other sounds were the chinking bridles, the creak of leather and the occasional terse word that passed between the men. They had left behind the worst of the weather, where snow was piled like cumulus on the mountains of Powys, on the Berwyn range and the giant shape of Mynydd y Cemais.

Faces were muffled to the eyes in wool; the men wore light half-armour and each carried his chosen weapon. Some of them were too young to remember the old days of Glyn Dŵr's rebellion but a race memory roared within them and they rode proudly, glad of the chance to strike one tiny token blow against the Saeson. Although they expected no fighting, even those who had never seen the man towards whom they rode were willing to die for him because they shared his blood. These were the tough mountain men of Powysland, men who could weep for a song yet kill with one expert thrust, coax silver from the harp yet chop and hack and ambush if necessary before the last note had faded. These were the ones of rebel strain, the poets, the lovers, the killers. Softly and swiftly they rode, coming like a wolf-pack over the border and southwards on to London. Huw rode in the forefront, his eyes grim and aching above his muffler.

The sky was clear, pale blue in places, the sun declining as they entered the snow-laced forests skirting the city. The leader bared his face and smiled, his teeth white among his black beard and moustaches. We're in good time, he said to Huw. You're a fine guide, boy. And Huw said, shivering: 'We are too early!'

'Better early than late.' The company reined in within the heart of the forest. Steam rose from the horses. Will it snow? someone asked, and the swarthy man, Theodor, squinted up to where the sun was firing the whitened treetops and a cold little star had appeared. No, it will be fine, he said. There's the thaw coming. Clumps of melted snow slid from the branches and dropped softly around them in the clearing where they waited.

'That was a great performance he gave, that night at Windsor,' said Howell ap Llewellyn, shaking damp from his beard. '*Duw!* It's a crime . . .' None answered. There was no answer.

At that moment the seabird joined them, its wings waving languidly overhead, tired near the end of its long flight. One of the younger men, unable to resist so sure a target, fitted a bolt into the springald he carried. He fired straight and true into the pale sky silver with reflections of sun and snow. The bird's body was pierced clean. Its wings folded gracefully and it plummeted through the branches, bringing down a small avalanche and falling into a snowdrift. Its own weight entombed it. White within white, invisible in death. From a distance a bell began to sound for Vespers.

'It's time,' said the leader. He leaned and clapped Huw on the shoulder. 'Take us to him.'

They rode on, cloaked, weapons hidden, rode bunched together like all the other companies of merchants and travellers making their way home into the city. They came to Newgate and waited, dispersing a little to ride unobtrusively up and down, in and out of the gathering shadows, while the snow-light gleamed in their eyes and the cold little star was joined by another and another, and the white roofs blushed under the dying sun.

Within the jail, Nickson had thrown caution away, and had locked himself in with his charge. He sat on the side of Owen's plank bed. The Welshman's lips were blue, his face like ash. A terrible groan made Nickson leap up. He found himself muttering: 'Don't die, for Jesus' sake, don't die. You cannot die. You must stay here for ever and let me drink your life, your experiences. You are all I am not, all I ever wanted to be . . .' The Welshman was clawing at his heart, his eyes tightly shut. Nickson looked round wildly. In his frenzy he had neglected to fasten the door connecting the passage and the main jail. Alison was hanging about. Nickson shouted at her. She pouted and wandered off to stand beneath the torchlight at the entrance to the main jail.

Owen's eyes opened, dull where they had been so bright. He began to gasp, long intakes of tortured breath. He was holding his left arm. He said weakly: 'Nick. Ah, Nick.'

'Master Meredyth! For Christ's sake! What is it?'

'Help me, Nick. I'm dying.'

'No, no!' Nickson cried. 'You'll be well. Just lie quiet.'

'Nick,' he said through his teeth. 'We've been friends . . .'

'I'll get a doctor.' The keeper started for the door. A terrible groan halted him midway.

'For the love of God! I must have a priest! I've led an evil life . . . killed men . . . lied, I've lain with women. A priest . . .'

'I'll get one.' Nickson fumbled with keys, their great weight dragged at his belt. He locked the cell behind him and ran through into the main jail where the prisoners were sitting or lying in apathy and the jailers were stoning the rats. Alison was making her bed, spreading straw about, he nearly tripped over her as he ran, rushing through the gatehouse and unlocking the outer door. There, as usual, stood the priest, hands folded, head as usual bowed in prayer. Near him stood the Welshman's servant.

'Father!' Nickson seized the priest's bony arm, drawing him inside. Huw slipped in beside them, and the keeper said: 'Oh, *you're* here . . . your master's sick. For God's sake, come . . . do what you can.'

They went through to where Owen lay. Nickson locked all four of them inside the cell. Huw fell on his knees beside the bed. The priest took out his crucifix. Owen looked deep into Huw's eyes. They were full of tears. *Annwyl Crist!* he thought. Something's gone amiss. The priest bent over him, masking his face from the jailer. Owen frowned savagely at Huw. He whispered, barely framing the words: 'What's wrong?'

Tears ran down Huw's face. Owen thought: how tired he looks, but shaped his lips again almost in silence, saying: 'Are they here?' and Huw whispered incoherently: '*All.* I saw the witchwoman . . . her fox bit me!'

Praise God. He got to Glyndyfrdwy. Nickson was shuffling nearer. Owen began to groan and mutter at the priest, watching the cadaverous face, the knowing eyes. The priest said sharply to Huw and the jailer: 'Stand back! I must hear his confession!' and began praying. He raised the crucifix, a blessing, a signal, and began another rapid salvo of prayer. Owen expelled every ounce of breath from his lungs and lay still.

The priest touched him on the forehead and turned to face the others. 'This man is dead,' he said soberly. 'For the love of God, open the door of this vile place to give his spirit passage!'

Nickson turned the key and flung the cell door wide. Then he took the few steps to where Owen lay. The eyes were half open. He could see a thread of white, a glimpse of pupil.

You died, he thought disgustedly. How dare you die! He bent closer with a vague idea of trying to fathom what had been so entrancing about that face, and so greedy for more stories that he would have torn the dead lips open to get at them . . . and later, much later, explaining himself away to the Constable, the justiciars, and to Gloucester's henchmen, he found himself saying: 'Sirs, he *was* dead! I saw him dead! I swear it!' He had never seen anything, bird or beast or man, move so fast. Faster than a whip uncoiling, Owen came up off the bed and had him by the throat, crying: 'Huw! the keys!'

Huw dived for the belt, but the keys were latched tight on to the ring. Nickson kicked and lashed out, catching Huw a hard blow on the side of the head. Owen felt his hands losing their grip, thought: *Duw!* he's stronger than I dreamed, prison has weakened me, and hung desperately on the jailer's throat, with his two broken fingers hooked behind the man's ear, hearing the priest cry: 'Hurry!' as he stood in the open doorway of the cell. Nickson's face was turning claret, but still he struggled and kicked and struck, twisting, dragging Owen down on to the bed, rolling on him, then being rolled on. The bed collapsed; they fell to the floor with the keys crushed beneath the two flailing bodies and Huw tearing at the jailer's belt, cursing, and the priest hissing: 'Be swift!' and Alison waiting at the entrance to the passage, listening and trembling and afraid. Owen felt the strength leaving his hands. The jailer spat in his face, temporarily blinding him. Then suddenly he felt all resistance cease and saw Huw's knife-hilt protruding from Nickson's side and the keys in the boy's hand. You've killed him, *bach*. A sacrifice. Aerfen has had her blood-gift.

The priest rushed over and hauled Owen upright, thrusting Huw before him to the door. They ran from the cell together, not looking back to see Nickson crawl upright and hold his wound in utter disbelief. As they raced along the passage, Alison set the jail on fire.

Over the days she had hoarded new straw. Her face was scratched bloody over battles for its possession. She had stolen chips of pitch from the torches and fat from the rushlights. She had torn up her ragged underclothes and mixed them with the straw. And all day she had meandered up and down the jail wall on the dry side, away from the drain, strewing the mixture, adding little billets of wood. The other inmates had laughed at her. Another victim of jail-madness. She had ignored them, carrying on with her privileged task. *R'wy'n dy garu di*, Master Meredyth. And now, leaping high, she seized a torch from its sconce and threw it at her carefully prepared trail of combustion. The straw exploded and a wall of flame blossomed the length of the jail. Panic erupted. Women screamed like slaughtered pigs, people ran from the blazing area knocking one another down, while the rats came out from the burning straw with their fur on fire, spreading trails of flame as they dived for the safety of the drain. The jailers, half-blinded and choking, rushed to douse the fire. Owen and Huw and the priest came through along the burning side; sparks and red-hot wisps scorched their clothing. They saw Alison, standing quite still, smiling against the already dying flames. They ran through the gatehouse and unlocked the doors and they were out. Not only free of Newgate but of the City itself. The sun was nearly down and quite soon the gates of London would be closing.

The cold air hit Owen like strong drink, making him falter dizzily for a moment before running on. The starlight and sunset blazed in his eyes, restoring instantly all their old beauty and brilliance. Still running, with the priest going like a deerhound beside them, he turned and seized Huw by the hair and gave him a smacking kiss on the mouth. Then he laughed, running, and from every corner of the network of little streets and from the entrances of alleys and courts and tavern-yards and from the road to freedom and the open fields, the strong shadows came hurrying to greet him, some riding, some leading horses; the men of Wales, bloodkinsmen all, some unknown until now, some known from childhood, those whose fathers had grown in wildness under the law of the Lord, Glyn Dŵr. His cousins, the fighting bards, Howell ap Llewellyn and John ap Meredyth reached him first, clutching him in their arms, kissing him, clouting his back with great blows that drove out his breath, talking wildly, crowing with laughter. Then Rhys and Gruffydd, Llywd and Hywel and Gwylym and the Theodor cousins from Penmynydd who had scarcely set foot in England the whole of their lives . . . all of them, crowding him into their embrace, ruffling his hair, exclaiming over his thinness in the snow-blue shadows and starlight and setting sun. They had a cloak of thick Welsh wool for him, for he had on only his doublet and hose, and their love and loyalty and shared triumph had set him shivering and near to tears.

And the beloved tongue fell sweetly on his ears once more, the full vowels and guttural consonants, each syllable a song, rippling with laughter and pride and loving mockery.

'We've come to spring you, Owen, boy!'

'Ah, well met, well met, my little one!'

'But you didn't need us, did you? Not with this villain!' and Gwyl ap Vychan smote the priest such a clout on his back that his thin frame almost doubled, and he felt wildly to see that his purse was intact.

'Nor with this one! Ah, God! there's blood on you, boy!' said John ap Meredyth with terrible pride as he looked at Huw. And Owen embraced Huw again, feeling more tears on the boy's face, saying: 'Don't cry, you fool! it's over . . .' and snatched up the reins of the strong fresh horses that had been brought for them. The priest had already mounted his; there seemed a lot of noise being made so near to Newgate and his skeleton's face was worried. The leaders were of like mind. The black-bearded Theodor raised his hand. Some of the excitement was tempered.

'Time we were away!' They mounted, the horses' whirling hooves churned silently in the melting snow. Howell ap Llewellyn's horse bumped up against Owen's mount. Hywelis wished us well, he said. She awaits our coming . . .

The horses sprang forward. The leaders began to set a fast pace towards the meadows of Smithfield and the outer ward of Farringdon. The company rode close, cloaks lifting to reveal weapons glinting in the snow-bright evening. The sky was turning a delicate lilac, more stars were out. Faster they rode, past cottages, with their little plumes of smoke, away from London. The horses' hooves were a mere ghost-beat on the soft ground. Owen rode in the middle of the pack.

466

He was dazed and disorientated after the long months without sky or air. They had travelled half a mile before realization thrust at him. He forced his mount close to the leaders, hauling on the reins so that the whole company jostled to a cursing halt behind him.

'For Christ's sake!' he cried. 'This isn't the way!'

'It's the way home, boy,' said Theodor.

Owen seized the leader's bridle. 'Devil damn! Where are we going? We must go back! Back, before they close the gates! through Ludgate and past St Paul's and over London Bridge!' He wrenched the horse's head round, it screamed and reared. 'South! Over the river! Or we shall be too late!'

They pressed about him. Howell ap Llewellyn and John ap Meredyth were closest, their faces stark and silent.

'Why in Hell did you think I sent for you all?' he cried.

Most of the men were quiet. Yet a little chill whisper arose.

'*South!*' Owen shouted, as if at deaf madmen. 'To fetch my little girl away! *Cathryn!* To burn down bloody Bermondsey!'

The horses stood quietly in the starry snow. In the distance St Paul's great voice sounded. John ap Meredyth began to speak. His words faltered and faded away.

'Oh, sweet God. Sweet Christ. Owen . . .'

He turned to Huw and said: 'Damn you, boy. Didn't you tell him?' Huw bent his head, weeping.

Howell ap Llewellyn was the bravest. He reached out and took Owen's hand, crushing it as if the pain might somehow shield him from the words.

'Queen Cathryn died over a year ago, Owen. All your sons are safe and well. But your little girl is dead.'

Owen withdrew his hand. He rode forward apart from them all. He looked up at the sky. There was one star, most beautiful and bright; it grew larger and longer until it spread itself across his sight in a blazing blur of silver, invading his mind so that for a time nothing else could enter. Only the soft voices of his friends, and the feel of their arms about him as they rode close to steady him in the saddle. Then the star shrank again, becoming for ever distant in the amethyst sky, as he remembered the tolling bell in the winter's night more than a year ago.

And he knew that the dance was over and the dream was done.

He looked back. He said: 'Where is she?'

'In St Paul's. Owen . . .'

Not their entreaties, nor their curses, nor even their weapons could hold him. Theodor attempted to detain him with some force, but saw his eyes and was afraid for the first time in twenty years. Owen turned his horse towards London. The priest, scarcely comprehending, looked at him; the eyes looked back, communicating their dreadful wound. *Shrive me, priest. This man is dead.* He turned from them all and rode back through the closing gates of the City towards the source of the tolling bell.

He walked through the great dark doors of St Paul's. He made no attempt to claim Sanctuary by touching the High Altar. He did not have to seek the place where she was; it drew him unerringly into a side aisle, quiet and almost hidden from view. The tomb looked very white against the other aged monuments. It was low and flat and plain; unembellished save for the arms cut into the top and a Latin frieze denoting whose mother and widow she once was. No flowers, no birds, no words or tokens of what had been. Nothing.

And across this nothingness he laid himself down. He let its bitter chill embrace him. Some time during the night priests and monks, unheard, unseen and unaware, moved softly to the High Altar with prayers and candlelight.

Her tomb bore no effigy. He became her effigy. And there he stayed until morning, when he was discovered by those who came to take him unresisting back to Newgate.

Epilogue

Pembroke Castle, 1461

He looks so fine, so fair, in his red doublet. It is new velvet with a high collar. He let me help him put it on. I saw where his blood will soak almost invisibly into the red. He is mine, and has always been mine, and was never mine. I know the date and time and manner of his death. I have seen it in all its tragic nobility. I have heard his last words upon this earth. He will be brave. Will I? I have not told him.

He looks more than ever like the Lord these days, except that he is clean-shaven. His face is very gaunt, a fine falcon's face, like the Lord's, and he is about the same age as Glyn Dŵr when he died. His eyes are still very beautiful. This past month the last of their bitterness seems strangely to have departed. He holds himself very straight, and he is pleased to be going again to the fighting. He has outlived most of his enemies and friends, and all but one of the three sons, Jasper.

Golden Edmund is dead these past five years, slain fighting near Carmarthen against the Yorkists, at the age of twenty-six. In time he will be re-interred before the High Altar of *Dewi Sant*. His purpose was accomplished. Although Edmund never saw his son, he, Henry, is now the one. The seed is sown. The line is pure. The dynasty is founded. Henry is five years old. His mother is Margaret Beaufort, great-niece of the Cardinal. She was fourteen when she bore Henry. Neither comely nor gracious, she is aware of her part in the whole pattern of good and evil and passion and war. Edmund was the one. Edmund was the child got in anger after the valets at Windsor had degraded Owen for his liaison with the Queen-Dowager. The bloody anger ran in Edmund, and now in his son, Henry. Wales will rule England. But first, there must be blood and sacrifice again. The foes who now rage are the enemies of the dynasty to come. It is war *à l'outrance*. York against Lancaster. Worse even than the French wars were.

All the black one's efforts were in vain. The force beyond the spheres, known to my own tormented spirit, the cone of

471

power raised by our mystic heritage, finally saw her damned and disgraced. She was discovered about to administer poison to the King – to 'Little Harry'. The ensuing search was thorough – the black books, the corpses of animals, the secrets of herbal and alchemy – all was revealed, and Eleanor was stripped half-naked and flogged through the streets of London as a witch. And seven years ago she died, an outcast, and blackness had her.

Humphrey of Gloucester is dead these past fourteen years. The last seven of them he lived disgraced for Eleanor's crimes. Suffolk murdered him. Some said that he fell in a stroke, but I know otherwise.

Suffolk himself is dead, beheaded for his allegiance to Lancaster – to 'Little Harry' – on a log of driftwood on Portsmouth strand by the raging rebel Yorkists who seek supremacy now. This is the beginning of the last long struggle initiated by Richard of York. For Richard's dead, his head spiked on the Bar at Micklegate in York. And his son, the giant Edward, rides forth in vengeance. The giant, bred by Richard and Cicely Neville.

Cardinal Beaufort died the same year as his old rival, Gloucester. He died peacefully enough, having laid up treasure on earth, and lies at Winchester.

James of Scotland is dead, murdered by his nobles at Perth twenty-four years ago. And so is Joan.

And Owen's little Owen. He lived long enough to take holy orders and died at Westminster.

And Cathryn's dead. *Cathryn's dead.* How many hundred times have I heard those words? I had to cling very tight to sanity when he returned to me as the Lord had promised he would, or we should both have been swallowed by grief and darkness. He came back to me quite soon after that second time in Newgate. He was there for only a few weeks, until they realized that he was of some notability and Little Harry roused himself from his holy trance. They took Owen to Windsor in captivity for some further time. Windsor, of all places! with its sublime memories. And then came mercy. Little Harry, aided by his favourite councillors, recalled that there was such a person as Master Tydier, for whom he had professed love in this very spot by the black and purple rocks of Pembroke. A general pardon was issued by the Council. Master Tydier was absolved of all his nebulous crimes.

And he came back. By then I had a house ready for him. The Howells and Meredyths helped me build it. He came back, mad and gaunt and grieving. More than once he struck me because I was not her. He began to drink himself to death. I brewed the white bryony for his madness. I smashed the jugs and poured away the drink. I gave him an amethyst to wear against the demon. And then I took him to my bed, where I had always longed for him. I held him while he wept and cursed life and prayed for death and vengeance and turned to me with a terrible passion that made me bleed, and he could have killed me to ease himself, but then he would have been left unprotected.

Hour after hour, month after month, he talked of her. How she looked, how she spoke, how she loved him. The first time, the last time, the times in between. He unrolled their life together like a blazing parchment before my sight; it burned and blackened and was finally blown to the wind. He need never have described her to me. I saw her. Although she was not my charge or care as he is, I took my spirit in charity, to ease her death.

She died very soon after being taken to Bermondsey twenty-four years ago. While she lay, quite pale and lovely, her life ebbing from the recent birth, I heard and saw them harassing her to repent her carnal sin. It made me very angry. I saw them dictate the will she made asking pardon of her son the King. She repented, but only with her lips. She was already far from them, a frail vessel riven by the madness of Valois. But I helped her. I took her mind within my spirit's hands, and brought her safely through the gate. She saw me. She smiled. She called me Belle. I believe she once said: 'We shall all be one love, having expiated our sins.' At least, that is what Owen told me she said.

And then I went to him in a dream to try to prepare him while the bell tolled on and on. He did not understand. He has never understood that he and I are one.

I was never jealous. I know that she was good and generous

and utterly true in her love for him. She gave him a season of rapture which he swears was the greatness I once spoke of. He has no idea of the greatness to come.

It was far harder to reconcile myself to Davy Owen's mother. Three years ago he brought her home. He had met her in the house of one of his Denbighshire tenants during his stewardship of the King's parks and forests there. She had long dark hair and a wanton smile. Old as he is, he looked at her once and she left her husband and came with him. They stayed together for one week. He knew a bitter disillusion. She returned briefly within the year, presenting him with some high words and with Davy. But even Davy Owen has his part to play. The smoke has shown it to me. Davy will be a great knight. He will be one of those to come ashore on this coast, at Dale, near Milford Haven, with the army of the prophecy, under the Dragon banner.

My essence was with him when needed. In Southampton . . . the wound on my mouth took months to heal. The few folk I saw shunned me. By the time it had mended he and she were safe, deep in their joy together at Hertford.

Edmund, created Earl of Richmond, and little Owen are dead, but Jasper will be safe. Strong, martial Jasper, who has proved himself so well already in the fighting against the House of York and in his support of Little Harry will live for many years, and be part of the glory. He will prepare a haven for Edmund's son in Brittany, keeping him safe from the vengeance of the giant. Jasper's arm is dedicated to Little Harry, not for the honours he has showered upon him (though it's pleasing that Jasper now has Gloucester's Earldom of Pembroke!), but through the King's mercy and kindness to Owen. Little Harry writes to Owen as *'our beloved Esquire'*, but all the accolades were reserved for Edmund and Jasper. Owen has never been knighted. Neither has he been married, although he swears over and over that he and she were married. He believes it. Many believe it. It is now tradition.

She lies no longer in St Paul's. King Harry had her re-interred in the Lady Chapel at Westminster. Owen has never been to the tomb. Neither have I, for I follow him everywhere. Last week I saddled a horse and went after him through the winter gales. He rode to a certain beach along this coast. He would rather have been alone, but I do not let him from my sight. I knew then that I had so little time left of him. I stayed some way behind him while he walked to a cove and stood looking at it, while the surf lashed the rocks and the seabirds mourned. Then he turned and came back, his face very calm and sad. He put his arms round me. The seawind blew my thin white hair about. I thought: could I only have died in beauty, as she did! and – how long since that moonlit night in the valley! He said: 'Hywelis.'

I looked at him. I looked all about him, and my heart grew sick at what I saw.

'Hywelis,' he said, 'I should so like to be with her again. Will I be too old for her now, I wonder?'

And I looked away out to sea and said: 'Owen, my little one. There's no age or time in that place. I have seen. Everyone is young *yn y Nefoedd*. The maimed are whole. The blind see. Everyone's young in heaven.'

I could have told him then. He has only thirty days left. The corpse-candles were shining about him, the merry little fires dancing red and green against the rocks behind. I could have told him, but he did not ask, and the words outmatched me. Instead I looked again out to sea and saw the time to come; the great fleet approaching from Brittany, with Jasper and Davy Owen and Edmund's son Henry, standing on deck under the banner of Cadwallader, ready to do battle with the Great Boar.

The Great Boar's name is Gloucester, too. A gentler, nobler Gloucester, Richard of Gloucester, one of the chosen victims of destiny, defiled, unjustly accused. He will fall to Wales at a place named Bosworth Field. Now he is a child, the brother of Edward of March, the giant, Ysbaddaden the Terrible. In twenty-four years this will come to pass. The smoke has told me. The Lord has told me.

I seldom need to look in the smoke now; the visions come unbidden. I see the battle to come within this month, when we ride into Herefordshire, Owen in his red doublet, Jasper keen and strong and bound for safety. Little King Harry deep in his inherited madness, praying and singing even while

475

the battle roars. And his Queen, Margaret of Anjou, as full of war-passion as Jeanne d'Arc ever was.

I see the rout at Mortimers Cross, the *galanastra*, the slaughter. I see the captives taken and brought to Hereford East, in the Market Place. The Lloyds and Howells, and Owen. I see the giant Edward of March, victorious. The future king of England, the future destroyer of Little Harry. I see him full of vengeance. He fears the dynasty to come. I see Owen in his red doublet. I see the block. I see the axe. Owen will not pass Ysbaddaden the Terrible . . .

Last night I built the smoke and wept into the fire. Glyn Dŵr came to me. He took a long time answering.

'Girl,' he said at last, 'what is destiny? What is greatness?'

I answered, half-mad with grief. Destiny is a candle burning down to its bitter black end. Greatness is a man and a woman in bed. Destiny is foxes mating, pentacles and charms. Rain and sunlight. Good and evil. Heaven and Hell. Flowers and mountains. Jewels and blades. A bay horse and a white bird. Greatness is a delusion. Destiny is the child of murder. Greatness is the seed of love. Destiny is the axe and the block. Oh, my father, what can I do? Can destiny be cheated?

And he answered, with a look that said *you should know better*, then one of the other swirling faces leaned and whispered to him and through the thinning smoke, he said:

'Do you recall the old custom that honours the gods of Wales, after the moment of death?'

The candles. Not the corpse-lights that presage the end, but the candles lit about the severed head by night. A hundred or more, burning about the head where it is placed on high.

'It will be a still, frosty night,' said the Lord. 'He will shine in death as he shone in life.'

'He is no god,' I said.

'No,' they all answered, 'but you can make him one. The people of Hereford will think you mad. Do it.'

I will do it. I will do it. Now he is ready to ride forth to his last battle, so straight and handsome . . . and time plunges me forward, too fast . . . I suffer doubly, always, through my terrible vision.

I see them rip the collar from his red doublet as he kneels

476

before the block set among straw in Hereford Market Place. For a moment he looks about him as if expecting a reprieve, for he has never asked me when his death shall be, and trusts on pardon and grace in vain. But now he knows; the crowd is waiting for his final words. I see his faintest smile. The words are not for them, but for himself.

'This head shall lie upon the block, that once did lie upon Queen Cathryn's lap.'

His blood will run down and soak the straw. It will trickle down the Market Cross, where they will impale his head upon the highest point. Crisp clear evening will be falling. I will have more than a hundred candles ready to make him shine. The people – even the Yorkist partisans – will mutter as they wander away – what a good death he took! How meekly he put his soul and mind wholly unto God. I shall begin to light the candles, more than a hundred, the token of our gods. I shall climb the steps of the cross and wash the blood from his face and carefully comb his hair, and set my candles burning all around him.

He is no longer Owen ap Meredyth ap Tydier, Esquire.

He is Owen Tudor, founder of the greatest dynasty that Wales ever set to rule over England. It is done. He looks so young, so bright.

I will weep awhile, and then be silent.

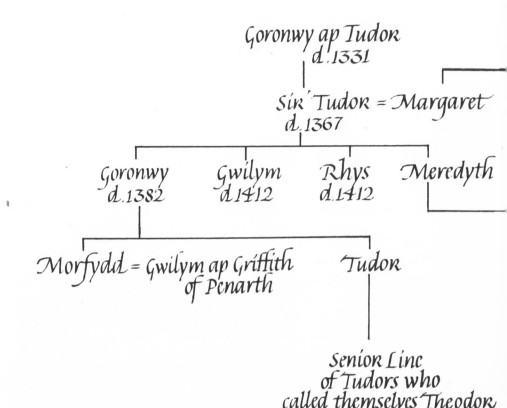

Goronwy ap Tudor
d. 1331

Sir Tudor = Margaret
d. 1367

Goronwy   Gwilym   Rhys   Meredyth
d. 1382   d. 1412   d. 1412

Morfydd = Gwilym ap Griffith   Tudor
         of Penarth

Senior Line
of Tudors who
called themselves Theodor

HENRY VI = Margaret of Anjou
1421~1471

Prince Edward
1453~1471

TUDOR PEDIGREE

NAMES IN CAPITALS ARE THOSE

OF KINGS & QUEENS OF ENGLAND